BLUEBIRD CANYON

Also by Dan McCall

The Example of Richard Wright
The Man Says Yes
Jack the Bear
Beecher

BLUEBIRD CANYON

DAN McCALL

CONGDON & WEED
New York

Copyright © 1983 by Dan McCall

Library of Congress Cataloging in Publication Data
McCall, Dan.
Bluebird Canyon.
I. Title.
PS3563.C334B5 1982 813'.54 82-7402
ISBN 0-86553-032-7 AACR2
ISBN 0-312-92057-1 (St. Martin's)

Published by Congdon & Weed, Inc.
298 Fifth Avenue, New York, N.Y. 10001

Distributed by St. Martin's Press
175 Fifth Avenue, New York, N.Y. 10010

Published simultaneously in Canada by Thomas Nelson & Sons Limited
81 Curlew Drive, Don Mills, Ontario M3A 2R1

All Rights Reserved
Printed in the United States of America by The Haddon Craftsmen
Designed by Irving Perkins
First Edition

Bluebird Canyon is a real and beautiful place in Laguna Beach, California. *Bluebird Canyon* is a novel; the imaginary characters in it are not intended to resemble real persons.

for Kathy

BLUEBIRD CANYON

1

NEVER HAD a family. Being adopted makes you different from the word go—and those kids on the schoolyard don't let you forget it, when you're a-*dop*-ted, a-*dop*-ted, it's a stigma, you never really get over it. Not having had a family of my own undoubtedly contributes to the fact that, as a lot of women know, I am not exactly a day at the beach.

At 6:37, Labor Day, I get a call, a two-car accident, no-injury, up where Thalia turns into Temple Hills. I respond promptly, arrive on the scene, and these two are having a verbal shootout at Generation Gap. Standing there shouting insults at each other. What happened was the old geez had pulled over to grab a view of the sunrise over the Pacific (oh, the sun always comes up in the west), and the hippie kid rear-ended him. Drove his terminal Woody right up all over the '67 Caddy's fins. The kid's girlfriend is sitting in the front seat of the Woody, having hysterics, and the males may come to blows. My patient reasoning, stern expression, and a few well-chosen menacing phrases do not prove effective. So since the kid clearly does not have both oars in the water, I spread him against the Woody. Of course he's got some dandy controlled substance in his pocket. I take his driver's license, go back and sit in the patrol car, call in a 10-28, and all of a sudden my clipboard and my ball-point and my sunglasses and everything are flying all over everywhere. I'm whiplashed. It's the kid, who has climbed back up into his Woody, put it in reverse, floored it, and slammed into the blue-and-white to the tune of at least a thou. This gets me excited. Then the hysterical girl runs away, charging up Temple Hills. The geez from the '67 Caddy trots after her in his shiny white shoes, calling, "Miss? Oh, miss, we mustn't leave the scene of an accident!" Girl turns around, gives him the finger running backward, and falls on her can. Then she gets up, gives him the finger with her whole forearm, and continues running. The geez walks back, shaking his head like "What is this world coming to?" The hippie kid beside me is smiling and making a sound like an electric train. Now Labor Day traffic is backed up, it's just after seven A.M., when I am supposed to be on my way home to home-sweet-mobile-home. I turn around to see Miss Nordland, the elderly widow who does all the religious paintings of Christ and Roy Rogers. Old Lady Nordland's big gray Imperial with the I'M A LAGUNATIC bumper sticker is feebly chugging backward across Temple Hills. Before I can yell "Stop!" (not to mention "Halt!"), she picks up a little speed and hits the patrol car on the driver's side. Knocks it into a kind of teeter-totter position on the side of the cliff. Ol' Vehicle 28 has had enough this morning, and begins to puke oil. Mrs. Nordland gets out, shaking her gray hair, and says quite earnestly, "Officer Bodley, you know I always look both ways before backing out." She chews her lower lip. "Has there been an altercation?" Yeah, I think, an altercation. The blue-and-white is bashed in in the front, bashed in on the side, two separate incidents, four disabled vehicles, one big mess. By this time traffic is really May Day. I direct it until the Chief comes down from his new home on Cerritos Drive (Cerritos! It sounds like a breakfast cereal.). The Chief pulls his Ranch-wagon with its Kiwanis-Club-type nifty gumball into Miss Nordland's carport. Walks over like Gary Cooper, surveys the scene, and says to me, "Well, Triphammer, you've had a busy half-hour."

Which is the way my shift ends and my day begins. Finally Butch Ravelling comes up in #26, and we all spend forty-five minutes getting traffic moving again. Calling wreckers from Buzzi's, taking statements. I was bent over, measuring skid marks for the yellow sheet, when a flotilla of skateboarders damn near took my ass off on one side, my right hand on the other. My feet are killing me, even though I've really only been sitting for eight hours. For months I knew something was wrong with them. The podiatrist said I had bursal sacs and bone spurs. I asked him what causes those, and he says senility. That's fine, I'm thirty-seven. No, he says, it's bursitis, used to be called fallen arches. He wants to surgically break my fourth toe on each foot. In the meantime he takes a scalpel and

2

cuts off four calluses, and my feet bleed into a bedpan. If you don't catch it, it can go up to your knees, then your hips, and you got ghastly back pains. So he made plaster casts of my feet, and now I wear these "Orthotics," little molded elevators inside my shoes. But they hurt worse. After a few hours of them, I get terrible cramps. So I'm not too inclined to stand around back at the station house, and finally at 8:40 I don't even care about controlled substances, which like a pro I lost somewhere. The kid isn't going heh-heh-heh anymore, he's come down to his normal state, which is a ferret. I let him go, with three moving violations, to go find his girl. She sure looked good running up Temple Hills. I seriously doubt she'd ever be cited for Failure to Yield. I'm tired, really ready for bed. I don't even shower and change at the station. I go home still in uniform. I don't even stop to have a Duke's Burger and flirt with that new waitress. I am so weary.

But when I get down to Treasure Island, and am entering my trailer, thinking that's the way it is with an 11–7 Graveyard, nothing happens for seven-and-a-half hours, then everything happens at once, I see things are not over yet. There's a paramedics unit there, and a dozen people standing around. I discover what has happened. A kid's dead, a two-year-old kid. He electrocuted himself in his parents' trailer. He was playing with some keys and stuck them into an electrical outlet. He was standing on a metal heat register at the time. I talked with a paramedic from South Coast Medical Center, and then they brought the stretcher out with this little tiny form covered with a sheet.

I can't take it.

A college boy from Pepperdine who's got a summer job with the *Sun-Post* is there, bothering the mother, taking down her words. She's a very skinny, gaunt lady, except extremely pregnant. Stringy hair. She's saying, "The keys were just sticking in the wall outlet, and Dougie—Dougie's laying there." She called an ambulance, and the paramedics responded but could not revive him. Suddenly she goes real white, sits on her trailer steps, and begins complaining of labor pains.

I take her up to the hospital in my car, following the paramedics. I sit in the emergency waiting room. Two years old, keys in a wall socket, standing on a heat register. The doc comes out and says the woman will stay for observation. There's nothing I can do. The father comes in. Douglas Sr., he's wearing a blue plaid flannel shirt. I look down immediately because his eyes say somebody's told him to get up to the hospital, it's Dougie, but nobody's had the guts to say *dead*, and I don't want to be the one. The doctor does it, properly, but the father passes out, flat out. We get him into one of the stalls where you whip a curtain all around

3

the bed. He comes around, and the news is hitting him in stages, you can see it hit him. He says, "I kept pushing myself so I could get home. For some reason I just wanted to get home. When I come home late, Dougie comes in and eats with me. Even if he's eaten before." The father has a gentle voice, like he always knew the world would kick his ass in. He goes down again, comes up again. "He liked to wake me up in the morning and crawl into bed with me."

The last thing the father said, before I left, was "God must've had one darn good reason for taking him. There is going to be an empty spot."

On the way back up Coast Highway, in glorious sunshine and heavy holiday traffic, I have a cigarette. I think: Dougie's dead, keys in a wall socket, standing on a register, inquisitive little guy. Families who lose a child never recover, it's in their eyes.

At home—home!, that's a laugh—I sit in the black Barcalounger and watch an old rerun of "The Andy Griffith Show." I've seen it before, but I'm afraid to sleep. So I sit there, totally useless tears in my eyes, and blow smoke rings.

The phone wakes me up. The Chief says we have a domestic at the Hooker mansion; the Hookers call it "Summer Snow." Chiefie Baby says, "The subject has an emotional problem." My head isn't too clear, and my first thought is that ol' J.O. has popped off or Mrs. H. has had another attack. But the Chief mutters on—Rex Hooker, the son, is apparently trying to commit suicide.

Now, this makes me sit up.

I'm told that since I am acquainted with the Hooker family, I better get over there.

I realize I have not taken my uniform off. I fell asleep in the Barca-lounger. I slap on some Brut, and only when I'm in my car do I discover it's 2:05. When I arrive at the Summer Snow house, in North Laguna, there is already a patrol car there. It's Butch Ravelling. He's in the house; I don't know why a rookie is dealing with this. The Hooker Seville isn't there in the big circular driveway, only a black Trans-Am with plates KINGS X, and a red Mercedes with plates ROLLEM.

I stand there a minute, looking at the house. Except I don't look, my eyes and my mind turn away from it. I'm embarrassed. Hurt. "Summer Snow" is beyond me. The first time I saw it, twenty years ago, it was beyond me. The Hooker family owns three acres, easy, of beach property, all the way from the water's edge up to the top of the cliff. The house sits there in the middle, kind of emerging from the cliff, or like it's the mother ship just landing. Enormous, all that pure white, all that glass, and

4

looking so goddamn *clean*. More like a monument than a house. World, Take a Look at Me. I don't know how I ever got the idea it was "Spanish Colonial"; it's the opposite of what that means. It's the world of tomorrow, you'd never think it was built forty years ago. I guess that's why it caused such a stir at the time. And does today, because we're still catching up with the architect, old J. O. Hooker. He was into solar energy while the rest of the country was fighting a Depression. And there are real lovely things about the place, like the rose garden for his wife. One whole side of the house is that huge rose garden, with dozens of varieties—J.O. gave me a copy of the booklet they used to pass out to tour groups—Sutter's Gold, Grand Slams, Golden Talismen, Texas Centennials, Madame Henri Guillots. The hybrid white rose gives the house its name, the big bed of Summer Snows. All dotted with Pinks and Blaze.

But as I say, I don't quite want to look at it; it blows my fuses. Probably goes back to the first time I saw it, at night, when I was in high school, and half in the bag. Way back in 1960, when Rex and I were seniors, out in the Coachella Valley. The Hookers had already built their massive compound, "Medjuhl," in Palm Desert. I was living with my aunt and uncle in Indio—I was student body president, a second-string quarterback who was voted "Most Inspirational" at the Awards Banquet at the end of the season. But I do not want to bring all that back—Rex and me. The desert. It was the first year I was called Triphammer, instead of my real name, Oliver Bodley. Which is another thing. I hate my real name. Oliver Bodley sounds like an obese kitty cat. Or Class Twit. But I surely did not behave like a Triphammer when Rex Hooker needed me that summer of 1960. Maybe he's forgotten. No, no way, you do not forget something like that. I don't know, it's odd. Back there we didn't have smog, and the world was simple. People behaved themselves. I-Like-Ike was president, and right was right and wrong was wrong. I really thought I was going places, I had a football scholarship to Iowa, which at that time was National Rankings. I pretty much convinced myself I would be heard from someday. I was on the guest list to Summer Snow. Of course we all thought Rex Hooker, the world-famous architect's son, was living on his dad's rep. But Rex was a real talented actor already, and a musician, he had a rock'n'roll band that played the bop dances at Legion Hall. When the band took a break, Rex would carry around this animal—it was a wombat, named Charles, and Rex said it ate linoleum, he fed it linoleum. So he invited about thirty of us to his family house in Laguna Beach, to a "formal affair." We had to rent tuxes, and buy corsages. Rex, then, whenever he met anybody, he would say, "Well—(the name of the person)—how the hell are ya?" That was what you might call his tag line,

5

he always said it. And in 1959, or '60 even, saying that was weird. The kids of today have no real understanding of what it was like to be a kid in the Eisenhower Years. We were really uptight back there. I mean, today, in sixth grade, they say, "Yo, pussy, what's this motherfucking shit comin' down?" Twenty years ago, in twelfth grade, we said, "How do you do?" And Rex Hooker always said, "Well, ——, how the hell are ya?"

So we were all given maps for this party. We and our dates in a convoy of about a dozen cars followed the maps and came to the mansion. In our rented tuxes and the girls in gowns, and a little crocked if you were lucky, which I was. And there was J. O. Hooker's Summer Snow. A colored guy parked our cars, and they'd put a dance floor over the swimming pool, they had a band, and tiki torches. Couples wandered in starlight. The Guest House, with its little water wheel, was turned into a gypsy camp, all nestled there in the Monterey Pines, and this bucktoothed old crone told our dates' fortunes by reading their palms. Between the Guest House and the main house was the "Edifice Rex." It's a brick maze about eight feet high that Rex designed and built when he was twelve years old. It's full of crisscrosses and dead ends and blind alleys. We graduates had to check that out. Got all juvenile in there, boisterous. And then we went into the big house itself, the mansion, and wandered about with our jaws dropping. Summer Snow is not only a massive thing from the twenty-first century, but the furniture is like what you'd see in a historical exhibit. Real lush and heavy. Antiques. If you're inside, you'd never think the outside would look like that; the inside and the outside are two things that don't go together. Like Summer and Snow. At one point my date and I found ourselves on a little bridge that looks down three stories to a rock garden with a lagoon where the surf pounds in right under the house through a retaining wall. Darleen and I peered down and thought we were in a pagoda in the Himalayas. We made out like it was our last night to be together. Which, unfortunately, it was. Old Darleen kept repeating "Summer Snow" in this singsongy way like it was "Love Is a Many-Splendored Thing." I rather lost my head. And went into exile in the billiards room, where there were all these plaques and trophies and cups. Photographs in frames all over the walls, J.O. with Earl Warren and Thomas Kuechel and Goody Knight and Bill Knowland and all those big shots that ran the state of California when I was a boy. And the Hookers with the Walt Disneys—the walls just plastered with photographs and plaques. A huge aquarium with Siamese fighting fish and little neon tetras that lighted up, the whole school going zip zip zip. Connecting the two main floors is a big spiral staircase. I spent some time studying on that after my fight with Darleen. While everybody else was dancing outside. Ol' Rex, on his way back from a phone call, found me there, and told me it was Honduras mahogany. Been stored in a hogshed for fifty years until his pop found it in '36—I remember Rex saying the year, "thirty-six," and telling me his pop soaked it in vats until he could bend it to the right shape. And then he put it in the Grand Entrance Hall where it circles up through space and ends in this pretty little cupola. The stairs themselves are inlaid parquet. Stained-glass windows on three sides, gigantic things, yellow-white and gold, with ruby panels. It was all way too much for me, a teenager, drunk on my ass.

I still remember that fight with Darleen. Me going it alone like Admiral Byrd and pitching camp in a huge bathroom under a skylight and admiring the Pullman sinks. Getting trapped in a secret passageway with a bottle of red wine and a big collie dog named Floribunda. I ripped my rented tux pants and was sweating like a pig, and finally got out and went down to the rose garden to try to relocate Darleen and apologize for roughing around her hooters. I cooled off and thought, The world is quite beyond me. Resented all wealthy, ostentatious people. And then the band played a fanfare and Mrs. Hooker was introduced—the First Lady in this long beaded gown. That's when we discovered the trick. She did an imitation for a few seconds, with a bandana and fake teeth, and goddamn, she had been the crone, the fortuneteller, and now she was so lovely. She'd taken us all in. Darleen and all the girls laughed, and Mrs. Hooker was full of mischief with a twinkle in her eye. She took the girls for a candle-light ceremony on the beach, and brought them back like they had been through initiation into a sorority. Then we were all standing around in the music. Rex semisloshed with Charles the wombat on his shoulder, feeding it tiles, Rex leaning against his date, Miss Rancho Mirage, this all-time chick named Marge Stivers. Old Man Hooker, also in a tux, came in about midnight from some statewide Republican affair and wandered down to look in on the party, and, I don't know, everybody—we just went kind of nuts when the World-Famous Architect, J.O., the man who had built it all, he moseyed over and said to his son, "Well, Rex, how the hell are ya?"

That night is crystal-clear to me now as I stand here with Butch Ravelling. And right away I feel danger signals. I feel strange kinds of shame and pangs of guilt. It's a shock to my system.

But I go in, toward the sound of high-pitched voices. I pause in the trophy room. A gold eagle on rosewood. Abe Lincoln on a pillar. Greek gods and goddesses holding up wreaths and flames. My, my.

I could hear a woman's voice, full of anger and fear, back inside somewhere.

And then Rex appeared. He didn't recognize me. But even after nineteen years, I could see who he was immediately. Those brilliant blue eyes and that blond hair, almost white. He's very tan, but he looks absolutely terrible. He's almost as tall as I am, a little over six feet. I've put on about twenty pounds, and he's lost about the same. Since I was heavier to begin with, now I've got maybe fifty pounds on him. He's naked except for these little tiny shorts, white shorts. And he's severely cut himself here and there and everywhere, some of the wounds still bleeding. A couple of days' growth of beard. He seems to be drunk out of his mind, carrying a huge glass of brown liquid, and you can really smell it. He's swaying around like somebody should yell, "Timber!"

Now, this is not what we want to see.

He sees me, and doesn't see me, and says, "Would you remove your hat?"

I wouldn't have, under other circumstances, but for some reason I took off my hat.

He finally sat down on this low little intricately carved walnut chair with maroon velvet upholstery, and said to nobody in particular, "This chair is older than this country." He stared at a fencing sword. Pulled it down. Butch got a bit nervous there in a high archway, put his hand on his gun. Rex saw it. Rex said quickly, "I'm not going to say, 'En garde!' " Then he sighed and said, "We will simply hold a damaged sparrow in our hands, and its heart will go db db db db against our thumbs."

Butch looks at me.

And my heart is going db db db db against my ribs. I figure it's my obligation to tell him who I am. But I do not do it. My, the square footage in this house, I had forgotten just how big it was. The color of this room

8

is mulberry, or plum, rose-colored vases with bouquets of pink and white heather spilling out. It gives you such a feeling of space and freedom, those big windows to the sea. But Rex is obviously not feeling too free, more like all cramped up, hugging himself and smearing little streaks of blood. He's completely shaved all the hair off his chest and one leg.

I feel pretty sick. Then the woman comes in, a very striking woman, tall, maybe five-ten, black hair, this long black hair, and no bra under a dark green dress. Her eyes a bright hazel-green. Very stately, very distraught. She says real low, husky, "We better go."

Rex is still sitting there. "This chair is older than this country."

So he's making a lot of progress. I couldn't take my eyes off anything, Rex, the house, the way this tall woman was holding herself.

"Well," Rex said, "I suspect I should be clothed." He started up the Honduras mahogany, and tripped, and almost fell. But he caught himself, kind of half-turned there, and Butch put his hand on his gun again, didn't mean anything by it.

Rex said, "May I please be allowed to get my clothes?"

Butch was annoyed. He said, "Buddy, where you're going, you won't need no clothes."

That wasn't necessary.

I do not want to be here. Nothing to do but wait. Butch wanders to the balcony and looks out to sea; he's on shark alert.

A car pulls up in the driveway. It's the Chief, checking in. The Chief wearing a red blazer, blue and white check pants, a white shirt, and blue tie. Jesus, he's Uncle Sam. The Chief takes me aside and whispers, "You've answered calls up here—you know the family."

I nod.

"My function is already in progress. You take care of this." And the Chief salutes me with his hand waist-high, flat, and disappears out the door.

Our Leader. Whenever there's trouble, he's at the other end of town. His function is already in progress.

Finally the tall lady walks down the spiral staircase, with Rex in his white shorts and a dark blue suit coat, that's all he has on, those cuts on his face and chest and legs. They stop at the last bend. She says to him, "David is due at three-thirty."

Rex wails. "But honey—you said he was going to Bluebird Canyon."

"I didn't know you were doing it again."

"Well—*dear*," he says. He really means it, he leans on the word *dear*.

She says, "This is what it's all about. I can never depend on you anymore."

9

He says, in a soft, slow voice, "And why is that, Jos?"

She turns and disappears back inside.

Rex wanders around like a sleepwalker, vaguely flapping his dark blue suit coat. Finally lies down on a huge white couch that kind of engulfs him. He coughs, a real heavy hack, and just lies there. Coughs again, like his lungs are coming up. He says to the ceiling, "Sorry about the cough. I did it yesterday in the Safeway parking lot, leaning on the trunk of a Pontiac with New Jersey plates. A chipper old man said to me, 'Came to California a little too late, didn't you?' " Rex smiles. Then he puts his hands to his face. "And, gentlemen, sorry to bother you. Any man who puts on the uniform knows that at some moment in his life he will be forced to stare down the barrel of the gun—of the enemy—of the society —whose safety and whose ideas he represents."

Say what?

Rex is very quiet, real sad. And then he gets up and walks outside as sweet as you please and gets into the back seat of my blue-and-white. Butch and I look at each other. I go out and lean down at the patrol car window. I ask Rex if he's all right. He whinnies.

A kid about ten on a Spider bike zips down the driveway, does a long, slow skid next to the Mercedes, and says, "Can David play?"

The lady comes up behind me, and Rex sees her. He says, "Please, darling—don't—please don't let them take me away. I really couldn't bear it if you"—and then he stopped and he whispered, this wince on his face —"don't put my mind behind bars."

Darling steps back and looks at him.

He's still whispering. "I know that sounds a bit *strained*—but I mean it, honey, it's not bullshit. Please don't . . . please don't . . ." He says it again, the tiny whisper: "Don't put my mind behind bars."

Her face all panicky. Then she grits her teeth and gets into the patrol car.

I watch Rex. He's scared. But his eyes are moving on to something else, the way drunks skid from one emotion to another. Except he can't be drunk to talk this way.

The kid on the Spider bike is holding his breath. Eyes big as saucers. This is quite a story for his parents.

Rex says soft in his throat, "King's X. King's X, guys."

It's 3:20. I register it as we haul ass up the driveway, through the Monterey pines.

Dr. Hans Brandsma, our all-pro headshrinker, is a big bucket of lard. Never there in the crunch. A month ago we had to bring in a physics

10

professor at UC Irvine, drunk and miserable; he had clearly fallen out of his tree. Brandsma checked him over and released him. Next weekend I was the one who had to fish the professor's carcass out of the bloody bathtub where he had slashed his wrists—his wrists were all gouged and dug out, more like he excavated than slashed.

I left my hat at Summer Snow.

When we get to Brandsma's home office on Agate, I think I better go in, as a silent partner. The wife stays outside, after Rex kisses her on the shoulder. A very deliberate long kiss before he goes in. Butch is back to work—we've received on the radio some trouble down at Aliso Beach with a club of bikers. If Butch is wise, he'll cite them for littering. I actually did that once, cited some Hell's Angels for littering. They gave me an honorary membership and a 1-Percenter card—99 percent Animal, 1 percent Motherfucker. I help Rex along—he can't walk a straight line—into Brandsma's office, a tax write-off home office, all leather and mahogany and books. There's Fatso himself, with his granny glasses. He jumps right up, poppidy-plop, comes around his desk, and gives Rex the brotherhood handshake, my main man. Rex stares at it and says, "You have, in effect, deprived my thumb of a fulcrum."

Hans Brandsma looks puzzled. He sits down and motions to the couch for Rex. I stand like a guard, which I am, at the door.

Hans Brandsma says, "Well, Mr. Hooker, your wife is pretty worried about you." He ponders, looks up over his granny glasses. "You've been drinking rather heavily, haven't you?"

"I have been spilling more than drinking."

"What triggered it?"

"Poor hand-to-mouth coordination."

"No, I mean the drinking."

"Well . . ." Rex sat back in the couch and crossed his bare bloody feet. "Kevin's half-brother Darrell arrived and begged him to take Bambi back for Nina's sake. Eugene is convinced Tracey can resume singing at the club on the lake after the mastectomy. Oh, and my sister Kate. Who helps me die. Donna squealed to Trish about Viv's abortion. Perry and Kim bedded together in Acapulco. We saw them in towels. Lucille feared the Changs would win custody of Dorian—"

Hans Brandsma looks at me. I look away.

"How would you characterize your physical and mental condition now, Mr. Hooker?"

Rex thinks. Finally he says, "Withering, euphoria, and tumescence."

Hans Brandsma writes on a yellow pad.

"Which one did I miss?"

"Go on, feel free to talk it out."

"I knew 'tumescence' was wrong, I *knew* it."

"Mr. Hooker, don't play games with me. I am a busy man."

"Gosh, I am hardly a knockabout."

"I must determine if you are a danger to yourself. I'm not kidding, Mr. Hooker."

"And I, while kidding my heart out, am about as dangerous as a meadowlark. Look, I'll tell you what, uh, 'triggered' it. Last month, when the folks were in the hospital again—and Jossie was in Mission Viejo, and wouldn't see me—it was our fifteenth wedding anniversary. I didn't want to go bonkers, so I devised an antibonkers strategy. With Marge Stivers, my bestest girl."

Marge Stivers? Miss Rancho Mirage? He's still seeing her after nineteen years? Been married and has a kid and still sees Marge Stivers?

"After an afternoon of tennis, Marge and I sent out for a pizza, and the Domino Pizza truck, you've seen them, those itty-bitty trucks with the neon domino on top, brought us a mushroom-pepperoni. We was in our tennis whites. Then we got bombed and all dressed up—Marge is on my show; good God, the way that woman comes alive in front of a camera —do you watch?—and we ordered another pizza four hours later, at the pad on Pearl—"

I'm standing there beside Hans Brandsma's door, and pricking up my ears and thinking about that gorgeous blond knockout, Marge Stivers. I can remember when I was in high school working at Pete's Texaco on old Highway 111, and she'd stop her red MG, she'd be in her swimsuit, I'd see the little blond pubic hairs at the crotch, she had just fantastic jugs and perfect pins. I can still see her thoroughbred ankles above her flip-flops.

"—Well, the same Domino driver brought a sausage and olive pizza to Pearl Street, and was a little startled. And then Marge and I realized we forgot to lock up Sissy's cottage, and we drove over there at approximately three miles per hour, on the bike path, and by the time we got there, we were hungry again. So we ordered a pizza, and the same driver came, with a shrimp-and-green-peppers, but I had put on Marge's blue velvet gown, only of course I couldn't hook up the back, and when the delivery boy came the third time to the third place to the same two people, and saw me in that blue velvet gown and heard Marge's voice calling from poor Sissy's bedroom—'He's tied me up, I'm afraid of what he might do'—the delivery boy's eyes rolled back into his head and he got into his itty-bitty Domino truck and, shit, he ran right into a power pole."

By this time I am smiling a little in spite of myself. I catch Hans Brandsma regarding me sternly, so I wipe it off.

"But the sad part, Doc—the sad part is how my wife found out. Jos told me how. She and he, our son, David, she and he were having a Fourth of July supper at A Fine Kettle of Fish, before the fireworks on the beach —and we always used to do that together, as a family, for ten years we did it, and we'd go out on Pop's yawl, the C #—the S-e-a Sharp—but now we are landlocked, all this vicious rotary motion—and whoever Marge had told the story to was at that very moment telling it to her boyfriend, at the next table, and my wife, and my son, they had to sit there behind their menus, just sit there, and hear it. I wish that could have been avoided." Rex is real melancholy now, and he whispers it. "I wish that could have been avoided." He looks up. "And in the car—Jossie told me, it breaks my heart, she always has to tell me—I so hate to see her struggle, I never saw a face that could make grief so incandescent—she says she said to David, simply, 'Well, it's the fact of the anniversary that makes the whole thing not merely crazy." And then, she told me, my son, he's only eleven, he said to her, 'You don't have to explain my father to me.' And she—she said it was like she had been hit."

Long pause. Rex sighs. "Aw, well, let me go home, Doc. I'm exhausted and scared. Let me go home and sleep. I shouldn't treat depression with a depressant. I know. Let me go home and sleep."

Hans Brandsma says, "If I were on that couch and you were in this chair, I'm sure I'd say the same thing." Hans Brandsma chews his granny glasses. "We're only trying to help you."

I know the law. I know 5150. My feet are just killing me, the Orthotics. Another silence, maybe half a minute.

"Now, Rex," said Hans Brandsma, "I wonder if you could define a list of words for me. This is just standard procedure." He wanted Rex to tell him who invented the airplane and who discovered America. He gave Rex numbers in sequence and numbers in reverse order. Rex was cooperating like a child. I went out of the room for a moment. The wife—Joslin— jumped up, and I shook my head. Her green eyes looked right through me, like she was trying to focus on something painful in the distance. She was clearly all worn out and badly shaken. Had to do something and didn't know what. I needed a smoke. I stood out on Agate Street, and I thought about how it was really my responsibility, man to man, to tell Rex who I was. This is too much of a shock for me, I'm trying to bury it all and be an Officer. I looked out at the ocean. I can't tell him "I just do my job." I thought some more about Dougie, the two-year-old, posted. And Douglas Sr., and his wife in false labor. I thought about the Woody-Caddy

13

nonsense on Thalia and Temple Hills. The girl giving the finger and falling on her can. I hate the Chief. Shit, I am the one who ought to be committed, I can't keep my mind going in a straight line. Dougie will never grow up to drink beer at fifteen, never touch his girl's tits in the back seat at a drive-in, never experience happiness. Or sorrow.

I went back into the room. Rex had turned the tables. "May it please the court, I should like to ask you—come on, Doc, name six states of the United States named after European monarchs."

Hans Brandsma sighed and looked out the window. He was nervous. He said, "Louisiana."

"Good on ya."

"Georgia. And Maryland."

"Out-*stand*-ing. Even the best guys usually miss dear little Mary-land."

Hans Brandsma said, "There are six?"

"You already got three. This is a character-builder, Doc."

Hans Brandsma shook his head. "Carolina?"

"Counts for two. Oh, honey, go for the gusto."

"I really think I should be asking the questions," Hans Brandsma said, and he snapped his fingers. "Virginia."

"Attaboy."

Hans Brandsma was pleased with himself. Hans Brandsma was having a good time.

He said, "Now let me come back at you, Rex. I want you to take into your mind three words—*chair, box, dog.* OK? Now I won't ask you any more about them for a few minutes."

"Exactly so. But first you tell me the two biggest cities in the British Empire in 1750."

Hans Brandsma stopped. "Well, London . . ."

"Yes."

"Calcutta?"

"Nope."

Goddammit, I could sleep or help out somewhere.

"Seventeen-fifty? Ah, New York."

"OK, OK, it's Philly, I shouldn't have pushed you."

"Philadelphia? I don't think—"

"I kid you not. I shit thee nay."

Hans Brandsma looks at him. Then his mind shifts to another track. I know what's going on in his mind. He has to decide. 5150. Hans Brandsma may have to commit Rex Hooker. And he remembers that UC Irvine physics professor, he blew that one, he knows it. "Rex," he says, "do you really want to go home? Tell me, truth-time, are you suicidal?"

14

Rex reached over to the table, tried to light one of Brandsma's Benson and Hedges. Burned his right eyebrow. He sighed and said, "OK, truth-time, I think I should mention something very dark in my personal history. Very dark. Perhaps too dark altogether. It's irresponsible for me to sit here and not tell you about it."

"Yes?"

Rex smiled, uneasily. "I'm not sure I dare tell you."

"Don't be afraid, Rex."

"Well . . ." Rex whispered, "rocker, vagina, police."

Hans Brandsma didn't get it.

Me neither.

Hans Brandsma put his fat white fingers to his forehead. "What?"

"Chair, box, dog."

"What?"

"Please stop saying 'what?' To da problematik dese zignificant rez-ponzes are. You told me to remember three words, *chair, box, dog*. I did. Now a *rocker* is a kind of *chair*—and my rocker is what you people think I'm off of. *Vagina* is what *box* is a slang word for—it is also something I want to get into, as a casual passer-by can readily visualize. Then, Uncle Skeets, *police* is a kind of *dog*—and they, the police"—he turned to me —"the police have provided an escort here, which is, as opposed to our medial term, something I want to get out of. Off of, into, out of. My prepositions meet your propositions. Your chair, box, dog is modulated to my rocker, vagina, police. Man, don't you see? I'm not nuts, I'm verbally inventive."

Hans Brandsma was nailed. By a skinny rummy with cuts and gashes all over his body. It was kind of fun to watch. And then Rex blew it. He took a step too far. "Or to put it another way—I'm not suicidal, man, I'm homicidal. And it's all a case of mistaken identity. When I drink, I don't fade away, don't quietly drown my inadequacies in self-pity. Hell no, I go after me *with a fucking bullwhip*. I gonna kill the sucker. He's mean and ugly. I swear, I gonna kill him. *I* want to live—and I can't do it until *Me* dies. It's I against Me. I'll kill Me—I'll kill Me—let I do it—because Me is ruining I—and all the people I care for and with whom I am biologically obligated and fatally contracted. Give I time—I'll kill Me— and then I—*I* can live again."

Those words just poured out of him in a low scream. I saw Hans Brandsma make up his mind. Rex Hooker stepped over the great big line. He's going to the funny farm.

And at that point I couldn't really say it was wrong. Not if I had to make the decision myself.

Hans Brandsma said, "Rex, I think you understand everything."

Rex said, "Doc, I warn you—'therapy' has cured a lot of honest observation."

"Just have a seat, Rex."

"Did you hear me? Understanding is the easy part."

"I hear you. Easy now, Mr. Hooker. You wait here."

"Doctor, I have to be home when Mother and Pop get back from Scripps. I *have* to be there—"

"You won't be much use to them in this condition."

"OK, O-K, you want to know Dante's definition of hell?"

"We've had enough of these riddles, Rex."

"No riddle. Listen. Hell is 'proximity without intimacy.' That's what —that woman—out there and I have. Proximity without intimacy. That's hell."

"Sit *down!*"

Hans Brandsma went out. Rex had a little fit, sneezed maybe ten times, real fast. I got him some Kleenex from the shelf. Rex shook his head, and sneezed again. He looked up at me. "Do I know you? I know you from somewhere."

I have to tell him, I have to.

He said, "Brandsma really ought to watch that short-term memory loss." Then he said into another sneeze, "Ah-ah-ah—*fuck!*" Squeezing his nose with the Kleenex, he looked at me. "I *do* know you."

I am very confused, and unhappy and guilty—guilty, like it's all my fault. I am feeling sad for him. But I am also furious at him. For letting himself become this way after having every advantage in the world.

Then it gets hairy. Hans Brandsma has conferred with Joslin. We are going to do it. I see Joslin really doesn't want to, but she's at the end of her rope. We go with Gravely Disabled, 5008. Detainment Advisement. Brandsma signs the form. I do. I begin to rehearse: You may bring a few personal items with you which I will have to approve. We go back in to fetch our boy. Brandsma has a real cautious look on his face. "Rex," he says, "your wife, and I have concluded that you've overextended yourself."

"It's a dirty job, but somebody's got to do it."

"You need a rest. There are people who are trained to help you. We want you to spend a few days with them."

"Now hold on here, you can't—"

"Yes, I can, young man."

"*Young man?*"

"It's a very good hospital—"

"Hospital?"

"They specialize in problems like yours. I've called an ambulance—"

"Young man, hospital, ambulance? What happened to chair, box, dog?" Rex bolts for the door, but I am standing in front of the door. "Hey —Jossie?"

Hans Brandsma says, "She'll be going with you."

"*What?*"

"She will be riding in the ambulance with you."

"But Doc, you can't do this to me, you can't drag a man naked out of his own home. I mean, if I was driving a car all over the road, or showing my dingo to liddle Suzie Cartwright down the lane, or just a public nuisance—but I was minding my own business in my own home.

"Come here, Mr. Hooker, I want to show you something."

So Rex goes over, and Hans Brandsma opens a little bathroom door. He has Rex stand in front of a full-length mirror on the back of the door.

Rex stumbles closer, his nose is almost pressed against the mirror. He says, "Come out, come out—I know you're in there." Then he whips around, grabs this big glass paperweight on Brandsma's desk, and pitches it straight into the mirror. Now we got glass all over the shag carpet. Rex is barefoot, and Brandsma doesn't know whether to shit or go blind. He shouts, "You self-indulgent *ass!*"

I move them both away from the broken glass, huffing and puffing a bit.

I hear the ambulance outside; the driver pops a couple of blips on the siren as he pulls up.

"Mr. Hooker," says Hans Brandsma, "you may not know the law in this state. But when a member of your family or—"

"No way, no *way* I don't get a call. Let me call Marge."

"Mr. Hooker, watch your step there, you've already cut yourself rather badly, you said you were going to do it, you said you'd kill yourself—"

"No, no—kill *him*, kill the fucker in the *mirror.*"

"Now, calm down. Please. Please read this." Hans Brandsma holds up a pamphlet or something, it looks semilegal, and he says, "Read this sentence."

Rex does. He says, "This is horrible. This is simply ghastly."

"It's the law."

"No way, no way. Here"—and Rex lunges toward me—"you read it, Officer. Don't you think that's grotesque?"

Like a goddamn fool I take it. I know this official legal shit anyway, but I read it: " 'Occasionally a patient's judgement is seriously impaired by illness and he may be admitted and retained against his will.' " I hand it back.

17

Rex says, "Isn't that horribly wrong, Sergeant?"

I say, "I don't want to debate philosophy."

"Philosophy? Phil-*os*-ophy? What we're talking here is *spelling*. On this side of the Atlantic there is no medial *e* in *judgment.*"

Hans Brandsma and I look at each other.

Rex goes for broke. His wife screams. I finally do something useful today and tackle Rex at the outer office door. We thrash about. The door opens and it's the driver of the ambulance, a pretty good-sized kid. With Rex and me and now the driver, we go round and round. A lamp falls over. Hans Brandsma is not your most dependable partner in a tag-team match. He cowers in the background, and Rex may be underweight and cut up and drunk, but he's got a lot of fight. He slugs me in the gut and knocks the wind right out of me. I could take him out pretty easy, but I do not want to hurt him. Finally I've got him up, both feet off the ground, Rex writhing like crazy, *"You can't do this to me!"* There's only one solution: strap him down in the ambulance, we have to do it. And we do.

It was going to be about an hour's drive, what with Labor Day traffic. I was in the back with Rex, the wife up front with the driver. Siren blasting, we whipped right along the middle lane at about seventy. Cars bumper to bumper on Laguna Canyon Road, cars hitting the shoulder, we gunned between them up 133 to 405.

Rex said, "Gang, this is really a poor choice." He was panting from the struggle.

I could see he was picking with his fingers at the straps on his wrists.

The kid driver was up to a hundred now, muttering: Goddammit, people who are really sick need this vehicle, and here we are driving a drunk to detox. We passed a dead skunk, and you could smell him, still ripe. All the holiday families getting the hell out of the way. This kid knows how to drive. Overhead, choppers coming in, skywaying to El Toro USMCAS. There are several types and sizes of choppers, but this lead one was the worst kind for me. Its blades hit the sky with a thud, rotors going thud, thud, thud. I feel Vietnam terror, like I'm a farmer and my ox'll get wasted, I've sent my family to safety. Sound makes me think crazy like that. An ache in my chest.

Rex calls to the front seat. "Really, Jos, David and I are something too precious for you to impair. Please listen—I know what you think of me, but David is a perfect little gentleman."

Joslin says back, "No he is not. He is a gallant little boy."

Rex gets tears in his eyes. "I stand—I lie—corrected. That's right. Our son is not a perfect little gentleman. Our son is a gallant little boy." Rex looks helplessly up at me, the restraining straps cutting into his wrists. He starts to say something, then shakes his head and says something else: "Look, we got this idiotic ride on our hands, no point in getting maudlin, let's pass the time with another word game. Sergeant, are you up for a word game?"

I look at him, I'm sitting cross-legged.

"I'll say a word, and you say the opposite. OK? *Love.*"

"*Hate,*" I say.

"Yes, of course, but when I asked my, uh, gallant little boy, I was waiting for him to say *hate,* and he didn't. You know what he said? *Neglect.* Oh, my, my, my." Rex looked away for a minute, and then said, "Well, it can't be helped. OK. What's the opposite of *vulgar?*"

I thought. Now, why am I doing this?

"Pop," Rex said, "oh, boy, my pop—he said the opposite of *vulgar* is *precise.* Not bad. Linguistically correct. But my favorite, my very favorite, was when I asked him the opposite of *stubborn.* And he said, real quick, *weakness.* Ah, me, there's the glory, there's the problem. Now then, Sarge, the opposite of *good.*"

"*Bad.*"

"Aw shit, I was hopin you'd say *evil.* The uniform and all. Say, ask me. You give me one."

I just looked at him. "*Drunk.*"

He just looked at me. "*Happy.*"

Well, moving along now . . . I looked out at the Datsun we were going by, and the sonofabitch driver had on a rubber conehead mask.

Rex whispered, "*Summer? Snow,* obviously. I thought of getting a license plate, SUM SNO, but folks'd just think I was runnin' nose candy. Give me another one."

I wish this was over. Love. Neglect. Drunk. Happy.

"Come on."

I shook my head. "I don't know. *Job.*"

"Say, that's not bad. Let me see—I—are you somebody I knew at Stanford?"

"No!"

"Jesus, man, bit my head off."

I looked at my hands. Now, that was uncalled for, shouting at him like that. I've got to tell him.

"The opposite of *job,*" he said. And then, "My job now is to take care of my aged parents. And what annoys me about that job is that I do all sorts of things for 'em they're not supposed to notice, and then they don't notice!" He hummed a little bit. Whinnied again. Said, "Ah, me. Six

19

states named after European monarchs. My face in the mirror, my mind behind bars. Magic casements opening on the seas of faery lands forelorn."

Then he was quiet for a while. We were all bouncing around at ninety now. I recognize this miniature golf course that my ex-wife, Sheila, and I played at once, the yellow windmill.

"Jos," he calls in this falsetto voice, "what's the opposite of *cheap*?"

No answer from up front.

I wonder what happened to the opposite of *job*. And how could the opposite of *vulgar* be *precise*? And why am I letting my mind bop around on his wavelength?

We are moving along real good. Only another ten or fifteen minutes, even with the traffic, that kid playing Barney Oldfield. I have to wonder how Rex got into this condition. He's blown it real bad. It bugs the hell out of me that I haven't told him who I am.

He says his bladder's going to burst, it is extremely painful, he's gotta take a leak.

I'd let him, but I'm too fearful of untying the straps. I look at all the cuts on his body. He must've come really close to putting an eye out. Gashes all around his blond-white hair and his nose.

"Please let me piss."

I shake my head, sorry. So he sighs, and he calls up to the front seat, "Jos, I don't know what on earth you think you are doing."

She shouts, "I am *saving your life!*"

"What?"

"In another twenty-four hours you would have been *dead*." She says it real hard: "*I am saving your life.*"

Rex says, low, "Well, excuse me all over the world."

We are off the freeway now, hauling ass into the hospital.

Rex whispers to me, "Ossifer, you know what tragic irony is? Remember this—tragic irony is to commit precisely the crime you wished to prevent. Which I am now doing."

Finally we are there, we swing into the receiving area. Now the problem is to get him inside.

Hans Brandsma must have phoned ahead. The kid driver went in for a couple of minutes, then out he comes with the biggest black guy I ever saw, must have been six-eight, 280, all muscle, bald as a billiard ball.

Rex saw him, and said, *"Oy gevalt miércoles!"*

But he insisted on having his piss. Right there in the afternoon sunlight. Taxpayers, mainly elderly, going by. We made a circle around him, for modesty. And he filled the quart plastic container—and then tied a knot in it, and the kid driver found another container—and Rex filled that too. And then he finally just let go on the pavement, a stream under the ambulance.

"Les go," said the giant black guy.

"But honey," said Rex, "these people think I'm screwy."

"We all has our ups and downs."

Rex smiled. "What's your name?"

"Hodge."

We trooped in. Hodge put Rex in a wheelchair. We went down a series of corridors, following those green arrows on the floor. Rex said, "Such handsome linoleum. How Charles would have relished a square or two."

I was looking at Hodge, wondering why he wasn't in the Rams front four.

Hodge strapped Rex down, in a little room. Legs spread, big leather straps, arms spread, big leather straps, big white bath towels on top, and tucked in the side. Then adhesive tape over the buckles—"Sometimes they bites 'em open," Hodge said.

Joslin is out at the desk with her medical insurance forms or whatever.

Hodge left the room. Rex turned his blue eyes to me. "David asked me what I thought he'd be when he grew up. He was probably expecting me to say president, or garbage man, or soccer star—and I said, 'Rough, and tough, and gentle.' It's what I do want him to be."

Joslin came in. Rex repeated it to her, "Rough, and tough, and gentle." And I guess she knew, because she smiled at him, almost affectionate. But that set him off again. He said, "It strikes me, Clancy, that it is vaguely inappropriate for you to assume any intimacy of tenderness, when, as you say, you are saving my life—but you never understand tone, *chotchke*, and you always assert your sanity by demonizing me. You bank on it."

Wham, she slapped him. Hard, right on the face.

Felt to me like all the air got sucked out of the room.

Rex said, "I'd like to respond to that, but I'm all tied up here."

She shuddered and stood her ground.

Rex whinnied, that sick horse sound. He moved a little, wincing. "Now —now—let me audibilize my real feelings here. Jossie, Jossie, I coulda been a contender, instead of a theme park, which is what I am. Truly, dear, is this what it all comes down to? Cops and hospitals? Is this what our marriage—our sex—comes down to?"

"Rex, I'm leaving now."

"No you aren't, no you are not."

Then Rex's voice gets real low and confidential. I think I should step

21

out of the room. Except I got to wait for somebody official to relieve me.

"One question. Ask yourself one question, Jos. 'Would *he* ever do this to *me*?' "

I'm averting my eyes, but I know she's moved closer to the table now. He goes on whispering to her.

"Jos, you know he wouldn't. In sickness and in health. Gentle fuck? When you lost your job at the UN, how I proved to you there is such a thing as a 'gentle fuck'? Or Kauai? When the Portagee Man of War attacked you around the neck? And Rex sliced the frond and put the aloe on you and the swelling went right down, sting went away? Kauai, babe? Fooling around that night, where the crew of *South Pacific* built that artificial chute out over the natural pool? You said my body was a silver shaft in the moonlight? And the urchin stole your wristwatch? Silver shaft in the moonlight? Or the miscarriage, how Rex—"

"Don't. Don't."

"—abided you. All them times you was sick, honey? And ol' Rex standin' watch over you? Make you tea and hold your hand? The fog lifting over Waiamea, and we could see the goats and wild pigs a thousand feet below? And the Menehunes? I think it's remarkable a man in my condition can say *Menehunes*. Oh, Jos, Jos, I know I'm in a bad way. I'm ill. You don't put ill people behind bars. You take care of ill people, abide them and heal them. Like Rex did for you."

"It's over now. Just stop."

"First time you stepped into Summer Snow? You said, 'I think we're not in Kansas anymore.' Remember, Jos?"

I'm standing there leaning back against the wall, averting my eyes. No way I can avert my ears. But I think she's weakening. She's going to buckle. And we'll have to drive the asshole back to Laguna. A round-trip supersaver. My feet ache.

"Jos, make you a deal. Take this shit off me and we'll do her without the Man. I'll sign myself in. Stay here three, four days, whatever. Just bag the bars on the windows. You're right, I've overextended myself, let me rest."

"I don't trust you."

"Obviously. But don't leave Rex here. You'll leave us here. The Magic Couple. The Us of Us. Jos, I love you."

"But 'I love you,' when you say it, 'I love you' isn't a gift—'I love you' is a demand."

"But honey, our s-e-x? Four times a night? Famished for each other? Can't leave each other alone? Acapulco? Diego Rivera's studio, that widow's talk about Pop, Señor Hooker? Oh, Jos, you can't leave Rex here. Bet you a thousand bucks you can't."

"You're on."

He raises his voice. "Officer—did you hear that? You hold the bets. California, welcome to Off-Track Betting. And we want to emphasize that, *Off-Track* Betting."

I look up. He's trying to point at his head. With his arms strapped down. I want to step outside. Twenty years ago, Rex and I were in a hospital together. July 1960. And he didn't stop talking then either. And it was sex then too. Shit, I got to keep my mind on my job.

She says, "Good-bye, Rex."

"Hey, dirty pool. We bet a thousand bucks. Gimme one more minute. Tell you why you'll lose our bet. Because nobody you've ever met—or ever will meet—wanted you as much—in every way—as Rex did, as Rex does." He's whispering again, whispering hard, can't quite catch his breath. "Because nobody you've ever met, or will meet, believed so deeply in marriage, believed in the institution of it, wanted so deeply to marry and stay married for the rest of his life—to marry *you*, to stay married to you for the rest of our lives—I mean, in bed, what we do with each other, in the bedroom, how does this sentence end? I dunno, you won't leave me here because of it." He's whispering. Panting. "Your pride, Jos, your pride in doing the right thing? You know this is the wrong thing. Cops? I'll voluntarily check in upstairs. No bars—I'll stay, I promise you. As that cop is our witness, I'll stay here, if you really want to save my life. And not punish me. You won't leave Rex alone in this little room. I know you, baby."

Crying. She's finally crying. I stand here and try to think what I am going to do now. If she calls the whole thing off, do I have the right or power or whatever to cancel all the legal forms? Do I get clearance from Hans Brandsma? She's all crying. I feel kind of obscene, listening in on such private matters.

Crying, she says, "Darling, I have to tell you something Rex doesn't know. Darling, it makes me sad." She's whispering too. "It gives me no pleasure at all to tell Rex this."

"What, baby?" Now he's ready to cry too.

"Darling," she says, "Rex just lost a thousand bucks." And she goes out of the room.

Kind of quiet in here.

For a while.

Just him and me.

23

And then he says, "Hear that? Did you hear that, Officer? What she said? The way she said it? Isn't she terrific? Oh, how I love her. Sergeant, I could tell you sex stories that would make your hair—or something—stand on end. That woman and I, for fifteen years, scientists think it has to do with something deep in the earth, but it was Jos and Rex, the Magic Couple."

I just stand guard. Though there isn't much point now, it's over.

Silence.

And then he says to me, "It's like a negative I have been carrying around in my mind, and now the picture is—I *do* know you, goddammit—who the hell are you?"

I don't want to, but I have to. I have to do it, I owe it to him. So I put my hands on the stretcher-table. I take a deep breath, and I say, "I'm Oliver Bodley. I'm Triphammer."

He doesn't get it, of course.

But then he did. He was real pale anyway, but now he just went white. He whispered, groping in his mind. "Trip?"

I stood there.

"And the leader of the gang was—don't tell me—it was *Duke*—Duke something. Oh—oh—what are you—what are you doing here? Oliver *Bodley*."

I just stood there. I'm sorry.

"Well, look, when this gets straightened out, let's have a drink. On the terrace of the Laguna Hotel. It's seen better days, but it's the past. All that matters to me now is the past. I'll have swordfish, like Pop always does, like Grandfather did before him, swordfish fillet, and you can have—do you like red snapper? Please be nice to Jos, she's a swell girl. This isn't her fault at all. Be nice to Jos."

I nodded.

"Well, gee, it's—it's so good to see you again, Triphammer."

I put my hand on his shoulder, the big white bath towel.

"This is just busywork. I'll pay you all back for your trouble. Could you get me—uh—ice water would be a blessing. In a tall glass. I'm going into massive dehydration. I think I cut this one a little close. My, my, though, Oliver Bodley—you're—you're Triphammer. They really kicked our butts in, didn't they? Duke . . . *Talis*, there we go. Well." He smiled weakly. "We can't go on meeting like this. In emergency rooms."

I went out and checked on Joslin, and the kid driver all eager to move out for legitimate cardiac cases. Joslin was looking at me strangely. I guess I looked a little strange myself. Finally made it into the cafeteria. I got a big Styrofoam cup of ice water, a couple straws. I went back into the little room and held it to his lips, and he drank. Trembling like crazy. Then he stopped and looked at me, and he whispered so it scared me, "God save us all."

My basic feeling is that I would rather have somebody pissed off at me for the rest of their life than dead. But Rex Hooker—it's way too hot for my professional expertise. It digs down to hardpack. We ride back to Laguna in the ambulance, Joslin up front with the driver, me bouncing around in the back by myself. Shows you what they think of me.

I would like to throw my Orthotics out the door. Going by the Disneyland Matterhorn, I'm thinking about the opposite of *job*.

We get stalled in traffic. This is no fun at all. The back of my mind says the opposite of *job* is—*garbage*. Oh yes, I'm cleared for takeoff. We get stalled again, a wreck up ahead. I have a cigarette. I'm shaky. And by the time we get back to Laguna, the driver kid is really beginning to bug me, carrying on for the ninety-ninth time about how this ambulance is for sick people and not drunks. He asks where he should let us off. Joslin says at the Hooker house on North Sunset. The driver kid has a fit and says he doesn't have to go up there—after three hours, he's worried about two minutes—but we do go up. He lets us out, and squeals away.

Joslin and I stand in the driveway. Trans-Am, KINGS X. Mercedes, ROLLEM. Joslin comes over to me, and she puts me on the spot. "You know Rex, don't you?"

Women's Intuition. I'll never understand it.

She says, "I told him, 'Rex, I love you—go kill the other you with the weapon of your choice.'"

I think about what he said in Hans Brandsma's office, about *I* and *Me*. I wonder how many times they've played that number on their marital jukebox. I smell the salt air of the ocean. The son, David, I guess, has been taken care of. But what about the family, the parents? J.O. and the Mrs.?

She says to me, "Did I? Did I put his mind behind bars?"

You might have thought about that before calling us, lady.

"Did I do the wrong thing?"

I left my stupid hat in the Grand Entrance Hall. I am going to need that hat at eleven P.M., when I go on duty, after all this R & R I have had, I feel very refreshed. My stupid hat, and I don't have a spare at the trailer. The Chief has a big neurotic hang-up about how we have to wear our hats. Forgetful Ollie.

Men who drink excessively, suicidal, high-strung overachiever types— it's a very serious problem in America. I know one thing has happened this day—Dougie put the keys in the plug, standing on the register. The kid is dead. That's what happened today. A two-year-old. Forget everything else, what happened on Labor Day in Laguna Beach is Dougie. He's cold.

Summer Snow, I look at it and don't. Nineteen years ago, that formal dance. When I moved onto the force over here, I'd answer a nuisance call, beach bums in the Edifice Rex, I'd clear 'em out, exchange a word or two with old J.O. in the driveway. I never mentioned July 21, 1960. Can't. Too afraid of it.

I go over to the rose garden. My aching feet on these white gravel paths. Roses, all about me, in the dusk. I got to think about this. But I don't want to.

What I want is my hat. I hobble on my bursal sacs and bone spurs back to the doorway, check the knob, and it's locked. I step back to see if there's a window open somewhere. No, this house is all closed up. My mind isn't. I walk between the Guest House and the Edifice Rex, down past the swimming pool, all the way out onto the beach. I sit down on the sand.

Just look at that sunset. I wonder why God didn't quit right there. If he had, I'd be out of a job. I know what's bothering me. My hands move in the warm sand. I know very well what all this brings up. Women and booze. I don't want to open up those chapters of my life. Keep the book closed. Your wife betrays you and you fall into the hootch. I don't need Rex Hooker of all people to rub my nose in that. I am making warm little mounds of sand on both sides of me, I am in uniform, patty-cake patty-cake baker's man. I know very well what is bothering me.

Sheila Kite. My first wife. My only wife. I thought we were happily married. Relatively happily married. For four years. Sheel never really enjoyed sex, never got her jollies. I was not exactly too keen on making my own supper. She was never there. I couldn't get up the heart to go into restaurants, I'd just walk by 'em. I was packing my own lunch. But I never questioned it. And she mowed the lawn. We lived in that little place in Coachella. Nice neighbors. The American Dream. Cookouts in the backyard, watermelon feasts, relatives. Sheel always took care of things, like the checkbook. One day I go to my mother-in-law's place, it had never dawned on me that anything was amiss. I say, Is Sheila here? Her mother didn't know, hadn't seen her all day. But Sheila had said she was going shopping with her mother. When she comes in that night, I ask her where she has been, her mother hasn't seen her. Sheila says she has been with a friend at the Salton Sea. Was this a male friend or a female friend, I ask. She was very calm. I said, Isn't it time to be truthful? She looked at me. I said, I think you owe me the courtesy. I'm trying to

26

hold in these waves of nausea. We had had a big church wedding, my uncle was my best man. I said to her, You got something going with this male friend? Kind of, she says. Nausea like a tidal wave. So I shower and shave and show up for work about half shit-faced. Feeling pretty sorry for myself. I figure that's the only thing I can feel, that, or go after her with a tire iron. I'm so ashamed. Next morning was kind of quiet. Not much was said. That's when I began sleeping on the couch.

What are we going to do about this situation? That drums in my head, both when it is clear and when it is pretty foggy. She had real nice legs, I've always liked legs, and hers were tops. But I knew it was never going to be right again. She had herself a new job over in Palm Springs, at Robinson's; she always had good taste in lingerie. I bought her a new car, very spiffy, a Mustang with a black vinyl roof, a high-performance engine. Mustangs were quality in those days, not the junk they make now. She always wanted a 'Vette, but that was a little out of a patrolman's price range. As it was, we were in debt over our ears. But she had a pretty good life. She had me, if she'd noticed. I would have done just about anything to keep her. And things seemed to be ironing themselves out. But one day I was on my way home, dog-tired, anticipating a nice Italian supper, some of that green spinach noodle she used to do, with clams, a little split of dago red, candles—and when I opened the door, what a shock.

She'd moved out. She took the TV set. Not a thing. Not a thing. She had left me, actually, one fork, one spoon, one knife, one cup, one plate, one saucer, one broken can opener, some ice cream in the freezer, one towel, one washcloth, one bedsheet, one blanket, one pillow, one roll of toilet paper, one alarm clock. She took the shower curtain. I lived there for a year. I bought some odds and ends. I used to sit there. Like a kid who comes home and somebody stole all his toys.

I did a lot of drinking, gave up my extra jobs.

It took me a long time to recover. Years. Paying her alimony, although she took the checkbook. I am sitting there looking at one knife, one spoon, one cup, one plate. One day, drunk, I just put all that stuff, one of everything, out into the shed I had built with my own two hands. I felt resentment. I felt betrayed. I guess that's it, I was deceived. Work so hard those years and have nothing to show for it.

It took me a long time to trust anybody. I kept asking myself, What did I do wrong? She said I never put the effort into the marriage that I put into police work. It was like my job was her enemy. And the better I did—that time I got a commendation—made it worse. See, she said, you can do it on the street, but you can't do it in the sack. Once she actually had the nerve to wake me up to say she was relieved I fell asleep so she could do it herself, with her fingers. This does not build confidence in the American Male. I went back to sleep, and when I woke up the pillowslip was covered with perspiration. I couldn't believe this was happening to me. Lots of other women, I eventually found out, knew I could do it in the sack. Most Inspirational. For someone who never read the instruction book. But I didn't love them. Now I can't even see Sheila's face. In my mind. Just her legs. Those legs—I try to go up, to get a complete view, and I always stop about midthigh. And her face is all gone. Except a picture of it I have when she was laughing and happy, the kind of gleam she'd get in her eyes when she was playing pinball and going for an extra game. Shit, I can see her, I'm lying to say I can't see her.

Never when I was married did I cheat on Sheila. But after the divorce I didn't pass up a thing. I took it everywhere I could get it, and you can get it everywhere if you're halfway decent and a police officer. The uniform turns them on. But I did not love them. And I hated them to talk serious. I'd give them my hanky. I never took them home, always to motels. And I'd frequent young people's places. I felt like a dirty old man, and I was thirty-one. I hate to remember the sound of my laughter then, I can still hear it, laughing because I was so miserable and didn't know what to do about it. I think I was an alcoholic. I started to get sick. Hangovers beyond belief, stomach cramps real bad, terrible permanent trots. One night I was far gone, my head on a bar, I was really blue, I was *blue*, and I had this girlfriend with me, she didn't drink, my head just lolling on the bar, and I said, "This isn't for you! Surely this isn't for you!" And she said, "No, it's not." And I wasn't talking to her, I was talking to *me*.

There is no way I can ever forgive Sheila. But I don't enjoy thoughts of revenge. She hasn't remarried. Of course then she would lose the alimony and I wouldn't have to live in a trailer park. But life has a way of evening things out. I still hurt inside. Sheila sits there in my mind like all the things I've lost in my life. I can hardly think about it to this day. And then sure enough I'm doing it, I catch myself right here on the sand, you dumb suck, you are thinking about it. You try to keep up a buffer. Certain things filter through, of course, feelings arrive all unexpected. Being adopted is not the worst thing that can happen. It means I was chosen. I was chosen. I know that before I was born my real mother worked as a cleaning-lady-maid-and-cook for my "aunt" and "uncle." My real mother was nineteen when she got knocked up, and what could she do? You can't raise a kid on zilch when you don't know anything and have no wherewithal. It was nice of my aunt and uncle to step in, they were far from wealthy. They raised me as well as they

28

could, taught me to love and trust and watch out. I'm as good as anybody else. So what if those little rodents on the schoolyard wanted to stick pins in me?

Look at that house up there, "Summer Snow." All peach-colored now, the setting sun is a personal spotlight dead on it. It's a wonderful house. I can't look at it properly because it reminds me I've done a bad job with my life. Old J.O.—how much brains and money and creativity and luck does a man need to build Summer Snow? To get opposites together? I remember I tried to build dollhouses, the first year Sheila and I were married. I don't know what put that into my head. I thought I'd sell them and pick up Christmas money to buy her presents. A scale of one inch to the foot. My own little Summer Snows, I guess. Building dollhouses is like building a real house, just smaller. I sheetrocked mine, put in real glass windows that went up and down, shutters and siding. I'd hold the brad nails with tweezers, even tried my hand at twelve-volt DC wiring. It was hard to cut the little boards, they'd splinter all over. Sheila decided she wanted to be an Avon Lady, so we went to that organizational meeting at the Chinese restaurant. Seven women and me the only man. They asked her what her husband does for a living, and she said, "Oh, this one builds dollhouses," and they looked at me that way. I wonder what Sheila thought I did do for a living, actually. After an Indio Police Department picnic, she said I just wasn't cut out to be a cop. Said I wasn't like the other men. She said I'm too smart to be a cop. Which shows Sheila's high opinion of peace officers. Also shows she had me down right—I only flunked out of two universities. But she's right. I don't have the temperament. Take things too personally. My mind fusses all the time. I crouch down in a garden, looking at a robin, trying to decide whether that feather is gray or brown. Concentrating so hard on the feather I don't realize there's a fucking gorilla coming up behind me.

I had to leave the desert finally. People are afraid of their own feelings. I have no talent or special skills, but I do not want to waste my life. There are many explanations for why people behave, like sex, power, all the religions and systems of philosophy. But I know one thing for sure, people want their lives to have meaning. If you argue with that, you might as well argue with the law of gravity or the fact that the wind blows. People want their lives to mean something to themselves. That's Bodley's Law. Although even with the best of intentions and all the effort in the world, good people lose, really lose it all. And Bodley's Other Law is that most people are so screwed up or lazy that they stop going for meaningfulness. They go for lesser things that they don't really want. So even when they get 'em they're unhappy and reminded of the fact that they chickened out back along the road somewhere. Some people don't get what they want, and it makes them crazy. But most people just slide, they don't set their hearts on much. If they did, they'd have to think seriously about what they want deep down and have to try for it. And that just might be too much of an effort, it'd demand too much of them. So it's easier to muddle through and complain. It leads to very twisted attitudes. What everybody calls facing the real world. But it's not. Just the other day, in the station house, we had a rape victim, I interviewed her, and I really admired her self-control and her intelligence and courage. But after she was gone, Butch said, "Why would anybody rape her? She's *ugly!*" The Chief said, "Well it was dark." I had to leave the room. I have no use for tirades from boring Women's Lib ladies, I'd like to see one try to do my job on a busy day, but I had talked with this girl. She was only nineteen, and very dignified, very self-composed after what she had been through. I had to hand it to her. It is disgraceful foolishness to talk about her the way Butch and the Chief did. It is not doing your job. I wanted to say, "What's the matter with you clowns?" But it won't do any good. If you tried to lay Bodley's Law on those people, they'd just scoff. Because they're prisoners of Bodley's Other Law. But I'd scoff at me too, the way I think I know it all. Babble on, little brook. That's my mind, Bodley's Brook.

And here I am all by myself. On the beach, in uniform. I hope no strollers think I'm on duty. I don't goof off. I do my job. I do my job well. After the divorce and all that wasted time of alcohol and womanizing, when I finally got myself straightened out, I tried to pour all my sadness and my energy into the job in Coachella Valley. But it just wasn't right, working for the Indio P.D. I was always the former football hero, "Most Inspirational." People thought I had flunked out of college because I wasn't smart enough. But that wasn't why. And then when my "uncle" died, it had a profound effect on me. You can't prowl around as an adult where you used to be a kid. Although it is an advantage in police work, knowing where everything is, right down to the number of steps it takes, and the way things smell, you can figure out the world just by the slightest change in the aroma. But I had to leave. I transferred laterally. When I was interviewed by the Chief here at Laguna, I decided beforehand I wasn't really in the running. But I guess he saw something in me. So he must know something. I had accumulated thirty credits at the College of the Desert, in the Criminal Justice Program, and almost had my associate of arts degree. I had two civil service commissions. This affects the wage scale. I had to leave. There were other factors, but I know the truly compelling reason was Sheila, losing her, just when I could have started a real family of my own. Family would be the way I could mean something to myself. And I know it wasn't all her fault. I didn't clean myself up until after she left me and I went through all that agony. The man she was married to was a confused kid, bitching about little things. I cannot believe how young I was. I have fantasies we could meet again, pretend it's the first time. Behave silly at our age.

My hat, for Pete's sake.

I get myself up, and my knees pop. I brush the damp sand off my uniform. I walk back up through the Edifice Rex, get lost in there, have to retrace my steps a couple of times, swear at Rex, and finally get out. I look over at the rose garden. It's so beautiful, sometimes you wish the whole world could be. I'm a dreamer. I stand in the driveway, bareheaded, looking about, trying to figure how I can step in for a moment. What's going to happen when J.O. and the Mrs. come back from the hospital? Find the house deserted and a police officer's hat sitting there.

But the house isn't deserted. I hear somebody inside. The front door opens and I just about faint. It's not possible. He couldn't do it, he hasn't had enough time. But there he is—with a cue stick in his hand. Fresh white duck pants, a blue and white striped dress shirt, cleanshaven and blown-dry, calm as can be. He turns and sees me. When Rex Hooker smiles, those blue eyes just light up. "Well, Trip, how the hell are ya?"

2

I DON'T see him for twenty years, and then I see him twice in four days. Four days later the sucker tracks me down. I'd spent my own little morning painting Butch's house. Butch and I were supposed to be a team, but Butch disturbed a nest of yellow jackets and had to be put to bed with an ear the size of a zucchini. So I was going it alone, killing myself on the chimney. Without warning, there is Rex at the bottom of my ladder, giving it a shake and almost sending me into the forsythia bush. He had called the office and traced me all the way to Butch's house on Tahoe Way. He calls up, "Trip—come meet my son."

I got Exterior White all over me. Rex looks like somebody who knows very well that people look at him and wonder what he does for a living. Rex knows who I am now. It kills me. Everything kills me. The opposite of *job* may be my mind.

"Come on, Trip," he says, "we got to talk over old times."

"Oh," I say. "There's a lot of stuff I got to do—"

"Wouldn't you like to come to the San Diego Zoo and see their newborn baby orangoutang?"

"It's not too high on my list."

"I know, I know."

32

I back down with the paint bucket. I want to know how he managed that Labor Day Shuffle, getting out of the loony bin so damn fast.

He says, "My son. And Mother. And Pop. Come with us now, to the land of yesteryear."

Well, shit.

But like the fool I am, I followed him. Followed his red Mercedes, ROLLEM, in my battered Oldsmobile, 1 GROUCH. All the way to Summer Snow. We got out and walked down to the pool where the kid was puttering with a skimmer, removing leaves and bugs. I could see, immediately, what much of the trouble with Joslin must be about. In the ambulance, that exchange about a perfect little gentleman versus a gallant little boy. He was a kid. Healthy kid, sandy-haired, strong body, eleven years old. But his eyes—they weren't the green color of his mother's or the spooky blue of his dad's. They were gray. Clear, hopeful eyes. Really innocent eyes. And rather thoughtful at the same time. High-potential eyes. This kid has learned to store away things that most people never even learn to recognize. But he wasn't precocious or anything, not a smarty-pants. I shook hands with him, a firm grip. We had a little talk about his soccer playoffs. He said he got a trophy. Right away I think, Uh-oh, this house has already got too many trophies, and I ask him what it's for—only he thinks I mean the soccer league, not the trophy, because he says, "Pride. Fun. Meet kids." I don't know a blessed thing about soccer, but he says he lags a little too much at halfback, always plays better when the weather's hot. At the championship game, the wind felt like a hurricane, kicking up the dirt. He liked everything about soccer. Even getting up at 5:30 for away games, reading comic books in the coach's car, stopping at Burger King. Fine little fellow. Pride, fun, meet kids. I could never tell this boy how shitty the world is.

Rex was checking us out, pretending not to, but he was very, very interested, fussing with the pump on the pool. After a bit, he broke in to say, "So let's go to San Diego, guys. See the great apes. And Trip, the folks are coming home from the hospital today. I know they'd love to see you."

"But," I said, "I'm covered with paint and I smell like something flies would ignore—"

"Man, we sees you rode hard and put up dirty, but I got some spiffy duds from my corpulescence. Back there when I waddled along to all-time-hits-not-sold-in-stores. Surely you can squeeze into *some*thing."

But Sundays are when I recharge my batteries.

"Could you come?" David says. He's made up his mind about me.

So I go into Summer Snow, into a basement shower, and stand there and watch the paint from my hair cascade onto my chest. Why am I doing this? I get out and dry off and comb my hair. There are paint specks on my sunglasses. Rex looks fine now, no scars or scabs from where he cut his face. I wonder how much he really wanted to hurt himself. Do damage. Well, shit. I clench my teeth. Kill the fucker in the mirror. I stand back and sigh.

In my Day-Glow bell-bottoms and floral print shirt I ride shotgun in a pink Seville. Rex driving with a fingertip, his head leaned back, speaking slowly to David about Marge Stivers. "She's real worried about her sister, son. Sissy Stivers is trying to kill herself again. I don't know why. She has a crazy old Greyhound bus with dolls from all the world's countries in the seats. Sissy is a strange person. Very unhappy person."

"Dad?"

"What, honey?"

"Well, you mean she really wants to . . . *kill* herself?"

"Yes, I'm afraid so. Never kill yourself, son. You might miss something. Like the point."

Silence, moderate traffic on 5, beautiful day, just love those brown hills. After a few more miles the kid says, "Death is a beautiful woman."

Rex turns, and says in a shocked voice, "What?"

"I *said*, 'Death is a beautiful woman.' "

"Oh, right."

"My homeroom teacher said so. This girl who sits next to me, Magali —that's her name, a Hebrew word—she's in love with me and always tries to, in the coat room, you know—"

"I'd watch Magali, m'golly—"

"Well, we were talking about death. And we asked Mrs. Tsoules with the silent *T*. Our homeroom teacher. And she said some people think of Death as a skeleton, and Edgar Allan Poe thought of it as a beautiful woman."

"You know where Edgar Allan Poe ended up—thinking crap like that?"

"No. Where?"

"Baltimore." Rex shakes his head. "Death is a beautiful woman." He says it again to himself, kind of smiling, his fingertip on the wheel.

We drive along, past what are rapidly becoming nude-beach exits. I hope that ordinance doesn't go through this time, I really need to restrain hordes of marines on tit-duty. Rex is a total incompetent with the tape deck. Finally he puts in a cassette of Marge Stivers's second husband playing banjo, a bluegrass serenade. It's not bad. And then some whistling, real nice whistling. Rex sticks up his driving finger and says, "That's me in the background on blow job," and David in the back seat whistles along, and the tape stops, and Rex says to his son, "You want to cop a few zees, honey, you look tired—didn't you sleep well last night over at—what's his name—?"

"Matthew Bretter. No, I just couldn't. You know how it is in a strange bed."

"I wrote the book on strange beds, honey."

"When you're in a strange bed—I mean, a *new* bed for the first time, you know, it just doesn't smell like sleep."

"Exactly." Rex kind of hums to himself for a while. Says, "Smells like sleep." Then says to me, "Kid's all right, Trip. I knew that years ago. When he spit into my hand."

"Excuse me?"

"Well, Pop always did it to me, when I'd get hurt and cry, he'd stand there with his hand cupped at my face, as if to stay, 'C'mon, baby, cry into here, put your tears in here, liddle crybaby,'—it used to make me so mad, just furious. And then one day when David was about two—this story doesn't reflect very well on me—anyway, he hurt himself when we were playing popguns, I jumped out from behind the kitchen door and said, *'Die, commie devil!'* and it startled our thundering toddler, and he hit his head against the kitchen table, and cried, and such a shlemiel I am, I did what Pop used to do to me, I cupped my hand to catch the tears, and you, David, you little bastard, you took a look at me—"

"Yeah?" the kid says, leaning his chin on the top of the front seat beside his dad's shoulder.

"And you *spit* right into my hand."

The kid goes heh-heh. I turn and see him just enjoying the hell out of it.

"And that," Rex says, "that was when I said to myself, 'David, you're going to be all right.' " Rex goes on chuckling. " 'Son, you've got it, you're gonna be OK.' "

At the San Diego Zoo Rex got hold of this pretty lady, Donna Brown-miller, about thirty, who works there. We walk around checking out wild animals, and Donna tells David stories about her trips to the Amazon and wrastlin' anacondas. I can tell Donna and Rex have been bed partners. Come to think of it, I bet Rex called ahead while I was showering; Donna seemed to be expecting us. We strolled around and stopped at a pool with two baby hippos. The hippos were also being watched by a Hell's Angel and his old lady. Rex said, "God, they're ugly mothers, aren't they?" The Nazi biker turned, and then Rex immediately leaned way over the railing, trying to make clear he meant the hippos. I had trouble not laughing. We had hamburgers and fries and Pepsis. Rex had a chat with Donna. I had a cigarette, and David and I watched some spider monkeys chasing each other all over their area. Children and grownups were laughing, and David said, all seriously, "A single monkey is a dead monkey," which made me sit up, like "Death is a beautiful woman," and he says Donna told him that "they're so dependent on each other—monkeys can't live alone. They can't survive. Like Dad."

Check. Then this middle-aged lady came up to Rex, her eyes furtive, and she says, "It *is* you—you *are* Steven Kelly."

Rex smiles. "Hello."

The lady turns to her friend, who looks like she's on a day pass from Leisure World. "It *is*—it's Steven Kelly."

The women are wearing flowery muumuus. They fall all over themselves, and say they know it must be such an annoyance, but they take out their pens and ask him to sign their map of the San Diego Zoo.

Rex does.

I look at David, who is rolling his eyes, Here we go again!

The two ladies go on chatting with Rex, and he's golden.

The younger lady says, "Are you and Jessica ever going to reconcile?"

Rex shrugs and says softly, "I don't know—I just don't know." He looks at them seriously. "You think we should?"

"This one does—but I go back and forth. We were so pleased when you conquered the alcohol."

The timid one says, "It seems that Jessica ought to give you a second chance."

Steven Kelly? Jessica? Conquered the alcohol? Run that by me again.

At three o'clock the zoo officials brought out the big brown orangoutang, Suzie, who was carrying this teeny-tiny baby, making a big fuss over it and nursing and cleaning it. Then they let out the father, Sabang —Donna told us his name—and he's bright orange, he's got an enormous neck pouch, and he weighs 400 pounds, just enormous. He sat around being huge for five minutes, and then he larded over to Suzie and the baby —and Donna and the keepers realized they'd made a mistake. Sabang smelled Suzie. Donna said Suzie was lactating, and old Sabang really wanted to mate with her, and Suzie just wanted to be alone with her teeny-tiny new baby. Now 400-pound Sabang was just whammin' away at her, grabbing her, trying to enter by the back door, and Suzie began screaming and trying to get away and protect the baby. Sabang had this El Monstro penis, and children were crying and yelling because their parents didn't want to let them see the monkey's "fight." Suzie swung up on a rock, Sabang right after her, and she was screaming skasksskakaskaskakska, and right behind me I heard this little old lady's voice:

"Just like a mn." Not "man"—*mn*. The old Jewish woman—I guess she was Jewish from her accent—said, "You expec sumding better from a munki? Just like a mn!"

Then a black dude in a white San Diego Zoo uniform came up over the rocks. He started yelling, "Sabang, leave Suzie alone—c'mon, man, get off her." He was shouting, "C'mon, man, now you leave Suzie 'lone," as if Sabang speaks English every day. Finally they had to get a big water hose and go after him to restore order. Some children were really crying, frightened. And their dumb-ass parents making it worse.

Donna had to get back to work. Rex and David and I drove back to Laguna, playing Ghost and Geography. They were both quite expert, but I held my own. I am not exactly used to driving all the way to San Diego, to watch orangoutangs engage in difficulty, but I'll file it away in a lower drawer, with what the Jewish lady said. And put Kelly's triumph over alcohol there in my in-basket. Sheila always said I was no fun, never got out much; needed somebody to light a fire under my ass. Me, the dunce, picking up the phone and hearing it go dead, I thought they were crank calls from somebody I'd hassled. Ollie on the Alert. I even had dinner with one of them, a threesome, and when Sheila said something of a truism, he said, "You bet your lily-white ass." I thought it was a bit gauche, in a restaurant. It didn't occur to me until long after that he knew, he'd held it in his very own hands. Excuse me, I seem to be getting a little carsick.

Mrs. Hooker was sitting on a maroon velvet settee. She was all in a sky-blue robe—and my God what a difference, she must weigh only eighty pounds now. She holds out her frail arms to her grandson and says in this merry, piping voice, "Well, my precious, tell me all about the orang-outang!"

I saw Rex and the kid exchange glances, and as David went to her, he said to the floor, "It was the first one born in captivity."

Mrs. H. had sort of assembled herself there, with classical music coming from speakers everywhere. She was like a queen, bidding her musicians to play. But she was in pain, I saw it in her face when I was introduced. I felt like I should leave, if I added any extra strain. Blew my fuses, the thought of her disguised as a crone, and then taking our dates to the beach for that candlelight ceremony. She sits here in a beautiful gown and holds herself up until David runs off to play. Rex and I go toward the bar, but

I turn for a moment and catch sight of her. She hasn't moved, she hasn't moved at all. Maybe she's just listening to the music. But I get this eerie feeling she's far off, in a foreign land with it, all by herself.

I still feel foolish in Rex's old clothes. I say to him at the bar I guess a little Scotch and soda can't hurt me. I know very well it can, but I allow myself a touch now and then. Never have been blitzed since the bad days, except that one New Year's when I woke up the next morning like a rummage sale. I know the danger is always there.

Then old J.O. himself comes on down the spiral staircase, shuffling along, slightly stooped, eighty now, he don't give a shit, he's made his millions. He was muttering about how the solar panels weren't working right, he'd kill the crook from Lumber Emporium. He said to me, "Well, tell me, Sergeant, has Tokyo fallen?" He was wearing a scarlet silk robe with black velvet lapels. He wears it everywhere. I remember once I came up here to clear some dumb fucks out of the Edifice Rex, and he met me in that robe, with a shotgun, at the front door. He asked me, "Have they captured those wolves that have been ravaging Pasadena?" I guess that's where Rex got it—saying anything that comes into your mind. J.O. went in to be with the Mrs., and Rex and I strolled onto the deck. The old western sky was ablaze with the sun going down, Catalina like a stencil under fluffs of pink and silver in the north. Some jerk-off in a Cessna buzzing surfers. Down below us, David's letting off steam with two big Labrador dogs, Rex says their names are Procter and Gamble. The kid is slapping their snouts, standing astride one and scrabbling around his throat. I can't put my finger on it, but for no good reason I am deep-down scared. The Scotch and soda warms me up; your problem isn't your first drink. Behind me I hear a big car roar into the driveway; the engine goes vroom vroom, and shuts down. Rex grins at me. "Marge!" But he doesn't go back to greet her, he stays put, and sure enough he's right: Below us on the beach there she is, at top speed, tits flying, Marge Stivers. In this absolutely black bikini-bikiniest bathing suit, she might as well be naked, her golden hair streaming. She cries, "Out of the road! Out of the road!" at David, and whips by him, her flipflops shoot off, and she goes right into the surf. She comes up, "Whoop! Whoop!" I've heard her give that sound ever since high school on the desert. She lies on her back, floating, and spies us up there on the deck, and waves. Rex raises his hand, the one with the drink in it. Then he puts it on a round white table, hunches his shoulders, looks at me like he's got permanent brain damage, and skitters along, toe-to-toe, heel-to-heel, toe-to-toe, heel-to-heel, with his elbows hanging out broke and his hands flapping loose and his neck going like

38

a rooster: "She's as solid in the sack as she is in a saddle, and that, mah fren', spells *ro-de-o*!"

I say to myself, Poor devil.

We go in, to the dining room. There's a damask tablecloth and shiny pure-black dishes and black candlesticks, absolute black on blinding white, settings for six. Rex and I hike down into the poolroom on the second level, the trophy room, walls covered with plaques and photographs. The kid comes in, showered, a little dressed up, white shirt. A revolting development turns out to be that this eleven-year-old is better than I am. He shoots pool with a baby stick. I hammer the hell out of it, and the kid says, "Bouncy-bouncy." Then he lines up his own shot and says, "Two, grab a cush, and the eight down there." Then makes it! With a goddamn baby stick. It's a lovely old table, fifty years old or more, and over it are antique lamps with gold braid—and I flash in my mind to the Cues 'n' Cushions in Palm Desert, all those years ago, the night Duke Talis cleared our pipes. I look at Rex, he's on a pretty healthy tumbler of Jack Daniels. I take my little sips of Scotch and soda. The kid is really on a string; he says, "Ten in the side," and shoots an amazingly soft shot, the ten-ball hangs on the lip, then drops in so quiet you hardly hear the little bomp. The kid's knees go in and out, like he's prancing in the end zone after catching a TD pass. I'm waiting for him to spike the baby stick.

I shoot like I'm ready to commit mayhem. The cueball goes all over the place, popping off cushions but not grabbing any balls. The kid says, "Bouncy-bouncy" again. Only slightly infuriates me.

Marge joins us, showered down and lavendered up, not wearing a bra. She takes a relatively easy shot and makes a three-point play, jumps up and down all excited. I watch her jugs, and I say, "Bouncy-bouncy." I can hardly believe I said that. But Rex laughs, and Marge gooses me with her cue.

Rex has told Marge who I am. She saw me play football way back then, or says so now to make me feel good. Marge Stivers is just so handsome, born and bred in money. Wilhelmeena Thundertits. I stand back from the pool table and cast glances at Marge's legs. I think what it would be like to have them wrapped around my back. She'd be the cowboy and I'd be the horse, and we'd escape from the Indians by her riding me upside down with her hands and feet clasped around either end of the saddle. OK, no problem.

We keep playing pool, and David offers this Howard Cosell imitation, "*Da*-vid *Hook*-er adds a whole new di-*men*-sion to—"

Rex says to him, "Watch it, boy, I don't want you to be precocious."

39

"I am not pre-*co*-cious, I am ma-*ture.*"

"Like that. Now stop it."

David looks up at his dad, scared for a moment, afraid he's crossed some invisible line. Real tears in his gray eyes. I never saw it work so fast.

Marge Stivers bends over to shoot, and that lavender blouse opens up. I really can't believe I said "bouncy-bouncy"; I've got no manners at all.

We play Stars and Strips, and David and I win. The seven-ball is called "Marge," it's the ball's name, because, Rex says, "She goes down easy."

Rex has had a few. And has another. I say he can freshen mine just a touch. Americans drink too much. Though I hear the French are worse, the French drink all day long. I don't see how they can, and hope to be an industrial power.

David and Marge want to have a playoff, so Rex and I go up to the Grand Entrance Hall and the main living area. Old J.O. is fixing himself another one, from his private stock. He says to me, "Sergeant-at-arms, never submit to insults except from the King." Words to live by, I think, as he slowly shuffles out onto the balcony to fuss with his telescope. Rex sees me looking around and he says, "You understand, Trip, the house is not *on* the seacliff—it is *of* the seacliff. The house and the land have a good marriage." We are now in the Music Room, as they call it, which is also a kind of library, with a grand piano and books from floor to ceiling. Rex hops onto this little moving ladder and slides along. "When Pop was young and foolish, he wrote a book about it, and the title is from dear old Emerson—see?"

He hands me a scrawny little old book. I put my Scotch down and open it. It's called *Build Therefore Your Own World.*

"Pop had it privately printed—says it was published by the Hooker Light & Power Co. Mother says it was published by the Hooker *Gas* Company." Rex grabs the book back from me, and we sit in matching blue and silver chairs, the last of the sun streaming in. David and Marge's laughter floats up from below, through the classical music on the stereo. I hope Mrs. H. is OK. Rex pulls out a sort of Indian humidor; he's got a lot of joints in there. He puts one in a roach holder with jewels on it. I wish he wouldn't do it around me. Or drink excessively. I remember our Labor Day ride. He's an alcoholic.

"I dig it, Trip, because I can hear his voice in it—like a John Philip Sousa band—listen—listen—" he's shuffling through pages, and he reads: " 'Overdressed wood walls cut with big holes for the big cat and little holes for the little cat, walls becorniced and bracketed and scalloped and ridged and swanked, gabled and tipped to madness, bedeviled in entirety. Window frames, corner boards, plinth blocks, fantails, rosettes, general jigger work. Wood-butchers! Into the ha-ha with them!' " Rex looks up, and says to me, "A ha-ha was a ditch in eighteenth-century pastures, covered over with grass, so that the sheep wouldn't wander away, but a stately gentleman might not see the ditch over-covered with grass, and fall into it, and then you could say 'Ha-ha!' " He smiles at me, all alive, and says, "That's true, Trip. Well, anyway," and he goes back to reading, " 'We must have our corner towers escalating into a candle-snuffer dome like an inverted rutabaga. Boy, take down Number 34 and put a bay window in it for the lady! Inside, littler boxes called *rooms.* Cellular sequestrations designed by some imbecilic neurasthenic whose ancestors were all too familiar with the insides of penal institutions. Sleeping boxes! with scores of doors and endless partitions—the inhabitants would have to spend the major portion of their lives turning around. What shall they ever know of sublime repose? How shall they ever live, in Emerson's great phrase, "glad to the brink of fear"?' "

Rex sighs. "Mother and I read it aloud every once in a while, and Pop crawls down a hole and says everybody's young once." Rex holds in the dope smoke.

I say, "You're sort of proud of your father."

"I have the goddamn right. Talbot House, O'Reilly House, Elsinore, the Seabreeze Gold Club, Norman Terrace, Sunset, Hettinger House—here, Summer Snow—museums and colleges and—well, now he's kind of a waste of time, cranky cuss, but he says it's his turn to be an old fool. And he's so much fun. Build Therefore Your Own Ding-Dong is just full of 'sermons against the somber'—Pop's always been that way—'Let us *play,* let us decorate with relish. Beware the prophecy of Frollo, the book will kill the edifice—heed the wisdom of Blake, exuberance is beauty.' "

I see. Rex, his blond head held back, his blue eyes so bright, all those words pouring out of him. Labor Day, the words pouring out of him then.

In the background I hear something that gives me the willies. It's old J.O. asking Marge and David a riddle. I think of the riddles Rex laid on Hans Brandsma. The old man says, "What are the four state capitals named after presidents? Cleveland wasn't named after Grover. Ain't the capital either. Come on, you two pool sharks."

Marge says, "Madison."

Silence.

David's voice: "Lincoln, Nebraska."

They're coming up the stairs. Marge says, "Jackson, Mississippi—no, wait—"

Rex yells out—it jiggles the Scotch and soda in my glass—"Jef-ah-son *City!*"

41

J.O. and Marge and David come in. We have a community sing, Rex at the piano. Marge is all sexy—"You Took Advantage of Me"—she's good. J.O. has a little buzz on, he's funny, and he stands up to sing an old favorite, but he changes one word, he sings, "I Abhor the Girl Next Door."

Mrs. Hooker calls, "Will you people come in before my dinner gets cold?"

So we get up and walk along, bouncy-bouncy, toward the dining room.

On the way, Rex says to me, softly, "Joslin couldn't stand the way Pop uses words like *wop, spic, nigger, kike*. Once Jos asked him, 'Why do you hate Jews?' and Pop said, 'Why leave *them* out?' "

Rex says, very low now, "Pop was sitting in a hotel at Big Bear in 1951 and a bullet came right through the big window and killed the man sitting next to him."

I look at him. Is he drunk, or stoned, or both? There won't be a scene, will there?

At the table we all hold hands and bow our heads to say grace. David on my left simply says, "Bless the food and bless the family. A-men." Rex says, "Rub-a-dub-dub, thanks for the grub. Yay, God!" Mrs. Hooker says to her husband, "Now would you please stop talking and cut the roast?" J.O. says, "I'll cut the roast, but I hate to stop talking." Prime rib, a beauty. And yams, and asparagus, baked potato, fruit cups and two salads and baby peas and corn on the cob and broccoli with cheese—good night, is all this for us?—sweet pickles and olives and celery, food all over everywhere. Mrs. H. explained to me that the shiny black dishes might seem rather morbid, but they were the very height of fashion in 1930 when she married "that old fool." Rex and Marge—she must have brought her own stash and toked up downstairs—they were both pretty stoned and giggling at everything. I wonder if J.O. and the Mrs. know. I wonder if the kid knows. Rex puts jumbo pitted olives on the ends of all his fingers and asks us to name our all-time favorite male movie star and all-time favorite female movie star. Marge thinks and says, "Greta Garbo," and Rex says, "OK, and who's your favorite female star?" Marge goes haw-haw-haw. Then the kid and Leela are discussing a hand of honeymoon bridge they played yesterday, and Leela says, "You just would not *stop* with those scoundrel things," which David remembers and says, "I know—Dad, I had eight diamonds." Marge says, "I used to have eight diamonds," and Rex says yeah, but we all know what we thought of *him*. J.O. doesn't mind, he's feeding his face. The kid and Rex both reach for the same bun, and have a big fight over it, tear the bun to shreds, and

42

a candle almost goes over, and David slaps his dad's hand and Rex goes on this fake crying jag—"'That *hurt*, you *bully*"—and David whispers to me, "My dad says if I ever grow up to be a bully, he'll beat the shit out of me." I nod.

This dinner is delicious, and it's fun, but my hands are shaking badly. I just do not feel at home in Summer Snow. Mrs. H. seems to have cooked the whole feast by herself. With their wealth, why the hell don't they have servants? Marge asks for the butter, and Rex looks at the butter in front of him and really gets into the concept of butter, but forgets to pass it. I do, even though I'm so fucking shaky I almost lost it into the centerpiece of roses. Mrs. H. checks her rolls in the oven, and gets more milk for David, she's up and down and up and down all the while, yakking away with Marge about people in Switzerland, I can't follow it at all. J.O. sits back with a kernel of corn on his lip, probably thinking about some theoretical problem in architecture. He comes back into earth orbit long enough to ask David, "Now, you are trying to get to Camelot, and you come to a fork in the road, and in the fork is a house which contains two extraordinary twins—one always tells the truth and the other always lies. Now, you don't know which fork to take—one road leads to Camelot and the other road leads to the swamp where the pythons romp. You knock at the door, and you don't know which one of the twins answers. How can you find out—if you have only *one* question—which road is the right road?"

I myself tried to figure it out. If you tell me this fork is right, should I take it? No. Would you tell me the truth if I asked you . . . No. Rex was no help because he said rather than going to Camelot he'd stay with those twins and run some Gestalt therapy on them, verbatim. Marge kept talking rapid-fire to Mrs. H. breezing along, and they'd laugh. They were gossiping like fiends. Marge passed me the string beans with almonds, I was just delighted to discover a dish I hadn't seen, but I also noticed Marge was making a point with Mrs. H., a little zinger about someone they obviously didn't like at all. Marge and the old lady were solid, running their own world.

When we were all filled up, and I was wondering if I could handle another sliver of pecan pie before I hit the fruit and cheese, David said to his grandma, "May I be excused?" She said of course, precious, and he walked around the table, picked up an olive that had fallen off Rex's pinky, ate it, and went to his grandpa and bowed low. He looked at ol' J.O., and said, "What you say, Pop, is this: 'If I asked your brother if this is the right road,' "—and he held out his right hand, pointing—" 'would he tell me to take it?' " Old Man Hooker waited a minute, and then

43

grabbed the kid and hugged him up, twisting forward so that he tipped his chair. *"That's* my grandson," he said. "I knew it skipped a generation."

"Well, tell me, do you truly like your work? You must feel it is a genuine contribution."

That's what the old lady said to me, just the two of us left at the table; everybody else went off to play some dumb game with flashlights. I was smoking one of the cigars Rex had provided, and I was afraid Mrs. H. didn't like cigars; she seemed to have a headache. But she said no, she'd learned to cope with cigars forty years ago. She was looking over a tiny chip in one of those pure-black coffee cups.

"I think," she said softly, "I think of our Rex, when he was just, just David's age now, and he was playing baseball on the beach, with his pals." Her nose was running and she daubed at it with a little lace hanky. "He hit a home run!" She gestured, her frail arms in the blue sleeves. "And the ball came through that window over there"—and I saw she was on pills, she had really worked her heart out making dinner—"and—and thousands of pieces of glass, they lodged in my hair, and Rex—our boy was so ashamed, he didn't come home for two days. I had been preparing a buffet lunch. That was when this house used to ring with a thousand voices. Before this—this pesky thing grabbed me."

I rolled my brandy in my snifter. Pesky. Whatever that illness is, ma'am, it isn't pesky. What I got is pesky. Just look the way the snifter shakes in my hands, I'm so thirsty all the time and have to pee every hour. And sleepy, and hard to wake up.

"Do you know Joslin?" Her eyes were like hot blue coals, staring at me. You can see where Rex got his eyes.

"Poor Rex—" She bit her lip and stared at me. Huge empty blue eyes. "It's not the easiest thing to have a world-renowned figure for a father."

I said, "Probably not that easy to have him for a husband."

"Oh—you *dear,"* she said. She clasped my hand.

I notice an ash from my stogie has zapped a burn in the tablecloth, really only a speck. But you can see it, red brown in the stitching.

"Joslin—Joslin once at Christmas, I said to her, 'Isn't our David a good eater? Oh, he's a wonderful boy.' I said it perfectly innocently, I presume. I said, 'Oh, he'll grow up to be as perfect as Rex.' Then—then Joslin said to me, 'No, he'll grow up to be as perfect as David.' " Mrs. H. held her napkin in her hand. "Well—well, I said, 'Of course,' and then—well, I certainly didn't mean anything sinister, I wasn't—I didn't mean to be the Mother-in-Law." She shook her head. "Rex said to her, 'Jos, why did you

44

have to say *that*?' He was quite angry with her. And I had caused that strife. By my innocent remark." Her hand gripping the napkin. "Perhaps, perhaps we are victims of forces we don't know." She looks up at me.

Well, I can't deal with it. Mrs. H. very faint, there in the low candlelight.

"He calls her Jossie-Possie. One Christmas I gave her my mother's mink stole, a truly gorgeous stole, and Jossie said to Rex, in the back bedroom, I heard her as I passed by, she said it made her feel like a—a whore." Mrs. H. didn't look up. "And now, now Marge is wearing Mother's gold engagement ring—whenever she comes to the house, but I suspect—oh, well, never mind what I suspect. . . ."

I'm just hydroplaning on sadness, watching her.

"I know I mustn't let myself brood. I know the family 'treasures' must not be—oh, mercy, the way Joslin talked."

J.O. came back through the room with a flashlight in his hand. He said, "Little bastard was hiding in the kiln." He stopped at the table, looked at his wife, and then looked at me.

Mrs. H. grabbed my hand again and held it up, and looked at her husband. "Isn't he a darling?"

Then David came in, all out of breath, with a flashlight in his hand. "Pop, your secret *pass*ageways—I had to crawl."

The old man, a bit tipsy, said, "Never crawl. Walk like the biped the universe decided on!"

Marge arrived, contributing her flashlight. "We can't walk all at once."

Way down on the lower floors somewhere, Rex's voice: "Hee-hee-hee, can't find me."

Marge says, "Walking can be difficult." She glances at Mrs. H. "Although *I* was walking at ten months."

J.O. says, "Hell, a calf can walk when it's born."

Mrs. H., in that Darvon world of her own: "Rex has the opportunity to *listen* to himself now—mind you, I saw Joslin coloring his thinking, but I didn't want to say—"

J.O. said, "Don't, then!"

The old lady was hurt. "Don't be forever reprimanding me, darling."

Rex came up with his own flashlight, spraying its beam. His mother said to him, as if the two of them were all alone together, "Surely, dear—surely now, the intermittent loneliness without her is far better than the constant frustration with her."

David pipes up, "You see, it's like pluses and minuses in algebra—and the lying brother is a minus and the truthful brother is a plus—"

All eyes go to him.

45

J.O. took his wife upstairs, after she pulled herself together and bade us all good night. Rex went up, too.

That's when the phone rang. David answered it and said it was for Marge, so she took it in the kitchen, and I heard her cry out, really loud. When she came back in, her face was all drained and contorted; she looked like she was going to scream again. But she was holding it in. I just stared at her, David was shying away. Rex came down and Marge reached out to him, buried her face in his chest. He looked over the top of her head at me, and I said with my eyes that I didn't know. He half-carried her back into the kitchen, and the kid and I could hear her sobbing in there.

David whispers to me, "Want to play pool?"

Rex comes back in and wiggles his finger at me. I go over to him and he says, "Trip, can you be of help?"

I see, over his shoulder, Marge leaning at the sink. Staring out the window at the darkness.

Rex whispers, "I wonder if you would be so kind—could you drive David to his mother's house?"

"Sure."

Rex walks over, kneels down in front of David, and hugs him, gives him a kiss. "I'll explain later, m'man. Got business to take care of, and it can't wait. OK?"

"OK." The kid bracing himself.

"OK, Trip? Help me on this one?"

Then there was all this rushing around, Marge and Rex. They went out and got into the car. From the sound of it warming up, it wasn't his Mercedes or the Cadillac. Very big engine, Marge's car. I wonder what I should do.

I play pool with David. And he beats me again.

Am I supposed to take David to his mother's house right now, or wait?

I'm tired of getting skunked by an eleven-year-old. We hang up our cues and go back upstairs. I stand in the kitchen drinking Pepsi when I see a funny thing on the kitchen table. It's like a miniature Arab caravan. Little wooden camels, each one carrying a giant date on its back, and the head Arab is one of those Spider Man puppets—all on real sand, with a little dune behind them. On one side of the dune are African Arabs, and on the other side it's like the beach here at Laguna, with a family on vacation, little plastic figures in a Model-A miniature car. A dollhouse-size picnic lunch basket is on the back seat with a grape and a raisin in it, and a father doll and a mother doll and a kid doll, and some miniature fishing

46

poles, and little suitcases. David smiled, and opened the suitcases. There were dimes in 'em.

I was puzzled. I looked at the kid. He said, "She's been doing it ever since I was real little. I know, I *am* a little old for it."

I was just looking at it—she must've done it all while we were playing pool.

"I remember when she made the circus one. With a trapeze artist. And a tightrope walker. And it had magnetic monkeys hanging from the Big Top. And clowns, and sawdust."

I stood there.

"The one I remember most vividly was the house on fire—"

"On fire?"

"She put a burning candle for the flames, behind the walls of her old dollhouse. She had a hook and ladder. And a pumper. And a chief's car. And a mother in the window holding a baby in a blanket." The kid goes heh-heh. "It was neat. But it could have caught fire." He went over and stared at the Saudi Arabia–Santa Monica thing, with a real gentle expression on his face. Never saw a kid so protective.

All of a sudden he turns to me. "The whole family is just petrified of fire."

This I do not know.

"There have been a *few* fires in Summer Snow. Over the years." He laughed, snapping out of his dreaminess. "One time Pop almost burned the whole place down. He was building his huge redwood desk—he was oiling it and varnishing it, and he left all the rags near the furnace, and it smoldered, you know, and burned a huge hole in the workroom wall." He shook his head. "But it turned out OK because the desk was so big he couldn't get it through any of the doors. So he took it through the hole he burned. And Dad, when he was just my age, *he* got fascinated with fire. Used to burn up his tin soldiers. And years later *he* almost burned the house down. When he came home from Stanford, and was sleeping in the solarium, and the electric heater next to the bed tipped over and set the blanket on fire. Nobody knew he was home because he drove in about two A.M., and he was, you know—" The kid doesn't quite know whether to say it or not. I suspect alcohol is a pretty big issue around here. So he goes on right quick, "It's a family joke—he tried to beat out the fire with a pillow, and ripped open the pillow, and so he was mumbling "Fire, Pop. Fire, Pop," with the flames jumping and feathers flying all over the solarium. Pop came down and threw a bucket of water on him."

"Is that what happened?"

"Well, I wasn't born yet, of course."

The phone rings again. The kid hops to it and says, "Hi, Mom!" Then he blunders a little, and he says, "No, but Daddy's friend, Mr. Triphammer, is."

I smile. "Daddy"—not "Dad." And I am amused to discover that I am *Mr.* Triphammer, Daddy's friend.

David says into the phone, "No, he went somewhere with Marge," and then I see him wince, like he knows that's not the coolest item of information. He turns and says his mother wants to speak to me.

Her voice is not exactly the friendliest. Real cold, in fact. She says she doesn't like to call, but Rex's message was confusing. And it's an hour late. I say I'll bring David right over. She says it's not Bluebird Canyon, she's in the Mission Viejo house, David knows the way, and hangs up, fuck you very much.

The kid's got his eyes on me. I say his mother wants him home immediately.

"Toot-sweet," he says.

Yeah, toot-sweet. So he gathers up some things, and we go on out. He digs my license plate: 1 GROUCH.

So he's sitting there beside me, and I see his muscular soccer-player legs in the dash light. He's a little nervous, but OK. He seems to trust Mr. Triphammer, Daddy's friend. I light up a cigarette, and some dimwit in a Datsun goes through the red light on Forest, goes right through it.

"Is it a good job, being a policeman?"

"Sometimes."

"Do you arrest people?"

"Sure."

"For murder?"

"Not too often."

"For burglary?"

"Yes."

"I know a kid whose brother stole a car once."

"My first arrest here in Laguna was a stolen car."

"Really?" He turns in the seat. "Tell me."

"Well, it was about two in the morning. Around midnight they broadcast a stolen car, a Camaro, blue, stolen up near the high school. The plates were the owner's initials, BJK. So I'm tooling along in the patrol car —it was a starry night, two, two-thirty, and fwooom, there he is: BJK, blue, Camaro."

"And you got him?"

"Finally. But first they took off. Doing sixty in the city. Took a sharp left by the old Safeway, then up through a parking lot, up Anita, down an alley, up over to Thalia. I had my siren and my red light going. They shot across Glenneyre, and then we came to this dead end with a high fence. I figure he'll go right through it, but he went around in a skid, parallel to the fence. And then he hit this guy's garden. The dirt really slowed the car down, and he went into the garage."

"Into the garage. He went inside?"

"No, I mean he hit it."

"Oh."

"Both car doors fly open, and the two kids are running in opposite directions. I'm going after the driver, I'm stepping on this guy's tomatoes. I didn't even stop to turn off the motor, just jammed it into Park. This little flake goes through the tomatoes in front of me, the sticks and stakes flying, and he's up onto the fence, and I got him right by the belt, I'm pulling his jeans off, I got his belt and he's not going anywhere. He's trying to kick me, and I'm tellin' him to get off the goddamn fence."

"This is neat."

"Well, I've already called my backup, and now he comes, and the other little puke runs at him, and Butch just opened his door, and the kid ran right straight into it; it dumped him right on his butt."

"Gee, what a great job."

"Well, you help people out."

"Sounds to me like you get 'em into trouble."

"No, they were in trouble the minute they took a car that didn't belong to 'em."

"But if you hadn't caught them, they might have just left it somewhere."

"When you go joyriding through town at high speed, somebody better stop you. Before you kill yourself. Or somebody else."

He sits there thinking. "That's true." He brightens up. "I really like the part about the tomato sticks and stakes—and pulling his jeans off."

"You should have seen that little dip's ass, his cheeks staring me in the face."

Heh-heh. "Cheek to cheek."

Heh-heh yourself.

On Laguna Canyon Road, on the way to the El Toro turnoff, cozy in there just beyond Kubiask's Antiques, I see Butch dozing in a blue-and-white. Speed trap, dozing in the dark. I cut my lights, pull to a crawl, and then gun it, and he doesn't wake up. Lazy incompetent. Beside me the kid takes it in. He says, "Are you really one grouch?"

"I am." I check in the rear-view; Butch is dead to the world. I've seen him take on three marines, big muscular suckers, you want Butch on your side, he loves righteous blood. But craps out on community service. He's not completely grown up.

I say, "You sure get along with that old grampa of yours."

Kid doesn't say anything.

"He's had quite a life." And then, when the kid still doesn't say anything, I look at him. He's troubled. I say, "What's the matter?"

"Nothing."

So I let it drop. Kids don't like to talk about things that bother them. Adults have their world, and kids want to be left out of that world's problems. Kids got their own very important little worlds. Twice as true in divorce situations. Taking sides. Guilt trips. Leave me out of it, I want to go swimming. That's the way kids respond.

"Well, I love him, of course, I just worry about his temper."

"He's sure got a temper, ol' J.O."

Silence, leave it alone.

I wait for the light at Moulton Parkway. They're carving up these beautiful hills. Not that I am an environmentalist; I just hate to see them ruin the land.

And then I felt like a prize fool. Here I was thinking about shopping centers destroying the land and suddenly the kid, David, he's crying. Beside me there, just sobbing. I pull into a liquor store parking lot.

"If—if people—could only—"

I am concerned about his well-being. I am also thinking how it will reflect on everybody if I show up at his mother's house with him in this shape. I let him cry it all the way out, and discover I'm very shaken. The way he wipes his eyes and cheeks with his hand.

We sit there and settle down. Fortunately I have some Kleenex. He is having trouble breathing. I try to get him back on the track. He calms down a little. He breathes and breathes, blows his nose.

"Once my mom shouted at my dad about Pop, 'What does that man stand for?' And my dad said, 'J.O. stands for Excellence.' And Mom said, 'Bullshit.' And my dad said, 'Oh, he stands for Bullshit too.' And Mom just walked out of the room and slammed the door pow.'" And now David was kind of laughing. But he was seeing the scene in his mind. "Oh"— he lets his head go, thunk, sideways against the window. Goddamn, his head hits the window hard.

Joslin was staying up in the Saddleback foothills. I don't know why, when they've got that big place in Laguna. When we pulled into the

50

driveway, Joslin came out immediately and swooped the kid into her arms: "Hey, Superstar, I've been worried about you."

She sent him on in, and then walked down to me.

"So Rex and Marge have gone out on another bender?"

"It wasn't a bender."

She waited. "Rex told me about you and him. High school. When you were beaten up by that gang."

I nod. I say, "On the way over here David got a little upset. He's a little young to process all—"

"I don't need an employee of the Hooker family to tell me about my son."

"Employee?" I looked at her. "Sort of a disgusting thing to say."

"Sort of a disgusting thing to be."

Well, holy shit.

I just looked at her. And then her face changed, and she said, "I—I'm sorry."

I muttered, "Kind of an emotional night."

She smiled. "I am not unfamiliar with your clothes."

I look down and realize what I'm wearing, and I say, "Rex just gave me the clothes for the day."

"Be careful what Rex gives you."

Huh?

"He may want it back. In spades."

I don't want to talk anymore. I get into my car, and pull out of the driveway with my low beams on her plates, KINGS X.

On the drive back, on La Paz, I think about the kid. What was that he said in the car on the way to San Diego? First night in a new bed doesn't smell like your own bed. No, he said it doesn't smell like—sleep. Doesn't smell like sleep. Officer Bodley drives along, sniffing, trying to smell what sleep smells like.

When I reported for duty at seven A.M., I found out what had happened. Sissy Stivers, Marge's sister, committed suicide. She hanged herself last night.

Right away I steel myself. I figure I better whip up to Summer Snow. Whenever I have to announce a death, I always go through my mind how I'm going to do it. I don't have the problem on my hands right now, because Rex and Marge know. But I'm in the mind set anyway, it just hits me. You want to do it softly and reasonably. You want to say: I have a very tragic piece of news. It takes a few minutes to sink in. If an older

51

person is involved, you try to find out if there's a physical problem, like they could have a stroke. Maybe you take a neighbor or a clergyman. You never telephone. It's just not right procedure to telephone. How do they know it's real? Maybe it's a crank call. But if a policeman shows up, and they have to look right at him, at the uniform, it's valid. It's the real world. Of course, it's harder for the officer, he has to go through the emotional experience, and you never know what people will do. You have to try to control them, keep them from hurting themselves. And carry the whole scene with you after you're done. Go home and try to cook with your hands going twitch-twitch-twitch. Sheila used to say, "Calm down, you're making *me* nervous." And me, "I *am* calm," twitch-twitch-twitch, why don't they package this broccoli shit so that you can open it? Shit, there's broccoli all over the floor. Sheila in that voice of hers, "Why don't you get a *decent* job?" That isn't tomato sauce bubbling there, that's blood. I think maybe I'll hold off on dinner a half-hour, work in my shed, send dollhouse siding all over everywhere. Sheila says, "Another dinner ruined," runs sobbing into the bedroom. "I hate it, I hate it, hate it, *hate* it."

No wonder she developed a wandering eye.

So I pull up Sunset and into the driveway. There's Rex, sitting on the trunk of his Mercedes, his gold boots propped on the top of the plate, ROLLEM. It's a hazy day, gray air. He's smoking, drinking a can of Coors. I check him out, he's not drunk. I notice a big mug of coffee on the asphalt.

Rex says, "I just missed you, over in Mission V. David was still in the pool when I got there. Jos is going to have to see another judge if she thinks—Goddammit, he's mine."

"Where is he?"

Rex motions with his head. "Asleep in his room. Where he belongs."

So I took the kid all the way over there, and we go through that, and then he gets picked up and brought back here. No wonder he breaks down. Treated like a Ping-Pong ball.

"Come in for a cup of coffee. Since you're here, I guess you've heard about Sissy."

I nod.

He gets down off the car, and I follow him in. J.O. is sitting in his red robe with the black velvet lapels, his white hair sticking out, there at the kitchen table with his coffee. He's playing with the camel caravan–beach resort "Breakfast Arrangement." Looking at it out of the corner of his eye, starts fiddling with it, moving a camel, he's eaten half a date—and he sees

52

us standing there, and the old man says, "You know, when I married her, she was a sane woman."

J.O. looked at me. Then he looked at his son. "So. Tell me."

"I'm afraid it's the Stivers family, Pop."

"Murietta? Not Murietta?"

"No. No, it's the—girl. Sissy."

"I remember Sissy."

"Well, Pop—oh, Pop—"

J.O. put his hand out, and he caressed his son's hair. "Sissy has come to harm?"

Rex sat back. "If harm is taking your life. She finally made it, Daddy."

J.O. drank his coffee.

"Last night she—she took her life, she hanged herself."

The old man didn't move. He raised the coffee up to his lips and put it back down, exactly, without a sound, onto the saucer.

"Jesus, Pop, she was in and out of institutions. I told you how she strung that barbed wire between the trees where the dirt bikers used to trespass, to get 'em in the eyes, and the night when she—"

"She tried to kill you with her Greyhound bus."

"Little dolls from all the world's countries in every seat. . . ."

Silence.

"Last night Sissy picked up a couple of black dudes at the Deep Six, took 'em home with her, got plastered, and before it was even dark it got out of hand. I don't know, I don't know, they beat her up—one of her earrings was embedded in her neck—and took turns raping her."

Silence.

"The nurse—the housekeeper got there, and they bashed her on their way out, so she called here, to Marge, but Sissy went out into the garage —she hanged herself in the garage."

"Murietta . . . ?"

"—is in Switzerland. As usual."

Silence.

Then J.O. said, "We won't tell Mother."

"*Chiaro, chiuso.*"

Rex drank from his Coors. "Damn," he said. "David's going to be up, and I don't want him to see me like this."

"Don't you worry about that guy. I'll take care—"

"*I* will take care, thank you."

Silence.

J.O. said, "They got the niggers?"

Rex said, "What?" Then he understood. "Oh, don't say that, 'niggers.'"

"Excuse me. The Distinguished Black Sodomites." He turned to me. "Anything?"

I said not that I knew of.

Rex said, "Marge kissed me, and she was smiling, and she said, 'No more pain, no more pain for Sissy now.'"

J.O. said, "Isn't that remarkable?"

Rex sighed. "Marge—shit—we're too much like brother and sister."

Silence.

J.O. said, "Are you going to be all right?"

"Of course."

The old man went upstairs to his wife.

I said I had to get back to work. Rex shrugged, and we went out and stood among the automobiles. He said, "I remember once I was really drunk, right in that kitchen. I was holding Mother in her white robe, and she was crying, I was totally zonked, this was about five years ago, and Pop was furious with me for—for letting the family down."

I smoked and looked away.

"He punched me in the face, with all his strength—"

I don't want to hear about it.

"Mother crying—sobbing, in her white robe—and I didn't stagger, or drop her or anything—I remember it, I remember just how it felt—" He was finishing his Coors, and put it down on the hood of the Mercedes. "My slippers, Trip, my slippers had suddenly gone down ten feet through the floor, and I felt, somehow, carved. Then I carried Mother over to the spiral staircase, I carried her up it, and I put her to bed, and when I came back down Pop said to me, really soft, 'Son, I will carry that punch to my grave.' And I said to him, 'Hell of a right cross for a seventy-five-year-old man. I could have dropped her.'"

Rex looked at me. "You know, I'm terribly ashamed—when you saw me—when you and Jos put me in the cackle factory. I assure you, it's not negligible grief. I am aware that it's negligible behavior. Oh, Lord, I came down and Pop said that, and upstairs Mother had been gasping into my ear, 'Oh darling, oh darling, he loves you so, he loves you *so* dearly—'"

This family really gets off on hurricanes. They're like loose wires, skipping on the pavement. I just listen. Bombs going off in the cold in my back.

Rex says, "It was only a matter of time. With Sissy." He shakes his head, as if he's trying to clear it. "Goddammit." He begins to sing, "That silver-haired daddy of mine." He sighs again. "Pop never asked anybody for help—never in his whole life. It's what makes him so heroic—and so —so *irritating.*"

He walks over and huddles into this ground-level window. His feet trampling a huge coil of green garden-hose. He raises the window and says,

"Hey, fart-face, waffles or pancakes?"

I hear David let out a sleepy groan.

"C'mon, man," Rex says, bent over there. "Waffles or pancakes?"

Another groan. Then, "Waffles."

Rex walks back to me and makes that sick horse-whinny noise. He whispers, "From high atop the Summer Snow ballroom, this is Steven Kelly posing the musical question 'What's the difference between a duck?'" He slumps, puts his hand on my shoulder. Squeezes my shoulder. Looks at the ocean. "Marge's face, when she said that, 'No more pain for Sissy now.' You should have seen her face. Oh, Trip, that woman is— when I think about all the ways she's beautiful, I—" He stands there and can't say. Then to himself, "Waffles. Right."

3

I'M SUCH a coward. I don't want to remember. Rex told Joslin. Well, if he can stand it, so can I. I will remember. But I hate it. Duke Talis. That happened. It happened, and I guess I feel, irrationally, that I didn't stand by him. But that's not true. Anyway, at two A.M., in my trailer, I can't sleep. I sit in the black Barcalounger and go over what's digging at me in the dark. Rex and me, nineteen years ago. July 21, 1960. It still torques my jaw.

Both of us fresh out of high school—he was going to Stanford in the fall, and I had that football scholarship to Iowa. I may have been "Most Inspirational" and saved the day in the Coachella Valley, but there was no way I was Big Ten material. It wasn't exactly a scholarship per se. I was hardly even recruited, no letter of intent. Scholastically speaking, I wasn't even Indio High material. I had the brains, I just didn't have the incentive. In my sophomore year I always used to wear my coat to class, and got expelled, my collar up, Elvis. I must have got about 150 blue discipline cards over a period of two years. And then I had nephritis, inflammation of the kidneys, my ankles all swelled up. I had to stay in bed all summer and watch the happy kids go by. The one doctor we went to said I had too much sugar in my blood. Which explains my sweet disposition. The school sent somebody up to administer the Regents to me. I didn't pass. And finally, when I went back to school, I was a year behind all my old buddies. But we'd drink beer and smoke, hide underneath the lecture room. We had a little group, we ran the school, football, basketball, baseball—only I didn't do much because I was still weak. But I worked out as much as I could. When I failed the Regents the second time, my aunt shipped me out to my other "uncle's" garage for tractortrailers, in Blythe, with gas pumps out front. I got all the shit jobs that summer. Anything dirty and grubby, Oliver would catch it. I was changing tires and greasing rigs and cleaning out the grease pits. I looked like the Tar Baby. After three months, in desperation, I call my aunt: Just please get me a bus ticket; I am going back to school. And I got straight 1's, Honors, from then on, no more 5's, no more forging excuses and getting caught fishing. I took a job in a florist shop. My aunt knew what she was doing.

Now, of course, I can see it from the other side. Kids are all the same. You can see right through 'em. They lie terribly. They reconstruct a story and they've got a person in three different rooms at once, they fall all over themselves. I say, "How come you said it was suppertime when five minutes ago you said it was lunchtime?" You just chip away, chip away. You say, Well, we can do this the easy way or the hard way. I feel sorry for them, with parents who don't give two shits. And it's always the followers who get caught, never the ringleaders. Somebody says, "Let's go put Janey's garbage can on her roof." And it's always the follower who is up there hanging on to the chimney with one hand and the can in the other. I understand they want to get their feet wet a little, but I hate to see them sign off on the future. One little guy at Indio High, who had a briefcase, today he's got a Rolls-Royce, he's an executive for Westinghouse. In tenth grade he was the puniest little dweeb I ever saw, pale as a sheet, trousers too big for him. He'd drag that briefcase up and down the halls with his slide rule and chemistry books. I took those courses too, like trigonometry, made a lot of paper airplanes in there. Everybody picked on him. Once we nailed his briefcase to the floor, and when the bell rang, he jumped up and it damn near took his arm off. So high school social life was a misery to him, but now he answers to no one, he's got his.

And July 21, 1960, Rex Hooker and Oliver "Triphammer" Bodley were sitting on top of the world. Rex would always strut around like Uptight Dudley Do-Right, with that white-blond hair; he had a way of walking that made people want to get him. But there had been that amazing graduation party at Summer Snow. I was impressed. In the spring term

57

I even took Speech Class, because I had illusions that the ability to give a speech would come in handy after I was too old to play and eventually went into coaching. It never in the world would have occurred to me I'd be a policeman. What a humiliating thought. We all hated the fuzz.

So on that night, July 21, we were half in the bag on Cutty Sark from his famous architect-father's liquor cabinet. We'd been hanging out in his mansion in Palm Desert, named "Medjuhl" after the big luscious date. I remember dates, because flying by us at about a hundred mph on Highway 111 there was that big shop that advertises "The Romance and Sex Life of the Date." Rex eases up on the Fleetwood, and we roll into a place called "Cues 'n' Cushions." Rex already had a Stanford jacket, red with white leather sleeves, and we shot some eight-ball on those tangerine tables. The gang sat around eating banana milkshakes and potato chips. Rex's girl, Marge, was spending the summer with her parents in Switzerland, and I had no girl. Nobody would ever have guessed at that point I was a virgin, but I was, I had done everything except. It bugged me when guys would say, "Shit, I don't know what went wrong—I didn't get lucky, and I promised her the moon."

Rex and I bagged the poolroom, got back in the Caddy, and stopped for gas at a Chevron station. A guy named Duke Talis pulled his head out of the guts of an old Ford. I didn't know him much at all, except that he was twenty-five, a dropout, had been in a lot of trouble, reform school. He was a good natural singer, had the lead in the operetta, and guys in Concert Choir said that before he was expelled he could lift a piano in the air, one end with one hand. And he killed a wino with a knee drop in Thousand Palms. He had long dirty ducktails. That summer night he was stripped to the waist—the temperature even at night can go over a hundred in the desert. He had grease and grime all over him and crazy brown and yellow eyes.

Rex seemed quite in control. "Fill her, Duke."

Duke put the hose in the tank and went for a windshield squeegee.

Then Rex and I went to the Sun-Air Drive-in, just beyond Cathedral City. A fat elderly couple were sitting in shorts on folding chairs in front of their powder-blue T-Bird. The movie itself was bad news, so Rex and I went into the Snack Bar for Cokes and chili dogs. A guy in sawed-off Levi's said, "Hooker."

Rex said, "Hey, Snipe. Learnin' anything this summer?"

"Nothin' like what I have learned in the past half-hour." The guy leaned over and whispered, "Marla Talis is doin' it for everybody. In Jordan's Buick. I've had her twice already."

Rex smiled. "She's doin' it for everybody?"

"Yo." And then Snipe looked at me. "Hey, podner, who are you?"

Rex said, "Oh, sorry, Snipe, this is Triphammer. Big Bad Bodley, student body president at Indio. He's goin' to Iowa this fall on a football scholarship."

Snipe and I shook hands. He said, "Iowa—bitchin'."

Rex looked at me. "Shall we?"

I still can hear him saying those two words, "Shall we?" Like "Shall we dance?"

I said, "You go ahead."

Snipe said, "No shit? Those Indio dollies got you infected?"

So at the Sun-Air Drive-in, Rex and Snipe and I walked over to a beat-up 1950 four-door, four-holer Roadmaster Buick—green, parked all by itself in the next-to-last row of speakers. Four guys were standing around it, smoking. The back door opened and a guy got out and went to another guy to bum a cigarette. A big blond crew-cut guy slid into the back seat and closed the door.

We stood there. Watching the movie sometimes. We were cracking jokes and laughing, sort of high-pitched. I stood off to one side because I didn't know these turkeys. When the back door of the Roadmaster opened, Rex pulled away from the circle. He said, "I'm going in."

Snipe said, "All the way in, Hooker."

The big blond crew-cut guy was coming toward us. He said, "She already forgotted it, but I going to treasure it in the memory book of my m-i-n-d." He farted.

Those Palm Springs chaps just exuded class.

Snipe said, "You gonna rip off a little bit of that, Iowa-bound?" And then he said, "I'm sorry, I been drinkin', what's your name again?"

I told him.

"Oh yeah, now I remember." He stood there. "Hooker's going to Stanford." He shook his head. "I really wanted to go there. Stanford. But my folks want me to stick close because I need parental super-vision. They're right. But Riverside, shit. I want to be a Stanford Man."

I think Riverside is not a very good college, but it *is* part of the University of California system.

"I'm gonna try to transfer, junior year. Man, get me a motorcycle . . ." and then he trails off, he's not wrapped too tight, and we stand around and stand around.

Rex comes out.

Snip says, "Hey, daddy-o, you got your ashes hauled."

It's my turn. They're looking at me, and I'm from little ol' Indio, so I get in. To the car. And in the back seat of this green Roadmaster I could

59

see that Marla was high. People forget the fabulous sixties didn't start until about 1965—we didn't do drugs; I thought she was just very, very drunk. She only had a little pink blouse around her shoulders, unbuttoned down the front, exposing her drab titties. Dark hair, dirty, and a little face that looked pinched, you could say starved for affection. Her head seemed too small for the body, and her curls were wet with sweat and matted on her forehead. Nothing on, except that unbuttoned little pink blouse. I pulled down my pants and she grabbed my two-by-four penis and said, "Give it to me, honey," and pulled her legs back. I braced myself over her, staring down at her face. When she looked up at me, she didn't know where she was. I sat down awkwardly on the seat, between her legs. She rubbed her foot on my thigh and said, "Hey, honey, I won't break its pretty back." It was like she was walking in her sleep. So I waited until my penis calmed himself down and I could get him back into my pants. I simply could not touch her at all. It's not exactly morality; I suppose I was thinking of myself. I did not want to remember for the rest of my life that I stopped being a virgin that way. It's hard to get at what you feel at seventeen. I know I did not want to say the wrong thing to any of the guys standing around the car. When I got out I was relieved when Snipe said, "Quick worker."

We got back in the white Cadillac, Rex and I, and tooled around in Palm Springs for a while. I had a sour taste in my mouth. Rex wanted to put a brick through the window of a home furnishings store to get Charles some linoleum. We waved and flipped the finger at people in dune buggies and 'Vettes on Palm Canyon Drive. I had a fake I.D., so we bought a six-pack of Oley. We drank four of them in the parking lot of Robinson's department store. A guy sauntered by in lime-colored chinos and a white turtleneck. Rex gave him a can of Oley and talked to him for a while. The guy said, "Who's going home with whom?" Rex did a fairly good imitation of Judy Garland singing "The Man That Got Away." We were fairly tipsy by this point.

The desert is pretty much of a down in the summer, most everyplace closed because of the terrible heat. Rex and I started home. But when we were humming past Sambo's, Rex said, "Duke!" and I said, "What?" And Rex was staring into the rear-view mirror, leaning up. "Duke Talis." I turned around and it was the old Ford that Duke had been working on in the Chevron station. I said, "What does he want?" The lights on the old Ford went on and off, three times, and Duke started to pull up around us, on the left.

Rex stomped on the gas, and the white Caddy tried to pick up.

I said, "He's heard about Marla."

"I'll lose him," Rex said.

I thought, How? That Ford, in this Caddy? Rex tooled off the main highway and cut toward the mountains on a little gravel road. The Caddy was all over, fishtailing. He cut the lights at the Smoke Tree Dude Ranch —and in the desert moonlight we sliced back and forth for fifteen minutes. Rex was really one excellent driver. Duke did a complete spin-out and his Ford stalled—if it hadn't been for that, he might very well have caught us.

We stopped out on the desert floor in an isolated spot up on the bank of a drainage ditch in a wildlife preserve. Rex and I got out and stood in the moonlight. The white Caddy sat real heavy on the sand.

Rex said, "Might as well kill that last beer."

And we stood there together, leaning against the car, passing the Oley back and forth. Pretty damn cocky. Rex said we ought to exchange letters when I was at Iowa and he was at Stanford. He told me about a problem his pop, J.O., was having with the contractors on the College of the Desert. The troubles kept multiplying, the Agua Calientes Indians, some geez at the Desert Air Hotel, the people at Indian Wells, and the Teamsters—he rattled it all off. He said one day when he and Marge had been riding out here at Smoke Tree, they met Cary Grant, who picked up his little daughter, all in white, and put her on a white pony and said, "I fear, my dear, you must accede to this." Rex thought that was terrific, just terrific. That Cary Grant said that. Accede. He said it wasn't easy to have Gabby Hayes for a neighbor, always coming over and talking to your mother about Hoppy.

And then we saw headlights. About two hundred yards away. We watched them. Rex flipped the empty Oley can out onto the sand. He said, "Well, we better get back," kind of casual, but he was moving pret-ty quick. And so were the headlights, coming across the trail toward us. We were listening for the motor. I said, "Might be the Border Patrol." Rex listened too. He said, "No, it's Duke." I said, "He's got us. If we try to cut by, he can ram us." Rex said, "I can get around him." I said, "You can't, this car won't go in sand, you can't. Bag the car. Let's *go*," and your Most Inspirational Player started to run.

Rex said, "It's my parents' car. Those guys'll bust it up." Rex was not leaving.

Duke's old Ford had Gerber baby food cans on its tailpipes, to give her a nice dirty metallic whine. Duke drove up to the edge of the ditch, cut the motor, but left the lights on.

There were six of them. Not so terribly big, but big enough. With

Brylcreem ducktails and cowboy boots and studded jackets. Duke eased himself out of the door, walking slow. He said, "How you doin' tonight, boys?"

Rex said, "OK, Duke. What's new with you?"

Duke Talis stood in front of his five men. He glanced around with those crazy brown-yellow eyes. He said, "You are going to go to Stanford. Stanford U-ni-versity."

It wasn't a question, so Rex didn't say anything.

"You gonna be a doctor or a lawyer?"

"Indian chief," Rex said.

Well, now, I thought to myself, I really do not want to get the shit kicked out of me. But I think I see what is about to happen. The desert air was a vacuum, and I could feel the starlight, the Dipper drumming like needles. Duke all at ease. And then he said, "You boys gang-banged my sister."

We didn't say a thing.

And then Duke said, "Which one of you got off her?" He looked at the sand between his boots. "She not good enough for ya?"

Duke's five guys standing there with blank faces. The radio in the Ford was on very loud, playing rock 'n' roll. Duke repeated himself. "Which one of you she not good enough for?"

I was thinking it was fifty-fifty, maybe we were not gonna get beat up. But our ass was grass, I knew it. If we had had the common sense to stand there a few minutes longer, it might not have happened. The big white Fleetwood solid in starlight. I am the one who blew it. I couldn't stand the waiting. So I jumped for it, grabbed the door handle, and flung the door half off its hinges. I was inside, behind the wheel, trying to turn the key in the ignition. I just don't want them to hurt my hands.

And from that moment we were ruined. Duke and his boys had to do their thing. I was thinking to myself, Cool it, just cool it, like after the play is over, don't let another middle linebacker come down on me. But the world don't work that way. There's always another linebacker. In this case, six. They were all over us, pulling me out of the upholstery and the blue steering wheel and the buttons for the windows, and the others slamming Rex tight against the back door. They started to work us over.

Rex said, "For the love of God. For the love of God and the Holy Virgin," but Duke and his guys weren't Catholic. For a moment Rex got free, scrambling up the side of the ditch, and then he got tackled, and they rolled him over. Duke pulled out a knife and held it—way up there, a thousand miles high, except it was only a few feet. I was writhing against the car, saying "fuck" and "shit." Trying to get to Rex to help him. Even when my eyes were closed, the knife was there over us, and I thought they were going to cut our balls off, then we'd have no balls, no children—

Duke took a couple of little slices, nasty, on Rex's arms. Those three guys were just pinning me against the back door of the Cad to *watch*.

"Fuck 'em," Duke said, and turned his back.

Those guys, all in their twenties, I guess, had skull-and-crossbone rings. One of them pulled back his arm, and Rex was able to squirm away again, going a few steps up on the side of the ditch. But it wasn't a tackle this time, it was a spin, and then all the air is gone with that cowboy-boot ferocious kick in the nuts, all the air on the desert is gone, gone from the whole planet earth.

I smelled hospital smells, medicine, and thin fumes, all mixed up with sand. They got boards from their Ford, and they hit him until he lost consciousness. Then they came after me. I saw a lot of blue lights and red star-fires. At one point I saw Mickey Mouse, when they tore away my right ear (which is still not sewed on properly; it's slightly crooked).

Them standing around our bodies. I remember legs. Boots. After a while Rex coming around, huddled into himself. He said something.

Duke said, "Can't hear ya, boy."

I can see it as clearly now as I saw it nineteen years ago. I can see it more clearly, because at that time my eyes saw everything double for thirty-six hours.

Rex trying to get up and stumbling and falling back down into the ditch.

I felt this little bubble of blood on my nose. Blood, sand, my ear—

Duke cleaned the blade of his knife.

Rex sat up. I thought he was blind. I cannot believe how dumb he was, he said, "You better kill me, motherfuck—I am going to bring down on you everything I got."

The whole world double and smelling like metal and gasoline.

Duke said, "Rape."

Rex lost his balance again, and his face was on the sand. I helped him sit up.

Duke said, "You raped my sister."

And I thought to myself, as well as I could think, that the guys at the drive-in would swear—Snipe, and that crew-cut, and those two others— I was trying to think how you could work it in a courtroom.

Duke motioned to his guys, and they took off.

Rex and I must have been there for an hour. We didn't know yet what the damage was. On the way to the hospital, in the front seat of the Caddy, me driving, Rex was coughing and bleeding. "Can't," he said.

"Can't." He passed out on my right arm; I almost went off the pavement. I watched his hands operating after his brain had stopped, his hands trying to pull his balls back up into their sockets.

Somehow I drove the rest of the way. When they brought out the stretcher at the emergency entrance, Rex regained consciousness a little. And then he said this fantastic thing. A doctor said, "Can you make it, kid?"—trying to help him onto the stretcher. "Can you make it, kid?"— and Rex said, "Doc, I live clean." For the next three nights we shared a room. In Casita Hospital. My "aunt" was there, all disturbed, and Mrs. Hooker, a constant vigil. Rex's balls swollen up like apples, stitches all over him, and J.O., out of his mind and never raising his voice, just Death Jaw —he didn't believe it was just a street gang, because of the litigation on the College of the Desert. He blamed it on special-interest groups. The man had just turned sixty, and one night he almost shook my teeth out, but Rex told me not to tell who did it.

The Hookers owned about a third of the land from Rancho Mirage over to old Highway 99, a lot of it from Rex's mother's father, who had been there since 1906, made several million dollars; Rex told me about it as we sat there in bed and watched "I Love Lucy." And finally J.O. wormed it out of me. Rex was embarrassed and pissed, but you don't say no to the man's Death Jaw, my goodness' sakes, I just want to go to Iowa City and freeze to death.

And his father took us, Rex and me, in that very same Cadillac. Old J.O. took us both up to the Chevron station in the night, and neither Rex nor I was feeling quite on our feet yet, and there was Duke, with a car in the air. J.O. parked the Fleetwood away from the light. He strode out and went over to Duke and said, "Hit this old man."

Standing there in the bright white neon of the Chevron station. J.O. said, "You put my son, Rex Hooker, in the hospital. And his friend. Now, come on, you hit this old man."

I couldn't believe it, his gray-white hair all mussed up and sticking out every which way—he was staring Death Jaw at Duke Talis, who wasn't worth his own snot rag, but J.O. had a son with apples for balls, and he braced himself on his own two feet and shouted it, "Hit this old man!"

Duke got the message. He saw that the old man would tear him up and feed him to the coyotes. So Duke went into the station and turned off all the lights and locked the door and got into his Ford and drove away. You do not mess with that.

I can still see in my mind the blue front seat upholstery that hadn't been cleaned, the dried blood, and Rex sitting beside me. I turned and saw this little smile on his face. I can still hear those words of his father, J.O., bouncing up the canyon in the hot darkness, "Hit this old man!"

I was really looking forward to the weekend, and it was no fun at all. How could I allow my hopes to get so high? Bubble-gum bitch pulled a sob story on me. I wanted to get laid, she wanted to solve her life. But it's my fault, I never give a woman a chance. I am so on edge, just waiting to get burned. Sheila would relish the job she did on me if she ever stopped to think about it. Women get the impression I'm not respectful, and that's not it; the painful truth is that I am such a case of arrested development I'm too chicken to give them a chance. It looks like childish arrogance and it's really childish fear. I catch one glimpse of that look in their eyes, I bail out.

My mobile home phone rings, I hope it's not her, I hope it's not her. With tuna fish stuck in my teeth I say hello, and Rex's voice says, "You like to come over for our Sunday football game, Trip? Join us for beers and a few good licks."

I look out my little kitchenette window at a yellowing frond.

I haven't played football in a dozen years.

I mull things over. The world is full of assholes, and eventually they all turn up at the beach. Friday the whole city school system received foul milk. The dairy doesn't know what went wrong, it didn't taste bad and it wasn't fatal. But it had some bacillus in it that the kids couldn't detect, so they drank it right down. Kept it down for about an hour or more. And then it starts coming up, and we have, citywide, about 700 up-chucking elementary school students, one by one, dozen by dozen, in music class all over your recorder, puking on your neighbor in math. Some kids held it longer than others, and so the teachers and administrators called parents, and the whole bus system really took a beating—and eventually we had vomit running all over the streets of Laguna like cottage cheese that died. All these kids barfing on each other all over town. I was receiving calls from about three dozen places, and what am I, a doctor? I don't know. Paranoid parents think it's everything from a communist plot to Proposition 13. I must have picked up at least ten kids that I just spotted hacking at curbside. One brother and sister act, twins, about seven, were horriding on each other, he really filled her hair. I take them home to their bisexual father and go to the fire station and hose out the blue-and-white.

Saturday is easy-traffic tie-ups, minor fender-benders, couple of rich old women fighting in Boat Canyon over lap dogs. I am thinking about tomorrow's football game at Summer Snow, remembering all that great stuff when I was on top of the world, my days of triumph on the gridiron.

August back there on the desert, pad practice. Hernandez, weighed maybe 220, 230, I can remember him running around the track, four times, a mile in full gear, the poor bastard, he'd have to stop and rest, and all of us sitting on our helmets watching him finish. Our QB was Joe Sneller, he could really scamper. He averaged over seven yards a carry in our junior year. All I could do was throw, so I sat on the bench, a charter member of the Pine Patrol, picking splinters out of my ass. Coach "Bulldog" Francis Carpenter—his real name was Francis and your ass was grass if you ever dared call him that—Coach Carpenter would yell and scream and jump up and down. A guy would miss a block and Coach would show it on the films, run it three, four times, just to make you feel terrible. Football is living in fear. That's what's supposed to build you up. Getting put down. Make everybody ashamed. Humiliate you to the point of near utter hysterics. But the bus trips I always liked, teasing each other, in the back calling "Coach *Fran*-cis," he never could figure out who. We had this one Italian guy, Bolgiano, his mother would fix him cold-cut subs and stuff his duffel bag full of food and Pepsi, and we weren't supposed to eat, because it would make you logy when you'd play, but Bolgiano was running this sausage factory, the whole bus smelled of it, hot meatball with cheese. He'd bring it just for friends, not the whole team, and we'd always grab a six-pack of beer somewhere.

Except then it happened. In the fourth quarter of the Coachella game, with us holding on to a 6–zip lead, in the last minute, on a TD scamper by Sneller and a missed extra point by Bolgiano. We are backed up way down to our eight-yard line, and Sneller calls a 45-Blue, only somebody in the center of the line misses an assignment, and this huge Mexican guy from Coachella comes ripping through, and Sneller tries to be tricky, to hide the ball behind his thigh, and he drops it. It takes a crazy bounce, and he's got it again, but he sees this UFO snorting chili pepper and lookin' at the ball like it's the last enchilada in the universe, and Sneller sits down—nobody's touched him yet—he sits down right on his arm, crunch. Breaks his arm. So Oliver Bodley is called on. Francis is having catalepsy: *"Bodley—get in there!"* We'd all been up, the clock only had fifty-six seconds on it. I put on my helmet, and realize I have got to save the day. My first varsity appearance.

I still don't quite believe it—although I have seen it on the films, to my utter humiliation, so I know it actually happened. Afterward, the guys told me that when I came in, in the huddle, I really called a sneaky play. Apparently what I said was "Holy shit! Holy shit!" The Thinking Man's Quarterback. And Hernandez snapped it to me when I said something like 69-Chartreuse, I don't know. Then, with remarkable presence of mind, what I actually did was turn around and walk—not run—to the nearest exit. Like I was a referee. It's all there on the films, like I was stepping off a clip, I turned and walked directly out of the end zone. The sweetest little part of the sequence is that when I went by it, I hit the goal post with my right shoulder, really I never saw it, but apparently I hit it fairly hard, and looked at it as if to say Oh, pardon my clumsiness. Then I was out of the end zone, when the Coachella line hit from all sides at once, and you can see the ball squirt up into the air onto the running track.

But that's a safety. We won 6–2. I was a genius.

But we had five games left to play. So Francis goes ape with X's and O's, he completely redesigns us from a running team to a passing team. He goes out and persuades basketball players and guys on the track team to be ends, we need height and speed. Van Damm, the center from basketball, has a knack of getting open; being six-seven, he just jumps up in the air, trying not to lose his spectacles. A sprinter, black kid, Jim Wright, he can *fly*. And by Turkey Day we are a fairly respectable club. Which is how I got noticed by Iowa. I laid up a lot of floaters in five weeks. And drilled a lot of high mortar fire to Van Damm's google eyes, gave Jimmy some room to work with. I was a mess every weekend because I was always so dizzy from getting up off the bottom of piles. Hated to get hit from the side, and I developed this permanent scab on the bridge of my nose from my helmet getting slammed down into it. But the worst, the absolute worst, was when somebody would step on my hand with his cleats. I just hated to have my hand stepped on.

Francis wanted us to play—not exactly dirty, but definitely on the rough side, where it was questionable, especially in the middle of the line, where the refs are blocked out. When the Iowa offer came in, he made a big deal of coming over and talking to my aunt about the satisfactions he got from devoting his life to building character through interscholastic athletics. My aunt didn't like him either; she could spot a fraud.

At the Awards Banquet, they ran the Season's Highlights. Coach at the projector, it was at the Valley Inn, all of the team and our dates and parents and boosters. They ran nice shots of some of my stuff to Van Damm and Jimmy. But then Coach said that he knew he had "his" new quarterback when he saw this unparalleled example of field generalship. He screened that play on our eight when I walked out of the end zone and hit the goal post. He played it twice, and then once backward. Everybody about died. Then they gave the awards. I was sure I was going to get "Most Improved." Anybody can win Most Improved if he's bad enough to start with. But instead I got "Most Inspirational." When they called my name, I was quite surprised, and the Homecoming Queen gave me the trophy. I didn't know quite where I was, after she handed it to me, in all the applause. I went home that night and polished my trophy all up with Kleenex until I put teeny little scratches on it. I got my picture in the *Daily News*. It's not too often the world pays you back for what you put in.

In those days we had one student body president for fall semester and one for spring semester, not one for the whole year. And when the principal, Old Man Berry, announced the nominations, my first thought was Oh shit, they're making fun of me—like when they nominated Karen Neal, a mongoloid, for health commissioner; teenagers can be very cruel. I thought they were making fun of me. And then it sank in. I came off the bench and made an ass of myself, but then I led the team, I did all right. And I was elected president. It really got to Sneller. He wrote in my yearbook:

To Ollie—
WHO CAN DO EVERYTHING BUT HOLD A GIRL.
YOUR FRIEND,
THE SNELLER

Slimy bastard. I can't do everything. And didn't have a girl to hold. And he wasn't my friend.

I was really into those useless memories in my trailer, getting dressed for Sunday's game. I let it all rattle around in my mind. I don't really want to open it up. Sheila. My whole past life. Leave it alone. Napoleon said, Let China Sleep. And Napoleon had his wits about him.

I go. The day is unreal, semighostly, not exactly overcast, some kind of layer inversion, and Summer Snow looks like a fairy castle. About a dozen men were standing around on the beach and running out for passes and yelling at each other.

Some of them had already had a few beers, and a few of them were pretty clearly on uppers, downers, a shot or two of the hard stuff. Especially a guy who wore a blue sweat shirt that said BIRDBATH in yellow letters, he was pretty wobbly. Rex was wearing a fluorescent black helmet. A big black guy was wearing a Pittsburgh Steelers jersey and mirror glasses. Two men were throwing passes, twenty- and thirty-yarders that never rose more than fifteen feet off the beach. And there's ol' David scampering about. Pride. Fun. Meet kids.

Just as we were choosing up sides, Marge Stivers came prancing down onto the beach in a gold sequined bathing-suit-type costume, with white cowboy boots, twirling a baton. We all stopped and cheered. She was excellent—threw the baton way up and caught it and twirled it around her shoulders and between her legs.

She walked up to Rex and said, in a loud whisper, "Rah."

Rex kissed her and she went to sit with the keg and do needlepoint. I think about her sister, and wonder about all the aftermath of that, and feel gloomy. I stare at those beautiful legs of hers, which I can remember from way back at Pete's Texaco, when she wouldn't give me the time of day. Twenty years later the pins are still perfect. Swell.

We're fourteen, seven on a side. The black guy's name is Ed Munday, he's their QB. I am a roving linebacker. Their man named Bob Short, who must have been a flanker at some major power like UC Santa Cruz, got behind Rex on a bomb and just danced into the end zone.

Short grinned at me, tossing me the ball. "Score one for the Fairy Fly."

"The Fairy Fly?" I say, thinking at least I know a Flea-Flicker.

"Well," he said firmly, "I'm gay."

I sort of stare.

"Not *lewd*, jerk-off—*gay*."

The fog had started to lift, the sun coming out. I was beginning to sweat. After twenty minutes my opponent was out of gas—so he had to stop for a beer and called for a substitute. Marge took off her white cowboy boots and came darting out barefoot to take his place. When she was halfway to the huddle, Ed Munday said, "Now they gonna rip in— we got a hole in our line."

Marge wanted to know what I thought was so funny.

Ed completed a surprise little ten-yarder to her, and when Rex tackled her he was extremely slow in getting up. Then BIRDBATH ran for another ten, later calling to Marge, who got by Rex this time but was hauled down when she accidentally bumped into Bob Short. He got up right away. "Pussy makes me so *nervous*." He stood there and said some of Marge's sequins looked like "incandescent vermin," while others appeared to be "comatose bees." That pissed Marge off, and she went back to the keg to pout.

My hands, Duke Talis, this house, Sheila, what sports have meant to me, I can't believe how much I am sweating. But I am thirty-seven, after all. The two big Labrador dogs come out of the house, somebody let 'em out, they are so frisky, they're all over us. Rex puts one on each team, which doesn't work at all. This UCLA philosophy professor who's slightly cross-eyed says our offensive problem is "Things fall apart—the center cannot hold." Another guy, John Huge, spaced out, kept mumbling in the huddle things like "We don't *have* bodies—we *are* bodies." While I was diagraming a play in the sand, John seemed to be paying attention and then he said, "Do you know that when pelicans get horny, they grow knobs on their heads like eggs?" The sun was really beginning to boom. Bob Short did his bat-out-of-hell number again, and got behind Rex for the second "Fairy Fly," all alone on another perfect bomb from Ed. Rex said, "You gonna pay, *faygeleh,* you gonna pay. Try that one more time, you won't get six inches."

Bob Short said, "I probably couldn't get six inches from *you,*" and Rex started chasing him with murder in his eyes. Bob Short fell down and said, "Look at this marvelous *shell.*"

Our team is called the Washboard Weepers, and I ask Rex what that is, and Rex says a gentleman never discusses his guests. John Huge says he won last year's Santa's Chug-a-Lug Big Board Classic at Newport, but then gets all lost in thought. He points to David and says, "Do you realize we'll completely convert to solar energy in his lifetime?"

David himself is a little pissed off; he's being left out of the main action. Kids like to excel.

Rex sees it, makes a quick little motion with his head, and pulls us around him. "Gents, my boy is bored. Let's run the ol' Oedipal Confusion —King's X?"

This guy Farley says to John Huge, "You rode a seven-footer on your *head?*"

"K?" Rex says.

John Huge says, "An erection is the absence of self-doubt."

The UCLA professor says, "You never met my wife."

Ed Munday says, "I hate white guys."

Rex calls, *"Da-*vid!"

The kid shrugs, and comes up to us. "Yeah?"

"All right, men," Rex says. "Ready?"

Mr. UCLA says, "First a question for David."

David looks at him.

"If a tree falls in the forest, and there's nobody there to hear it, is there any sound?"

David looks at his dad, looks back at the prof. "Sure."

"But sound is the perception of waves by the auditory nerve. If nobody's there to hear it, how can there be any sound?"

David says, "Squirrels."

The professor kicks up his foot—"I refute it *thus!*"—and falls flat on his back. He lies there. "Genius consists in immense memory."

Bob Short says, "I have such terrible dreams."

Ed Munday says, "Always hated white guys."

So the Washboard Weepers kneel in the sand for a team prayer. And Rex says, "Hike it to me, I'll fake a pass to Trip." Then he was drawing in the sand. "King's X—and then you just stand there and wait for me to come on back and I'll lead you. Follow Daddy."

We went up to the line. I hiked it after Rex called signals: "Hair Pi —three point one four one *seven.*" I cut back to block, David got the ball, and then all fourteen of us were running everywhere, David charging away, Rex sprinting sideways in his black fluorescent helmet along toward the ocean, screaming "Follow Daddy! Follow Daddy?" He speared UCLA and then we weaved and Rex said, "Stutter step—stutter step," as John Huge threw his Chug-a-Lug champ's body in the air over Ed Munday, who was so horrified at what white guys can do that he just backed into the surf and sat down. I ducked a towering inferno, Farley, and Rex said, "Good on ya, David, good on ya! Follow Daddy! Follow Daddy!" and then BIRDBATH blind-sided Rex, clotheslined him pretty terrible, and they both went down hard, and I heard BIRDBATH say, "Follow Daddy, my *ass!*" Bob Short was yelling to David, "Wrong way, you're going the wrong way," and I turned and started back, and Rex said, "Don't listen to him, go the other way." Bob Short screamed, "Why can't everybody go *both* ways!" The men were taking clips and running into anybody, even if he was on your own team. It clicks into slow motion in my mind, Procter and Gamble tearing about, we were running all the way up the field, all the way back down the field, and then all the way up the field again, Rex screaming, "King's X, King's X—" and finally David spiked the ball in the sea and turned around, and all the guys were flat on the sand or on their knees, and Farley was walking toward the keg spitting a little slit-stream of blood. Marge got up and started prancing, with her baton, "I wanna be a football hero—I want to—" and David turned to get the football before a breaker carried it away. He had tears in his gray eyes, but just in case anybody saw the tears, he dived on the floating ball and went under.

Follow Daddy, follow Daddy!

When we all got back to the keg, Rex said to him, "Nice run, peckerwood."

Big platters of ham and cheeses and roast beef and sprouts and avocado and bread and shrimp and schooners of beer and wine and fingers of dope. I eat a lot until somebody tells a sick joke and I completely lose my appetite. I see too much of that sick stuff on my job, and it's not a laughing matter for me. Down on Buena Vista, the Goldsmith kid sticks things up his pecker. I took him to the hospital with a nail in it. And I also took him to the hospital with a number 2 lead pencil, unsharpened, up there, all the way up, that's how he gets his rocks off; apparently, you can go all the way up to the bladder. It gives me the willies even to think about it. My hole couldn't handle a Q-tip. And the things people stuff up their asses, shove all that debris up there. Or that girl who put razor blades in her diaphragm so when the asshole cheater comes in he's sliced sausage, except anybody who'd cook up such a plan is not to be trusted on the assembly line; of course, the blades came out inside her and she was hemorrhaging all over the porch when we responded to the call. It's all too sick, I can't think about it. Sex always makes me feel I'm spinning in darkness: having another stress trauma. But you're bound to have lingering emotional problems when you are a model for authority. Sheila was right. Once for a period of weeks I couldn't take out the garbage without putting on my gun. I don't understand sex or anything else. But I do know that the most interesting stuff is absolutely common. I have no desire for a gymnasium full of accessories and pronged aids. Nobody respects a policeman, much less thinks about the strain he carries home. No wonder. The Chief once said, at a function in progress, a Chamber of Commerce banquet, "If we don't all enforce the law, nobody will." To a round of applause. And I'm sitting on the dais thinking, What the hell does that mean? That is absurd. The truth is everybody *doesn't* enforce the law, which is why policemen *exist.* Why can the Chief say utter nonsense and have sensible men and their wives applaud? Sometimes I say it to myself out of the blue. Well, Trip, if we don't all have a cheeseburger, nobody will. If we don't all fuck this nurse's aide, nobody will. Ninety percent of what people say and do bears very little looking into.

I want to say something respectful to Marge Stivers about her sister, but I don't get a chance. Rex, nursing a Coors, is having a very animated discussion with the professor about the boundaries of human knowledge. Swell. I really need to be reminded of the fucking boundaries of knowledge. Of flunking out of Iowa and Stanford. The sky is brilliant and terrific, the beach down south loaded with people, the sun and the surf and the hillsides. Marge is talking with Farley's wife, a loud woman who has come to pick him up. Marge and her, drinking Bloody Marys. Marge is juggling limes, boobs falling out of that sequined white halter top. Anybody molest her and I'd have considerable difficulty restraining myself. In rape there is a stigma that attaches to the woman. Rape is a goddamn serious crime, because how does the victim ever get over it and enjoy sex again? It angers me when the Liberated Ladies say policemen are insensitive to rape victims. Being a cop means you get violated every day. I know quite well what it is to have something linger emotionally and be terrified at night just putting your key in the door. Which is why I wore my piece to take out the garbage. Sheila should have known it's no crime, or joke, for a man to be scared. Fear is not cowardice. I am getting to like Bob Short. He says that sailors' gold earrings involve an unwritten law: You never roll a sailor and "pluck his bauble" because that is the guarantee of his funeral expenses, the earring is his burial costs. I dig this fast-breaking news like I'm a city father on Dexamyl.

I watch Marge. The Bloody Marys, she's really puttin' 'em away. Too much laughter, a big belch like a gift, words slurred and not in the right order. Everybody else's windows are open anyway, but she's on a tear. I remember Rex's story in Brandsma's office about the three pizzas, and I still can't get over the fact that she is actually here at Summer Snow, nineteen long years after that party. It seems very sad to me, given what had to be done with Rex on Labor Day, that Marge is also a dues-paying member in this equal-opportunity disease. It won't bring Sissy back. It never helps a thing. Why oh why do people drink? I'd reinstate Prohibition in a minute. And now she and Farley's wife have climbed way up a white oak to a big treehouse, I guess it's David's, and they're looking for whales at this time of year, and Marge is yelling "Thar she blows!" Rex paying no attention to her. And then he has to, we all do, because crash-bam-crash she falls out of her tree, so to speak—literally, she comes blam-crash-sickening-thud down onto rocks and sand and a little salt-water inlet. Farley's wife shouts, Rex goes to her like lightning. Marge totters up all in a daze. Rex kind of half-carrying her, the sequined uniform all ruined and wet and ripped. She's had a really bad blow on the forehead, must've broken some bones, ugly cut on her foot. She's not crying or anything, maybe it's a concussion. Rex and Farley's wife take Marge into the house, she's in a daze, her lights are dimmed.

I watch the Labradors, Procter and Gamble, chasing the optic yellow tennis ball that David is throwing them. Finally Rex comes back out. Bob Short is stark naked in a tidal pool and has made his socks into hand puppets. A while later Marge comes out, showered and bandaged, with her hair up in a big white towel like a turban. The expression on her face is like a five-year-old girl's. She tries to smile, shyly, to say I'm very sorry I'm naughty, but something else too, like God is an odd old fellow to put me on his short list of good sports.

David wanders up. He's noticing everything, a little frightened, trying to be OK and not show anything, fiddling with the yellow tennis ball.

Gradually people drift away. Guys clap me on the shoulder. I try to stand, but my legs have really stiffened up. Marge's disaster has put a damper on things, even if she's limping with them up to the circular driveway. Rex asks me to stick around a minute. I do, just sit there by myself smoking a cigarette, my mind on cruise-control. I know there is no Truth, people are just committed to their versions of it, but I wonder. Things do come from somewhere—every chair, box, dog. I'd like to talk with Rex a little about Labor Day. Starting with how he got back home so fast. Many things. But I sure as hell am not going to tell Rex I was at Stanford when he was. After I flunked out of Iowa, where I was colder than I have ever been in my life. That icy wind whipping down, you just had to pack yourself into a doorway and pull your jacket around you. German is the most foolish language ever invented; no wonder Hitler rose to power. And so I came home and went to junior college, and then the coach at Stanford, Cactus Jack, gave me an opportunity. I got a little hole-in-the-wall apartment up in Menlo Park. I lasted two quarters and got my walking papers in spring practice. I couldn't rush, too many minus points, and didn't even pay a courtesy call to Rex; his "brothers" would have thought I was an escapee from Los Turkos anyway. I used to hang out at a bar, the Oasis, and drown my sorrows. I was a freshman when Rex was a junior. I'd sit in my dinky rattrap and know I couldn't cut the mustard. German got me at Iowa, and at Stanford it was Western Civ. On the midterm there was this question, "Was Oedipus guilty?" and I wrote "Yes," and got zero credit. I still think I should've gotten full credit —shit, yes, he was guilty. I've cuffed many a man who didn't *know* he was guilty; no way you can plea-bargain your intentions. And I remember the creepy feeling I had, sitting high up in the stands at the Big Game over in Berkeley, when my fellow students chanted in unison across the stadium, "We pay your tu-i-tion, we pay your tu-i-tion." Spoiled brats, like yelling a-*dop*-ted, a-*dop*-ted. I knew right there I was in the wrong place. Of course Oedipus was guilty.

Rex says, "Come on, man, you look so abstracted from your life, you'll wake up some morning and find yourself dead."

"*What?*" Don't you talk to me that way. Stanford Man.

"Hey, Trip, lighten up. I was just kiddin'."

OK, OK, OK. I look at the ocean. I can't even enjoy a game of touch football. I wish I were smarter. My mind is full of clichés. That's what the T.A. said to me at Stanford, that my mind was full of clichés. Even if it's true, it's kind of cruel to say.

"Look at that son of mine down there."

I do. The kid's perfecting his skim-board technique, does a little half-flip in the surf.

74

"How do I protect him, Trip? I don't want him to inherit our anguish."

I look at Rex. "Our?"

He smiles. "Come on, Trip, you can't fool me. You mean your life every bit as much as I mean mine. You just do it different."

Well, I'd really rather not talk about it. "I guess."

"Aw, sure, you gotta step back and think."

I try. But my mind's too full of clichés.

Out there, David yells, *"Dad*—did you *see* me?"

Rex shouts back, *"Yeah!"* And whispers to me, "I think it's about time I told him the story of E. Pericoloso Sporgersi, the Wop of the Waves, the Dago of the Deep. And his girlfriend, Vulva Sprezzatura. Shall I tell him, Trip?"

I sit there sulking. Do what you want. It's your son. It's your life.

Rex sighs, and touches me on the shoulder, and walks down to the water.

I sit there and think I'm no good to anybody. Like the bumper sticker I used to have on the Cutlass, before the Chief made me tear it off: ANOTHER SHITTY DAY IN PARADISE.

My vehicle's a mess, pop bottles and the *Enquirer* under the front seat, empty bag of cookies, crumbs. The Chief should discipline the men. We don't even have staff meetings. His divorce really cut the Chief off at the knees. Now he's moved in with his lady friend—that ridiculous house on Cerritos Drive with a bed in the middle of the living room, on a big plastic pedestal, with a mirror on the ceiling. I had to smile when I first saw it. Three sides of the house are all glass, and he had me over to help him wash the windows after a big rainstorm. I couldn't resist it, standing there with my Windex and telescope squeegee, I said, "Like me to catch the mirror?" He just looked at me. I think he's going through second childhood. They got a gigantic Jacuzzi on the first floor. I suppose he and the lady friend go down there at night for a little splishy-splashy. It's got fountains and all these weird plants and trees, and the water bubbles up around them. I visualize them down there playing with their rubber duckies.

At least he's got company, somebody to get him through the night.

The closest friend I've ever had was a policeman. It took years to build up the trust, which is the whole key to it, trust. We talked for years in a light bantering way before we could talk seriously, out under his apple trees. Policemen can't really have friends. Even Fred and I stayed away from things. Under the apple trees we'd catch ourselves, watch the conversation dribble away. All the way around, for everyone involved, it's better not to have attachments You go to a party and somebody always wants to talk speeding tickets. I come to the party wanting to eat, have a couple of drinks, discuss sports, talk about who's ballin' who. I am Joe Blow, not Sergeant Bodley. I really do not want to talk about California radar versus Florida radar, especially not Florida, where the radar is so bad they got trees going fifty miles an hour. But some jerk gets half in the bag and slobbers on my shoulder about how he was only doing forty-five, and I give up. I go talk to somebody's grandmother in the parlor, who doesn't know I'm a cop, and is deaf, and I talk to her.

I could feel Fred drifting. His wife left him and took their son. Fred couldn't handle it. The constant pressure of working and missing them. He let his uniforms go, began running around with his shirttail out. Face all twitchy. Made mistakes. A gear went loose in his mind. All he could think of was little useless projects. And then he didn't show up—couldn't locate him anywhere for days. Killing yourself is a hell of a thing to do to your kid.

Fred couldn't put the gear back in place, because—he told me under the apple trees—he had invested everything in his wife and son. When they left, he had nothing to live for. He never talked to me about death. He was always a quiet guy, although quite perceptive. Had the saddest eyes I've ever seen. I think he should've packed up his duds and moved to Oregon or somewhere. Far enough away to be out of it, close enough for the kid to travel. But now the kid is probably going to grow up to be in worse shape than Fred was. No father. I remember standing honor guard, and the flag over Fred's casket.

I get a prowler call about dusk, drive over there, and haul my backache out of the blue-and-white. I go up a little cobblestone path on Oak. I rip my sleeve on a cactus, naturally, and there's a plateau with gravel and a garden and a dinky barbecue that was probably quite useful in the 1920s. Beside a beautiful jacaranda is a skinny little black kid. He must be from Alabama or something; he's mumbling, but I can't understand a word he says. He has a strange look in his eyes. Only about eighteen or nineteen, confused, not drunk or on dope. He's dressed very shabby, wandering around a little tree, mumble mumble mumble, eyes going jump-jump. I ask him where he's from. He doesn't know. He seems to think his girlfriend is dead. He says his girlfriend is in the crick, three guys jumped 'em, and now she's drowned. He has no marks on him. Goes sniff-sniff, says the fire gonna git 'im. Or something. We are not exactly communicating. I say he will come with me and we will try to get this straightened out. Big white eyes in his inky face; he's very mixed up. He wants to take his dog. I look around. There is no dog. But he walks over to the little tree, goes through all these elaborate motions of untying his dog. Then we go down the cobblestones and get into the car. Kid pats his lap, and the "dog" jumps in onto his lap. The kid shuts the door. I say, "I hope that dog is housebroke. If he pisses on my seat, you're gonna clean it up." Kid says OK, OK, and he pets the dog all the way down the road to Glenneyre. But when we pass Albertson's and head up the hill, he forgets about his dog and goes crazy. He's after my gun. Today I wore my own gun, my .357 stainless magnum, which the whole department may switch to from the standard .38 service revolver. Now I have to hold him by one hand, drive with the other, and turn my body to protect my gun. I move the car over to park at the top of the hill, and my door comes open. The dome light is on, and people are driving by but they don't stop to help, oh no. I tell him I'll have to hurt him, and I reach for my night stick, and he calms down. Probably not because I said it—his little fit is over, and he's back to the dog. I'm not Bull Conner and he's not Dr. King, we're just two farts in the dark.

At the station he wants cigarettes. I give him a pack of Salems somebody left lying around. He opens the pack from the bottom. He lights up five of them, one at a time, and arranges them in a little tin ashtray. He says they are for his friends. He remembers an address in Dana Point, and empties his pocket. There's a phone number. I place a call. It's his cousin, a lady. She says she'll be right there. Which, after time goes by, she is —but not before he has another little seizure about how they are trying to kill him, don't let them get him like they got his girlfriend. His cousin is a nice lady who has brought him a bottle of cranberry juice. He goes off with her, trying to get his dog to heel. I have developed a kind of tingling in the fifth finger of my left hand; probably it's irreversible cardiovascular damage, brought on by excessive smoking. He had five of 'em there, for his friends. Sometimes my pinky fails to respond. I'd ask a doctor about it if I had the guts. But I don't. If the truth were known, shit, Oliver Bodley is still scared of the dark.

4

REX SAID "It's a costume ball—come as your illusion of yourself." I asked
him what that meant, and he just laughed. So I stopped by after duty
Saturday night. I'd have to say it was a bit orgyesque. Fifty or so people
all in costumes, the stereo blasting out all these old songs from the sixties,
Country Joe and the Fish, the Doors. The driveway was completely
jammed up with Caddys and Mercedeses and Porsches and a lot of little
Rabbits and a gorgeous antique Packard and a 'Vette. I had to leave 1
GROUCH on North Sunset. The front door was open wide. I walked
through people in costumes—they probably thought I was in a costume,
which I suppose is true because it is my "illusion of myself." All these folks
roaming around down in the rose gardens and in the Edifice Rex and
sprawled at the pool and gathered around a bonfire down there at the
beach. "She's a Twentieth-Century Fox," and "White Rabbit," blaring
away. One guy was Henry VIII, and a woman was Marilyn Monroe, and
four guys were the Beatles, and there was old John Huge, from our football
game, a polar bear, and Ed Munday too, big black Ed, Muhammed Ali
in boxing trunks, and a fine lady was "Liberty Leading the People." She
said so to a guy who said he was Edward R. Murrow, when I thought he
was Richard Nixon, with that five o'clock shadow. The lady had one boob

78

out, and I kind of latched onto it, visually. When she danced with Groucho Marx, I held her flag. Finally a voice behind me said, "Well, Trip, how the hell are ya?"

He was a Hell's Angel. Looked mean—he'd let his beard grow for a few days, he had leather and chains and an Iron Cross, he was filthy, with blue glasses. A lovely little plump brunette on his arm. He said, "Trip—Wanda. Wanda—Trip."

"Trip," she said—she was Wanda the Witch, I guess. All in black and you could see most of her bosom. She had this enormously long cigarette holder like a wand. "Trip," she said again. "Are you something we take —or something we're on?"

I looked down at my feet. I said, "And what do you do?"

She sighed. "I'm a freelance nymphomaniac."

Oh.

"Listen, bull, don't you dare take pity on me."

I don't know why I said it, I just blurted, "The secret with compassion is to keep it self-interested." My, listen to me.

Wanda went all serious. Looked at me like she had just discovered we were enemy agents working for the same country. She said to Rex, "Sweetart, save the cop for me, OK? He's a good one." And off she went.

Rex kind of ushered me along through mulberry balloons. The dining area offered huge platters of chicken and clams and shrimp and sausage, and a million hors d'oeuvres. Out on a deck, a barbecued goat was going. But they called it "Bambi." Booze everywhere, goddamn joints in little vases. Standing by the sink in the kitchen was a guy who could put his whole hand in his mouth. Impressive, actually. I wandered back into the rose light. At the buffet a tall, skinny black guy farted kind of effeminately and said, "The opinions expressed by my body do not necessarily reflect those of my mind."

Marge Stivers came bounding in with a platter of pigs-in-blankets. She saw me and gave me a big smooch. I immediately think of her sister, and immediately tuck it away. She has on a gorgeous pale green gown, and a pale green crown. She put down the tray and picked up her pale green tablet and torch. "I'm the Statue of Liberty, Trip—I'm the Lady in the Harbor." She danced with me. She said, "Wanna lift your lamp beside my golden door?"

Well . . .

She threw me around, she's really strong, like a man, I'll bet she plays a great game of golf. But I cannot keep her sister tucked away, and I do not want to say anything. When a guy grabs her, I scrunch into a corner and watch. Some people would think she's merely brassy, verging to slut.

Some more perceptive people would think she's really got her act together. Peppy, nothing'll knock her off her feet. But that's not it—she's something else. Way too complicated for me. But I know she's not what she seems. No sir.

And then here comes another load of crazy people, this six-foot skinny lady, overwrought and underfed, terrible acne and long orange hair like lace on her shoulder bones. Ragged pink bulky-knit sweater full of holes and open all jagged at the neck. Where you could see, if you didn't have the sense to look away, her pocked-up chest. She wore a black wool skirt with a lot of lint on it and these white veiny stockings on her stick legs. With her, two guys whose hair looked more brewed than grown, hair all ghoulishly coming up out of the Black Lagoon. Feathers and high-button shoes and fur chaps and finger cymbals. The pimple-covered girl was yelling in a man's voice, "I hated it, but then my dermatologist told me the causes—my incessant Cokes, nervous tension"—her voice was way down there, like she was a retired Coast Guard cook—"not washing every time you turn around, lack of sleep—I mean, it's me. My acne is *me*. So I *like* my acne."

But even she was drowned out by this old Beatles record. A middle-aged guy with longish gray hair came struggling down the stairs with a butterfly chair. Music pounding: *Help me if you can. I'm feelin' down.* The man was not doing too well. He tripped over the chair, fell over it, and lay there on the Honduras mahogany. *And I do appreciate you bein' round.* I nudged Rex, and he turned and smiled, looking at the guy. Rex said, "Steamboat Willie." *Help me get my feet back on the ground.* And the man was up again, working away in the dim candlelight of the stairs. Now he had the chair all the way down to the landing, and he put it there and fell into it. Instant sleep. Rex started to laugh. *Won't you please, please help me—*

Rex said, "See, Trip, life can go on." He offered me one, and I broke a cardinal rule. In uniform. I took a drag on a joint. Didn't do a thing for me, actually. What did do something for me was Marge fell out of her toga, her boobs just spilled out. "Rat shit," she said, and hunkered 'em back into place. "I would have had a happier life if I weren't so fucking *stacked*!"

"It's OK," I said.

Somebody took my hat. I frequently misplace my hat.

It wouldn't hurt to say something to Rex. I said, "She seems to have dealt with it successfully."

He wasn't really listening. "Her tits are always falling out."

I said, "No, I mean her sister's suicide."

80

Boom, he turned on me, and we ain't gonna say this twice: *"Don't."*

Well, now I'm feeling festive. As long as I'm breaking cardinal rules, I'll smoke one all by myself. And do.

By midnight there must have been a hundred people wandering all over everywhere. And I can't count how many I've had; I hope most of them were cigarettes. An hour ago, or perhaps seven minutes, Rex took me aside, which means he's still thinking about it, he doesn't take it lightly. Rex said, "You know what Marge's father did? You know what he did, in Zurich? Bag the fact that he didn't even fly back for the funeral, bag that—he enclosed one of Sissy's Keogh Plans that might have gotten lost in the shuffle. You know how alone Marge is? You know how *alone* she is?"

Tears in his eyes, Marge. Tears in his eyes.

They've about stripped Bambi clean. People are playing Giant Steps on the beach. On the moon. I run into a girl with a smile in a peppermint suit and red knee socks and white racing gloves. I have myself a little thrill when she says, "I love you." She grabs me hard, and I just stand there thinking, Here is the answer to my life. Then she ruined it by saying, "I love you, and I love everyone, because I love the baby Jesus." Her shoes had big number 5's on the buckles, maybe to indicate the number of toes inside.

She drifted toward a line of gay guys who were gathered in a can-can line singing, "Yes, We Have Our Bananas, We Have Our Bananas To-daaay!" I found Rex again. He was in the Solarium talking with a guy who had hair like a hatchet. Rex got up when I sat down, and introduced me to the guy, Peter Ingalls, who told me the sixties were ruined for him, because he'd been in Vietnam. "Khe Sanh," he said. I had somehow acquired a bottle that said LAMBRUSCO on it. But it's not alcohol that's doing this to my head. It's that stuff Peter's staring at, the joint in his roach clip made out of an old shell casing. "This soldier from the North Vietnamese Army, ARVN," he whispered, "his buddies were coming back for him, they just kept coming, we kept shooting, and he kept waving them back—so that they wouldn't sacrifice themselves for him—and then he shot his head off." Peter was really shaking. "I mean," he said, "that's what *we* are supposed to do. Iwo Jima and Mount Surbachi and the guy with both his legs blown off leading his platoon up the hill on his stumps. But *them*—I mean, those little gooks—man, I just walked around in a daze from then on. Guys would come up and ask me if I was OK, and for about three months, man, nothing. I knew I was in a plane and a hospital and"—Peter was squeezing my shoulder, kind of G.I. drunk, his head with that hatchet hair all bent down—"gooks—for *gooks* he blew his head off, little brown zeroo nippin' in the grass. God, what a mind rush. Just a rush. My brain is way over there, back there somehow—"

"Take it easy, man," I said.

"And you know, you know—'Where Have All the Flowers Gone?' 'When will they ever learn?' " He was actually singing it now, softly. "That's what *we* were singin'. I mean, like we were over there and in the newspapers and on the TV we saw long-hairs and all those peace signs and we knew a lot of our friends back home hated us for bein' over there killin' gooks. And we didn't want to be there—shit, really."

"I know," I said.

"I had this talk with my high school science teacher about it. When I was drafted. I was gonna go to Canada, and my science teacher said he was against the war too. But he said I should go in the army with a heavy heart. Go in the name of what America had been and in hope of what she would someday be again. And I couldn't figure out how I was going to kill a Vietnamese peasant with a *heavy heart*, but I went—I *bought it* —I bought the dead end in the middle of the road." He went on, sighing, leaning back on a rocking chair. "It was the number one song on the Khe Sanh hit parade. 'Where have all the young men gone?' I mean, where we had gone was *there*, Khe Sanh. And we'd shit on the peace freaks back home, but—damn, I thought I was over it, it's been years. I'm drunk. . . ." He looked to me for help.

I said, "Take it slow."

Peter stood up and put his hands on the glass walls of the Solarium. It's three flights down from that room to the rock garden. I thought maybe he was going to back up and then run right through the glass, but he said softly, "My girl, when I got back home, it was the shock of my life. She had lost an incredible amount of weight. The doctor said she was sterile. Her father owns a chunk of the Padres and her brother does Toyota spots. I went to visit her in Corona del Mar, a big mansion, and the level of operative life in there was down to about here." He held his hand down beside him, crouching. He gave me a sad little smile.

I said, "I'm not following all this."

"Her brother, Dick, Dick's got a dog, half boxer and half mastiff, and when it walks, it fishtails like a Lincoln. It was born in Africa. Striped. Maybe one percent zebra. Gorgeous dog. Kills anything. But terrified of cats. You know, that dog cost eleven hundred dollars." He spun around and sat back down in the rocking chair. "That mansion in Corona del Mar, a window blowing open. You see guards in gray raincoats out there in the dark. She, she was all in tears, thinking about how she's sterile."

82

Peter started to laugh, began to laugh hysterically hard, and ended up sobbing.

I was just sitting there.

Marge and Rex—Rex wearing a big Mexican sombrero, which went well with his leather and chains—came into the room, happy and laughing. Marge said to me, "Well, *there* you are."

The minute they came in, Peter shut up. And Rex's face suddenly got very serious. Frightened. Marge got it too, and all the party happiness went out of her face.

Peter lurched up, smashed against Rex, and ran out through a crowd of people. He knocked a girl against the wall, very hard, and her sandwich went sky-high. I started after him, but Rex grabbed me. He said, "Easy on."

"But," I said, "he's going out of his mind. Khe Sanh and a sterile girl —"

Rex was glowering behind his blue glasses. "I've heard all about it."

"What?"

"Let him go. He's never been to Khe Sanh and he doesn't have a sterile girlfriend."

Rex took a long pull on his Coors.

Marge said, her eyes a little baffled, "It's a mistake, it's really a mistake —"

Rex said, "Can it, Marge."

There was a silence.

Rex said, "Did he run the number about the eleven-hundred-dollar dog?"

Well—

"He sure works the piss out of that dog."

"Then—he's crazy."

Rex said, "Now you got it, Trip."

To hell with this dope and Lambrusco, I need a Pepsi. I went back into the kitchen. They'd done a job on the refrigerator, like a retreating army. But there were some Pepsis left. The man who had put his hand in his mouth was now munching on a fluorescent tube that he held up like a giant celery stalk. Sure has a mouth thing.

I took the Pepsi back into the Solarium. Peter—Peter Ingalls?

Marge was steamed at Rex. "It's—wrong," she whispered.

Rex's eyes were closed behind those blue glasses. He was scratching his growth of Hell's Angel beard, scratching underneath, at his throat.

Marge said it again, real low and private. "Wrong."

Rex said, "Were you asked?"

Marge in her Statue of Liberty toga. Woebegone. "Peter Ingalls—*Peter*, Rex—"

"I told you, babe—can it."

It was uncomfortable in there. So I took off, closing the sliding glass door behind me. Marge bugging Rex about Peter, she was really upset. The way she said *Peter* like that. Who the hell is Peter Ingalls anyway? I have smoked weed.

I saw Wanda, who was working her way from group to group, goosing people with her foot-long cigarette holder. I put my face close to hers, and stared at the beads of sweat on her forehead. I said, "We can't go on meeting like this." I'm so suave.

She said, "Don't toy with me."

"Let's dance."

The record was James Brown and the Mighty Instrumentals. Wanda and I were writhing around in the middle of the room. I love women dancing. I tried to catch the brass boob every time she came around, and now she was shimmying, and she really let loose—blabablebableabbblllla. I pulled her to me so close and tight; she could just squirt out of her dress, like toothpaste out of a squeezed tube.

When we finished dancing I did the one useful thing I learned at Stanford. I learned it from a guy in the Oasis. I said, "Have you had the opportunity to observe my cigarette bit?" I took the cigarette out of her holder. I said, "I loft the cigarette into the air, where it will describe a graceful parabola, finally coming to rest on my nether lip." I always say it just like that. I threw the cigarette up into the smoky air, and it flipped over the way it does in a slow circle, and I stuck out my jaw and the cigarette landed there, wagging on my "nether" lip, as the guy in the Oasis used to call it. I've only practiced it ten million times.

"God," Wanda said, "you're *mar*velous, you know about self-interested compassion, and you can dance, and now *this!*" She wound her hair in swarms. "What are your three favorite memories of the sixties?"

Rex goes by us with a bottle.

"Excuse me?"

"Your three favorite things about the sixties?"

Oh. I say, "Chairs, boxes, and dogs."

She screams. "You're *won*derful."

Rex'll tell you all about it.

"You have a place down here?" She says it real private, she's mine for the asking.

Oh yeah, I got a little place at the beach, just come down on weekends. I can't take her to the trailer, for crying out loud.

"What do you do?"

"I'm a police officer."

"What?"

Can't you see the uniform? I'm wearing it on the outside of my body, as a hint.

"Oh." She was thinking, standing there holding on to that foot-long cigarette holder, and now she used it like a riding crop, on my shoulder. "I didn't know"—and she left it right there. She walked away from me. She went through the door and out into the garden. And then she came back in. "Listen, buster, you're not running a channel check on me tonight—shit, you *are* a cop."

And she spit in my face.

I didn't move. I controlled myself. It was extremely distasteful. To have somebody spit right in your face, somebody you were cuddling and dancing with. She actually spit—spit in my face.

I ran into Joslin. Now, what's *she* doing here? She looked at me weird. I believe I have removed the sputum. Joslin was dressed sort of moderately and quiet. And obviously getting ready to leave. I wonder if Rex runs Marge and Joslin in shifts. What's going on? Joslin was talking with the guy in the butterfly chair, who was awake again. Somebody had put my hat on the guy. Joslin reached down and said, "Let's return this to whom it belongs, Al." She put the hat on my head, fixed the angle a bit, made it right. She said, "I owe you an apology."

So does Wanda the Witch.

"I had no right to speak to you like that, when you brought David home. It was a misunderstanding."

She's OK. Maybe she'd talk to me, calm me down.

Rex must have been watching, because he was Johnny-on-the-spot, right there. He said, "Babe, I just realized . . ." and he turned to me, squinting through those blue glasses. "I been on her case for an hour, because she wouldn't dress up as her illusion of herself, because she wouldn't *play*—but look—look—"

I looked. Gray pants and blue turtleneck, just dressed ordinary.

"I get it, hon—I get it." Rex took off his blue glasses. "I *got* it."

Joslin was rather animated herself. Her face getting eager. "Do you?"

"That's it—that's what I married. Jos has the most colossal illusion of all—"

"Yes?" She was cool and sophisticated, but also listening to a fairy tale.

Rex held her hands. "You have the most colossal illusion of all. You have the illusion that you are *yourself!*"

She clapped her hands, really delighted. And making fun of herself being delighted. Rex nuts about it. They kissed each other. Shit, I never saw two people make each other so instantly happy.

They went away.

Too bad it didn't work out. They really had something.

Marge came by, she had seen it too, and she muttered, wagging her torch: "*Out* of the road, *out* of the road."

The gray-haired guy who had been wearing my hat murmured singsongily, "The voice I hear this passing night was heard in ancient days by emperor and clown—"

I looked at him.

"The same self-same same-self song that oft-times hath charmed magic casements, opening on the foam"—he burped—"of perilous seas in faery lands forlorn." He looked at me. "Know what I mean?"

"No, sir."

"It's the top of the show. This is Jack MacKenzie welcoming you to 'This Passing Night.'"

I never understand what people say to me.

"Fifteen years ago, who would have believed it? That our little soap opera would be Rex Hooker's baby?"

I'm paying attention, I'm just not getting it.

"Fifteen years ago, he seemed like a nice-enough kid. A California Boy. A Stanford Man. Doing fine on Fifty-seventh Street. Don't Bother Me, World, This Is My Life and It's *Fun.*" The guy burps again, a little smile on his face. "Did you know him then?"

"I knew him in high school."

Suddenly the smile gets big. "Oh my, Rex Hooker in high school. Yes —yes, I can see Rex Hooker in high school." He sits there like an aging Buddha. "Did Rex acquire it along the way, or did he have it from the beginning?"

"What," I say, "does Rex actually *do?* On the soap opera?"

Old guy ponders. "Jack-of-all-tirades."

Oh. Then I see my girlfriend over there. "Does Wanda work on your soap opera?" I have to point her out to him.

He nods. "We've put her in—how shall I say it?—in a slightly less hopeful setting."

He says, "You're a policeman."

"Yes, sir."

"That's nice." He was a dreamy man. I felt fond of him. He said, "Our feelings we with difficulty smother, when constabulary duty's to be done —ah, take one consideration with another, a policeman's lot is not a happy one." He smiled at me. "A la D'Oyly, a la Carte." He reached down for a glass of white wine. Drank it. He said, "Want some real life?"

No, thanks, I've already had some.

He set down his wineglass and rummaged under his chair and brought up a box of Life cereal. He offered it, and I took a handful. And he did, and we sat there munching. I *am* stoned. First time in my life. It's not that bad. Munching. Must be the munchies. So this is what that means. My. I hope I haven't said it out loud. Which actually might have been better, considering that now I have said out loud, "After a certain amount of suffering, you lose your sense of humor."

He says out loud, "And after a certain amount of suffering, you get it back again."

Forward, munch. I like him. Name's Al, he says. And falls asleep again. Marge comes in with a huge candle affair that has half a dozen wicks floating up from wax pools which are mint and black. I look at her, trying to balance the thing. In my mind I say to her that I am very sorry for every bad thought I have ever had about you in my whole life. You don't know it, but I had lustful thoughts about you at Pete's Texaco. When you had that red MG.

"There," she says to herself softly, leaning over it.

You wouldn't have had all this trouble if you weren't stacked. But you are. And the trouble would be worth it, if you weren't so alone. I think of how Rex said that, Marge is so *alone*. How do Joslin and Marge get along?

"Buying or just looking?" she asks me.

Oh shit. What do I say out loud? Pretty eyes. "I was just thinking about your little red MG."

Now she's really looking at me funny.

Al says, "The crew could be out by vespers."

Marge says, "You guys are really gettin' into it." And she goes away, but looks back at me.

Now my head is going pound-pound-pound. I think it's time. It's time, but where? My legs seem to be a bit watery. Probably won't even notice it come April. I am now in the Music Room, where Rex and a handsome fellow are auditioning for the "Ted Mack Original Amateur Hour." They are whistling, like on that tape deck in the Seville on the way to Sabang, whistling; they are very good. I'll go over there and raise my hand above Contestant Number One, and then Contestant Number Two. I thought

I was right about that because Rex introduces me to the guy after they have finished showing off, and he *is* Contestant Number 2, this guy was Marge's second husband. I am a genius. But Rex is oblivious to my gifts because he has just asked me if I'm feeling all right. Not really. Got spit on in the face. Marge's Ex-Hubby Number 2 has freckles all over his face and works in the oil business. Ex-Hubby Number 2 has large, straight white teeth. Oliver, however, has destroyed considerable bone casing with his failure to floss. Everybody knows about Ollie. Perhaps they wonder why I do not speak to them directly. It is because you think you see me, whereas I am only a radio signal sent from the mother ship.

And the radio signal seems to be descending stairs. Ah, yes. The stairs lead down into a big workroom in the belly of the house where there's a little trolly car stolen from Knott's Berry Farm. Never been down here before. Golly, Ollie—it's a basement! Not only does Ex-Hubby Number 2 click into the puzzle via Marge, he was Rex's fraternity brother at Stanford. Got his first look at her on a Big Game Overnight. We were all at Stanford at the same time. Can you guess which item does not belong in this picture? So he stole Rex's girl. No, that's not true, Ex-Hubby Number 1 must have done that. Well, we've got that figured out. I have not fallen and will not require hip surgery. I hear a voice. I turn, and there's nobody there. Later, I suppose, they'll pinpoint this as when I lost my mind. I think I hear it again. Quite loud, actually. I say, "Who's there?"

And he steps out of the shadows. It's that Peter, Our Viet vet. He retreats to where he was. He's fiddling with a fuse box, kind of playing with it and muttering.

It's like I caught him beating off.

He snaps shut the little red metal door on the fuse box. He rummages through some old junk piled against the wall. He pulls out what appears to be a stuffed peacock—a beautiful thing, about six feet tall. The bird is mounted on a wooden perch and its tail just fans out so lovely behind. It comes down almost to the floor. Peter pats it on its back, raises a little cloud of dust. He stares at the bright blue neck feathers and strokes them and then gazes at the beak and the eye and the little feathery crown.

I think it's wearing off. I shouldn't mess with that shit, I can't handle it.

I walked out onto the sand and had a legal cigarette, and looked up at the stars. So this is some kind of anniversary party for the cast and crew of the soap opera. I guess. I'll have to watch it on TV. Why would Rex Hooker be a honcho on a soap opera?

I wend my way over to the bonfire, where this fairly old guy is giving a speech to some young people gathered around him. Old Guy says, "As the sage puts it, my children, the only thing impossible for a man to do is sit still in a room."

A handsome kid in a Levi's outfit, with schizzy eyes, says, "Shit, Jack, I did it for a year and a half."

The old man laughs. He has a big saggy belly. He's smoking a cigar. A little blonde with a mouth like a torn pocket suddenly explodes into laughter. "Ludes are soaps."

More laughter. The old man looks at me, my uniform. I say, "Oliver Bodley." We shake hands, and he says, "Jack MacKenzie." Now it focuses, I know him, he used to be a movie star. Westerns. Always the good guy. Sort of soft-spoken. He's really gotten old. He says, "Beautiful night."

Jack MacKenzie. Well, I'll be damned. I don't know what to say, so I say, "I certainly have admired your acting."

"Thank you, son." He mouths the stogie. "It's been a long, long trail" —and then he sings it, low to himself, "A long, long trail a-winding."

"Jack" says the schizzy-eyed kid, "Jack, sing it for us. Sing, Jack, sing."

Jack does. He looks at a moderately old woman, I'd say she's sixty, although she's still a real looker. He sings to her softly, "I'll be loving you —always. With a love that's true—always."

The gang at the bonfire picks it up, kind of dreamy, they're all getting off on it.

"When you need a helping hand, someone will understand—always— all-ways—"

Jack MacKenzie pretends he's got a microphone in his stogie, and plays talk-show host. He puts it in front of little groups of them, moving around with that pot belly. They sing well, and he's kind of lively, with his deep voice, hopping around the fire.

"Days may not be fair, al-ways. That's when I'll be there—al-ways."

It's sort of touching. It's pretty. Nobody's going to spit on my face here. I like this wing of the party, I wish I'd come down here earlier.

"Not for just an hour—not for just a day—not for just a year—but— al-ways."

Everybody applauds. And the kid says, "Speech! Speech!"

The aging lady says, "Life is full of noise and laughter—and the constant need for communication."

The lady has a little tremor. She says, "No greater joy, no greater happiness can come to a woman than an evening like this—to see that you are growing, all of you, by the grace of God, into honest, caring, hard-working people—"

"Work so hard," says the kid, "down at the plant, busting my ass—"

"Shut up, clod," says a strange girl. I don't know if it's "Claude" or "clod."

"We all must lead productive lives. That's one thing about the Kelly family, we're all livers."

"Gizzards!" says somebody. "Kelly Giblets."

The lovely big dogs, Procter and Gamble, asleep by the fire. Jack MacKenzie holds out his stogie. "All of us here can feel the soft touch of time."

A tall, hairy kid says, "Look who's talking about a soft touch."

Jack smiles. He turns to the lady. "I have been supported by the sweetest of women—" and he has tears in his eyes. "Tonight—tonight —I know that I am, I am—"

"You're *indicating*, Jack."

"Buzz off, buster." Mr. MacKenzie returns to his lady. "I feel tonight that I am surely the richest man on the face of the earth."

"And you owe it all to NBC."

Jack laughs. "She is my inspiration, the most beautiful and generous and most precious—she is still and always—my bride." Tears trickle down his face.

Somebody laughs, like it's all a joke. The weird girl says "Ssssh!" like it's not.

The spacy-eyed boy begins singing, softly, "Dancing in the Dark."

Jack MacKenzie and the lady are dancing in place, cheek to cheek. Kind of swaying there in the sand. "Dancing in the Dark." The singing voices go low, and everybody's smiling, and they applaud.

The lady says, "Just look at us. We're—"

"Ridiculous," says Jack MacKenzie.

His voice is the way I remember it in *Navajo Outpost*.

I stumble away, I don't understand. I go up to say good night to Rex. I am in my uniform. How would it look if the Department had a bust, and here I was. In this condition. I climb up through the starlit garden. I watch a beautiful nude woman swimming slowly like Esther Williams all alone in the pool. She's got liquid brown hair that comes down to a perfect ass. I stand there and watch her make a turn, kick off, with the longest legs in the world. She is totally preoccupied. With herself.

And here I thought I could pick someone up. I feel the usual sinking feeling of the American Male. Knowing he's going home alone.

The wind moves the tall trees, it's so soft and slow, the beach air, this passing night. Heh-heh, I say to myself, like David. This Passing Night —actually, I think I do recall Sheila watching a TV soap opera called that, years ago. Jack MacKenzie must play a kindly doctor or something. I'm not going to get laid.

With a love that's true—al-ways. I am upset. Dancing in the Dark. I have made a mess of my life. I know that. It probably comes off me like an aroma. Which is why I don't get laid. Animal disappointment.

And now I am sitting here in the main living room. I've stayed for the formal presentation. Rex is giving people big slices of a huge birthday cake, decorated with pink and black swirls and white frosting. "This Passing Night." He's in charge of a soap opera. Marge Stivers is smiling and social, however alone she is. Serving sleepy old Al a piece of cake. He'll probably top it with "Life." Marge seems to get along quite well with her ex-husband, Rex's fraternity brother. And after all these years Marge is still in love with Rex. My, my. I pick at my cake.

An auburn-haired girl whose black sweat shirt has STARFUCKER spelled on it in pink sequins comes halfway up the stairs from the rose garden. She calls to all of us, "Come to the Burning of the Bird." She really yells it: *"Burning of the Bird!"* People start to come out of the kitchen and the Music Room. We wander down past the pool, where four naked people are now piddling around the shallow end in the lavender light. One of the guys calls out, "Sexy Rexy, looky here, they gimme a big-eyed gal t'make me act funny 'n' spen' all my money." Rex says, "Hang in there, Turfbinder." I slow down and look at him—it's the country and western singer Mustang Turfbinder. The place is full of celebrities. Now everybody's moving down to the beach. And as we come around the cabana, I see it's that Peter Ingalls guy: He has brought out the peacock and screwed its base into the sand a few feet into the surf. He's brandishing one of the pieces of driftwood from the bonfire, standing there with it, like a torch, beside the peacock.

"Welcome, my children, to the communion of your race," he shouts. The burning driftwood waves back and forth.

We all stand there. Rex calls out to him, "Hey, don't do that."

Peter doesn't seem to hear.

Rex mumbles beside me, "Party's gettin' out of hand."

Peter calls it again, *"Welcome, my children, to the communion of your race."* A wave breaks and the surf sloshes around him. He keeps himself up by holding on to the peacock. He stares the bird in its glass eye. He holds the torch close to it and the bird's eyes glow—like it might come to life, and cry out, and fly.

Jack MacKenzie comes lumbering over. He says to Rex, "What is this, son, a location shot?"

Rex says, "That de-mented sumbitch goin' to comflagrate mah bird."

91

He starts forward in a little half-run. Peter sees Rex coming at him, so he wipes the torch across the base of the peacock's tail. The bird is so old and dusty that it catches fire immediately. The flames spread up it, and Rex stops at the water's edge. Peter staggers back from the fire, shouting, "Take wing—*take wing!*" I think the peacock is really going to fly. In the fire it almost seems to be shaking out its feathers. I could swear it turns its head, not as if it's a stuffed bird, but like a real live bird with a little chain connecting its ankle to the perch. Its head jerks in that robot way that birds have—jerk, jerk, jerk. A big piece of the tail gets caught in the sea breeze and lifts away, a separate piece of fire going up into the black sky.

Right beside me the STARFUCKER girl says in a little whisper, "*Dynamite.*"

I look at Rex and his face is strange, empty. He's not a Hell's Angel at all.

And then Rex moves in on Peter, who doesn't have much of a choice, unless he wants to swim to Catalina. He stumbles into the surf on his left, trying to run, and Rex goes to his right, waiting, slowly moving in. Rex lifts Peter, lifts him right up into the air with both hands in his armpits, and sets him on the beach. Jack MacKenzie and everybody else are starting to get kind of anxious, nobody is moving. The bird is all fire now, blazing away. It burns itself out and stands there smoldering while the tide comes in, the smoke smelling really ugly. I am going back up, get my 1 GROUCH, and go home. I've had enough.

And then I look down the dark beach and I see a little figure standing away back against the house, in a white dressing gown. It's Mrs. Hooker. In the middle of the night. I shuffle over toward her. She is standing at the bottom of a metal fire escape that goes from the beach all the way up five flights to their bedroom. She is standing there as if she's been sleepwalking and somebody has just awakened her. So tiny, with an old-fashioned hairnet on, her hands up to her face. Her eyes are frantic.

"Oh," she says.

"Ma'am, it's kind of chilly for you."

"What's happened? Is someone hurt?"

"No, no," I say, and realize I am shaking. "It's just a wild party."

"What was that fire—that terrible fire?"

"Oh, they burned up that old stuffed peacock."

She is searching my face with her fearful blue eyes. "And is Rex upset?" She is whispering to me.

"No. Not really."

"Why, Rex has had that peacock since—since Stanford. He had it in his fraternity room." She is really afraid. "All burned, so terribly burned." She is talking to herself, not to me. Those eyes, glowing out of that frail little face. I can see she's had a lot of medication.

"Ma'am, you don't want to catch cold."

"What time is it? What time is it?"

I look at my watch. "It's twenty to three."

"Oh. Good." Very slowly: "And everyone is having a truly *good time*?"

"They seem to be."

She turns. "That's the important thing."

I think she is pretty unsteady. I walk with her, back up the five flights. She stops at each level, to catch her breath. In their room, ol' J.O. is snoring away, making the windows rattle.

The Mrs. crawls in beside him.

I steal quietly out their door, shutting it behind me. I go down the Honduras mahogany staircase. I get in my car and drive home.

Rex is a soap opera. You kidding me? I wondered what he did for a living. I'm sure Sheila watched it. She would have gotten quite a kick out of that party. She'd have been impressed. I don't want to smoke any more of that shit.

My trailer's a mess, I couldn't have brought anyone here anyway, Chef Boyardee smiling in the sink. I got spit on, straight in the face.

I'm so weary I can barely get my pants off. At the prime of life I'm an old man. My pillow doesn't smell like sleep. Could you guys give me a break, just spare me the blazing peacock dream?

5

THEODORE HUMS. About five-five, five-six, probably in his fifties although he looks seventy, fat, wino, always drinking Thunderbird or Ripple—anything under a buck a quart. Theodore is his own musical accompaniment. Unbeknownst to me, he persuaded the two old Albanian ladies at the bookstore on Mountain to let him sleep in a closet. Or what is now a closet but used to be something else, because there is a big mail slot in it for junk mail. These ladies call in a complaint, and when I get there they are apoplectic. One of 'em says, "He is vun diskustink slob!" She points her finger, and I see it—this halfway decent-sized droopy semi-erection sticking out the mail slot. I go over to inspect it for distinguishing marks or scars, kind of apprehensive because who knows what is on the other end. Then I hear it: "Hmmmmmmmm." And I breathe a little sigh of relief. I say, "Theodore, I'm going to open this door now, and I don't want you to hurt yourself." "Hmmmmmmm." I think he's pretty damn lucky one of those old Albanian ladies didn't pick up a big book and whack it. I open the door, and there he is with his pants around his knees and a pint sticking out his back pocket, gassed, humming.

I can't seem to get rid of Theodore. Like he's my own personal whatever-you-call-them, not your alter ego, some little fairy or elf person,

certainly not your guardian angel. A magic fellow just for you. Trip &
Theo. One dark and stormy night I am going down a little alley that winds
up from Pacific Coast Highway to Legion. There's an alcove for garbage,
Laguna Beach Disposal, and tonight a huge cardboard crate for a refrigerator is standing beside it, because it was too big to shove into the bin itself.
It's just pouring rain. I'm checking doors, feeling sorry for myself—I'm
soaked, I will be soaked for many hours, I will not be dry until I go off
duty. Then I see a pair of feet, stocking feet, sticking out of the refrigerator crate. Maybe somebody's crawled up in there and died. I take my
flashlight, look in, and it's Theodore. He's taken off his shoes and he's all
covered up with newspapers. He's snoring. I'm bored and sopping, so I
take my night stick and bang like hell on the side of the crate. He wakes
up, puts on his shoes, gets out of the crate, and I duck behind it, so I can
see him peer up the alley and peer down the alley, officer of the watch,
hmmmmm. Then he climbs back into the box, takes his shoes off, has
himself another drinky-poo, pulls up the front page, and he's snoring
again. So, like the shit I am, I take my night stick and beat on the fucking
crate again. Theodore goes through the same routine, puts on his shoes,
gets out, looks up and down the alley, hmmmmmm, then climbs back in,
shoes off, slurpidy-slurp, snore. We do it a third time, only now I'm
getting ashamed of myself. I tell him to get the hell out of the alley so
he won't get run over or catch pneumonia. He gives me a sob story, so
I buy him a meal, give him a dollar. Take him over to the Laguna Hotel,
where the janitor will let him sleep in the basement until the rain blows
over.

A big black man with snow-white hair stopped me on the street one
day and said, "You don't remember me, do you?" I didn't. But it turns
out that five or six years ago I arrested him for stealin' Crisco at the
Safeway in Boat Canyon. While I was writing him up, he told me about
all the hungry mouths he had to feed. So I poked around, helped him out.
And now, years later, he's a chef—not a cook, a chef, probably makes
more money than I do. Snow-white hair above that black face. He said
he never forgot my kindness. He makes me feel fine. I paste it in my
mental scrapbook.

Only part of my job I absolutely cannot stand is packing a cadaver.
Bodies are a bitch, washed up on Main Beach, bloated about three times
their normal size. You take hold of an arm and it comes right off in your
hand. Dead animals are one thing, but I shudder at sea monsters that used
to be people. Especially if they've been around for a while, decaying, the
gases coming off them. First one I ever had to pack was in Indio, an old
guy who had had a coronary, been dead a week, he was all black from the

chest up, stunk like a sonofabitch. It must have been 110 degrees in that room. I went around opening windows, to get rid of the foul stench, and while I'm letting the fresh air in, I suddenly hear behind me—griiippp! —the new air got to him and his stomach exploded. The undertakers come in, wearing their big long rubber gloves. I help take the stretcher down the stairs, and the geez comes apart in the bag. And the bag leaked, we were negotiating a turn at the landing, and this juice comes trickling down my neck. I tossed my cookies right over the banister. I didn't get my uniform washed, I burned it. I was sick; the experience gave me the goddamn willies for a week. I took a lot of showers. But I could still smell it, I'd get a whiff of that juice and my stomach would flip right over.

I can smell it now, rainy November night, sitting in the blue-and-white. Haven't seen Rex Hooker in three weeks. Maybe he's dropped me. I resent that, somehow. Oh well, I think, I'd drop me, if I could. Oliver Bodley, a most inspirational bundle of aches and pains.

Guy on a bike runs by me. A vroom-vroom boy. I pull him over, get out of the patrol car, take three steps, and all of a sudden he guns it, and away he goes. Son of a *bitch*. It's raining pretty hard, and we go back down Coast Highway. He pops into that big parking lot across from Treasure Island. He's squirreling around—it's a Bonneville 650, a mean machine, ninety mph in a parking lot. I call the sheriff, and we go hauling ass up the highway again, for a long, long time. This is some kind of cross-country endurance test. I'm on the radio yelling for the sheriff and the CHP. We pass Emerald Bay and I'm way out of jurisdiction, but once you're on somebody, you can follow him to the state line. We are *going*, approaching Fashion Island. Where the fuck is everybody? I'm on the radio to KJOY. We're doing about one-ten, I can hardly believe it in the rain. We play the Fashion Island Dos-à-Dos, last dance of the night, I should be so lucky, vroom-vroom, and as he goes around toward the cinemas, there's this big steel lamppost, and the bike leans right over on the curve, the ass-end like a meteor, the crash bars are sparking, and his fucking shoulder hits the pole. The bike corkscrews, and I think he's going to dump it, he'll dump it sure as shit, but no, wawawohwoh, he's going again. I finally get some help, suddenly my radio is alive with hibernating spirits, the sheriff and the CHP. I am heading him toward John Wayne Airport, as they now call it because a conservative mood is taking hold, and they got a roadblock—good thinking, guys—my adrenaline is pumping so hard, why the fuck they set up a roadblock down there? We go down into a gully, and up and out, we're both airborne, wawawooo, and now I hear Butch has awakened from one of his slumber parties on El Toro and joined the fray. I've got him behind me, and Smitty from CHP, three of us all in a row, 1, 2, 3 behind the bike. Smitty says we'll run him right into the field, he knows the construction here, it dead-ends. But the kid on the Bonneville is playing Steve McQueen in *The Great Escape*. He pulls a right-angle slide right through the construction, and Smitty is the one who goes into the field. I'm yelling into the radio, "I ain't gonna chase him no more!" and now we've got five cars on him, when Dick Stoller of the Sheriff's Department says, "I'm coming through!" I hear him on the radio and feel the vibrations and noise rushing by—"Get outta my way, I'm coming through!" Jesus, he does. It's like we are sitting still. Stoller is doing 140 easy. He fucking passes the motorcycle! And then I see his plan—he is one fine driver, used to do stock cars for a living—he pulls across the road, and over the radio he says box him in, slap the cars into a **V**. We got our biker trapped. He slows down and stops. He stops. He stops three feet from Stoller's car, and we arrive and make our **V**. Then all of a sudden the guy revs his bike all the way, just like he did to me in the fucking first place, he pops the clutch, and goes straight into Stoller's car, wedges himself against it, his bike is actually embedded in the car. I dash out and try to get his helmet off, he's got this molded face-piece. I'm sure he's broken his neck because blood is pouring out, but what happened was he bit off the end of his tongue.

Take five, guys.

Butch and I sit there in the rain and smoke our cigarettes.

The kid didn't bite off that much of his tongue. He could talk. He says his girl don't love him no more. He says life ain't worth living no more. Stoller is quite upset about his vehicle; he should have been a pilot in the *Luftwaffe*. Butch reminds me we should go pick up Smitty, who's door-handle-deep in a sandy bog. The wind picks up the rain and throws it at us, those big trees bending and flapping around. Fog rolling in from the sea. Shit. I have an acrid taste in my mouth, and I spit and spit. I watch the kid pass out and slam the pavement. Everybody sees it and nobody moves to help him. Could have gotten us killed, fucker. We do help him. Ambulance coming, wow-wow-wow. We sit there and smoke in the rain.

It's my job. Standing here on the pavement in the rain, staring at that turd color on my wet cigarette, my body calming down, my heart beating. My job. When you just do it and think later. I would like to go home to a woman who'd know without my talking about it, she'd just catch my eyes, respect it, and be proud of me.

6

I **WAS** on another eleven-to-seven, actually cutting out a little early, a Friday night in the middle of November, with more rain coming down. I was heading back to the station around 6:30 when I heard the call to the fire department. I was mellow, one more shift finished, a weekend in front of me, my dick a bit stiff, it never loses hope, but when I heard that call I sat right up. A fire at the Hookers' at Summer Snow. The manager of the Edgewater Reef Motel said he had a boy with him who said the phone lines to the house had been cut.

I hit the siren and put it to the peg. Slid around the corner of Ocean onto Coast, a four-wheel drift, then gunned her up the hill. I'm making time, flat-out on North Sunset, past the motel, and into the circular driveway. Some elegant things have already been dragged out, and I skid into a lamp, knock it over as I fly out the door. J.O. and Mrs. H. were standing there in the rain, huddled together under a Monterey pine. She was in a pale blue dressing gown, and the old man was wearing that scarlet robe with the black velvet lapels. Leela was panicked out of her mind. Then here comes David out the window, packing the telescope, he's busy as a bee. "Precious," Mrs. H. calls to him, "don't go in again—*don't* go in again," but the kid docs. I say, "Fire department's on its way. Where's

Rex?" The big white mansion all dark with black smoke leaking out of it.

Leela said, "Oh yes—yes, they're in there—oh, J.O.—what—what?"

J.O. seemed stunned, eighty years old, trying to protect his wife. He wanted to go back into the house, but he couldn't leave her. So I went to the big front door and tried to open it, but I couldn't, it was bolted. I slammed at it with my shoulder, but it didn't give, not that oak door. Leela said, "Rex led us out through David's room." I was looking around through the smoke. Light rain just pattering down, I could see it in Leela's hair, in her hairnet. Then here comes David again through that busted window in his short blue p.j.'s, and he's coughing as he drops that fencing sword, clatterty-clatter, on the driveway. He's not really going in after the shit, he just picks it up on his way out, kind of absently, as he tries to get fresh air. His bare right foot is all bloody. Leela sees it and tries to grab him. But he breaks away and tears down through the rose garden. It was so dark, still before sunup, with the rain and the heavy clouds. I chased after him and yelled at him to stay the fuck outside, but the little bastard zipped back in. No, goddammit, *no*. Why hasn't the fire alarm gone off? It's smoke-activated. And now everything's all silent and that ugly black smoke is pouring out the big windows, like the house itself is one enormous head, coughing, coughing greasy smoke out of its eyes and nose and ears. You can see a little light in there, firelight, little patches of it in the Solarium and the Music Room.

Then I hear sirens coming up North Sunset, and I figure we'll be OK, as soon as the trucks get to us. I run back to the driveway just as they come pulling in, their sirens going hee-haaa heeee-haaaa, heeee-haaaa, like a wounded electric animal, and their huge lights, the beams blasting across the house. You can see the rain falling in the beams. That tanker is a hard sucker to drive, when it's half-full it pulls you and pushes you, it can tip over easy with tons of water inside. Most people do not know how many gallons to a ton, but it doesn't take too many, the water just yaws all over the place. The trucks come down the driveway and pull around the blue-and-white, which like a fool I have left in their way. Half a dozen guys come tumbling off the hook and ladder, and out of the cab. J.O. runs toward them and talks to one of them, and the guy has a big ol' helmet on, and he grabs an ax and runs to the front door. He plants himself, and swings back, and then really goes after it, just clobbers the living shit out of that door, and then kicks in what's left, and the greasy smoke pours out, blowing him back away from the house. The other firemen are running around, shouting at each other, pulling hoses off the trucks. I watch them almost knock down Mrs. H, and J.O. grabs her, pulls her back toward the pink Seville, holding her, with help from the manager of the Edgewater Reef.

Goddammit, I gotta *do* something here—10-70, 10-70. And then I hear Rex's voice.

It sounds like it's down by the pool, so I run toward it, and it is Rex, he's crying out, *"Woman—woman here!"*

I can't see very well, knocking through the wicker high-tea chairs, and then he's there, Rex, naked with gray goop all over him—and he's got Marge Stivers in his arms. She's naked, also covered with that goop. Rex is coughing so hard he can barely talk, but he says, "Mouth-to-mouth— *mouth-to-mouth,"* and I'm so busy grabbing her I goddamn fail to prevent him from staggering naked back into the smoke.

I work on Marge. She moans after a minute, so I pick her up, I've got her, and I run back up through the garden because the paramedics will have the equipment. And I fall down. Shit, I'm trying to protect Marge and instead I fall right on top of her. It terrifies me that she isn't crying or gasping; maybe she's stopped breathing again. I hit my head so fucking hard on something that I see pretty lights.

I get her up, she really is good-sized, heavy when she's limp. I flash on when she fell out of that tree. I get her around the middle, hoist her along, my legs banging into hers, like she is a rag doll. I make it to the first Monterey pine and through the rock garden to the circular driveway. J.O. sees me. The old man helps me get her to the little white truck that has just pulled in, and the guys take her. There, take her, take her.

The front door is a fucking mouth bellowing this huge stream of black, black greasy smoke, and the men have gas masks on. Semiliquid smoke pools up around the decks and balconies, really bad stuff like in a horror movie, it's all around us. Gas masks scare the shit out of me, and they use big torchlike flashlights, and hoses like huge snakes running from the tanker into the house through the front door.

It makes me furious that there are other cars parked out along the road. You know they've followed the sirens just for the fun of it, people with umbrellas and plastic see-through raincoats, standing out there, and probably some "guests" from the Edgewater Reef. Something to do, maybe get a big ol' thrill out of someone else's tragedy, a dozen gawkers already, and through the Monterey pines I can see headlights, more rubbernecks coming.

They have Marge on a stretcher, she's covered with a stained sheet, kind of glued to the nasty stuff, a big oxygen tank beside her. A fireman's there with a mask, putting it on, pulling it off, doing mouth-to-mouth in a way I've never seen before. And then behind me there is an incredible *boom!* like a jet breaking the sound barrier, like a bomb goes off in the house, and suddenly the whole Grand Entrance Hall is a big balloon of yellow turning into white, a pure—Jesus Christ, almost beautiful—sheet that billows. Three firemen come spilling out the front door, they don't have a chance against that, and then they crouch in the driveway, flooding the yellow-white sheet as it rises toward the sky. They lay some chemicals on it, really do a job, that explosion goes out as soon as the chemicals hit it. But the greasy belch-belch-belch of smoke doesn't stop, it keeps coming and the men in masks go back inside.

Leela is screaming at J.O., "Our boy—our—*boy!*" And it looks as if she is going to run into the house, and it also looks as if the old man is going to run in there, so there they are, each one trying to hold back the other and also trying to rush in. Leela screams "Rex! Rex—My *Boy!*" and J.O., his robe all fallen open now, he cries to one fireman, "Hold her, hold her," and the fireman takes Leela. Then J.O. starts toward the house, toward the front door, and Leela is straining—poor little old woman, she seems stronger than the big guy, and she gets loose from him—and then I think both of them are going to go into the house and die, going forward and holding each other back. J.O. is groaning—sounds, not words—but I grab them both and pull them back, and J.O.'s sounds turn into words. "You're hurting her, you're *hurting* her." I know he feels he's the only person in the world who knows how to take care of her, but he thinks his son and his grandson are somewhere in there. Leela's arm bones are like twigs and there is hardly anything left of her body. I almost fall again, we're about to knock each other down, that tiny woman and me, when she turns suddenly and says, "Where's David?" I don't have the heart to tell her, she must not have seen him go back in, or thought he came out again. I know he was going in after Rex, but Leela doesn't, and now she can't find him, and she's looking, looking, kind of all battering against my arms. Then this unearthly noise comes out of the house, a high, inhuman moan, a whine, like the call of some terrible space animal, and everybody stops for a second, frozen in the rain and the light of the fire. The awful noise goes on almost like a demented song, from another planet, you can't tell what would make a sound like that—and then I know what it is. Procter, or Gamble. It's one of the big Labradors somewhere down in the house. Its voice comes wailing out with the smoke.

I've got to go in. I start to move away, but Leela is sobbing. I wonder if Rex could be lost in a crawl space or in one of their secret passageways. Maybe he's mixed up in the dark and the smoke, he's lost his way. Leela breaks away from me, an insane angel in that blue dressing gown, her arms out to the smoke and fire, the light, her eyes popping out of her tiny

101

wasted-away face, like she's being burned up by the fire herself, screaming, not really a word, just a *mmmmaaa* wail, and the scream getting caught in her throat as she goes into the smoke. J.O. flies after her, they disappear in through the front door, and I tear after them, and then we are all three pushed out again by two firemen with masks, and one of them rips his mask off and looks at J.O. and Leela and yells out to me, *"Hold these people!"* What the fuck does he think I've been doing? My head, my head. By now the Chief has arrived, and he picks up Leela just like a baby, and I wonder why I couldn't do that, and that's when I know something's the matter with me, I hurt myself somewhere. A fireman has J.O. and is dragging him, J.O. spitting curses, "Cocksucker—let me—*cocksucker!*" —just that one word. And then he bursts out of the fireman's arms, and in that scarlet robe he's back into his mansion, he designed it, he knows every inch of it, he's engulfed in the goopy smoke. Leela is screaming, "J.O., darling—*nooooo!*" Her voice breaks and she's sobbing these little whimpers, and goddammit, I have to go in there, I'll never forgive myself if I don't make a run at it. I try to use my head, and I go down around the rock garden again, I have it clear in my mind—the outside fire escape, that long metal one, maybe the fire hasn't reached there and I can go up. But by the time I pass the pool—which has ashes and crud floating on it—and make it across the ground cover to a shortcut to the fire escape, there is already a fireman coming down it, very fast, spraying an extinguisher, but it isn't being sprayed at any flame, it's just shooting off into the air. He isn't even looking at it, because a bellow of smoke is following him down the stairs, and then he sees me and slams his hand against my chest, knocking me down toward the beach. He goes into the basement.

Rex and David and J.O. are inside, somewhere, somewhere on one of the five floors, trying to get each other out. Goddammit, they all *were* out, every one of them, and where do I start looking? But I can't, I'm dumped on my butt, all I'll do now is kill myself. But I don't give a rat's ass, I run across the sand and throw myself in the ocean, and all sopping salty I go back up and follow the fireman into the smoke. I can see his flashlight, the red circle around it that is just like a giant bug or something. I can't see the man, just the red light, and the smoke is like drinking soup through your nose, it is so greasy and liquid. I throw up and fall backward and crawl outside and gag and throw up again. I pull myself to my feet and make my way back to the swimming pool and up through the rock garden. Nothing is working too well, in my brain or my body. I seem to be passed out and awake at the same time. The ocean water didn't protect me, that was fucking dumb. My feet are aching so bad—they feel artificial, but they also have nerves, and I can't seem to support myself, I flash on it,

102

ridiculous, once I went back to the huddle like this, except then I was young, and could breathe, I can't get my breath, and I'm seeing pretty colors behind my eyes. I can't get my breath, and when I reach the circular driveway, they've moved the tanker down about twenty yards so it's almost flush against the outside wall of the Executive Wing, and a ladder is up to the window of the master bedroom. A fireman is there, his hose going in the window—and there is no firelight, just the smoke, the fire is out, but the house is coughing, throwing up oily goop.

And then I see them coming, very slowly, out the front door. Rex, naked, with David in his arms, Rex crawling out of the smoke, and David's covered with the goop too, in his sky-blue pajamas, which are just black rags now. His father is hauling him along, crawling—and then the Chief pushes by me, because he has seen them too, and then a fireman, and they get the kid, and Rex, who is turning around to crawl back in there again, he isn't really conscious, just going on instinct. And then two more firemen help carry them, Rex and David, their bodies. Rex is clearly alive; I don't know about David.

J.O., the old man, is still in there.

7

I'M NOT real sure who was in which ambulance. I think it was Rex and David in the lead, and they got Mrs. H. in the second. She didn't want to leave until her husband came out, but she went kind of crazy when her son and grandson appeared with all that slime streaming off them. The kid's foot was badly cut, and I thought he was dead except that the blood spurting regularly from his foot meant the heart was still beating. The place so jammed with gawkers in cars that the ambulances couldn't get through, so I charged up and helped clear the street. I guess I was pretty hysterical and surly. I just got people out of there.

When I came back to the driveway, they had the old man out, the sheet covered his head. J.O.

The crews were mopping up, hosing the house, driving that shit-smoke out over the beach. One of the dogs, Procter or Gamble, was limping around, topply, whining, like it was drunk. The Lab was a pathetic sight in the drizzle with the sun coming up and everything smelling horrible. The Chief, all out of breath, clomped over to me in rain gear and boots and ordered me to the hospital, said I should contact the families. And I should get myself checked out by a doctor. I looked down and my hands were all runny with blood, I don't even know where or how it happened.

The Chief asked me if I could drive, and I said yes, and squeezed my hands together. I guess the blood wasn't mine. You sure you can drive? the Chief said. Yeah, shit, I'm sure. I almost ran into a mobile TV unit going past the motel. I was trying to think who the fuck I'm supposed to get in touch with—Joslin, for one, but not Marge Stivers's parents, they'd already lost one daughter this fall, when Sissy hanged herself. Shit, how can I call Joslin? I got fourteen things racing through my head, trying not to think about anybody else dying on the way to the hospital. Downtown the streets are pretty well deserted, and I fly by Main Beach, my siren on, my bloody hands slipping on the wheel, driving fast and poorly.

Leela had collapsed in the emergency room. Doctors and nurses are running around and I hear one guy say, "The white count is out of sight, it's over the top." She needs treatment immediately, and everybody has their hands full. Rex and David and Marge are on stretchers, these teams in green smocks hovering around their bodies, and a doc looks at me, and I say I'm all right. He goes over to Mrs. H. and says something's wrong, and I'm waiting without getting in the way when I see a needle pop right out of her arm, and thick blood, Jesus, I never saw such blood, it comes out red mud, it just blew the needle right out of her skinny little wasted arm. The doctor yells at the intern, and I have to head out to the men's room down the hall and wash my face and hands and drink a long slug of water out of the basin faucet. I pat my face dry with paper towels, and for some reason I comb my hair before I put my hat back on. I check myself all over for injuries but can't find any, and I just stand by the sink breathing deeply, trying to think. I do notice that I have blood on my pants and my shoes. Where did all this blood come from? And while these details are zipping around in my addled brain, I am also thinking I'm a policeman, and it's my job to figure out the origins of this fire. The very first call said the phone lines had been cut. Right away I think of Peter Ingalls burning that peacock, but my mind is wandering around, I'm about as sure-footed as that pitiful Labrador. I don't know where I am.
Obviously I don't, because the door to the men's opens, and a black custodian comes in and looks straight down at me. This means I am sitting. I thought I was standing.
His broom goes clatterty-clatter, he helps me up and suggests I let the doctors take a look at me. I am only semicivil to him, embarrassed to be in this condition. Then I sneeze all over myself and it's black; I must've inhaled a lot of that shit myself. I grab the dirty towels in the janitor's pushcart and get rid of some grungy snot; clears my head a little. I stagger back into the emergency room. Leela and Marge have been whizzed away,

105

the teams are still working on Rex and David. I try to be a professional, go over to a doctor who is sitting down, crud all over his green smock, holding a Sprite can. I identify myself and say I have to get in touch with the immediate families, can he give me some information? Instead of answering, the doc stands up and starts messing around with my eyes, he's really kind of rough. Get out of my eyes, dammit. I explain the blood on me isn't mine. I hear a sound of vomiting behind me and a doctor's voice saying, "Good, good—here it comes, here it comes. How's the boy?"

"Nothing yet," a female voice says.

"Judas Priest, look at it come—"

A terrible retching sound.

"Foot finished. Goddamn, I should have been a tailor."

I hear these voices as I realize I'm on my back and this M.D. is fucking around with lights in my eyes. I see a little Jewish tailor in Poland, in his shop, it's summertime, the sun is shining, but it's snowing, I can see it so clearly, through the window, the lace curtains blowing in my face, little man sewing in the summer snow, hear his little voice singing to himself, singing and sewing.

When I wake up, I'm still in the emergency room. There's a curtain around my stretcher-bed. It takes a minute or two to get my bearings, then I get up and plunge through the curtain.

"Hey, whoa, big fella." It's Dr. Pepper. Dr. Sprite.

My legs are real watery, so I walk over and sit down on a plastic chair.

The doc says, "Whoa," again, like I'm a dray horse, and tells me I've had a bad blow to the head, a minor concussion. I say I'm fine, I have work to do, and he says he wants me under observation. I tell him I'll do the observing. I have always had a low opinion of medical doctors, with their prices.

I ask him how everybody is.

David and Rex are in the I.C.U. Almost asphyxiated, it was touch-and-go, but they'll make it. Marge and Mrs. H. are all right—Marge got out in time and Mrs. H. is in shock; the main problem for the old lady is her illness and the trauma. Everybody's unconscious or under sedation—I'm trying to take it in, my head is splitting—anyway, they're alive. But not J.O. His body has been moved to the mortuary.

I tell the doc I have to notify the kid's mother.

The doc is confused. He thought Marge was the mother.

A lot of people are rushing around—hospital personnel and media scum. Reporters. I want to get to a phone, I don't want the families involved to hear this on the radio. The doc takes me into an office, and

I am trying to think what to say to Joslin. That's when I realize I may do more harm than good—do I know what my voice sounds like? So I tell the doc all the information and he writes it down, scribble-scribble. I remember him saying, "The *Stivers* girl?" and looking at me, bewildered, and me saying "Marge—Sissy's sister—don't call the parents." My brain does a little blip. "And Joslin Hooker, that's Mission Viejo, and—and it's unlisted—you got to go through the phone company—" I cannot figure out what has happened to my mind, I'm like toast, I pop up and then somebody pushes me down again.

The Chief comes in, takes one look at me, and goes out. He looks terrific himself.

By late afternoon I've slept it off and sweated it out. I shower for a good long time. Butch brings me civvies. I check around. Mrs. H. is asleep, she looks like death. Marge is kind of groggy. I do not intrude. On my way to the I.C.U., I find Joslin in the hall, pacing up and down, her back to me. When she turns around, she sees me and lets out a little cry. She actually comes up and puts her arms around me, and we hug each other, oddly enough. I feel guilty, because I notice at a time like this how good her hair smells and how black and long it is. I'm actually at this tragic time feeling her boobs against my chest. God, I'm a puke.

"How's he doing?" I say.

"He hasn't—he hasn't—but he said, 'Mommy, don't cry.' "

"And Rex?"

"He's still unconscious."

It's cold in the hospital corridor. I say I'll wait with her.

We had a tasteless little supper in the cafeteria. And then we sat. I went in, every hour, to look at Rex and David with her. They had shaved Rex's hair away from his temples, to get at some burns, and he had lots of tubes running into him. He was so thin. Unconscious, coughing up that black sputum. David was completely spaced out. His mother would just sit there and hold his hand.

I called the Chief at home, and for once he actually seemed concerned about my condition. Still an asshole, of course. He said, "Well, after you conked out, I made some calls. You got to know how to handle people —it comes with the job." Thanks, Chief. He said the investigators had definitely come down on the side of arson. For the next week we'd be up to our asses in it, I should take care of myself and get back as soon as possible. I told him about Ingalls burning the peacock, and like the shit I am I said I'd gone up to investigate a noise complaint; I didn't say I was an invited guest.

The peacock interested the Chief; he said I should have reported it. I

107

mentioned that the doc told me I had a concussion. The Chief repeated that I should have reported the peacock. I look through the glass booth at Joslin sitting there. The Chief says we'll have a conference at 10:30 A.M., if I can make it. I say I can. He wants to know the condition of the hospitalized people. I tell him. I can hear his voice pause, and I visualize the Chief at his desk. He says this Rex fellow put us through quite a little circus on Labor Day, the mental hospital and all. Does he have any arsonist tendencies?

I get all ready to blow my stack—even though you can understand why the Chief might let that possibility buzz in his bonnet, he doesn't know the history. But as I step out of the phone booth, it buzzes in my bonnet for a second.

Joslin is staying the night. I should go home, try to prepare myself for the hours and days ahead. I get her a blanket, and there's one thing I have to do. I look at her pale face and her eyes. I say, "Who's going to tell them?"

Joslin is dazed. She looks at me.

"Mrs. Hooker, Rex, David—who's going to tell them?" She doesn't seem to understand, so I say, "That J.O. is—dead?"

She looks away like I slapped her, and then she grits her teeth, still looking away. "I will."

I start off, and I hear her break down. I start to come back, but she puts up her hand in this funny little fluttery go-away motion, her face hidden in her black hair. She wants to be alone. I turn around. And then I turn back around. She doesn't really want to be alone. But it's like pride. You don't intrude on it. So I go out and drive myself home.

Before I conk out, as the Chief says, I catch Channel 2, and they have thirty seconds on the death of the distinguished Californian, J. O. Hooker, founder of the Pacific Architecture School, with some shots of his greatest buildings all over the Southland. I don't know how these people get this shit together so fast, it almost makes you think they prepared it in advance. Then this morning's scene, in horrible living color. The minicam went into the Grand Entrance Hall, showed the Honduras mahogany spiral staircase all charred black. They went into the Edifice Rex—a "monument to excellence of architectural design"—shit, Rex built the maze when he was a kid, his father didn't design it, it's not a monument. I can't believe how the media gets everything mixed up.

The *L.A. Times* next morning had a big story, a photograph of Summer Snow looking like Frankenstein's castle. It said the "origin of the fire was in the lower floors, issuing up a stairwell serving as flu and chimney." Buzz

Barrett, "*L.A. Times* Staff Writer," mentioned the acrid, billowing smoke, said "it is not immediately clear whether there were flames in the east wing rooms," and that "solder from a ceiling light had fallen loose." The "Investigative Team," which Buzz Barrett also called the "Inquiry Team of the Laguna Beach Fire Department, Police Department, State Police, and Sheriff's Department," examined the "blistered paint peeling off in fist-sized flakes" and the "paneling burned through to cinder blocks." Apparently J.O. died from "smoke inhalation," not fire—only his left arm was burned, and there wasn't even a sign of burning where he was found. There will be a "coroner's inquest" because "evidence points to human carelessness or malice." The Laguna fire chief said, "J. O. Hooker was an internationally famous architect—this house would have passed any of our tests with flying colors." But the smoke detector and alarms had been disconnected; whoever did it was someone who knew the house. People were checking from the "Fraud and Arson Bureau of the American Insurance Association" and the "California Board of Fire Underwriters." Buzz Barrett said there had been reports of "previous fires at the Southern California landmark."

I decided to check in at the hospital before our 10:30 conference about the fire. Marge was checked out. In the room down the hall, Mrs. H. was dozing, she looked fairly peaceful. I didn't want to disturb her. When I got to the I.C.U., Joslin's blanket was lying on a plastic chair. I announced myself to the nurses. Rex was blotto, all the tubes still in him. A thing like an oscilloscope was going blip-blip-blip, very regular, and the I.V. was going drip-drip-drip, very regular, in his arm. But David had been moved out of the I.C.U. into a regular room. I went in, and there was Joslin with her son, both awake, quiet. I leaned over David's bed, and the little suck's eyes were just so pretty. His mom looked haggard.

When I got her out into the corridor she said she hadn't "told" yet. She said she almost told David, but—and then she groaned, "I buckled." Like she was ashamed of herself.

But she said to me, "I want to see the house. I have to."

It's 9:45 and I have to get to the conference, but maybe I can make it, and I think this is a primary obligation.

So I drove her there. I told her what I knew about the scene itself. Everything I said, each piece of information hit her like a punch, a blow. Even the names—even the dogs' names—made her wince. She said she just ran out of the house when the doctor called her—she forgot to get a sweater or anything. I noticed she was wearing slippers.

I was very careful about the possible causes. She hadn't heard about Peter Ingalls torching the peacock—she'd left the party before that happened. My mind flashed back to when ol' Duke Talis put Rex and me in the hospital nineteen years ago, Rex and me sharing a room, J.O. taking us in that white Caddy and shouting, "Hit this old man!" J.O., dead. The old man dead. We pulled into the driveway. Before we even got out of the car, just coming down that big driveway, she let out a cry—and she turned around and buried her face in the seat and then just as fast turned again to look.

We got out of the car and walked in the garden. An old black man was there, Joslin knew him, called him "Dibby." We stood beside the swimming pool. Dibby pushed his red baseball cap back on his woolly head, slowly breathing and trying to get his cigarettes out of his shirt pocket, his old black hand fumbling with the button.

No one was supposed to go inside, the house was blocked off with sawhorses—Dibby said that the "in-shaunce" men were coming at noon, he was waitin' for 'em. But Joslin had to step in the front door. The house had never seemed to me so huge as it did now, with the smell of ashes —and I guess part of it was the emptiness. The Honduras mahogany spiral staircase wasn't there. What was left of it was piled along the black wall. You could look straight out to sea, through the holes where the stained-glass windows used to be.

I took her back to the hospital and made a beeline to the meeting about the fire. I arrived at 11:10. The Chief was pissed I was late. Sixteen men were there. J. O. Hooker's death is no small potatoes. Peter Ingalls had been located—or, actually, he had not. He had been found, his name and place of lodging, but it was all cleaned out, nothing there, no clothes or anything. The Chief thought that pointed a pretty clear finger.

The Chief said my assignment was to interview all the members of the family. Oh swell.

The meeting was a dull affair. Chemists do not liven up a conference. Two firemen were out of action—smoke inhalation. It was a very dirty fire. The fire chief stressed it was not electrical and there may have been a contributing cause from chemicals. The expert on his left said whoever set the fire was a "sophisticated chemist." I didn't like his pencil mustache, but some of those guys make sense, and it's pretty hard to argue with all the technology.

We broke up at noon for lunch, and the Chief wanted me to stay. So he could ask me what my gut tells me, he always asks me that, he seems to think I have these remarkable powers of intuition. I don't. He still harbors suspicions about Rex.

It was a beautiful autumn day, blue sky, Catalina shining out there all

110

purple-green. Butch Ravelling gave me a friendly shoulder squeeze and said I could probably collect on the concussion.

I suppose Joslin didn't like Marge being there. In the fire. And she sure didn't like Marge being there in the hospital, Marge coming in drunk, and telling Leela that J.O. was dead. Oh boy. Joslin was just outraged. Marge, all made up, dressed to the teeth, and blitzed. If Mrs. H. had noticed it, she must have been extremely insulted. Only that's not what you feel when you hear your life's partner is dead.

I saw Marge in the hall. She gave me a big tearful, boozy kiss and headed for the exit. I waited until she couldn't see me, and then I followed her to the parking lot to make sure she had somebody picking her up. But she didn't. She climbed into a yellow 'Vette, and started to back out, and sure enough she clips a beat-up old Pontiac. It is my job not to let her go out onto the highway. So I walk over, put my hand on the door, and say, "Move over."

She objects the way drunks always do, they got their little booze world going, they don't like to be interrupted. But I am pretty firm. Besides, I am a friend.

While I drive, she cries. She fucking cries all the way out to her farm. My heart is in the right place, and besides, I am enjoying driving this 'Vette, it must get about three miles to the gallon, it's almost a struggle to hold it, would probably do 160 if she'd get it tuned.

When we get to "The Camp," as she calls it, she asks me to wait, she wants to talk to me, but first she has to take a cold shower. So I stand there staring at a big old Greyhound bus; it must be the one that belonged to Sissy Stivers, the one she tried to kill Rex with. I wonder if it really does have dolls from all the world's countries in its seats. I go to satisfy my curiosity, but the door's locked. So I stand in the sunshine and think about death and wonder if the soul is immortal. I doubt it, after all the dead bodies I've seen, except maybe they look that way because the soul is gone.

Marge comes out of her shower. She's wearing a white dress shirt, a man's shirt, and frayed white shorts, it makes her tan stand out. That reminds me of the three-pizza story Rex told Hans Brandsma on Labor Day, and I get a picture of Marge and Rex in bed. She's got a towel around her head, and she's muttering to herself, going for a bottle of Cutty Sark. Just the thing after a cold shower to sober you up.

Marge blows her hair dry.

I kill a fly, grab the sonofabitch right out of the air. I let him die in my almost-closed fist. I get a little wave of nausea, and then it passes. An aftershock of my concussion, I suppose. But I have had these spells for over a year now, and weariness. Couple of brief blackouts, in fact. At least it's never happened to me behind the wheel.

Marge comes back into the room, her hair all gold and billowy. She pours another Cutty Sark. That's something she and Rex have in common. Her liquor bill probably exceeds my car payments. I feel forlorn watching her waste herself. She's a good-sized woman, but even so, she can't burn up that poison fast enough, no metabolism can. She's crocked. I say, "How did Mrs. H. take it?"

Marge looks at me like I'm an idiot, slugging herself with the sauce. She mumbles, "When I went in, she kissed me, and she was 'utterly frozen,' that's what she said."

I imagine Mrs. H. saying that, the two words, *utterly frozen.* I hear it in my mind, a little whimper. How did Marge tell her?

"Look, I wasn't drunk when I talked to her."

Obviously, and you didn't back into that Pontiac either.

"Don't be so fucking superior, Trip. I did my job. I couldn't let *Jos*lin tell her." Marge banging around in the freezer, looking for ice. She throws away a bowl of popcorn that looks like it was made in September. She sits down and spreads her legs like a lady of the evening. "I still think . . ." she says, and then leaves it dangling, and puts down her drink. She pulls a ladder-back chair across the carpet, stands on it, and reaches up to a top shelf of books over the fireplace. She sways and I say, "Careful!" as she comes tumbling down from the chair with a scrapbook. She's crying as she hands it to me—a red scrapbook with a big gold *S* on the front, the cover flapping back and forth. And there it is, in the front—a photograph of her and Rex, way back twenty years ago when we were all in high school. Rex is in a tuxedo and she's in a formal gown. They look terrific. There's an inscription on the photograph,

MY LITTLE MARGIE, GOD BLESS,
REX
JUNE 10, 1960

"*Shit*, we were happy!" she says.

I don't want to hear this. I have things to do. My eyes say, Are you going to be all right?

She reads eyes pretty well, even when she's crocked, and she gives me the *re-*tard look again, like I am in left field and naked with my dink on display. So I say something here. I say, "I hope you didn't make it any harder for Leela."

Shit hits the fan. She's just cursing a blue streak at me.

112

I stalk out of the house. Now I have this little problem—no car.
I suppose I could hop on the Greyhound.

She's not done yet. Comes to the door and continues.

Torrent of abuse burning my ears. Seems I am on Joslin's side.

Fuck it.

At the highway a young guy in a red Dodge pickup gives me a lift into town, he's going to Dana Point. He tells me about a guy who had a sex-change operation, and now has hair growing on the inside of the vagina, suing the surgeons for ten million. He asks me if I've heard about it. No, I haven't. He lets me off at the station house on Forest and tells me to have a good one. The Chief wants to know right off where the hell I've been, he says I have to interview David, the kid was the one who reported the fire.

It's not that easy to explain to Joslin. She's still there, in the hospital corridor, like a sleepwalker, carrying around that blanket I brought her. Rex is now in a private room, he's out of danger. He's not supposed to do much talking, but he has ordered a suite of rooms at the Laguna Hotel. Joslin is supposed to get it all ready for them, the El Dorado suite. Tomorrow they'll be released.

David is OK. Given everything. I let her prepare him, she's ready to go through with the interview, realizes we have to find the arsonist.

I carry my notebook, and it's very quiet in the room. The kid is frightened. He doesn't want to say the wrong thing. I ask him to describe it to the best of his recollection.

His mother says, "Just remember it, sweetheart, as best you can."

He looks at her, he looks at me.

"Well," he says—and it's kind of pathetic the way he says that word, real slow, "well—"

His mother holds his hand, and I have my ball-point there, like a stenographer.

"What woke me up was this funny smell. In my dream it was kind of mixed up with salt water and seaweed. It was this smoldering smell." His eyes going from his mom to me. "I tried to turn on my light beside my bed. I clicked it and clicked it and nothing happened. So I got up and went into the hall. To that little lamp, you know, beside the phone, which is always on. But it wasn't. And the smell was stronger. I thought it was coming from the kitchen—maybe Pop left the kettle on low and forgot about it. But—it—it wasn't in the kitchen. So I went back under the stairs. And I could see a little light coming from my dad's room. So I thought that meant we hadn't blown all the fuses." David was struggling, trying to get through it right. "Except when I peeked in, it was candlelight. He had about a dozen candles. Dad was naked, sitting at his desk, and I said, 'Hi.' But he didn't turn around. I walked up closer to him, and he was asleep. Sitting up. Except he wasn't really, he was, you know—well, he was asleep." The kid was checking with his mother, his eyes going. "The room was a complete mess. He had out all the old photo albums. On the bed. Open. Like pages of me in Paris playing soccer when I was four"—he looked up and his mother smiled, and I'm not writing anything down—"and the wedding-pictures album, and on the bean-bag chair were those two pillows stuffed into those two red T-shirts with the gold lettering on the chest in French. 'We Are All Undesirable,' you know, *'Nous Tous—no—*"

"Nous Sommes Tous Indésirables," his mother said.

"Yeah." Heh-heh. "And I looked at the T-shirts, and I peeked around my dad's naked shoulder. Dad's head on his chest, and I saw a piece of white paper. On the desk top. It said—it said—"

"What did it say, sweetheart?"

David looked at me. "Will this get my dad in trouble?"

I said, "No, it'll help us catch the bad guy."

"What . . . well, what it said, Mommy—"

"Yes, sweetheart?"

"It said—" And then he began to cry. His face was so kind, like you wouldn't want to hurt this kid for anything.

"It said—'Belovedest, I only,' that's all, he was just trying to write you a letter—"

And now Joslin's having trouble.

"You're the only one he calls that, 'Belovedest,' you're the *only* one—"

"I know, sweetheart."

Holding hands and crying. This is really going to find our arsonist.

"So I—I—I just stood there. That smell was getting real strong. And I sneaked out, to leave my dad alone. Smoke was coming up the yellow stairs. I tried to go down to see if maybe something got knocked over, but it was so *strong*. And I ran back up into my dad's room, and I shook him awake, and I told him. And then he was *wide* awake. He hit the light switch on the wall beside his door. But the electricity was off there, too. So he ran out into the hall where the smoke was getting *fierce*, and he called, *"Fire! Pop! Fire!"* and he dialed the telephone, and dialed it again. And then he looked at it and said it was out. Then he yelled to Pop again about fire, and went over to where it was coming up the yellow stairs, and then he grabbed me by the shoulders and told me to run as fast as I could to the motel and get the desk clerk to call the fire department."

You could see the kid had to tell it. His eyes going real fast, from his mother to me.

"So what did you do, sweetheart?"

"Well, I *went*. But the front door was locked. And the knob was off. I couldn't open it. Dad was halfway up the spiral stairs—and I yelled at him, 'I *can't!*' And Dad came back down and saw the knob off. So he ran into my room and he smashed the window—he didn't open it, he smashed it open. He yelled at me, *"Eleven twenty-two Sunset,* tell them that, the end of Sunset Drive—" and he went up the stairs, and I jumped out, and I got a bad pain in my foot. I must have stepped on the broken glass. But my bare feet are pretty tough from hardly ever wearing shoes, right? But I saw a lot of blood spitting up between my big toe and the toe next to it, you know? I was all out of breath when I got to the motel. It was raining, and the door was locked, so I started yelling 'Help me, help me, fire, *fire!* And I was trying to find a big rock to throw through the window. Then a man came out through the lobby, and he had keys. I was thinking 'Come on, come *on.*' He opened the door and I said, 'Our house is on fire,' and I pointed, and I said eleven twenty-two, the Hooker house, and our phone doesn't work. So the man went right to the switchboard and plugged this thingy in, you know. And reported it. He was looking at my bloody foot, and I told him the address again. And he told them, and then he said he didn't know if it's inside the city limits, we got a fire here. He was p.o.'ed—I looked down and I was bleeding all over his gold carpet —and then he said to me they were on their way and I—I—"

Jesus, he was doing such an excellent job, but he was scared out of his mind.

"And then I went back with the man from the motel, and Pop and Leela were standing outside, but my dad wasn't, and so—so—I figured he was trying to get—" and David looked at his mother, and he stopped, and then he said, "I don't really remember too much after that."

I get it. He doesn't want to tell his mother about Marge. Isn't that something? I said to him, "Thank you, David. This will help us."

"I—I don't remember all the *de-*tails."

"Oh, you did fine. The smoke was coming up the yellow stairs?"

"Yes."

"And from nowhere else?"

"I don't think so." His eyes so forlorn, tears on his cheeks.

"This will help us a lot."

"But it—it doesn't matter—Pop's—*dead.*" His chest heaving, trying to get some air.

His mother put her arms around him.

I went out and paced back and forth in the corridor. Jesus, what a kid.

Rex was taking charge, leading his mother into the El Dorado suite in the Hotel Laguna, Leela in a dark blue robe. She saw Joslin and me standing there, and she said softly, frightened but with a helpless little smile—"Oh, Jos—"

Joslin stepped forward, and she and Mrs. H. gave each other a big long hug. Rex brought David in, the kid in a wheelchair with his foot all bandaged. I started to make my way out, when all of a sudden Rex said, "My dear Joslin, now please leave us alone with our grief. You walked out on this family—don't come crawling back."

Mrs. H. said, "Oh, darling, don't speak to your wife that way."

"My *wife*?" Rex stood there.

Jos helped David off the wheelchair onto the couch.

"Family-shmamily," Rex said. He turned to Joslin, his voice was very strange, his vocal cords must have been damaged, and he growled, "Blue-bird Canyon is *empty*, you see, Bluebird Canyon is *gutted*, so you will get out of here, *harlot*—"

This is fine.

He helps his mother. "Easy now, take it easy." He was shaking like a leaf.

I look at Joslin. Her ex-husband just called her a harlot in front of their son. The kid probably never heard the word *harlot* before.

I see something's gone loose in his head. He turns and faces Joslin, and in complete silence, forming the words with his mouth, but no sound coming out, he says real slow, "You fucking bitch."

The bellboys are bringing in the rest of the luggage.

Joslin runs.

I catch her in the patio, she's so frantic she can't even see. She hardly knows it's me stopping her. I have her in my arms. She was trying to do it, flowers and phone calls, and this is what happens. Shaking against my chest, she's so scared and deep-down hurt, and I hold her. I look up over the top of her head and I see Rex in the window. Goddamn asshole. So placid. He turns around, I watch him in the glass. Joslin sobs, "I hate him, I hate him, I *hate* him." I look up at the empty window. OK, Chief, what do I do now?

Rex was on the phone a lot. Calls pouring in. And he's heading off well-meaning people that show up and get in the way. Leela kept lists of people who called, and who needed to be called. Tons of flowers had arrived. A lot of them were sent to the McCormack Mortuary where there are visiting hours—where J.O. is, on view. And Leela had flowers sent to the hospital, to various wards. Leela does talk to some special people on the phone, but Rex steps in fast—and then they argue, and he takes the phone away from her. I watched it all.

Rex did finally have to talk for the record, but I guess I told him more than he told me. Blew his mind when I told him Peter had skipped town. Rex just went white. The two of us were sitting there in the El Dorado suite; Leela and the kid were with Joslin in the coffee shop. Rex blew his nose and threw the Kleenex on the yellow carpet and stood at a floor-to-ceiling window that looks out into the hotel courtyard. Then he turned on me. "You listened to Jos, Trip—taking me up to the loony bin. You, of all people—after what Duke Talis—years ago—when Pop—" Under his breath he muttered, "It was unforgivable. You knew it was me—Steve Kelly."

Steve Kelly?

"Now you see who's crazy." He looked at me, and there was no person behind his eyes. And then a furious person. And then a sad person. I looked at the shaved-away places on his temples. He said, in that gravelly voice, "Peter Ingalls, Senior, he was in a kind of partnership with Pop. Back in the late forties, after the war. Shit, I told the men from Sacramento."

Shows me how well the Chief keeps me posted. How can I do my job when I'm not on top of developments?

"And Pop—oh my Pop—in 1951, up at Big Bear, a bullet came through a window and killed Ingalls, almost killed Pop."

"What? Ingalls? You mean his father?"

"Yes, of course."

"But you didn't tell me the connection when—"

"What're you talking about?"

"You told me about Big Bear when we had dinner. The night Sissy Stivers hanged herself, and I took David over to Mission Viejo—"

"What? *What?*" Rex went back to the window, he was trying to control himself. It was absolutely silent in the room. Really eerie silence. I watched him tremble in the sunlight, try to hold on. He sighed. "Peter Ingalls, Senior, he puts up a building, cut corners, although he said at the trials it was the subcontractors. I don't know, I was a kid. But there was a—a fire. Look, Trip, I told the goddamn state boys."

I feel real abreast of the situation. I say, "You got any idea where we start hunting for him?"

Rex looks at me like he's going to kill me. Then switches to mournful.

Poor bastard is really in outer space. He mumbles, "After his dad was killed, they put Peter in a foster home. No. I think he went through a couple of foster homes. Some kind of bad scene with the other children in the first one. I don't know." He looks up at me with that don't-blame-*me* look. And shouts, "I don't *know!*"

OK, OK.

He sat down on one of the king-size beds. "I'm sorry." And then said something in Italian or French or something. And then a whisper, "Joslin."

I said, "She's doing everything she can now."

"She done enough for a lifetime," he said.

I'm thinking she hasn't slept a wink. And I'm thinking about Labor Day—I know Sheila would not have gone along with me in any ambulance. Shit, she would've called a garbage truck.

I mumble, "You don't know how you affect people."

"Jos has made a career out of self-righteous panic." And then he sighed. "I know. God-*damn* how I loved her. Bluebird Canyon—it was all for her. Pop designed the house for us. Mother used to come up, while we were under construction, she'd look out at Bluebird Canyon and say, 'It's perfect.' And it was. Jos and I were the Magic Couple. We disproved the rule. And she foolishly—stupidly—recklessly—willfully left Bluebird Canyon. It was *perfect*, and she made it a—a pain. How could she do that to me? And David? And Mother. And—and—" He stopped, like he was hearing voices. And he whispered, "That's not true. Rex destroyed Bluebird Canyon."

There he was, swinging back and forth, like a drunken man. Except cold sober.

"Yes," he said, "when Jessica told me, I knew we had a long, long corridor—"

"Jessica?"

"I mean, I mean Joslin."

"Who's Jessica?"

"Oh—it's—it's—" he started to say something, and then he just said, "Another name." He sat there. "And—and here they are now."

The door to El Dorado opened, and Mrs. H. kind of runs and falls, she tears into the bathroom. Joslin is behind her, a little slow, because the kid is on crutches, that foot all bandaged up. Rex says, "What's happened?" and Joslin says, "She—she got ill in the coffee shop," and Rex shouts, "Well, why didn't you *help* her?"

I look at David's face, just stark terror.

8

IT WAS late afternoon, about 4:30, and I was sitting with Joslin in Room 126. The kid was in the lobby playing checkers or something with a girl his own age, and Rex was with his mother. I had never formally questioned Joslin, and I didn't want to start now, but I did need to know some things. She was staying in Room 126, on the second floor, just down the hall from the elevator. It bothered her somehow, and she said the number aloud, "One twenty-six."

I said, "Well, it's a nice room."

"Sure."

Oh—?

Then she turned to me. "Leela's mother, Grandma Darr—she was sitting on that bed right over there." Joslin was smiling a little. "We'd just met, and she asked me, 'And what church do you go to, dear?' I told her, 'The Jewish one.' " Joslin's smile brightened. "And Grandma Darr nearly fell off the bed."

The memory seemed to calm her. She said "One twenty-six" again, under her breath, as she unpacked some sweaters. "Rex *would* get one twenty-six," she said.

"Why?"

"Because he'd know I'd remember. . . . Oh, this *family*. This family-shmamily." She looked at me, a black sweater in her hand. "Rex says those are the two cruelest words I ever said to him. Family-shmamily."

Oh.

"We spent our wedding night here. After the wedding in Summer Snow."

I look around. "Twin beds?"

She smiles and nods her head.

"Why here?"

"Because it's one twenty-six. Because this is the room. Forty years ago. The Darrs. Because this is the room twenty-five years ago. When he went swimming with Peter Lawford on the Hotel Laguna private beach. Because this is the room. Because thirty years ago. When he was seven and went swimming with William Bendix, who was in *Guadalcanal Diary*. Because this is the room. Because Family-shmamily."

Oh, now I've got it.

She sat on the bed, and almost slid off it. Like Grandmother Darr.

I say, "I kind of wondered why Rex wanted rooms here. This hotel has seen better days."

"But Rex can't see it anymore. He can't *see* it."

"He drinks too much."

"Oh—" She shook her head. "He used to get drunk. He used to be so funny when he was drunk. So *funny*. But—but—I was poisoning him. I had to get away. I didn't make him happy—we weren't good for each other—"

I let it sit there.

"When I realized we were going to get married—*married*—I had to laugh. All my girlish dreams. My Prince Charming would be a Frenchman, an Algerian, dark, political, a little too serious. And now Joslin Breuner is going to marry this blond from Orange County whose life is a soap opera, whose parents drive a pink Cadillac—what *is* this?"

She went back to unpacking clothes. They had been brought by Dibby —the black guy we met at Summer Snow yesterday. The guy who said, as we were leaving, "This family been struck by the hand of trouble." Winthrop Dibble, the caretaker of Medjuhl, the Hooker mansion in the desert. Dibby had been with the family ever since he was J.O.'s boyhood friend in Colorado on the cattle ranch. Joslin said J.O. was good to Dibby, but he usually talked terrible to black people.

Like a dope I told her something I'd heard from a CHP, he called black people "porch monkeys." Joslin screwed up her face. "Porch monkey?" I started to explain, but didn't. She was looking at me like I was going

120

to call her a Jewess or a kike or something. She said that whenever Rex made an anti-Semitic remark, and got called on it, he would just say, "Look, some of my best children are Jewish." So this is a fine little conversation. I look at my hat on the vanity. Somebody always steals my hat.

Joslin told me about the death of Dibby's wife, ten years ago; her stomach was all bloated up with cancer. Karabelle had to see "Miz Leela" before she died. So Joslin went along with Mrs. H. in the pink Cadillac, the old pink Cadillac, and she watched Leela in that run-down Dibble house, sitting with cancer-stricken Karabelle. Joslin says she just didn't know what to make of it—the old black woman and the Great Lady, Leela, and all the years between them. Leela in her perfect costume like a queen, and Karabelle had been like a "mammy" to Rex. Joslin said, "I told Rex it was like *Gone with the Wind*, the Hookers could have run a great plantation."

She stands there, tall, looking out the window at the sea. Then she turns back to me. "So what did Rex do? He reported me. To his mother. And then he reported her to me. He said, 'I told her, Jossie. I was hard on her. I said, "Come on now, Mother, if we lived in Charleston in 1750, you know we would have owned slaves." And you know what Mother said, Jos? The pause is everything. Mother said, "We *never* would have owned slaves—and we would have been good to them." ' "

I like the way Joslin tells it.

But she catches it in my eyes, and says, "See? *See?* Now I'm doing it —this family is all *stories*. The Hooker Story. Outsiders need not apply."

I do not need to look at her like this—like a sexual person. I'll look at my fucking hat.

"*Build Therefore Your Own World.* You see what's wrong with the Hooker world? They all agreed to be heroic characters in their own play."

I looked out the window down into the courtyard and out beyond the terrace to the ocean. It was blinding, the water just blinding in the afternoon sun. "Families do things like that."

She smiled at me, a little shy. "Family-shmamily." She finished unpacking, closed an empty suitcase, and I said, here, let me get that, and just as I brushed her in the big closet we looked at each other, real close in the closet. Probably all in my crude imagination, but I think both of us felt guilty.

She said, "They always go for broke. And they never go offstage. They're always *on*. Constantly colliding with each other. Pop—he *did* build his own worlds, they're beautiful, and now Leela is struggling, fighting for her life. I can feel her pain, she"—Joslin was not looking at

121

me—"and Rex, he seeks it out, he wants the melodrama, he craves it. It's as much a craving as the alcohol." She kind of sagged her shoulders. "But there's so much—so much *good* in him. He understands things, despite the way he talks and behaves. He really does—understand. And he can be so kind. He—"

She looked at me, real fast. She said, "You think this is *easy?* Why do you think it took me so long to get out? Oh, it took years. Years."

Looking straight at me, "Well, he's more powerful than I am, but I'm stronger than he is."

I said, "Is it a competition?"

She smiled.

"You still love him?"

"Oh—oh, don't. This is all hard enough."

"And the kid—"

"I was thinking this morning when I woke up, about—oh, several years ago, he was five or six—he saw, on television, *The Prince and the Pauper.* There's a scene where the prince, who suddenly isn't a prince, comes up to a group of children skipping stones on a pond. And the prince doesn't know how to skip stones, and the children turn on him. David said he thought the pauper and the prince, both, were stuck. I remember how he said they were 'stuck.' It bothered him, it really bothered him."

"What do you mean?"

She was still smiling. "That I like my son."

"Well, you love him."

"Of course. But more than that. I *like* him." We went downstairs to the terrace for sandwiches. Joslin was wearing a dark skirt and a dark blouse with a little orange in it, very small orange clusters. She said, "Rex wrote something down for me once—I still remember. He wrote, 'My morality is entirely personal and negative, there are certain things I will not do. The rest is energy.'"

I let the words sit on the salty breeze. "Is that good or bad?"

Joslin said, "What do you think?"

I stared at the ocean. "You sure remember things he says."

"He says memorable things."

"And he remembers what you say. You got quite a case on each other."

"Oh, Trip." She took off her black sunglasses, and her eyes squinted up from the bright sunlight.

"He said some pretty memorable things to me today. While you were in the coffee shop."

She looked at me, pretty sharp. "What?" It was like she was afraid of

122

something—and I thought about what he had said, she makes panic her career. Self-righteous panic. I said, "He called himself Steve Kelly, like he really thought he was."

She groaned.

"And he called you Jessica."

She groaned again, and pushed her plate away. The breeze caught her long black hair, and she put her right hand up, a funny little motion. She cleared her throat. "God, how I fought it!"

She didn't say anything more, so I said, "That soap opera thing?"

She laughed. "Yes—that soap opera thing. I think you better have him tell you about it. My version is too bitter."

I nod.

"I think what really destroyed him—was—when I wouldn't let David do it anymore."

I look at her.

"Oh"—she was getting a little panicky again—"you don't know? Haven't you *seen* it?"

I shook my head no, and she seemed startled. "You've never seen it? But didn't you wonder—after all this time—" She was looking at me like I was more a criminal than a cop. Like when Rex said I should have stopped the trip to the loony bin.

I said, "When is the show on?"

She let out another bitter laugh. "When is it *off*?"

I lit up a cigarette.

Then she said, "Ever since I took David away from it, from him—" She was ashamed of herself, and wiped her lip with a paper napkin from beside her pickle. "You better ask him."

"OK. But I don't understand what he does. Is he like a star of it? Or the producer, or—"

"Once he said to me that he'd even sew the costumes, but he keeps losing small motor control."

"Then he really sort of *runs* everything?"

She smiled.

And I was rather disgruntled. Felt toyed with. Tired of asking simple questions and getting trick answers. Except she was all fucked up about it. She said, "Don't tell him I said anything. And don't say I didn't want to talk about it. 'This Passing Night.' Magic casements opening on— Bluebird Canyon." She couldn't continue, her hand real jittery. She sighed. "Bluebird Canyon. Sometimes I think it's that show that keeps Leela going; she never misses an episode."

Now, if you don't want to talk about it . . . but obviously she did, and suddenly an idea struck her like a shot to the head and she whispered, "My God, what will he do with *this*?"

I didn't get it.

She turned to me, her mouth all kind of ajar. "He's put *every*thing into that show. For twelve years. He can't stop anymore—he knows he can't stop—" And then she just sat there like she was on another planet. Well, well. She shivered, and looked at me again. "He'll—he'll have to disappear."

"He'll what?"

"Disappear."

I couldn't figure it out. But I'll have to watch the show.

Joslin said, "When Rex and I separated the first time, David, who was just six, said to me, 'I know why you can't go to Leela and Pop's house —because you're Jewish.'" Joslin smiled. Full of disconnected memories. "Once Leela said to me, 'The soul would have no rainbow if the eyes had no tears.'"

She looked at me. "Rex asked me to come home. And I've always wanted to come home. But I've never known where home is."

"Family-shmamily," I said.

Kind of frightened, she stared at me. And looked away. She said, "David told me that Marge had seven periods in six weeks, and his dad was worried about it—David said his dad was also worried when she did not have a period. David explained, 'You worry either way.'"

I may have flunked out of two universities, but I've got some spark of intuition.

They are sexual again.

I said, "Doesn't he, at this point, have enough problems?"

Wham. I thought she was going to hit me, slap my face.

Instead she said, "That is an incredibly cruel thing to say."

I sat there. Well, of course it was.

"What can I say?" she said, "He's the love of my life." She looked at me again.

I said, "I'm sorry about what I said."

"Trip—cram it."

That word *cram* seemed peculiar. She can even say *fuck* or *shit*, but not *cram*.

So we sat there for a little while. The Hooker Story.

Finally she said, "David is so hurt—my 'precious,' as Leela would say—"

She bought into it, Joslin bought into it all the way.

"He wants me—she wants me—and David wants me—to join the family again."

And? I say with my eyes.

"It practically killed me to get out. How can I ever go back in?"

"You want to?"

"No. No, I do not. But to abandon them *now*"—and she grabbed her hair, her long fingers in that black hair—"but when I know, for me, it's just to help during a crisis, it would raise false hopes. I'm out. I can't go back."

"Didn't you raise—uh, false hopes—last night?"

She looked at me again. A hard look. "You know, Trip, you're really a teenager. I mean it, you think your little jokes, your smutty little asides —'porch monkeys'—and at a time like this—"

Well.

A teenager.

I feel disgusting. I think of myself like some wet thing in a closet. I handle everything wrong.

A teenager. A teenager.

We walked down to the boardwalk, past the hotel's private beach, past a volleyball game, and then turned around and walked back in the surprisingly warm November air. The sky was just aflame out there, bright pinkish orange. Huge sky. We sat down in the little park next to the hotel where I've busted more than one weirdo on everything from indecent exposure to public drunkenness to vagrancy, you name it. The place looks very pretty until some asshole brings you face to face with the real world. And I feel it like a left hook to the ear:

We are adults.

We are the people we looked up to and thought managed the world properly. When we were kids and teenagers, there was this other world there that adults lived in.

Is this the way they felt? Those *adults*?

I wonder if old people feel this way when they make it all the way to Senility Junction. Maybe you're always a child. Or maybe she's right— I'll never get beyond teenager.

Joslin said, "I had—a bad thought today."

"A bad thought?"

"When President Kennedy was killed, Malcolm X said the assassination was 'chickens coming home to roost.' Rex really admired Malcolm X, and when Malcolm said that, Rex was furious. Furious. And this morning, I—I kept trying to push it out of my brain, but the fire, Summer Snow going up in smoke—"

"You thought it was chickens coming home to roost?"

"*Yes.*" She was trying to catch her breath. "And I thought of myself as—as vile."

Whew.

I waited, watching a little baby about two years old wander toward the edge of the boardwalk and the mother shriek and go catch it.

Joslin and I sat there.

The little white sketchy clouds, mare's-tails, scattered above us, and the sun a beautiful red ball sitting out on the water. Joslin wanted to sit on the sand. Which we did. We sat watching the surf. I was wondering about a dozen things. It kind of scared me on the terrace of the hotel when she said Rex would disappear. I can't figure out what she meant by that. And the show, and David taken away, and it keeps Leela alive—I was just bopping around with questions. I wish I had had an education, except people in general so often seem to get dumber in direct proportion to their academic training. And professors, no doubt about it, they got their brains plugged into their assholes. But what I was really thinking was that I was violating a Number One Rule: Do not let it get inside you, do not take it home with you, it ruins your ability to be of assistance. And I'm afraid it's getting worse. Because I know I am falling in love with this woman; something about Joslin blows my fuses. It is obscene for me to be thinking about it. I am conscious of her eyes and her lips and her boobs, and now in the sand I have designs on her legs and her bare feet. I'd love to listen to the story of her life. I don't know a thing about her family. Her family-shmamily. Where does she come from? And I'm even thinking she would make a good policeman's wife. She's so fearful in general, she wouldn't have specific fears. I think she's kind of simple in a very intriguing way.

Then we saw a big brown Mexican guy, I've seen him several times before. His legs are like pipestems, maybe he had polio when he was a kid, and the rest of him is just huge, all muscle, and he's tanned almost black, and wears black racing trunks. He came jerking slowly along the beach, leaning on a pair of white canes, dragging those useless legs behind him. He dragged himself all the way down to the water's edge, and he stood breathing for a minute, then screwed his canes way down deep into the sand, balanced on his pipestems for a second, and just plowed into the surf. Water must be about fifty-five degrees. His huge hairy ol' arms pulled him through the waves, his legs dragging along. And those two canes, screwed deep into the sand, still stood there. As the tide came in, the surf just made it around the bottoms of the canes. I looked at Joslin and wondered what she was thinking—maybe of David, and his swimming, or just thinking of nothing and watching the man—and her flowing black hair, here beside me. I turned back to watch that Mexican guy, way out there in the ocean now, lazy like a sea lion, all at home.

I called the Chief, went over for two hours, and spilled my guts—about Ingalls and Big Bear and everything. The Chief listened, and I did not even call him on withholding Sacramento information from me, but I did say it was useless for me to interrogate the members of the family when I don't even know things of primary importance, like who Peter's father was and how he built a building that resulted in a fire, which led to dissolving the partnership of Hooker and Ingalls. The Chief looked at me, looked at me like I was crazy—and suddenly I realized the Chief didn't know either. I have this bad habit, when I am surprised, of thinking I'm the person who has purposely been kept in the dark. I always think I'm the last to know. It's from my childhood, I can't seem to grow out of it or shake it off. Always think people are tricking me.

Anyway, the Chief wanted a man on the family. But more than that, he wanted me personally. Didn't explain—just looked away. OK, Boss, and that night, almost ten P.M., I'd dozed off in the hotel lobby, in front of the tube, but I saw them come in—Rex helping Leela. I scrunched down in my chair so they wouldn't see me. I was embarrassed about snoozing. Rex went inside, but before I could make my exit he came back into the lobby and stood there looking at me. "Thank you," he said, "for taking care of Joslin."

I got up. "Is she in one twenty-six?"

"Oh, you know the number?"

I was flustered. I thought he was saying thank you. But maybe he can read my mind. I said, "She was upset."

"I know."

Right away I am on the defensive. I know how that works when I interrogate a suspect. Rex is no fool. He's got a line on me. Or maybe we're both just paranoid.

David comes bopping in on his crutches and says, "Leela needs you."

Rex goes to El Dorado.

I sit with the kid and have nothing to communicate.

I say, "How's the foot?"

"The doctor says I have to keep off it."

When I dozed off a minute ago, I dreamed that I set the fire. And Rex was coming at me across a field looking for cover under a sycamore tree. I turned and hit him with a bazooka. Then I dreamed David was my own son and I was flying a P-38 and went down in a ball of fire, and then had to tell him about it, and he said, My dad's dead, and I said, No, son, not while you have me to tell you. Now, what kind of sense does that make? I've gone insane. Dirt clods on the earth, as I crawled at them when the bazooka hit me, the weeds and undergrowth in my fingers as I saw the blood spout from my own mouth, and then the clouds in the sky, and a star, as my plane went down, and David's tears as I explained to him that I was dead. Good thinking, Sergeant, we're all behind you. You work on your problems in your dreams.

He said, "She got really mad at me."

"Your mother?"

"Of course not. Kathy."

"Who?"

"The girl I was playing Scrabble with."

"Oh."

"I had this Z-10 and X-12, and I just couldn't, you know? And she said, 'Well, Mr. David Hooker, can't you even make *one* word?'"

"And you couldn't?"

"Well, *no*. She was irritating me. So I told her to go fuck herself. And she ran away to tell on me. I think anyone who is twelve has to admit she's heard the word *fuck* before."

"I agree."

He's sort of humorous, telling me that, sitting there wearing a dark brown shirt with little white lines in it.

David wanted some water, and I told him to stay off the foot. I went to the water cooler and brought back a cup.

The kid said, "Did you hear the birds today? They were singing away. They don't know about any problems. And, you know what? People out on the terrace, maybe those people will always remember this day. And talk about it in 1990."

I'd give just about anything to have a son.

"By the fountain there must be a zillion ants. It's like rush hour on the freeway. You know, in the black dirt under the rosebushes?"

If I could choose, he would be my son. And I want to fuck his mother. And I love, and hate, his father. Other than that, I'm not in the least involved.

"My dad told his doctor to fuck himself. Have you noticed, everybody's language has—has just gone to shit?"

Rex came back in. He nodded to me, and looked at his boy. "She's OK now."

"Whew," said the kid. "No bleeding?"

"No. No more bleeding."

We sat there. Rex was wearing a black silk shirt and black pants and black suede shoes—black suede shoes, just like we wore in high school, I haven't seen shoes like that in twenty years. He kept clearing his throat, nervously, and his mouth had a funny twitch to it, and his eyes an I'm-not-in-here look. My mind skipped to Joslin. I hoped she was getting some sleep. She could go home, to her own bed, it'd smell like sleep. What does Room 126's bed smell like? Family-shmamily, probably. What does that smell like? And how do you fall asleep when you're breathing it? Joslin in bed, I'm just splashing around here in Bodley's Brook.

Rex pointed out the window to the courtyard. "Honey, beyond there, now it's a parking lot, but when I was your age it was all jungly. Lots of paths. They even had parrots."

"Parrots?"

"Yep. And macaws. Oh boy. Oh boy." Rex looked at me. "How you doin', Trip?"

"Ready for bed."

"Dibby tells me you've been up to Summer Snow."

"Joslin wanted to go."

"You're a considerate man."

Jesus, is he mad at me?

"I suspect we will bulldoze it. Plow it into the ground."

David said, "You can't. Dad, you can't."

Rex looked at him. He waited a minute, a few seconds. He said, "Of course not."

"Not Summer Snow."

"No—" his father said, kind of startled. "No, you're right. Out of the mouths of piss-ants—"

"Dad."

"Why did the moron throw the clock out the window?"

"To see time fly?"

"Right."

Silence.

"Dad, why did you say that?"

Rex said, "I don't know." He sat there like he had forgotten something and was trying to remember what it was.

David was looking at him. He glanced, kind of pleading, at me. Then he said, "Dad, could I talk to you?"

"Sure, m'man, sure."

"Like I have this big question."

"OK, shoot."

"Well . . ."

129

I said, "I think I'll get some shut-eye."

David said, "No—Trip, I didn't mean—"

Rex smiled at me. "Right, Trip, you're in it. I think my son here wants a refuge from *public* eyes." He looked at David. Two couples had come into the lobby, tipsy and laughing and talking, dumb realtors and their wives—*Have you hugged your realtor today?*—standing at the elevator. One guy said to the other, "You know how to tell a macho woman?" and the other said, "I bet you don't tell her much." Laughter. The first man said, "No—no—how do you tell a macho woman?" and the group waited, and he said, "She's got a kick-starter on her vibrator." They all got convulsed, and I myself smiled and looked at Rex, who must've heard it before, and the two couples went into the elevator, drunkenly laughing.

Rex handed me the crutches and put the kid on his back, piggyback, and we went down the hallway past the bar, into the "Card Room," which was all dark. Rex found the switch and flicked it, and a little fluorescent tube went on, a hospital kind of light. The window was open and we could hear the surf crashing away. Somewhere out in the China Sea there must be a storm.

"Well?" Rex said.

"I don't know where to start."

"Start at the end."

"Dad, come on—"

"OK, start anywhere."

"Well," David said seriously, "do you remember when I got upset last year? When Kevin teased me because I'm half-Jewish, and he said, 'Jesus doesn't live in David's heart, Jesus doesn't live in David's heart'?"

Rex smiled kind of sad. "Yes, I remember."

"Well—Dad—does—does Jesus live in *your* heart?"

Rex looked at me, *uh*-oh, and he said, "He's sort of a transient."

"What?"

"You know, in and out. That fucking Jesus, I never know where he is, I get his room ready and then he's off on a gig somewhere—"

"Dad, come on."

"I'm sorry, son. Well, it's—I mean—"

"Do you believe in God?"

"Oh, of course," Rex said, "don't you?"

"I—I don't think so. My mother doesn't."

"That's true. She's a crummy old atheistic Jew."

"Dad, please be serious."

"OK."

"You really believe in God?"

130

"Yes."

"And the Devil?"

"Oh, my son, yes—I do indeed believe in the Devil."

"Dad, I really want to be serious."

"I am serious."

"You—you believe in a guy up in the sky with a big white beard?"

"No. I believe in a woman in the sky with a big black mustache. No —wait—I'm sorry." Rex was looking at his hands in the Card Room, spreading his fingers out and turning his hands over, palms up, and then the backs of his hands. He said, "Trip, you gonna back me up on this one?"

Before I could say anything, the kid looked up at me, he didn't speak a word, but he was kind of measuring. His dad and me.

"Let me explain," Rex said. He was really tired, as exhausted as Joslin. "Look, sweetheart—you have asked me a very serious question. And you're eleven years old. I don't want to run a number on you, OK? I'll tell you right now what I think. Truly. OK?"

David, his eyes bright.

"Now, we, for a long time, you know what our—our religious affiliation is."

"Our what?"

"The church we go to."

"Oh, yeah. Episcopalian."

"Right. But Pop—Pop didn't much—well, I remember once after Holy Communion, Pop said he was tired of playing 'Swallow the Leader.' " Rex smiled. "It got Mother upset. Mother doesn't like—well, Mother takes religion very seriously. Especially since her illness. She says now there are times, especially in the night, when she wishes—Mother wishes—'what God has left of my body could be lifted into the arms of the church.' Do you follow, sweetheart?"

David shook his head, no.

"Well, honey, now—whether God exists or not—well, we're children now."

"What?"

"This, well, this thing that has happened to us, it makes us—it makes us children. This afternoon Mother and I had to pick out the casket. The casket for Pop."

"Yes."

Rex was whispering. "And in the car going to the mortuary, Mother was talking with me. It has to be decided where Pop will be—where he will be buried. Where he will—where he will lie."

131

The kid whispered too. "Yes."

"And Mother wondered if it should be in the desert, where he built such fine buildings, the College, and Medjuhl, and all—or if it should be back in Colorado where he was born, and grew up on the cattle ranch, where his mother and father and—well, where he could be with his—*people.* Or should it be here, in the Laguna cemetery, here where we've lived so many years. And Mother was saying that she didn't like to think of Pop in the desert, in that terrible *heat,* and then also maybe not in Colorado, it's so very far away, but she wasn't sure about Laguna, because of the fog in wintertime, and how on foggy days—"

I was watching Rex very closely, watching the trouble he was having, trying to talk.

"And, sweetheart, we know that a person in a grave can't feel heat or fog, we know that, right?"

"Yes." It was like the kid was listening to a fairy tale.

"And then—oh—we were looking at the caskets, and Mother still hasn't even gotten over Grandma Darr's death ten years ago—and, well, you know how sick Leela is."

"Yes." David, his brilliant gray eyes getting all glazed with tears.

"Please don't cry, honey. I can't bear to see you cry."

"I'm trying not to."

"Well, we looked at one casket, and Mother said, 'J.O. would like the rose tones.' You can hear her say that, can't you?—'rose tones'?"

David was hearing Leela say that, and I could hear it, too.

"And that's like heat and fog—what does Pop care about 'rose tones'? —but the way Mother said it—well, my son, there are a lot of things going on now. And they're religious. For example, it's not where Pop is buried —in the desert or Colorado or here in Laguna—it's not just heat or the past or fog, it means who his life—and his death—who he *belongs* to. And it involves the Hooker name, which you bear, it involves who we are, and how our family can handle our grief, and we"—he kept on whispering, but he was speeding up, talking fast—"and how we shall come to terms with ourselves, and we—we are children now, we are—in awe—and it is not an occasion f-for emotional collapse, we don't prove we're strong— although—although you watch Leela, you watch your grandmother, man" —he made it sound like a threat—"and—and we do anything for her, because she is blind now, she's blind, I don't mean she's got trouble with her eyes, but she's been kicked, kicked, and we have to—all of us—we have to regard ourselves rather closely, and be enabled to receive the— the unfolding of grace—of divine grace—"

"Dad?"

Rex was crying, really crying. "Hold on to me, my son," and he grabbed David to him, and he said, "In the smoke, in the terrible smoke—maybe the madman knew the only way to kill the world's pain is to kill the world itself—which is the annihilation of grace, you see—don't you see?"

The kid said, "Dad, maybe I'm a little young for this."

Rex stopped.

At least for a moment.

It's too much for the kid, this wasn't what he meant when he asked about God.

Rex said, "Maybe too good. But not too young. You see, son, in the smoke—somewhere—after I got Marge out, after I was sure Pop and Leela were out—and I got you out *first*, son, you were supposed to go to the motel and call—but you came back in, I thought you were safe—you disobeyed me—"

"But Dad, *you* were in there—"

"Exactly. And Pop came back in, son. For the same reason you did. Because I was in there, you in there—and I could see you, I could hear —I could hear—I suppose now I can try to reconstruct it in my mind, but I know—I know I knew—that Pop was in there, maybe a room away, and you were in there, maybe a room away. Get it? Do you *get* it?"

The kid's eyes.

"And then I thought, I thought I had you both, I knew I did, but I was half-dead with the smoke, and I couldn't get you *both* out, and then it was—a voice, Pop's voice, he had lived for eighty years on this planet, and he had—had a rich, full life, and it was, the voice—you want to know about God—Pop was saying something to me in the darkness, and he— he wrenched out of me my love for him and—and his love for you and my love, I—I—he wanted me to go for the eleven-year-old, not the eighty-year-old, that's what it was, Pop or David?—which—oh shit, I knew all along it was going up in smoke—which is the way—I heard him, his voice—'Go for the boy! Go for the boy!'—and his voice almost *smiled* at me—"

The kid was mesmerized. It was like a faith healer, like way too powerful, and I tried to pull back, too heavy to lay on the kid, don't do that to the kid, for Christ's sake—

"That voice smiling in the darkness, it was such a terrible, such a terrible love—Pop was just the dearest man—and that is where you need every ounce of your strength, when you love life so hugely that you'll die for it, and if that ain't God, honey, *sell* it—oh, in the very covenant as we are stricken—in the very sinews and bone, ashamed and begging in the blood, oh Jesus, I'm losing it, I'm *losing* it—"

"Dad?"

Crushing him, Rex was squeezing the life out of him. "Help me, son, *help* me—now we must be—we absolutely must be blessed—be *blessed*—"

"Dad?" The kid wild-eyed, his head thrown back, "Dad? *Dad?*"

The *Laguna Breeze* is a weekly. It had already been out for a day before we happened to see it. But when Rex got his hands on it, he went crazy. I looked it over in El Dorado and read the fire chief's words about how the fire was "well involved" by the time the men got there and that a "chemical accelerant" had been "employed." Peter Ingalls, "the chief suspect," was identified, and it told about how the "manhunt" was on. With no results yet. And there was an editorial, with a big black box around it, called "Sorrow and Sympathy," with a little story about the Hookers, "an extraordinary family." But what made Rex go nuts was a photograph on the front page, where you can see the outline of J.O.'s body, you could see how a man had been lying there, the body all outlined by that goopy slime from the smoke. You could see exactly how he had been lying, his legs and arms stretched out.

Rex's face went into Death Jaw, like his father's used to. He walked very fast out the Arcade, and I went along with him. He said under his breath, not looking at me, "Go away, Trip." Said it again, carrying that *Laguna Breeze*, bumping into people, who looked at him funny, and then looked at me funny, too, because here I was tagging along in uniform. He didn't wait for the light on South Coast Highway, cars screeched and honked. I should've cited him for jaywalking, but I held up my arms like it was police business, and stayed with him. He walked along Forest to the corner of Glenneyre, to the little *Breeze* office. Edna, the receptionist, knew me, of course, but Rex didn't stop to talk to her. He marched right into the office where the editor, Virgil Ault, was sitting in a white shirt with his sleeves rolled up. Virgil's not an old man, but he's bald, heavyset, and he said, "Yes . . . ?"

Rex held up the paper. "Did you make up this page?"

Virgil stood up and came around in front of his desk, looking from me to Rex.

"Did you approve running this photograph?"

Virgil, real startled—he must have been the one who wrote "Sorrow and Sympathy." He held the paper about waist-high, and I looked at the big gold watch on his thick wrist, and I heard his voice say, "Yes—"

Rex with that Hooker Death Jaw jutting out.

"Your—was J.O.—are you—?"

I was focusing on the hairs on Virgil's wrist when Rex's arm came out, pushing me back. He said, "Well, I have a comment," and he waited for Virgil to look at him, and they stared at each other, and then Rex slugged Virgil right in the face. Virgil fell back across his desk, a nosebleed gushing immediately.

Rex stood there. "You know what it did to my mother, to see that?"

Virgil's eyes were in shock.

Rex turned around and walked into some people—two men and Edna —who were hovering in the doorway. Rex went right through them, and I followed. We were outside in the sunlight on Forest Avenue again, Rex walking fast all the way back to Coast Highway, where this time he did stop, and pressed the button. He held his right hand with his left, and looked at me, and said, "Broke my fuckin' hand," just like somebody might say, "Ummm, I got a headache." Then he turned and looked up at the traffic coming down the hill past the Laguna Hotel.

I knew where I could find Rex, so I figured I'd better get back to the *Breeze* office, and check out old Virgil. I hope he doesn't press charges, or I might be in a pickle. I suppose I could have stepped in and prevented it, but I had no idea.

When I got there, Virgil was sitting at his desk with a paper towel, a cold soaking paper towel, on his nose. All the people in the *Breeze* office kind of buzzing. Virgil Ault, sitting there with spattery blood on his white shirt, he kind of looked at me sideways. Finally he said, "Bodley?"

"Yes, sir?"

"I almost didn't run that photograph—my better judgment told me it was the wrong thing to do. The young man made his point. Just one thing I don't understand."

"Yes, sir?"

"Did you have to provide him with a police escort?"

That made me feel pretty chipper. I sat and talked with him for twenty minutes. About the investigation, off the record. He had a little bubble of blood in his right nostril. He showed me J.O.'s obituary in the *New York Times*. I was pretty sure Ault wouldn't call the Chief. Virgil Ault had known J. O. Hooker for a quarter-century. "What a man!" he said. "Changed the face of California architecture. I even have . . ." He wheeled his chair back to a filing cabinet and reached up and brought down a little copy of that book, *Build Therefore Your Own World.* "See here, Sergeant—personally inscribed." He opened it and shoved it toward me.

135

Virgil sighed. "I was working for the *Mirror* then. J.O. was at his peak. He had a temper. He was explosive. And"—he wiped his nose with a Kleenex—"I see it doesn't skip a generation. What's the son's name?"

"Rex."

"Poor man." He sighed. "I wanted to attend the funeral tomorrow, but now I suppose—dammit, I knew I shouldn't have run that picture."

I said I'd be talking to Rex, he'd probably cool down.

Which he did. That evening he called me at the office. I was typing up a report on a little fender-bender. It sounded like I was about number 23 on Rex's list, you can often tell when people have been on the phone a long time. He wanted me to drive the family car to the funeral, noon the next day, and he'd like me to wear my uniform. My chauffeur's uniform? I thought, and then felt ashamed. His voice was kind of low. I mentioned Virgil Ault and the quarter-century, and how proud he was of the autographed book and how sorry he was about the photograph. Rex said OK, I'll call him.

So I did the driving. They had one of those monster black Caddy limos, Rex sat beside me in the front seat with—I was kind of surprised—"Dibby," and Joslin and David and Mrs. H. in the back. They were all dressed in black, except for David, who was wearing a dark blue jacket and gray flannel pants, but he had on a black armband. I picked them up at El Dorado at 11:30, the place overflowing with flowers. Leela was talking about their Episcopal priest, Father Darcy, and his "gentle strength and understanding." Rex said he used to get into playful arguments with Father Darcy, called him a "hippie," and tried to fix him up with Marge when she was between marriages. But he liked Father Darcy's work with draft resisters. Leela, I guess, had a weakness for men of the cloth, and had worked with a lot of them in her civic programs. I was sitting behind the wheel, picturing her broken body being lifted into the arms of the church, which I saw as Rex handing his mother's body to a holy man with a kindly smile.

I let them off at the main entrance to Saint Mary's Episcopal Church.

136

Butch was handling the parking; he gave me a funny look when he saw me driving the family. There was a spot saved for the limo. Butch said they'd blocked off the streets from Legion to Forest, and commandeered the municipal lot. There were at least three or four hundred people there, mostly elderly, but I recognized a few faces from that party of Rex's, characters from his TV show like Jack MacKenzie, and it pleased me to see that guy Al who carried around the butterfly chair that night. He and Rex talked together for a few minutes outside the church.

When we went inside, the organ was playing softly, the place gradually filling up. J.O.'s casket was on the wide step in front of the altar. I spoke with the Chief, who was in plainclothes, and then I stood at the back. Father Darcy said a prayer, and I looked at the stained-glass windows, all those pictures of Jesus and shepherds, the big gold cross against the brick, and old Leela was right about Darcy, he did everything with that "gentle strength." He spoke about the "joy" that J. O. Hooker brought to every person he touched, and about his tremendous contributions. I looked at Virgil Ault over on the side, his bald head. The whole thing was brief. David recited the Twenty-third Psalm from memory, without a hitch, his eyes on his dad. And then Rex read the "thy people shall be my people" section for his mother, and said a few words about the love between his mother and his father, and read from the Gospel of Mark. It was quiet and peaceful, the organ music and the flowers, very restrained. Then Rex said he'd like us to hear the only "modern" song his father could "stand," his pop and his mother loved it, and it surprised me. The Beatles' song, "Let It Be." But what shocked me was the singer—Marge Stivers. Her golden hair coming down over her black robe, at the altar, with the organ accompaniment.

> In times of trouble
> Mother Mary comforts me,
> Whispers words of wisdom,
> Let it be.

I was thinking, This must make Joslin real happy. I tried to see her reaction, but I couldn't, she was just sitting up there at the front beside Leela and David while Marge sang:

> Let it be,
> Let it be,
> Let it be,
> Let it be . . .

137

I didn't know she could sing like that—it was haunting, and I felt kind of doubly sorry because she had lost her sister only a few weeks before. And how rude I was to her when I drove her home from the hospital and she screamed at me.

We filed along, a pew at a time, past the coffin. I was way at the end. The face was at ease, his white hair against the "rose tones" of satin in the casket. Then I had to move pretty quick to get back to the Cadillac, it was my job, and I got it out of the lot and sat in it while Butch tried to keep people moving. When I saw the family on the steps, I got out and opened the doors. Rex told me later that the pallbearers were all architects—colleagues from the professional fraternity—and they put the casket into the hearse and then we had the long, slow parade with our headlights on to the cemetery, Calle de Eternidad. One guy was kind of boozed, it was Leela's brother, Uncle Andrew, he even talked when we were standing around the open grave, and Leela had to hush him. I would've liked to bop the sucker with my night stick.

About half the people at the service came to the interment, it was one of those foggy Laguna days, the clouds heavy and gray. Father Darcy did some more Episcopal stuff, and then turned to Rex.

Rex said, "Pop had a request. He mentioned it to me about a year ago. I would like us to honor it now." The wind in his yellow-white hair, Rex in a black suit. "As some of you know, J. O. Hooker was a cowboy, he grew up on a cattle ranch in Colorado. When I was a boy, Pop would tell me bedtime stories about his horses—Preacher, Tony, Rust—and about the roundups, the drives, the rodeos. Well, Pop said, 'When they put me in the ground'—which we now do—'let 'em sing a song—let 'em sing "Home on the Range." It's not exactly sacred music—but it was sacred to Pop. So please—would you join me, and sing it for him?" Rex started it, and then here we all were, in Laguna Beach, in this ghostly fog on the hillside, singing about where the skies were not cloudy all day.

> Home, home on the range,
> Where the deer and the antelope play . . .

I looked at Rex and David, holding hands, David's face real serious, singing along. David so solemn, the way a kid can be, holding on to his dad's hand, believing the words and the music and the people; he'll carry it with him the rest of his life. And Jack MacKenzie—I remembered him singing "Dancing in the Dark" at the bonfire—he came up and stood beside Rex and put his hand on his shoulder, his strong voice singing harmony. Everybody gathered there—"Where seldom is heard, a dis-

138

couraging word"—a chorus on the hill with the fog coming up around us.

Then the song was over, and people moved around and talked to each other. Folks went up to Leela, who seemed a little stronger now that it was over. Joslin quietly staying with her. Jack MacKenzie talked with Rex. Some blue-haired old lady in a mink coat was shaking hands with Dibby. Father Darcy was talking with David, and I just happened to hear this young chick on my right whisper to Marge Stivers, "Oh, he *is* cute!" and I followed their eyes and they were looking at Rex. I did not like that at all, it was so disrespectful. Cute, for Christ's sake. But then, life has to go on, and all the bullshit you say and don't mean. And finally do mean, I guess.

9

THEY'VE MOVED out. The desk clerk says the Hooker "party" has moved out, and the forwarding address is "Medjuhl." He gives me a phone number in Rancho Mirage.

Terrific. I am, at the very least, responsible for their whereabouts. And they blew it right by me. They're ninety miles away.

Then, no sooner do I turn around and go about my business and chase my own tail, I get a call. It comes into the station house. It's Rex. He says that they've just arrived in the desert and he's found a chemical brew, in a can, wrapped in burlap, in back of the power plant that's buried down in the nerve center of Medjuhl. His voice is scared. He says the glass dome of the greenhouse has been retracted. All the drawers in the desks have been turned upside down, it's a mess, he needs me there as soon as possible. I call the Chief at home. The Chief thinks it over and says yes, I should go. Take my own car. At twelve cents a mile.

I pack a little bag. Rex's voice sounded locked up in a vault or something.

I put my bag in the trunk and I set out. Soon as I hit the Orange Freeway, 57, I breathe a sigh of relief. I'm out of range of the beeper, I'm

140

going to who-knows-what, and I'm nervous as hell, but for ninety minutes I can just drive. 1 GROUCH.

I coast along at the double-nickel, past the Diamond, past all that old shit, Pomona, on 10 for a while, I give a rat's ass. Truckers blow their big rigs by me at eighty. I smoke my cigarette, and I know what I have been keeping in, I realize it, driving along.

My uncle's death. Ten years ago. I was still out on the desert myself, just twenty-six, still a boy trying to be a man. I was on patrol when the office found me and told me my mother had called. My aunt. He was in the emergency room. I tooled up to Casita Hospital. I knew it was coming. He'd been there before, for pneumonia, for emphysema. They had the oxygen on him. I checked in on him a few times, between calls, between wondering why things were bad with Sheila and me when we'd been so hopeful together. At least I had. Next day was Sunday. I sat with him from three to seven, and he didn't wake up. And on Monday at nine A.M. I'm at my desk, covering calls like a dispatcher, you never knew what your job would be in that Indio department, and I get this funny little feeling I should go over to the hospital. I put it out of my head. Then around 9:30 the little voice comes again. Somebody is telling me to go over there. I put it off once more. But at ten o'clock I get up from the desk. To hell with it, I'm not getting any work done, I tell the secretary to take care of things, and I go. I park the patrol car by the emergency room and go right in, up the elevator, his room was just around the corner. My uncle was sitting up, he looked good. We chatted. Then he said, "I'm never goin' home, Ollie. We'll never go huntin' this year." I figure he's just down in the dumps, the old hospital blues. But he says, "Make sure to get the key, that consolidated loan," and I know what he means. After forty-five minutes, I say I've gotta go, and my uncle says, "No, don't go." I knew my aunt would be there at noon. My uncle laughed, and remembered the Awards Banquet when I was Most Inspirational, the game film where I walked out of the end zone. He laughed. And that got him to coughing. He coughed real hard, I was afraid the tubes would pop out. I was still rawboned then, no flesh on me, I remember what my body felt like. Pretty square and innocent, just a boy. Though, for all I knew at the time, I was a man. I said, "I'll be back at three, when I get off duty," and my uncle said, "No, I won't be awake." I said, "Look at you, you're in the pink." He said, "No, I won't be awake." And then he said, "I just want you to know I love you." That freaked me out. My uncle had never said anything like that to me, never. But I guess I always knew it. Never said it straight out, though. My eyes got to feeling big. I didn't know what

141

to say. I squeezed his hand, my uncle's huge hands, I squeezed two fingers. I had a big lump in my throat. I was afraid I was going to cry, and back then, no man cried. I got up and turned, and there was my aunt.

So the whole rest of the day is shot. For three and a half hours I don't do a thing. I can't. I know he's gone. I call all the other aunts and uncles. Aunt Daisy in Merced, Aunt Babe and Uncle Charley up in Tacoma. Aunt Rose in Stockton said, "We just came in the house, Fred said up in Tahoe, he said, 'Let's go home.' We had a feeling." It was October. I walk in to the hospital at 3:30, and my aunt has a blanket under her arm, her tiny hand in his huge hand, the mattress cutting into her arm, her hand kind of lost in his. He's asleep, she put the blanket there to ease the strain. We wait. At five o'clock the doc comes in and tells me to see him in his office. The lungs are filling up with fluid, it has spread to both lungs. There is nothing they can do. No operation. You can't remove a man's lungs. The fluid will get to a point where it shuts everything off, and the heart will stop. He's got six hours to two days, no longer than that. I should inform my aunt. I say to the doctor—he had a pair of black-rimmed glasses, he was a serious sucker, and also kind of namby-pamby—I say, Oh no, oh no, *you* are going to tell her, she's been married to him forty-eight years. The doc doesn't want to. I say, You better tell her or we are not paying your bill. Why should I tell? You actually want me to tell? He says he certainly does. I say I'm not a doctor, she thinks he's going to get better. You tell her right fucking now. Me pretending to be a man.

The doc sends for some little dinky white pills, he says she's gonna need them. And he tells her. I come back in and she's weeping. We sit there all night—11:30, 12:30, 1:30. About three o'clock his breathing changes, there's about one breath a minute, wheee-shhh, wheee-shhh. I go have a cigarette—my uncle is dying of lung cancer and I've gotta have a cigarette —and when I get back, it's like one every two minutes. I think he's dead, his eyes closed—and then—wheee-shhh. But his chest didn't come up. He's gone. My aunt's asleep. I wake her. She's all over him with kisses. Now what do I do? Do I go get the nurse? I did. Only it was a lady doctor, how am I supposed to know? Nurses don't walk around with stethoscopes. Or maybe they do, I don't know. I went out into the corridor and I saw a nurse and I just grabbed her, I didn't mean to, I just grabbed. I wanted a doctor. All the lights in the corridor are off, and all of a sudden I'm crazy, this woman turning blue in my grasp.

Then she's in there, taking care of my aunt, and when I come back in with a grip on myself, I learn my aunt has taken the dinky pills, and they hit her real fast, or maybe she just fainted. I take my uncle's jewelry off, real carefully, the watch, the ring, I put that key in my pocket, and seal everything else in an envelope, and the nurse covers him up. I uncovered him. I didn't want him covered. They'll cover him up soon enough, so leave him like that, I don't want my aunt to see the sheet over his head. At home he used to say to me, "I want to tell you something, but not with this crowd around." The crowd was my aunt.

For the past year, he had tried to work, but he kept passing out. It affected his eyesight too, his pupils like a pinprick. When he tried to write letters, he wrote with a huge scrawl, he couldn't see the words. During one operation the docs had zapped him with paddles. Big paddles, and they inserted a catheter to get near the spot they suspected. They did it on purpose, to trigger the heart attack, bam, bam, with those paddles. He told me afterward that he had been somewhere you wouldn't believe, somewhere he had never been before. I thought about it when I removed his jewelry. He said it was a river, a big river, and there were a lot of people he'd never seen. It was a beautiful place, and he could stop and talk to the people—it gave me chills. The river had sand on both sides, no grass, but trees, maples and oaks. The trees didn't grow out of the sand, there was nothing in the river but water, deep and clear, and the people breathed the clean blue air, people dressed in gowns, real gowns—and my uncle was never known to have what you would call an imagination. And then he woke up with all these tubes in him, when he had just been walking along the river. It made me wonder. He could remember them zapping him with the paddles, and he knew the number on the back of the surgical cap. He said he had heard them talking down below him, and seen the body twitch with each hit, but it didn't hurt, he told the doctors and they discussed it. The number on the surgical cap was correct—and he would have had no way of knowing that at the time, being completely under. So how did he know? It was a four-digit number. You can't make that up. So I assumed there was a Hereafter.

I myself could be dead tomorrow. I'm not really afraid, because there is nothing I can do about it. Rockefeller had more money than Fort Knox, but if God says, Rockefeller, you die at midnight, and the clock ticks, who cares about all that gold? Winos never die—they live to be eighty and ninety, abuse their bodies something horrible. People who don't smoke, don't drink, jog every day, they take a piss in the middle of the night and fall over dead with their dicks pointed up.

Aunt Babe and Uncle Charley from Tacoma were coming down. And Aunt Rose and Uncle Fred in Stockton, they already had their bags packed. I took my aunt home. She was goofy, didn't know down from up. I gave her those pills for three days.

There was no autopsy. I kept my promise to him: Don't let them cut

143

me. I was nervous they'd do it anyway, but they know he died of cancer, no reason in the world for an autopsy. I would have to be there when they posted him. I suppose I looked suspicious. What is this guy worried about? Just don't cut him. I had taken his slacks and a sports coat to the cleaners. I told the mortician, Just stick with the incisions under the arms. Keep him dressed to the waist. I had to see it with my own eyes, for peace of mind. To be sure I kept my promise.

I buried my badge with him. He had helped me make sergeant, and he was always there, even bailed me out of some financial problems Sheila and I were having. I figured once he's in the ground, he'll be there forever. And I also went into my shed and looked around and found some old photographs, of my aunt and me when I was ten years old, and him and her, and me and him with a line of trout, and another one of us with our shotguns, and picnic shots. I put them all in a cellophane envelope, and sealed it, and when the coffin was being closed in the mortuary, sealed tight so no worms or water would get to him, I put the leather case with the photographs and my badge in his breast pocket. I had chosen that sports coat with the big leather buttons on the pockets, because he used to wear it when he went to the race track, hound's-tooth. I said good-bye to my uncle right there. The mortician left me alone for a minute or two. And then I made them close it in my presence, just crank it down to a perfect seal.

It was a beautiful day, the day we put him in the ground. Cloudy all morning, and then the sun came out. The trees, and the desert wildflowers like a carpet. And right afterward it started to rain. We just had an interlude. When he could walk by the river.

He loved desert life. Every time we went hunting, he talked about the arroyos, told stories about rattlers, roadrunners, coyotes. I stood by the grave and saw him working in his shop, making birdhouses. He used to shoot starlings because they took all the food and left nothing for the chickadees. He never hit many of them, though, he'd just fire away, cursing. He loved cardinals and waxwings, and he could make chipmunks eat peanuts out of his hands. After the niceties at the graveside, I took my aunt right home. She was starting to lose it, she'd been pretty good up to then. And I was all out of dinky pills. We had supper at home for relatives and friends. Most of the men gathered out in the yard getting blistered on peach brandy. Aunt Babe doesn't like to see people drink, so I played whist with her.

All of which goes through my mind as 1 GROUCH makes his way in the darkness through Beaumont and Banning, and past the old Lo-Ball poker parlor in Cabazon. I can do it all automatically, noticing the sudden rise in temperature, shooting through the pass, and San Jack up there. This is where I was born. Out of wedlock.

I like to think of myself as moral. Except I've got the hots for Joslin. Stop it. My headlights catch that old weatherbeaten sign, COACHELLA VALLEY—A BETTER WAY OF LIFE. And I remember my uncle one day after we caught about seven bass, he was driving the old Dodge and he said, "Coachella Valley—A Better Lay of Wife." He nudged my aunt, and she harumphed. She was pleased. They had a very full, very gentle sex life, year in and year out, forty-eight years. Pretty honorable people. No heroics. Just doing it.

I put it to the peg, and I made a hundred, ol' 1 GROUCH tooling it like a teenager with his first car. I wonder if anybody is still around, from the old days. I can smell the bass in the cooler. A better lay of wife, the only play on words I can remember my uncle making. I drive like a complete asshole, this is my turf. If sand can be turf. I remember the Hooker house. Old J.O. really let himself go when he built Medjuhl. Then 1 GROUCH came in the driveway, and I got out, stood for a moment to catch my breath, kind of shake the miles off. I had the key in the trunk when Rex came out.

He thanked me for coming, then took me right in and showed me the can in the burlap bag. There really had been an "attack" on the house. Desk drawers all overturned, spilled. Rex in white shorts, making coffee. Joslin is not there. Leela and David are, napping in the back bedrooms.

We sit by the pool. I can see he's blown apart. Very calm, though. We are extremely quiet. We swim in the pool, naked, under fantastic stars. We have more coffee.

Leela cries out in her sleep, and he races in there.

I comb my hair.

The burlap bag is moldy. In the morning I'll get a lab report on it. But I don't want to see the Indio chief—Farley Brumwell, the Hawk—I do not want to see him again. Rex has put me in a room with a little bathroom attached, so I arrange my Brut and Noxema and razor and pills in the medicine cabinet. It's real cold in the house, the air conditioning blasting away. I call the sheriff's office, identify myself to the dispatcher, and give the number where I can be reached in the morning.

My pajamas are ridiculous. I clean my gun. I'm not tired, so I wander out through the greenhouse, it's incredible, all those plants. The irrigation system goes on, it's run by an automatic timer, and it fairly scares the p.j. pants off me. Delp-delp-blup, fish zip in the pools. I go out to the patio, and walk by the pool, and look at the stars. I take a deep breath. The sky is so vast on the desert, so vast.

Rex talks. It's eight A.M., and he's right there. Over our eggs we talk particulars. I'm rather startled that he can speak so clearly. Looking out at the morning sun, drinking tea, body pretty sharp. He was on the phone real early, I heard him in my sleep-fogged mind. I showered, scrubbed the hell out of my scalp, came out, and just then the sheriff called, he'll send a deputy. I call the Chief in Laguna and tell him about the bomb, and we go over strategy.

A dumpy woman showed up, to get David, she was friendly, Swedish or Finnish, I think, and Rex put a Nerf football into the kid's satchel. "Take care, m'man," he said as they drove away in a Buick Electra. David was good pals with her son, they were going to spend the day messing around with Go-Karts. David was funny, he's hard to wake up in the morning. He smiled at me, like he was glad to see me, and then dozed off again over his strawberries.

Rex fed the surviving dog—Gamble, that was her name, her tits hanging low. He bent down with the dog food and put it in a big yellow dish. Leela's doctor checked in, talked with Rex, and went back to see his "star patient." Then the deputy arrived, and he and I discussed things for the better part of an hour; my, their new Dodges can go. I give him the chemical can and the burlap bag—he's young, very young, pimply, sporting a 'stache—we had to be cleanshaven in my day. He's a celebrity hound, says that over the wash they got a lot of pretty famous people to keep surveiling—Firestone (of the tires), Ex-President Ford, Ginger Rogers. He knows dink about weapons. I smell the air, the air of my youth, and look at San Jack over there. I love this desert. After the deputy takes off, I have a glass of Snappy Tom. Dibby comes around, and Rex talks with him.

The Medjuhl house is in the middle of nowhere, between Palm Springs and Rancho Mirage, all alone in the desert except for an old abandoned Medjuhl date garden that Rex says is a fantastic place for kids to play in, it's so sinister and dark in there with the fallen trees and ruined decaying fronds blasted off by storms. Other than that, it's just blank desert in all directions. Rex said the official name of the road to Medjuhl used to be "Sodom." It made Pop furious when the county put up the street sign —but it was mainly Leela who objected to "Sodom," it gave her chills. J.O. tore the sign down every time the county put it up. The street was named "Sodom" by an enemy of J.O. on the Board of Supervisors.

"So," Rex said, "Pop went and bought up a sixty-acre parcel of land

146

and started talking about tearing up the fourteenth fairway of the Thunderbird golf course, which the surveyors argued about, back and forth, going over old deeds, filing suits and countersuits. It took years, Trip, but when the dust finally cleared, Pop made a tidy profit and got his own way —he really meant his *own* way, because, as you can see . . ." He waved his arm toward the street.

And I smiled, because I hadn't heard that's how the street got its name. It's the legal name now, on the signs: MY WAY.

As you drive along My Way up to Medjuhl, you can see the house from a half-mile off because J.O. put in a lot of fill, to create a one-acre-square pad standing up six feet from the desert floor. The house is built on it, and you really don't know what the structure is as you get closer to it—a lot of igloos, or an American Stonehenge, or living proof that the Mayans made it this far north before they freaked out. There's not a single right angle in the house. Half of it is underground, because buried houses conserve energy, and it's completely self-supporting, with its own water system from an artesian well, and its own sewage-treatment system, and its own power plant. When you get there, you expect to see people wearing spacesuits, it's on the moon. Rex says the motto of the house is "Cranky, Diverse, Poetic, Humane." J.O. let his imagination run wild. And the house shakes you up at every curve. Really spectacular views of the mountains are blocked by concrete walls, the front door opens right into the kitchen, and the kitchen goes right into the swimming pool. There's not a tree or a lawn, just sand. But at the center is that massive greenhouse, a jungle, hundreds of exotic plants, orchids and gardenias and African violets and begonias—if you sit in there, you can hear it growing. The bedroom walls are deep red or yellow or blinding white, and there's a rainbow room, and stained-glass windows like the ones in Summer Snow, except these windows tell stories, like the goose that laid the golden egg. Over the family room is a giant stained-glass window that shows an ancient merry-go-round with silver chargers and black stallions and a swan boat and a Bengal tiger and a crocodile with a big grin.

Rex got out some salami, sliced it up with cucumbers and pressed turkey and bread. I watched him. Recovering from grief, living through it, doing things.

I go into the bathroom and take my "Bute," for my "ulnar neuropathy." I finally went to see a doctor about my tingling pinky. I made him write down the name. Ulnar neuropathy. Fifty-two dollars for twenty minutes. But the Doc knew what he was doing. He had a little plowlike gizmo, stainless steel, and he wanted to know if it felt sharp. Yes, on all

147

fingers, sharp, except I feel a bit like I'm entered in the fifth at Santa Anita, taking Bute.

The autumn heat is very comfortable on the desert until the sun goes behind San Jack and it gets chilly. We wandered down from the house to the corral to check out Tequila, the palomino, and Whiskey, the roan mare. Rex told me how he and his pop used to tear up and down arroyos, hunting coyotes. Comin' in with their horses lathered up and wiping them down and grooming them. Rex's blue eyes seeing the past. Rex learned to ride on Whiskey's mother, and his ass still hurts when he remembers how he got thrown and J.O. shot the rattler that had spooked the horse, and made a bracelet with the rattles. Rex's eyes, very troubled and clear. Trying to get through the days, his father's ghost all heavy on him.

Sometimes I think people who were not born and raised in Southern California can't possibly understand how we live. I know I have no idea how somebody born and raised in New York City goes about his business, subways and Harlem and snowstorms and foreign languages and no way just to get out by yourself and be alone. David didn't get back until dinnertime. He was covered with dirt and grease and sand, he'd had an outstanding day with the Karts. Rex made him scrub himself in the shower, and then Rex fixed tacos for us, and we had a fight with olive pits. Leela wanted to see some home movies. David is all excited, I can see it's a family tradition. Cartoons come first, old silent cartoons, *Puddy the Pup Down in the Deep* and *Andy Panda's Pandamonium,* they've been around since Rex was a little boy. Then the travelogue, as Rex calls it, he's running the projector, a big twenty-minute reel. Then sequences of Rex growing up, all spliced together, and Leela and J.O. wearing those crazy old clothes from the 1940s, and J.O. coming back from the navy, and all these cornball dramas they made up for Rex surfing and skateboarding to a musical accompaniment, and the wedding with Joslin, and them chug-chugging into the sunset in a Model-A with shoes and junk on the bumper, JUST MARRIED. There's a Shakespeare series with J.O. as Shylock, Rex in *Othello* with black makeup and a turban standing next to the candle with Joslin asleep on the bed, Rex as a religious rock star playing a *git*-ar and singing "Ave Maria" to the tune of "Be Bop A Lu-La":

> Ave Maria, she my baby,
> Ave Maria, don' mean maybe,
> I got a gal, she's just my size,
> She pull the wool over Joseph's eyes.
> I got a gal, you know what she did,

She gave birth to the holy kid.
Ave Maria, don' mean maybe . . .

and on and on in living color and stereophonic sound—Squaw Valley for
Joslin's ski lesson, Joslin whizzing by with a terrified look on her face and
her black hair with snow and ice in it, and Leela playing the harp, J.O.
on harmonica, a lot of it spliced together all crazy. They've got a sequence
of David singing, the kid standing with his hair all combed, dressed up
in brown slacks and a yellow and brown cowboy shirt and brown cowboy
hat—the cutest liddle five-year-old—and you can hear Leela's voice from
somewhere behind the camera, "Sing, David." He stares at the camera
and then there he is singing away:

> Going west in a covered wagon
> Get along mule, in spite of the danger
> Goin' through Indian country
> We're going to cross the Cumberland Gap,
> The Cumberland Gap.
> Where a man isn't judged
> By his money or his name,
> Where you walk up to a stranger
> And say howdy just the same,
> And the only thing that matters
> Is your courage and your heart
> 'Cause the past is all behind you
> And you make a brand-new start.
>
> Where a woman's dreams are planted
> In a special piece of land,
> Where a castle is a cabin,
> Every timber split by hand,
> And she has no silks or satins,
> But her heart is filled with pride
> Because she's building up a future
> With her family by her side.
>
> Where a boy can climb a pine tree tall
> And nearly touch the sky . . .

Man, he's really getting into it, singing his heart out. Leela murmurs,
"Such a lovely tonal quality." Rex says, "When Pop was a boy, he really
did ride in a bona fide covered wagon full of forebears and niggers and
Jews and horse thieves—"

The movie just whipped right along into Leela giving a lecture on horticulture, she's standing in front of a red velvet curtain and J.O. is hiding back behind it with only his big arms coming out, so it looks like his hairy arms are Leela's arms, and as she talks about begonias, those big arms flail around and fold under her bosom, and a big ol' hand comes up to scratch her nose, and then one hand gets a little close to her tit and she turns around to whack J.O. with her own real arm—and it's over. David goes for the pool, and Leela goes to the shower, just to let the water beat on her. It's hard on her to see J.O.

Rex and I get some brandy. He looks through the reels of film, packs it all into a cabinet, closes down the screen. He wonders if maybe the movies were too tough on her. But he knows. That's the funny thing about Rex. You think he doesn't, but he knows. He says, "After they were married, Trip, it was hard for Mother to get used to the wild Hookers. Uncle Tom, Pop's brother, was tickling her once at a family gathering and he bit her ear. Pop got real down on poor Tom, for bitin' his bride, and Tom went out to the barn to get even drunker. And Mother was twenty-two years old. J.O.'s new bride, at a gathering of the Hooker clan, and the blood just wouldn't stop flowing. She was crouched in the sitting room with a cloth to her earlobe." Rex puts the projector away. "It took her a year to get used to Pop at bedtime, getting undressed, in his garters, those garters knocked her out. And once they were roughhousing, a pillow fight, and she kicked him on the rear, her bare foot hit Pop's cast-iron butt, and she broke her toe. When they called the doctor and he examined it, he said, 'Well, young lady, have you been kicking your husband again?' " Rex got out an old family album and showed me J.O. and Leela's love letters. J.O. would write things like "My Pretty Red-Wing, you know those cheeky old boys who wrote the Bible never intended the stuff to be taken literally," and Leela would sign her letters "Your little heathen."

Family-shmamily.

I asked him about Joslin's family. I hadn't heard anything about them. Rex told me both Joslin's parents had passed away, but she has an older brother, Ernest, in Connecticut, who has a very fine legal mind, but is also very ill, almost an invalid.

We wandered out to feed Tequila and Whiskey, and Rex was at home with the horses, and we leaned against the corral in the desert twilight and he sang "Home on the Range." He told me Gramma Hooker was a fine woman who'd lived through all sorts of disasters, deaths of her own children and her children's children, fortunes won and lost in cattle, land, mining, construction—she was always serene and the world's best Chinese checkers player. When J.O. came home from college, her only son to go

150

to college, he challenged her to a game and she cleaned him out. But when J.O. and Leela were married, Gramma took Leela aside and said, "Well, dear, you got the difficult one—but you got the smart one."

Now, that's the sort of Hooker story that Joslin gets so panicked about. Rex tells it like he was there, but he wasn't even born. Joslin can't deal with it. Stories. I don't know how I feel about it. Everybody's got stories, even me, who has no blood family.

Way late in the night I got up to pee and I saw him, naked, lying out on a chaise by the pool, and in his left hand he had this big marble he had shown me before we went to bed—about twice as big as a golf ball, a glassy, with red and white and blue swirls inside—it was given to him by J.O., who was given it by his father, who got it from his father, and it's David's now. Rex was singing in his sleep, and I looked at him, his white-blond hair, his thin body, Rex, where the deer and the antelope play.

I peek in on David, he's spread out on the bed, the covers kicked off, breathing evenly.

I hear a noise. Must be in the garage.

I freeze. I go get my gun, spin the chambers, get set. I move like behind enemy lines through Medjuhl, out the back, around to the garage. I am not breathing, I come up behind 1 GROUCH, and then I reach in the open driver's window and hit the lights.

It's a rabbit, eyes frozen in the lights, a jack rabbit, he goes bong-bong-bonging away like a kangaroo, zip off the "pad" onto the desert, bounding away.

Me with my .357 braced, shaking like a leaf.

All I accomplished was to wake up Rex. He came in from the patio, naked, and we sat in the kitchen. He was talking strangely. "As Dr. Steven Kelly would say, the key element in the arsonist's syndrome is the flame of warming, achievement, peace." Rex sleepy, hung over, he fell back into his thoughts for a while, and then bumped up again, and said, "Post-orgasmic," as if seeing that I had the wrong idea, and correcting me. He nodded his head and cleared his throat. "Has to beat off watching the flames, but seeking an infantile quality—in fire, to achieve quiescence . . ." and his voice trailed off. He looked up at me, and I looked away.

Then David came out, all sleepy, and Rex snapped to, gave him some milk. David said he heard voices. Rex said, "Trip's and mine, m'man." David finished his milk, and Rex hoisted him up—"You're not quite big enough yet that I can't carry you"—and took him in to bed, and sang him a lullaby.

151

David's fishing for a dream,
Fishing near and far,
His line a silver moonbeam,
And his bait a silver star.

The word *star* is a high note, and Rex's voice was clear and soft.

Sail, David, sail,
Over the bounding sea,
Only don't forget to sail
Home again to me.

I sit in my room and clean my gun. The Academy. They give all sorts of courses there, public awareness, paramedics, fire prevention, and investigation. I'm pretty top-dog now, I run the firearms training, two weeks in April, eight hours a day. I teach it at the National Guard Barracks in Riverside, where they've got jeeps and tanks, and trucks running around all day long. But I was not top dog seven years ago when I gave my first lecture. On "Long-barreled Weapons"—rifles, shotguns, and submachine guns. I got all my slides ready, on two of those carousel things, and I had studied hard, it was letter-perfect, I had the fucker down cold. If I had worked like that at Stanford, I would have been Phi Beta Kappa. I pulled down the screen, went back to the podium, and I start, "This is a . . ." and immediately I panic, my hands all shaking. "This is a twenty-two-caliber long rifle rim-fire twenty-two-inch barrel-bolt action." I've got thirty weapons to cover, I'm not even looking at the slides. "This is a Thompson submachine gun, forty-five-caliber semiautomatic" blah-blah-blah, and everybody started laughing. I look up, and on the screen is a double-barreled shotgun. I thought I had gone crazy, flipped out, forgotten where I was. "This is an Ithaca Lefebvre twelve-gauge shotgun," fucking forgot where I was, "1939 slide-action gas-operated"—and shit, the slide was a single-barreled shotgun. What finally dawned on me so cruelly was that while I was in my room studying my notes, the supervisor had changed the slides around, he had deliberately fucked up my presentation—put the sucker in a hole and see if he can recover. I felt like J. Edgar was staring down at me.

I sit here in Medjuhl. And I'm scared.

We have already lost sixty-three officers in gunfights this year. Eighty percent are killed from within twenty feet. If those guys had taken my course at the Academy, they'd be sitting down to breakfast now, most of them. You train and practice and work so that when the time comes it

152

is automatic, your body thinks for you, like when I played football and people had to tell me later what I had done. Thinking is what gets you killed. The candidates I get now, most of them, it's like they're out in the backyard plinking. They've never had formal revolver training, none of 'em know how the hand should come up on a single action, how to put your thumb along the hammer frame, how to bring your thumb down around the pistol grip in double action. I tell 'em they've got to know, they're policemen, this is part of your *job*. Nowadays I'm lucky to get even one natural shooter. In the generation coming up now, there are fewer and fewer, they aren't hunters. I always was. Used to go deer hunting with my uncle, bag a buck about every two to three years. I even used to go by myself. I haven't in several years. The last time I went, I took some coffee, homemade vegetable soup, some crackers. You sit in the car, up in the mountains, freezing your ass off. I take my camera to get pictures of does, which of course you don't shoot, and I fall asleep when the sun's out, huddled against a tree. Deer walk by, they could be standing right next to you, I once had one come up and sneeze on me. It's not easy, at least I don't think it's easy. Once I followed a deer for fourteen miles, it was snowing like a bitch up in the mountains, and eventually I found myself in a little woodsy clearing and realized I have one hell of a problem —how do I get back to the car?

I should go up again this winter. Nobody to bother you, no radio, no TV, no newspapers, no beepers. It's a different kind of being alone. You don't feel lonely at all. You feel happy. Most people don't understand. Sheila, her mouth ran so much she never even saw a deer. You don't walk, you tiptoe. My uncle had emphysema, used to smoke cigars and watch the deer. One night he came back to the cabin, I was asleep, and my aunt wakes me up and says Oliver, you got to go get your uncle's deer. He was coughing so hard he couldn't bring it in. So I go, and pretty soon I see a mound of leaves, it's a nice six-point, with tongue hanging out, eyes glassy, and my uncle had tied it to a tree with a rope. Just in case it got up and walked away?

A woman like Joslin, she'd probably think deer hunting is pointlessly killing innocent animals. Which, I suppose, it is. But it also isn't.

I've hunted deer ever since I was eleven. When I was fifteen I took up archery, practiced all summer, every day. I bought stuff to darken your face, that camouflage shit, I really was going to get one with a bow and arrow. When the season opened, I was in the woods sitting on a log, sitting there communing with Nature, it was about ten o'clock. I see a buck, he's got a hat rack, sixteen points, maybe twenty yards away, and I pull my bowstring back, the arrow goes six feet, hits a limb, and breaks in half.

153

I've got four more arrows. So I take another one, and it's almost home when the buck puts his head down. Those arrows cost $2.49 each, I had to buy them out of my own money. I sat there all the rest of the season, on days when I should have been in school, and I never saw another deer. Then one day I take a canvas chair and climb up into a big old oak tree maybe five feet through, with craggly limbs. I worked all night, got my chair up there, and I sit down with my bow in my lap, arrows in the quiver, I drink my coffee. It's a beautiful crisp day, warm, noon, one P.M., and next thing I know I'm on my back on the ground, all my arrows are broken, the camp chair is on top of my head, I must have dozed off, and how I never got stabbed with an arrow I don't know. Oliver Bodley, Woodsman. "Man is in the forest," it says in Bambi. Doesn't say he's on his can, covered with equipment and cold coffee.

Well, I see I've got to do it. It would leave a bad taste in my mouth if I came out here again, years later, and did not look in on things in some official capacity. It would be cowardly not to. I'm fearful, but I am not a coward.

So Monday morning, bright and early, before the rest of Medjuhl was up, I left Rex a note and said I'd be back by noon.

Then I put on my uniform. My Laguna Beach uniform. To pay my respects to the Indio Police Department. Where I spent years in my Indio uniform. I have to do this properly. Neatly. I shaved and dressed, quiet as a mouse. I backed my car down off the pad before I started the motor. Then I aimed 1 GROUCH straight down there, saying to myself all the while, I have got to, if I don't I won't feel right. When you don't face up to things, you kick your ass everlastingly. And now, winging my way past Indian Wells, I feel better already, affirmative.

They've built this whole area up. You'd hardly recognize it, except for the beautiful little hills and the smell of the desert air. I take a big inhale, and light the always-the-best first cigarette of the day. This uniform doesn't look too bad. I change speed drastically as I wipe my shoe tops on the backs of my pants. I make sure in the rear-view that the razor cuts on my Adam's apple have finished bleeding. I drive into the official vehicle lot. The C.V. Savings and Loan revolving time-and-temp says 68° and 8:45. I pollute the ionosphere with some Binaca. I've got my marksman medal on my left titty, I am a professional to be reckoned with. I check my fly. OK, here he is, folks. I'm a little shaky with anticipation.

Ta-*da!* And it's one goddamn mess, no wonder I left this place. New girl at the desk. Suckers standing around, looks like a PAL convention.

I wait. I wait for five minutes, and then I am announced—God, the furniture is just as dilapidated and forlorn and out of date—and the chief who comes out is not the Chief, he's not Chief Brumwell the Hawk at all. It's Captain Darling, Charley Darling. I remember when he was the old sergeant here just as I am the young one now in Laguna. Charley Darling, who chewed gum and never clipped his nostril hairs, had acne scars, was overweight. He's the *chief?*

Yes, he is. He does a double take and says, "Uh—uh—*Bodley!"* Which gives me the feeling he's not glad to see me but he's proud to have remembered my name. Which is the way he always was, self-conscious. So this is it? And I spent an hour getting dressed up? Charley sends the dispatcher for a cup of coffee, and she just unplugs the switchboard, who cares if people are murdered or die, fuck that. And then Charley says he has a better idea, let's go around the corner for a bit of chow. He clearly admires my marksman medal and my stripes, and he must have nothing better to do.

Out on the sidewalk, he still walks with that ponderous roll, I remember it, as if his ulcer has put marbles on his feet. He says that in the wee hours three tons of melons were stolen from the C.V. Yard in Thermal, he sent Officer Crenshaw down to investigate. I think it's a joke, and I say, "Were they Crenshaw melons?" He looks at me as if he has been hurt. "I didn't remember you as a kidder," he says.

Well shit, *Crenshaw*, I thought . . . he holds the glass door, and we sidle into a booth, and this G-rated waitress says, "Hi, Chief." He gives her a wink. "Bob Crenshaw," he says to me, "fine young fellow from Red-lands."

We get our coffee, and he orders a big breakfast, I have scrambled eggs and home fries and juice. I look at a couple of guys at the counter, down on their luck, dressed real shabby, losers. Let's face it, Indio is not much of a place.

Charley wants to know what I've been up to, what brings me back to my "old stamping ground." I say I'm working on a case. Then I tell him I've been concentrating on ballistics and weaponry, I mention my activity at the Riverside Academy, and I am getting fairly annoyed, watching him spill the cream, which speckles in his coffee. I want to show him who is boss. I ask him his opinion on the CER, the semijacketed hollowpoint versus the old round-nose lead variety.

Charley Darling doesn't know what I am talking about—the chief, the chief of police, he doesn't even know. I say that a controlled expansion round is getting a lot of support from the paper-pushers—I say that pretty carefully—they don't increase medical damage. The tests show it, when you fire into blocks of gel with a density similar to human flesh. But I myself am not convinced.

He nods, like he understands, and misses it completely.

The food comes, and he eats not so much like a slob but more like a dainty slob. What he does with his pancakes makes me ill. Here I thought I could justify twelve cents a mile, a conference with a supporting department, and the old fart doesn't get a thing. He says, "You experts have decided it is a superior round, have you?"

"I could sit here for hours and tell you why the other one is a superior round."

"Oh, well, Bodley, you know our routine. Yesterday a collie dog led three officers a merry chase down Caranza. Owners requested us to use restraint, the pooch had a delicate heart. Got a call from a housewife who said some sand was blowing into her backyard. How do you stop the sand from blowing? Am I right?"

I nod, yeah, I know.

"I asked the men working in the adjoining field to wet down their operation. We still get bee calls."

I am thinking, B-calls? Aren't they on a 10-code yet?

"Lots of swarming bees. Owls are trouble. Snakes in the kitchen sink. It hasn't changed. Tell me, how's the wife?"

Shit, he ought to know Sheila and I are divorced. That was a contributing factor to my leaving. I hang my head without moving it.

I sigh and we play an eyeball game. He's not completely dumb, he must have had some skills to move up. His uniform is a bit forlorn, that old denim stuff that went out years ago. He tells me the former chief, my chief, Brumwell the Hawk, had a coronary, it was a sad day for everybody.

I think, Yeah, except you. I wish I had known. And maybe I'm too harsh, Charley really seems moved. Though it doesn't hurt his appetite.

I realize a lot of years have passed. I've been living a whole different life. I'm thinking like a snob—which I suppose is always what happens when you come back to the same old world and notice you're different. It makes you feel superior. I've gone off and seen the sights, and you guys are still stuck here, middle-aged and mired down. I feel like an asshole. But I also feel honest. Guys kidding at the counter and reading newspapers, the sports page of the *Enterprise*, I can remember reading that in here when I was seventeen.

I tell Charley about the Hooker case. It seems I have to underline it with my voice, to get his attention. But I tell him this special assignment I am on has some links with Sacramento and I'd like him to be informed, and all of a sudden he feels important. He's like a cartoon. I hate him for the way I myself see him. But he's talkative now, and I answer questions, and then I see he's beginning to respect me, and you always like to feel respected, so my feeling mellows out. Charley didn't expect anything, he didn't get all dressed up for this, he's just putting in his time. He says he appreciates it, and he'll be "much obliged"—"much obliged"—for my input.

We get a refill from the girl, who when it gets down to it is all thighs and backside.

Charley gives me a Pall Mall. I smell it and remember what a really good cigarette smells like. After football season that spring I smoked Camels, and used to smoke Chesterfields; Philip Morris tasted like beans. He tells me the schools today are full of shit, his youngest reads Tennessee Williams in tenth grade, can you believe it?

Yes, actually.

"Well," he says, "guy calls in, 'Help, quick, my car is being stolen—oh, it's my wife.'" Charley pokedy-pokes his Pall Mall in the ashtray. "Guy called and said someone stole a rifle from his front porch. We investigated, and he figures out why the rifle's gone—he's not at his own home. Been up all night playing poker at a friend's house." Charley laughs, he's told this story before.

The man talks like me. I am going to be this man, and forget to clip my nose hairs and neglect my uniform. This is the future. Some asshole that showers with Brut is going to look at me, twenty years from now, and think what I think about Charley.

He took the check from the waitress; her left eyelash was falling off. On the way back to the office he told me about a drug bust, a guy tried to throw hashish out the window and it landed right in Crenshaw's lap, and Crenshaw looked up and said, "Thank you." They'd been coordinating it for weeks.

Charley stood there on the sidewalk. The bank said 10:14, 77°. He was, again, "much obliged" for the information. He said how-de-do to passers-by, and introduced me to the new city manager. Charley seemed to like me, and said if I ever wanted to return to "my old stamping ground"—he kept repeating shit like that—he knew we could work something out, although I was probably used to a "higher life style." I said I'd check back, right now the arsonist was still at large.

"Well, when they find him," Charley said, "they'll probably find some bras and panties in the nearby oleanders."

I looked at him. He's not a bad man. He's an awkward man. Always has been awkward, for fifty years. Those acne scars. I think he could have run a very successful hardware store, helping people with gopher traps and

157

light fixtures. But he's a cop. He puts his belly over his shoes, stands pretty strong, and blows out bad cigarette breath.

I said it was good to get back in touch.

He shook my hand, said he had work piled up on his desk. He said, "We can't just sit on our hands and watch the world slip through our fingers."

When I got back to Medjuhl, that phrase was going in my head. I told Rex, who was delighted. He said, "It's the 'watch the world' that does it —'let the world' wouldn't have been near as good." He commandeered David to the breakfast table and told him, and it took David a second to grab it, to get it, and then the kid went, "Oh—gross!" and laughed like crazy, the first time I'd seen David really laugh, just a spasm of hilarity.

I laughed along with them, but I felt like Benedict Arnold. It is funny, but I guess I shouldn't have repeated it. I sat there in my uniform, downright spiffy, and felt that I'd betrayed Charley. I guess I was in a vengeful mood. Charley scared me, all the way down. Getting old. I went down to Indio to show off, and got disappointed, and came back and took it out on a man who maybe is a good chief. Jesus, when you hate yourself, you keep adding to the reasons.

Leela came out, wearing a white velvet robe, Leela with a poached egg and toast, she just lives on those eggs. Rex kissed her good morning. She was afraid she was coming down with a cold. David was getting some grapes out of the fridge. He looked at me with a big smile on his face, probably thinking about Charley Darling's remark, heh-heh. He says, "I'm going to fill an ice tray with water, and put a grape in each thingy, and then freeze it."

His dad says, "Why?"

David says, "Because I had a dream about it."

Rex says, "You want me to explain what the dream means?"

"Nope," the kid says, popping over to the sink.

Leela says, "It's bad luck to discuss dreams before breakfast."

I turn around and look at the three of them. I'm real frightened. I'm not a policeman.

$$10$$

JOSLIN'S VOICE: Want some milk?
A BABY'S VOICE: Weea hi hi waawa
REX'S VOICE: Did you see that? He's so goddamn precocious—see, he did it again.

    It was a tape, pretty loud through the whole house, playing on their sound system. Leela had to hear some of the old tapes. The baby was David.

JOSLIN'S VOICE: Rex, hand me a washcloth, I've got—
DAVID: Hi hi
REX: C'mon, Squid, up—up—
LEELA'S VOICE: Procter is drinking out of the toilet again.
REX: Flush, Procter, flush.
JOSLIN: Will *some*body hand me a washcloth?
J.O.'S VOICE: Where are them goddamn nail clippers?
JOSLIN: I am trying to . . . come on, David, come on . . .
J.O.: I had them right in my dear little hand.
REX: Don't help him, let him do it himself.

J.O.: Someone's hidden them just out of spite. Procter, get away from the
    toilet—
LEELA: Here you are, dear.

It was all a jumble, a tape recording of the whole family in the bathroom
getting into each other's way. Leela sat in a big black velvet chair, scrapbooks on her lap, her eyes closed. She was smiling, listening to years gone
by.

David bopped in with the mail, and there was a card from his mother
addressed to Leela. The old woman opened it and read it and cried, and
read it aloud—it was a piece of thick light brown paper with a green design
on it:

> To know someone here or there—
> with whom you can feel there is
> understanding in spite of distances or
> thoughts unexpressed—
> that can make of this earth
> a garden

It was by some German poet. Leela stared at it for a long time, and said,
"My Joslin—" in a long sigh, and then she said it all aloud again, very
slowly going over "that can make of this earth a garden."

Rex got up and said we ought to take care of the horses. It was one of
those days you get on the desert when the wind really picks up and the
sand starts moving around and the sky gets black. It was going to be a
beauty. I used to hate to be on patrol during those storms, everybody
getting spooked, big electric flashes, poles coming down, pets running
away, and your windshield all pocked from flying sand. Many times I was
sure I'd be electrocuted. Rex and David and I went down to the corral.
It was blowing around real good, and Rex looked up at the sky and said
c'mon, perfect time, we got an hour before it breaks. He asked me if I
was a cowboy, and I said thank you, I'll skip this one, I got enough trouble
without falling off a horse. So he and David saddled up Tequila and
Whiskey, and Rex gave me the dirt bike just inside the stable door. We
went off into the windstorm, Rex on the palomino, David on the roan,
me on the dirt bike, the sand kicking around in our faces and our hair.
I was having fun, and Rex was going like crazy, "Hyp, hyp, hyp," down
into a little wash. I almost lost the bike coming up the other side, and then
we were way out in the middle of nowhere, the sky getting blacker and
a few droplets of rain.

160

"Now," Rex shouted at me, "bet you a hundred bucks—Jesus, Trip, turn that bike down, it bugs my filly—I'll give you ten to one, go 'round the property, David and I both beat you, horses against the bike, OK?"

Property? Nothing but yucca and scrub and tumbleweed as far as you can see. "What's the course?"

"Just follow us."

"But," I yelled, "if I follow you, how do I win?"

"You don't—that's why I give good odds. Go!" And he and David went off, they were both yelling, and I come vrooom-vrooom behind them. We were tearing along in the wind, the rain starting to come, big chunks of sagebrush rolling around. We made a huge square, rounding off the corners, no fences or signposts that I could see. Tequila got spooked and began to buck, Rex holding on and flying around. David took the lead, really going on his roan, hunched up like a professional jockey. And then Rex blew right by us on the left, "Hee-*yaa!*" I gunned it, went down into another wash and up and back to about where we started. I was completely out of breath, and the sky opened up buckets.

Rex and David rubbed down the horses and groomed them and fed them oats. Rex said to me, "You know whose land that is?"

"Yours," I said.

"Nope," David piped up. "It's mine."

The rain was beating on the tin stable roof. Rex found a dead cat in the straw and threw it at me. Filthy thing, I almost caught it and then jumped out of the way.

"I got it for my birthday," David said.

"I'm sorry it died."

"*No—*my *property.*"

"They give you all that land and you're only eleven years old?"

"*No,*" he said again, like he was getting a little fed up talking to a retarded dirt biker. "When I was *born.*"

"Pop gave it to him," Rex said, brushing Tequila's flanks. "And you hold on to that land, son"—Rex talking like a good ol' boy—"that there land is priceless—it's a hell of a parcel, boy, pure gold—"

I said, "It's just a bunch of sand."

"Now, you keep holt your tongue, pecker-face, that there land is forty acres of the future. Son, you just wait. Del Webb or somebody gonna want that land for Son of Sun City. Some *consigliere* goin' to walk into your office in 1992."

David was giggling. "I'll be filthy rich."

"But remember, boy." Rex came around to comb Tequila's tail. "More than all the money in the world, first comes—"

"First comes all the money in California."

"Goddaymn right."

We ran back into the house—well, David and I did, but Rex forgot about the swimming pool on purpose and just went straight in, clothes and boots and all. He dried off, and we had muffins and avocado and clams, real balanced lunch. Leela was still poring over scrapbooks and fighting her cold. She said she'd like to hear some dance music. Rex popped up and said yes, that was an excellent idea, we had taken care of the barbaric virtues and now we should attend to the civilized amenities. He said he'd give David a dance lesson.

"Oh, Dad—"

"No, come on, I'll teach you, honey. I am not only your farter, I am Herr Doktor Professor, and it iz zimply time dot ve haff a longg tawlk about dese tinks, like danzing." He took a yardstick out of the broom closet and rapped it on David's head. "I vill giff a demonstraaation in der lexicon of de danze, und ve furst turn our attention to de Charleston— dis Charleston must be zeen in its full economic und *pol*itical rrrramifica-tions. De Charleston is ein daaaanze about *voman,* expressing de ambigu-ity of voman *e*-merging to de new freedom after Vorld Var Vun. *Nota bene* de combination of zexual aggressiffness und coyness vich vun has alvays in dis dance felt, und it begin to make senzzze."

"Oh, Dad."

"De complexities of der *lindy* is a speecies of mutual audition for young peeeple looking for surfival in hard *times,* de young man saying, 'I am fast, see vat I can do, how good I am.' "

"Come on, Daddy." The kid was really enjoying it, embarrassed and tickled, looking at me and back at his father.

"You must appreciate de full deeper shtructures of dis danzing. My assiztant, Fräulein Clitoris Tingle, vill show you dot vat I zay is de truth, for Miz Tingle is a teatrically powerful danzer like myself, who is alzo articoolate about danze, und dot is a rarrre creatchur!"

"God you're an idiot, Dad."

"Dis alzo is true."

Rex put on some nice slow dance music for his mother, and we played a little poker, stupid games like Whore's Fours and Anaconda. I kept dealing seven stud, and David loved it—"Staying with you, Trip," and me saying to him, "Can't bluff me, little pisspot." This eleven-year-old kid knows everything, I never knew one-tenth of the shit he knows when I was his age. It was nice, the music gliding around and the rain pouring outside. We played for a couple of hours, until dinner. I won $25 and David won $16. Rex was ranting and railing, "I want a hand of

Chowchilla Indian High-Low No Peeky Monday Night Baseball Texas Hold 'Em—you board-whackers, 's all you is, board-whackers!"

David crouched behind his cards and sang, "Every time you throw some dirt, you lose a little ground."

His father stared at him, real fiercely, until the kid broke up. David's got a great laugh, it goes completely out of control.

After dinner and some TV Rex put the kid to bed, and Leela retired to nurse her cold—she said "knock myself out"—in her room. Rex found his copy of our old high school yearbook. We stared at photos of ourselves back then, Jesus. And he showed me the autographs you get from friends, the little messages. Marge Stivers had covered a whole white page opposite a photograph of the front door of our school. I sat on an orange staircase that leads to nowhere, and I read her blue ink on the thick white paper:

Rexy—

Well here goes, I guess I'll have to say just everything so that it will be a long long time before you forget me. But it really has been an experience knowing you for all these years and I don't think I'll ever forget my first impression of you. Of course you know that I couldn't stand you but after a lot of thinking I began to realize exactly what you were like. I have been trying to think of a subtle way of saying this but I can't even say it teasingly. I have given you so many compliments, but you always ignore it or laugh but I really mean to say this and I'll be honest. Rex —oh, I can't say it. I just always like to be around you because you're always so happy. I guess that's all. I'll have to mention something about that first date, that gentlemanly date we went on, and you didn't have me fooled as to what kind of guy you are, and you still *seem* to respect me, at least I can hope. I was very serious, and I was so shocked—more than anything—when you laughed. I knew somehow that you weren't serious, but I didn't really care, after that dip in the pool with the handsome stranger, in his arms, and that delay of three weeks didn't help! You really have been a wonderful *friend*, too. Although I know you could never love the daughter of a cattle rancher, I hope someday you will stop being a snob. I won't hold my breath. Rex—sincerely—you have more talent than anyone I know, and I'm positive you'll impress all the girls at Stanford, but once in a while when a Stanford Man comes home he just might remember that there is a Valley Girl here who knows him, and knows how sincere he can be. Most people don't know it, but I do. I want you to promise to stay that way as long as you can because you're the only boy I know that way. And please continue to kiss as

163

tenderly but let's please keep it sincere. After all I forget things easily but some girls might not. I know one. I'll truly never forget you and I hope you continue to be as successful as you are now. Happiness to you and may all your sweetest dreams come true.

> Always with the sincerest of tender love—
> Margie

I looked up and Rex was sitting there in Leela's black velvet chair with a glass of cognac beside him. I don't know, he seemed like my brother or something. Although never having had one, I can't compare. "How come you didn't marry Marge?"

He shook his head. He held up a cigarette lighter, a sterling silver cigarette lighter. It had an engraving: EMPEROR AND CLOWN. He said, "Marge gave me this on the tenth anniversary of the show. 'Emperor and Clown' is from the prologue, 'This passing night . . .' You've never seen it, have you?"

No, I shook my head, embarrassed.

" 'In ancient days, when emperor and clown,' " he said. "It's so nice —so nice. Hell, I don't know why I didn't marry Marge. I always loved her without ever really thinking about it. With Joslin I *thought* about it." He turned the lighter over and over in his hand. "Would you like to come and see the show, Trip? See us film it? This Friday is kind of special." He sighed. "Lord, for ten days now, I been talking wills and probate and property and insurance and bonds. Pop had money all over the lot, and lawyers and—and"—he motioned with his head down the hall—"and Mother."

I nodded. I heard the automatic sprinkler in the green house go on; the storm had blown by. Rex sat there. He suddenly started to talk about "paranoid ideation" and a wealthy widow who sees cockroaches having cocktail parties in her kitchen sink. "Yes," he said, "Dr. Steve Kelly will figure it out."

"That's the character you play?"

"No. Rex is the character I play. Steve is who I am." He went to the window and looked out at the clearing night sky. "Good moon. I remember Pop looking up at the moon and saying that for centuries it has been an inspiration for poets, but by the year 2000 it'll be 'just another airport.' He said that a few years ago, we were standing out there, and I knew he was an old man." Rex put some classical music, real soft, on the stereo. "Everything OK here at the Grief Clinic, just gettin' into the Thorazine Shuffle."

I fiddled with the old high school yearbook.

164

I know who we are. I know who we are. Marge Stivers, Rex Hooker, Oliver Bodley. We're people who went to high school together.

There was a whining noise coming from the garage. It was the dog, Gamble. Rex let her into the kitchen and fed her, talking to her, "Where you been, little mother? You're wet, hon. Come on, hon. Why do you bump Leela all the time? You blind? I wonder what goes on in your mind, when you sleep you go *heh-heh-heh* in your dreams, do you enjoy bumping Mother in your dreams? Yes, you do. Yes, you do. Lost Procter, din' you? Poor baby."

He turned to me. "I just found—Mother found—this wonderful letter Pop wrote to the *L.A. Times* three years ago. I remember him standing right here—right here"—Rex put out his hands as if he could touch him —"and Pop was just—oh, he was ecstatic. He wandered around Medjuhl carrying that newspaper, with his letter supporting a bill to 'save the coastline,' a thousand miles of it, 'from those goddamn developers' and to preserve it for 'generations to come.' Pop had the old look in his eyes. He was comin' up to eighty—and he was *young* again."

"You miss him."

"*Miss* him? The world doesn't exist without Pop. *Build Therefore*— I was reading it again today. Listen, listen, just one paragraph, here, about this Baptist church he built on a promontory at Seal Beach. Have you seen it, Trip?"

"No."

"Well, if you'd seen it, you'd *know*. Here—" Rex got the little old book, flipped through it. "Here: 'Our problem was a plot of ground two hundred feet by a hundred feet composed of forty feet of liquid mud overlaid by six feet of filled soil the consistency of hard cheese.'" Rex looked at me. "I can put my lips together, Trip, just like Pop did when he was five years younger than I am now, when he actually wrote down 'the con-sis-ten-cy of hard cheese.' My tongue is Pop's tongue."

He was going to lose it—but he didn't, he caught himself, and he went on reading, " 'Water at high tide came to within a foot of ground level. In short, a tidal basin. To me it was a fine cushion to relieve earthquake shocks. I would float my church on the mud, as an ocean liner upon the sea. Indeed, outwit the quake!'—Oh, Trip, listen to him, 'outwit the quake'!—'outwit the quake, instead of fighting it, so that the building might settle again unharmed.' " Rex looked up and sighed. He closed the book. He sat there with his father. Then he came back to me. "And he was right, Pop was *right*, goddammit. During a big quake in forty-seven, everything around there fell down except the Calvary Baptist Church, the mother moved around a bit, and the cross fell off, but the building 'settled

165

again unharmed.' " He smiled. "The minister thanked God from the pulpit and thanked Pop over the phone."

He relaxed for about a minute. We were just sitting there. But then he said, "I could have saved him."

"You saved David. You saved Marge. You tried to save him."

"Trying is no points."

I said, "He was an old man."

Rex shot a glance at me, but then his face softened down. He said, "Working with him at Summer Snow. When I was a kid. In the yard. And when he'd help Mother with her roses. Fussing around the soil, worrying about their diet, their vulnerability to fungus. His sombrero and gloves, shooting dead needles off the pines with a hose. I never saw him —never see him—stationary. Always moving." Rex turned. "I'm going to have one more cognac, you want one? Anything?"

I said maybe a beer.

So he poured from the wet bar, poured from the fridge, and came in. He picked up the cigarette lighter. "Emperor and Clown." He looked at me. "Mother wants me to get back to work. She's right. Come with me to the taping on Friday?"

Oh, I don't know.

"Jos and Pop never got along. Right from the start. And he was helping. He saw the difficulty Jos had with Mother, Mother's overt displays, too much *holding on*. Touchy-feely. He took Jos over there, by the fridge, and he looked her in the eye, and he said, 'Listen, woman, you're part of the Hooker family now, and you have to understand my wife, your mother, thinks that means you have to kiss somebody every time you change rooms.' " Rex swirled the cognac in his snifter. "Oh, Pop." Then he looked at me, "Joslin and I were married, the third time, right in this room."

"The third time?"

"Repeated our vows, after David was born. The first two times, well, we were married in New York at noon, and at Summer Snow at eight P.M., same day. New York, Jewish; Laguna, Episcopal. In New York I about broke my foot—Jos's crazy brother, Ernest, was supposed to wrap a glass in a napkin for me to step on, like they do in Yid weddings as a symbol, and poor Ernest wrapped up a *shot* glass, and I stepped on it, and then stamped on it, and stomped on it, in my black patent leather shoes, and while I was chasing the shot glass around the room and breaking my foot, I was thinking, 'This Jewish shit is gonna be harder on me than I thought.' " Rex sighed.

"On our wedding night, our first wedding night, holding a glass of

166

champagne, completely happy, she was just sitting there on the other bed, in Room one twenty-six, and I cried out, 'Unchain the Jewess, she has found favor in the eyes of Rex—unchain the Jewess!' " He finished his cognac.

"Why did you marry her?"

"Oh, I don't know. Character is so erotic."

"What?"

"Goodness is sexy, Trip." Then he looked at me. "She hasn't—hasn't behaved badly in all this."

No. I sipped my beer.

"I don't know—Joslin, well, she started life with nothing. And made such a splendid person out of herself." He sighed. "And I was born with a silver spoon—with a whole silver place setting—in my mouth. I just so admired her. She—her becoming became her." He looked at me. "Tell me, Trip, do you know why your marriage went wrong?"

I thought about it. Well, if you come right down to it, I guess I don't. Except Sheila was such a complete cunt. I told Rex about it—how Sheila took everything from me, how I came back to the house that day and found one spoon, one knife, one fork, one cup, one saucer—one of everything, and how she took the shower curtain.

Rex was really listening. He looked kind of astonished. Almost embarrassed. He was blushing when he said, "One of everything? One cup, one spoon, one knife—?"

I told him again, each item. Sheila, that bitch.

He said, "And the shower curtain, she took that?"

"Yep."

He still had a really odd look on his face, and he excused himself, I could hear him muttering for a minute in the bathroom. I drank my beer. Well, I hate Sheila and he still loves Joslin. I think he ought to marry Marge Stivers and start a new life.

We start for bed. Just at the hallway he stops and says, "Oh, my dear Jos. It's so—so terrible that we never really had the house in Bluebird Canyon. By the time it was finished so were we. The Magic Couple never made it to the Magic Place. And Joslin and Pop—they could have loved each other, they should have loved each other—they both came up from nowhere. Pop used to speak of her, during the divorce, Pop would speak of her and he'd get a little wet in the eyes. Once he said to me, 'All your married life, you and Joslin were listening to two different radio stations —and then you'd argue about the program.' " Rex smiled and looked at me. "Pop didn't like me to say rotten things about her. He thought she was a goddamn Jew bitch communist whore, of course, but he was oddly

167

touched by her. And Joe didn't understand that the way Pop talked wasn't the way he felt, it was a way of protecting himself from what he felt. She didn't get it. Pop—Pop respected her."

Oh.

"You try it, Trip. Just look in that woman's eyes, and you know she has a—a great staying power." Rex tossed it off with a jerk of his head. But it was the first time I ever saw him self-conscious.

Wednesday morning Rex wanted to go to Disneyland. David all-over brightened at that, he'd never been on Space Mountain or any of the new rides. And shit, last time I went was with Sheila on our honeymoon. So OK, Rex got the Swedish woman with the Buick Electra to take care of Leela, who had decided her cold was the flu. And we went. On the way we played black dudes, we had to "signify."

"That chick backin' up tryin' to say my breaf stank."

I said, "You makin' us all sick."

Rex said, "All you think is you hopes her draw's fall off so you can have some 'citement."

David, kind of bashful, said, "Close yo mouf."

Rex: "Ma jokes is foul. I need to go home an res'. Shit, I need to git ma tongue pierced."

We hummed along in the Coral Cad, nobody in here but us porch monkeys. It was idiotic. We played Ghost, and I was no good at all. When I said *f* and David said *a* and Rex said *r*, I was thinking of *farther*, so I said *t*, and Rex said, "Trip, you just cut one," David went into his giggle fit, and I felt completely illiterate.

We parked at Disneyland and got Jumbo books. First thing we had to have a few moments with Mr. Lincoln, and Rex told David that when he, David, was a little boy he didn't believe it was a robot. David denied it. But we listened, and as we filed out, Rex said, "Interesting choice of text." It was a Wednesday in November, not too crowded. Rex had brought a camera, and he got three Mickey Mouse hats with "Trip" and "David" and "Dad" stitched on them, and he took my picture with David, with our caps on, and then I took them, and then David took us. Disneyland had changed, lots of new attractions. David was having a swell time. We panned for gold, climbed all over Tom Sawyer's Island. Pissed me off, Disneyland is so clean, you can't throw a cigarette butt down before some guy in white whips it up. Rex had brought along a joint, which still unnerves me. At least he didn't moon on the Matterhorn. David had to go on Space Mountain, but I chickened out, I have enough of that in real life. We clanked around the Autopia. The target practice

168

wasn't real. Rex said Pirates of the Caribbean was his favorite, because it had such vaginal implications. He and David loved it. Rex said an old Stanford fraternity brother of his had been the "Imagineer" on a section of it. Rex was stoned, sniffing away, had to have a candy apple and a hot dog. We went on the Jungle Cruise and heard all the old jokes from the tour guide: "You have now been taken through the Dark Continent; thank you for being taken." Ha-*ha*. A skeleton in the outhouse in frontier land was the "head man," ha-*ha*. But Rex got upset going into the Submarine Ride because he remembered doing that with Joslin when she was pregnant with David, and the Disneyland person saw Joslin six months along and said to the people behind them, "Let the newlyweds go first." I guess it was funny then, but now Rex sat depressed and stoned in the *Nautilus*. He perked up some when we got into a conversation with a guy in a lion suit, the King of the Jungle, wearing a crown and a purple robe, and the lion checked David out for "navel residue," meaning bellybutton lint, and Rex said, "David, don't listen to him, he's not a-tellin' the truth, he just a-lyin',"—which made the lion say that in the jungle they called that a "two-finger joke," and he put two fingers to his lion's mask and spit. But what made Rex happy was the lion's pun, when he wandered away and said, "I'd like to go home with you, but I have my pride."

The frightening part was the Haunted Mansion. We were in the little black cars, going past those ghostly transparent figures feasting and dancing and laughing in the ballroom. I was with David in the car ahead of Rex, and for a split second I thought it was part of the ride, David caught it before I did, it was his dad, maybe the big room seemed to him too much like the rooms at Summer Snow, because when we were going past the mirror where there's an optical illusion that a light-green ghost is right in your car with you, the high moaning we'd been hearing turned into an awful noise, and Rex jumped out of his car, and they had to stop the whole ride. A girl in uniform came down and helped us out and took us up some stairs, Rex howling this awful "Baaa BBBaaaa—BBBAAAA—" like a robot that had jammed.

It took him a few minutes to get hold of himself. "Sorry about that, guys," he said, breathing pretty hard. He kept shaking his head, trying to clear it. We sat and had lemonade. David looked frightened to death. So we went to the Tiki Room, that was pretty harmless and dumb, and the Big Thunder Mountain Railroad, and watched America on Parade, but we didn't forget the Haunted Mansion. Rex must have seen J.O. in there.

We went into the old-time cinema; Charlie Chaplin is so funny. Then Rex and David had silhouettes made, and they bought a little blown-glass piano for Leela. Rex let David pick it out. But Rex was hurting, he felt he had let his son down. I told him to forget it, and he just muttered, "Inexcusable." On Main Street, as we left, he said, "You know, Trip, Marx insisted the mind is a toy." The way Rex whinnied, that hopeless way of his.

On the ride back to the desert David fell asleep in the back seat, stuffed full of food, his Mickey Mouse cap askew over his eyes. When Rex saw the kid asleep, he went into his Dr. Steven Kelly thing again, talking about the "arsonist syndrome," about "competing with the father—and punishing the mother—who neglected—kicking out the rivals from Mother's womb—watch fire and achieve peace—" Rex driving along, me sitting beside him, the kid asleep in the back. "Never got mothering, urge to excel, never felt he could measure up to Father—inarticulate, big ambitions—" It was crazy, it made me very uncomfortable.

Back on the desert David woke up, and his dad gave him a driving lesson, the kid took the wheel of the Cad himself, and we went up to the wildlife preserve where years ago Duke Talis and his boys did the job on us. David had trouble controlling the Seville in the sand. It gave me an eerie feeling when we stopped at the exact spot and Rex inspected it, climbed up on the rocks and looked down at me and David leaning against the Coral Seville. Years ago it was a white Fleetwood. Rex looked at us for a long time. He had a peculiar little smile on his face that made me wonder if he was hearing "Hit this old man." Jesus, it was weird just to stand there like that, all the shit from twenty years ago coming back. Nobody for miles around. I fired a few rounds from my gun and let David have three tries at a beer bottle. He wasn't even in the neighborhood, too spooked by the weapon.

When we got back to Medjuhl, Leela was sure her cold was pneumonia. She hadn't seen her doctor in Laguna since the fire, and now she was all panicky. Wouldn't let the kid see it, but Rex told me. He whispered about it, out by the pool, and said a couple of times, "More here than meets the eye." I was uncomfortable—I mean, is it just a cold, or what? Anyway, I was supposed to drive David back to Laguna in 1 GROUCH, to his mother, and Rex would follow along with Leela. And while I was getting my stuff packed, I heard him babbling on the phone to Marge Stivers. About Peter Ingalls. Jesus H. Christ.

So I was confused and upset enough when I realized something was wrong with David. In the car. I knew it could be a lot of different things, but he didn't seem to want to talk. I asked him what was eating him. He said, "Nothing." I said I could see that. Finally, in Cabazon, I said, "It's me, I guess, you don't want to ride with me, you'd rather be with your

Dad. That's why you're sitting there like a bump on a log." He said, "Of course not." I turned the radio on, and he said, "I hate that kind of music." So I flipped her off.

I think I could wear my Mouseketeer hat on duty. To command respect. I ask David what he thinks of the idea. He looks at me, his head in his hand, his elbow propped up there on the arm rest. Suddenly he gives a little laugh and says, "Dad took me through the Roy Rogers Museum. Last summer. Dad was kind of, you know, stoned?"

"I know."

"Roy Rogers's horse—Trigger—the horse is stuffed, in a glass case. And Dad was bent over staring between the back legs. I asked him what he was looking at, and he said, 'Just wanted to see if Trigger was cocked.'"

I smiled. At least I got the kid talking.

"My dad is pretty gross."

"You like to go places with him, don't you?"

"We have hairy old times. I guess that's why I'm cranky. I'm sorry. I'm mad at my mom."

"Your mom?"

"She won't let me go to the studio. I used to be on the show, you know, until I was seven. And then Mom wouldn't let me anymore. She said it wasn't good for me. But I think it was because she and my dad separated."

"You were on the show?"

"Starting when I was six months old. I was the *baby*. Danny. I was on for *years*."

"You?"

"Yes," he said, "*me*." Sarcastic little twit.

"Well, maybe your mom's right. A kid shouldn't be on TV all the time. You got school and everything."

"I had school right there. A tutor. Sara Rose."

"Why'd your mom think it was no good?"

"Because I wasn't around kids my own age." He said it like for the millionth time.

"I think she has a point."

"But there were lots of kids. From other shows. We got into all sorts of trouble. And lots of times I wasn't in the script, so I went to regular school, too. I had the best of both worlds, Dad always said so."

"Still," I said, "a lot of child actors grow up to have unhappy lives."

"A lot of *children* grow up to have unhappy lives."

I looked at him. And he got embarrassed. I think of what he's going through, so I stop pushing. It's a beautiful day, we cut through Riverside, the temperature drops. Humming along.

So he thinks his mother took him off the show not for his sake but because of the divorce. Maybe his dad popped that little sliver into his head? Would Rex do that?

David says, "The last show I was on, I remember it so clearly. Mom was there, and Dad was still hoping she'd change her mind. They were still friends. We had a big lunch in the commissary, where all the people from other shows eat too, you know?"

I try to picture it, I see the Indio High cafeteria full of grownups in costumes.

"We were standing in line waiting for a table. And Dad got a menu from the thing where the hostess stands? We looked at it, and Mom said, 'Oh, David, try the Chinese chicken salad, that looks good.' And then this guy in front of us, in a tuxedo, he was just *huge*, this big black guy in a tuxedo. Like a *mountain*. He slowly turned around and looked down at me, his hands were about twice as big as my whole head. It was Rosie Grier. You know Rosie Grier?"

"Sure. Played for the Rams."

"So Mom said to try the Chinese chicken salad. And Rosie Grier peered down from way up there, in his tuxedo, he was in costume for some show, and he looked right at me and said, really slow, 'No, man, go for the Vegas burger.' "

I looked at him.

"So then when the waiter came and said, 'What will you folks have today?' I just said real fast, 'Vegas burger.' I didn't even know what it was."

"Was it good?"

"Oh, it was *ex*-cellent."

I kept 1 GROUCH steady at the double-nickel.

He was kind of revved up now. "Like I don't want to make a *career* of it. Dad doesn't want me to anyway. I'd just like to go back and see everybody again. Besides, he needs me."

"He needs you?"

"For this little part. Only it's not exactly little. He finally found out."

"Found out?"

"That I—" and then the kid stopped. "I'm not supposed to tell. It ruins the whole concept."

"Concept?"

"Well, that's like the *idea*—"

"I know what a concept is." My turn to be sarcastic. Little bugger thinks a police sergeant doesn't understand the term *concept*.

"No, I just mean everybody always wants to know. What's going to

172

happen. Not only real people in the real world. The other actors, too. They get you off in a corner and ask questions."

"They do?"

"Dad is also the producer, and he knows the Bible."

"The Bible?"

"Yeah, the Bible is what's going to happen over the next six months. Some actors think, since I'm his son, he might tell me. Or even that if they're nice to me, buy me candy, help me with something, then Dad will like them and they won't get killed off or anything and they'll still have a job."

"I see."

"It's their bread and butter. If they get killed off, they don't eat."

"That frequently happens to people who get killed off."

It took him a second, and then he said, "Well, you know." He smiled, checking out my car, peeking around.

"Well," I said, "I tend to agree with your mom. Although I don't take sides. You should be out playing baseball and riding your bike and flying kites."

"I do that, too."

Going to have a lot of heartache in your life, David. I'd bet on it. Very smart, but very innocent. Still believe people are decent. It's going to chew you up when you find out they are not. "Well," I said, "I've never even seen the dumb soap opera, so—"

"It's not a dumb soap opera."

"Well, I've never seen it."

"So how do you know it's dumb?"

Got me again.

"What I mean is, you won't spoil the story for me. I was just asking you why, if your mom feels the way she does, why does your dad countermand her wishes?"

"Counterman?"

"If she says no, isn't it all decided?"

He thought, staring at his sneakers. "But they don't preserve the tapes. And now when he finds out that—uh-oh, no way, you were trying to trap me."

No I wasn't, I don't give diddly-squat about the story. "If I do go up there and watch them tape a show, a little background might help. So I can understand it and not be completely lost."

"Oh." He thought about it.

Some flagmen were out, they're paving a section of the road, and we sat there in the pass, David and me, looking at the lovely hills. No smog,

173

nice November day. I have got to have kids of my own before I die. If only I didn't have to get married. If I were a woman, I'd go out to a university setting, find a smart engineering student, he wouldn't even have to look good, as long as he's got smart genes, and I'd get knocked up and then live with my wonderful kid. Except I want to be a father, not just a parent, I want to be a father.

"Well—OK," David said, "but don't tell anyone."

"I won't."

"Well, finally—finally Dad has discovered that I am not really his son."

"What?"

"What?"

"For years he thought I was. But I'm not. He's sterile."

"Your dad?"

"My biological father is Josh Kelly. The black sheep of the family. Who was adopted."

"Oh, right."

He sat there.

I took my hands off the wheel. "Look, I don't know anything about the story, you can't expect me to figure it out all at once."

"Well, OK. Now, Dr. Steven Kelly," he said, "that's Dad."

"I understand that."

"And he was married to Jessica. Who is Mom. I mean, in real life, not the actress. And they had me as their baby, which is both. But Dad—Steven Kelly—didn't know he was sterile, because when he was a teenager he had the mumps. Dad had them when he was six, so it was OK, but Dr. Kelly had them in adolescence. Like George Washington."

"Oh."

"Did you know the Father of Our Country was sterile?"

"Come on."

"No, it's really true. They were Martha Washington's children by her first marriage. All the children in the paintings."

"I don't think that's true."

"Well, even Mom says it is."

"I guess that settles it." Jesus Christ, the Father of Our Country was sterile. No wonder Joslin wanted him away from there. What's he supposed to do, give an oral report in Show and Tell?

"And Josh Kelly isn't really a Kelly. He was adopted. And had amnesia. He came back from Korea, and he and Jessica had me behind Steve's back."

"Check."

"For years everybody knew. Except Steve. My dad. And now he's found

174

out. And he's having a nervous breakdown, *right at the point when—*"

I laughed. I had to, it was just completely weird hearing him talk so seriously about it.

"Are you making fun of me?"

"No, man, I'm not laughing at you, I'm laughing with you."

"But I'm not laughing."

Shit. "Maybe I shouldn't know too much about it." I saw a middle-aged lady standing beside a Riviera, rear tire in shreds, lady standing there on the shoulder looking helpless. I pulled over. The lady was upset, she was on her way to a convention, already late, and could I drive her to a phone so she could call Claremont and say she'd be there "come hell or high water or even a flat tire"? She had buckets of flowers in the back seat, roses, gladiolas, all these nice floral arrangements for "the sisterhood," she was afraid they'd wilt. She had a Triple-A card. But it was no problem, I checked, a good jack and a brand-new spare blue whitewall, so I just changed the tire for her. David watched, and got me a crescent wrench from the tool box in 1 CROUCH. The lady chattered away pointlessly, and I got some grease on my new slacks. I swore a little, which offended her not in the least. So I swore more. She asked David if his "daddy" was a professional mechanic. David said I was not his daddy, I was a policeman in Laguna Beach. This got our lady to wondering what was up—probably thought David was a runaway. Anyway, her flowers didn't wilt. She tried to tip me, and I said we're not allowed to accept gratuities. So she went sailing off, a fairly wealthy lady, nice, scatterbrained.

I hated that grease stain on my new slacks, and my hands were semi-wretched, so we stopped at a Taco Bell where I made a mess in the men's, and David wolfed his burrito, his mouth and chin stained orange. I figured a little Good Samaritan shit wouldn't hurt him, probably work in my favor —not that that was the reason. I frequently do it alone. But the little bugger had me self-conscious about motives. I figure the kid can smell a rat. Good kids always can. I turn it over in my mind and add some taco sauce to the grease on my pants.

I said, "You really miss your pop, don't you? He was a great man, old J.O." I just flat-out said it, looking at the lacy clouds.

He was chomping away at that burrito, needed extra napkins. He seemed to trust me. "You know, he was kind of *foolish.*"

I would have objected, except he said it so affectionately.

"The way he said things all the time, you know? He'd give me a newspaper and say, 'Here's a want ad, David—"Wanted: man to wash dishes and two waitresses." ' " The kid looked at me. "Get it?"

"Yes."

"Or he'd say, 'David, If God didn't know we'd get into trouble, why did He give each of us different fingerprints?'"

I liked the way he said it, preoccupied with his sticky fingers. "Pop told me an excuse. You know, an absence? From school? 'Please excuse Suzie today, she's ministering, and in bed with Gramps.'" David shook his head. "Get it?"

I nodded, eating.

"Just thousands of 'em."

I sat there at the picnic table. I'd order another taco if it were not for my peptic ulcer, or whatever. I also notice my ulnar neuropathy is acting up again, I probably need a refill on my Bute. I said, "I suppose all that shit—all that was just his way of saying three little words."

"Three little words?"

"'I love you.'"

He gave me a strange, hurt look.

"You know, when you love somebody, you want to play with them."

He got tears in his eyes. And I say to myself, Lighten up, Trip, lighten up.

We got back in the car and tooled away, after dumping our garbage in the receptacle.

I think of Rex and Leela, behind us somewhere in the Coral Cad; maybe they even passed us while I was changing the tire, but Rex would have stopped. Or they could have passed while we were having our Tiajuana Two-Step; my bowels are already rumbling away, I hope I don't have to stop. I think that there is something I have not been told, there was a strange tone in Rex's voice when he talked to Marge. What was that all about? Peter Ingalls? There's something hidden. But I can't ask David. Although I'd probably learn a lot. Often with a suspect you ask seven questions that you already know the answers to, and then just ask one that's big, but the suspect's mind is on the other shit, and the key thing comes plopping out right in your hand. I wouldn't do that to David. Except I would if I thought it would help. Anyway, I changed a lady's tire. If you can't fix the big shit, fix the little shit. I am thinking all this in my adult belching way, the taste of the taco, heartburn.

David says, "Since the tapes are never stored—Dad always objects to that—they need me. Now. So Dad can see I'm not his son. He's going to be sitting at a piano, playing all the old songs. 'Danny Boy'—you know that song?"

"Oh Danny Boy, the pipes, the pipes are blo-o-wing—"

"You *have* seen it."

176

"Well, everybody knows that song."

"Dad didn't write it?"

"No, of course not."

"Oh." He sits there, looking at his sneaks. He says, "Silly me."

"What?"

"That's what my dad says when he finds out something everybody else knew—he always says, 'Silly me.' "

"Did he tell you he wrote it?"

"No, I just thought . . . did anybody else write 'Jessie, You Mean the World to Me'?"

"No." I mean, I guess not. I never heard of it.

"Good."

We were heading onto 5 from the Riverside Freeway, past the Angels' stadium. The Rams. I wish life had been different and I had had a shot at management, I could be a fantastic scout. Mission Viejo next five exits. We pass by the Irvine Ranch. Poor little rich boys and poor little rich girls all sent up to Stanford to play together and study together and marry each other and then come back and go into the family businesses. If I had just paid attention in Western Civ and English. Goddamn it, I could have been a Stanford Man. Rushed a jock house, made lifelong valuable connections. Now I'd be at the wheel of that Porsche Turbo. Saddleback is lovely over there. And Mount Wilson in the rear-view. I resent it, mountains are God's handiwork, I deeply resent it, I don't even know what clothes to wear when I am invited to a function, my jacket's not real leather, it's vinyl—

David says, "Are you a bachelor?"

I look at him, and light my first cigarette. I know the kid doesn't like cigarette smoke. I've been not having one for him. "A confirmed bachelor."

"Mom's friend, Sara Rose—"

"I thought she was your tutor."

"Dad says 'tootress.' Or 'tootrix.' " He sighs. "One time, years ago when I was eight, Dad had to make—on the show, Steve Kelly—he had to make an *agonizing* decision. And he took me, Danny, into his arms, and he said, 'Son, I have to do the only honorable thing.' "

"Did he?"

"Yep."

"Good."

"But the point is"—David, sitting there—"after the show, Dad asked me if I thought it was good, you know?"

177

"That he did the honorable thing?"

"They tell me, Mom and Dad, I don't really remember it, I don't remember saying it, but they tell me I did, I said, 'I really liked it when you said you had to do the only considerable thing.' "

I looked at him.

"See? I messed it up—I mixed up *considerate* and *honorable*, and said *considerable*." The kid sighed. "Dad said it was more than an honest mistake. He said it was a splendid mistake. He said only *I* would make that mistake."

I thought about that, and we drove a mile in silence.

David said, "My dad always says that a sense of humor is not the best defense. But it helps in the long run."

I turned to him. "Well, I imagine you'd have to have a sense of humor to work all those years on a soap opera."

"What?"

"Well, you know, soaps are sort of—well, you know."

"No, I don't."

"They're sort of dumb."

"They are not."

"Well, why aren't they on at night?"

"Because they're supposed to be on in the daytime."

"But that's when people are at work. You only watch TV at night, or on weekends, when you're not working."

"But that *is* my dad's work. He works *hard*." David was quiet for a minute and then he said, "My dad doesn't make fun of *your* work."

So that's what I was doing—I do not see how I can be so stupid, asleep at the switch, asleep at the wheel, I was just thinking about goddamn Sheila and how she loved soap operas, sitting there in the house all day eating bonbons. Lulled by the freeway, resentful of Stanford Men—I hardly realized I was talking out loud, thought it was going through my mind.

I lack class. I got him on my wavelength, teased him out onto the tightrope, and then I just walked away and left him. I probably shouldn't have kids.

"Why didn't you turn?"

"I was going down to La Paz."

"You were supposed to take one thirty-three, the Laguna *Free*way."

"But last time I took you to Mission Viejo, that's where your mother lives."

"*She does not.*"

"But we went to her house there."

And now, goddamn it to hell, he's crying, his tears really are spilling. "It's not *our* house."

Oh, I am just so manly and calm and good. Once again I am going to return this guy to his mother in bad shape, drop him off in tears.

"It's the *Roses'* house."

I take the El Toro exit, I can get to Laguna almost as fast that way. The kid sighs, tries to catch his breath. I'm such a fine person.

"It's my dad's *and* my mom's house. In Laguna. It's at the, the—top."

"I know. I know the house. I just thought she had moved over here."

"She was *house*-sitting. For the Roses, while they were in Hawaii."

"How am I supposed to know that? Sir, will you please forgive me?" I hate myself saying that goddamn "sir." I pull back, ease off, for just a second I think I might express my true feelings. Apologize. But that's not what he needs. I cut across Paseo de Valencia and make my way up to Moulton in the late afternoon, fighting the sun. I feel like a shit.

"Look, David, don't blame me. You know I never even saw the dumb soap opera—"

"It's not *dumb!*"

"I didn't mean that—"

"Then—then stop—saying it!"

OK, OK. Kid crying, I'm completely upset, no use talking. Rat's ass.

He sits there, crying away, while we climb up through Bluebird Canyon to the mansion at the summit, a deckhouse overlooking the canyon and the blue Pacific. He wants to hurry, he says can he please get his bag out of the trunk? I put a fairly strong hand on his arm. I say, "Now, how is your mother going to feel if you show up this way?"

His eyes are belligerent, looking at me bloody murder.

"I'm sorry if you think I insulted your father's work. But I couldn't, not even if I wanted to—I told you, I've never *seen* it. Only a fool would criticize something he knows absolutely nothing about."

"Only a fool or—or a *pig.*"

Hey, now, just a fucking minute.

I guess my face must have shown something because he said, twice, "I didn't mean that, I didn't mean that."

I stared at the instrument panel while he cried. I breathed a bit. I said, "If you cry, you know, your mom won't blame it on me. She'll blame your father. You want your mother to hate your father?"

Jesus, I'm so good with kids. I bully them.

"She's probably not even home."

"Well, I'll wait in the car." I am feeling miserable. No wonder they threw me out of Stanford. "I—I think your father is a fine man."

179

"But you said mom was right."

"I was talking through my hat. I don't know a single thing about the show. How can I, when I've never even seen it?" I am talking in circles. "Why—why do you want to be on it so bad?"

"Well, I can't"—trying to catch his breath, stop his tears, his face all scrunched up—"don't you see? I—I can't leave my dad *now*."

Oh, break my fucking heart. I got his bag out of the trunk. I can't leave my Dad *now*.

The door to the huge house opened, and there was Joslin. Little blue sun dress, her black hair braided down her back. Kind of a rehearsed smile on her face.

She sees, immediately, David wiping his eyes with his bare arm. She does not ask me to come in.

David stalked inside with his bag, leaving us there in the driveway. I made "Who, me?" motions with my eyes. I was hurt, we were really doing swell when I changed the lady's tire and we had the Mex food, when we were talking, it was just the last ten miles.

"Thanks," Joslin said. "I can see he's in good shape."

I said, "I guess I said something wrong."

She said, "I guess you did."

This big house, top of Bluebird Canyon, the day so beautiful. How can anything that starts so good, and continues good, turn out so bad?

I said, "He thought the Vegas burger was *ex*-cellent."

She said, real cold, "I don't know what that means."

"It was OK, until just here. I thought I was supposed to take him to Mission Viejo, and it upset him."

"I'm supposed to put up with this? You bring my son home in such a state he can't even talk?"

"He was OK until a few minutes ago."

"I'll bet."

Good luck, no use trying to explain.

"You stay away from him, Trip. Just stay away."

"I was trying to help."

"Don't play innocent with me. Where my son is concerned, I become a wolf." She was trembling.

"Look, I am not your enemy. I said something wrong about that soap opera. I called it dumb, and he got real loyal to his father."

She was staring at me, trying to figure out if this was a right-wing plot or something, but I just looked back at her.

Finally I said, "He's a gallant little boy."

Her startling eyes. She said, "Call me when you have news, I have to

180

. . ." and she made a gesture toward the house. She actually smiled at me. The whole thing flipflopped emotionally, she went from hating me to liking me. Without the clutch. Jesus.

So I got back into 1 GROUCH and drove away. It was blamming around in my head—"I can't leave my Dad *now.*"

11

PROBLEMS COMPLETELY piled up at the office. Some sucker named Olene Arthur Matthias reported a theft of 800,000 dollars' worth of private papers and said he had been beaten unconscious with a baseball bat while searching a house where his estranged wife was staying. Next day his brother-in-law charged him with assault with a deadly weapon. I talked to the maid, Maria de Jesus, through an interpreter. I contact the D.A. to see if this is civil or criminal calendar. Then a lady up on Los Olivos reports her gold Buddha has been stolen. A two-foot-tall replica of the Kamakura Buddha, whatever the fuck that is, with a diamond in its forehead. I surely will keep my eyes open. Then at exactly 11:27 P.M. I see a dune buggy zipping all over Main Beach. Drunk in the moonlight, doing wheelies and figure-eights on the sand. I go on foot, although he'll probably try to run me over, I've already called my backup, and then the guy stops dead. I walk up and there is a little kid about three years old just screaming bloody murder, and I see why, a razor-thin steel cable caught in the differential, jerked tight around his foot, and amputated it. His whole little bare foot is sitting there, blood all over the place. I race back and call for paramedics, and then I try to apply first aid, blood gushing everywhere. The driver, who later turns out to be his brother,

182

seventeen, is so blitzed he can't see straight, but he sure can see the foot. The cable was just like a big motor-driven scalpel. Finally the paramedics arrive and take the kid away, and the foot, and I don't do a thing to the teenager, but it is very hard for me to restrain myself. Crazy people, the world is full of immature, careless, crazy people. And in the night I dream about the foot, I knew I would.

Next day I get a call from a lady over on Agate that her porch is on fire. But no, it was my old buddy Theodore, he was sleeping under her porch, and smoking. So I hassle him, I take out some of my pent-up emotions on poor defenseless Theodore. I tell him he has an arrest card of at least ten pages; the next time I bring him in, the judge will put him away so long he'll forget what it tastes like. I am sick and tired of all this disorderly conduct. Theodore just stands there going hmmmmm. And then that evening I am shooting the shit a little with a cabby on the corner of Thalia and Glenneyre, and I see Theodore go into the Patio Liquor Store. So I wait, and Theodore comes bopping out with a big bag full of bottles, and I say real sharply, *"Theodore!"* and he jumps so high he drops all his bottles. A big puddle of wine spreads on the asphalt. Theodore says, "Now look what you done. Now look what you done to them bottles. Them weren't mine. Now you broke all my bottles." I ask him why he's buying this booze anyway. He says, "A guy paid me to get them. Them weren't my bottles." He pokes around, finds one not busted. "Here is one for Theodore. This one for Theodore. This one didn't break. Hmmmmm." He toddles off. Poor old rummy.

But when I get back to the station, I see the day is not over yet. Not by a long shot. Butch is calling for help, there's a guy up on Temple Hills who is holding a little girl at knifepoint. So I haul ass up there, and sure enough, Butch is facing off with a wild-eyed young man who is weeping and shouting, "I love her, but I'll kill her before you take me in." He doesn't like us one bit. He shouts, "I been persecuted by police all my life." He's crying, says he'll kill anyone who tries to stop him and don't care if he dies doing it. The little girl is panicked out of her mind. Butch and I stand there helpless. Butch tells me it all started with a Disturbing the Peace report, a neighbor called that the man was irrational and violent. He threw his wife to the ground, dragged her across the gravel, and then grabbed his little girl. Now he says, "I'll count to five and then I'll kill her if you don't leave." Butch turns to go, but I say, "Look—let her go. I won't charge you. I won't jail you. I won't handcuff you. I'll take you to the hospital." I spell it all out, real calm, being as nice as I can. He says he wants it in writing. Sure, that's fair. Christ, he's got the butcher knife right at her throat. People standing around in the dusk, maybe a dozen people behind us now. I get out my pad, my ball-point. I write it all down. He has me read it out loud to him, and says, "Sign your name." So I do. He wants Butch to sign it, too—and Butch does, his handwriting all shaky. We make the trade. The man gets the paper, I get the girl. Then I give the girl straight to her mother, who hugs her in tears, and I cuff the asshole and take him to jail. When we get there, he seems to have had a little accident along the way, his face is rather cut up and there's a mouse on his eye. Mercy me, I don't know how on earth that could have happened. Butch neither. Everybody thinks I'm Mr. Nice Guy—just scare me real bad sometime and give me serious trouble.

I checked with Rex, he and his mother were safe in the El Dorado suite. I guess Joslin didn't say anything to him about David's condition when he got back. I still don't know quite how it happened. The docs were working on Leela's "cold," Rex had begun supervising construction at Summer Snow. Determined to have it all rebuilt by Christmas, he has to have Christmas in there. And he'll probably make it, the major damage was smoke.

I mull over Peter Ingalls. At Big Bear years ago, J.O. and Ingalls, Sr., were sitting on the couch, near the fireplace, watching a football game on television. The bullet came through the window and struck Ingalls in the head. He was killed instantly. Deputies investigated but found no suspects. And even after all these years, no one knows. It could have been a professional killer, from organized crime—just one bullet, right through the head. Its trajectory proved it was not a wild errant shot. According to ballistics, it was fired from less than fifty feet away, from a high-velocity-type rifle. But what's that have to do with anything? I'm barking up the wrong tree. I doze off, I'm exhausted.

David. I'm so fond of the little twirp, and twice now in my car I have made him cry. I go over it to find the spot where I blew it, but all I see is his eyes filling up with tears, and I am not really seeking an answer, I am just trying to get out from under the burden. You'd think a grown man, a policeman, would have a little more control over his emotions.

I am afraid to go to bed, because the other day I had a dream that David died. My own voice, crying out, woke me up. I sat in the kitchenette, naked, and had a cup of tea, read the sports section in the *Times*, and stared at my dick all huddled there. This is no way to live. What is the fucking matter with me? David died, and there was nothing I could do about it. In my dream he was going down in the sea, just going down, and he smiled at me, like he was happy to die, there were bubbles in the ocean, he smiled. Why would I have such a nightmare? My dick lies there

184

between my legs. I wonder why, when girls go swimming, their nipples stand up rock-hard, and when guys go swimming, their dicks shrink into worms. I wonder what David will have for breakfast, and what it will be like for him to go through puberty, which he will soon do. If he doesn't die in the sea. I don't know what's going through my head. But whatever happens, nothing happens to that kid. That's where I stand, I will not have that boy touched.

What am I talking to myself for? Look at my dick. Oliver Bodley. In the middle of the night. Talking to himself in his trailer.

Rex really wants me to see them make that soap opera. "This Passing Night." So I work out my shift with the Chief. Rex said he'd pick me up at four A.M., that was a surprise. And I didn't know what to wear. I got all spiffed up in a tie and sports coat, but when his red Mercedes arrives at five minutes to four, he's wearing Levi's and a sweat shirt.

Has a thermos of coffee. I warn him that I never watch soap operas. But when I tell him what David told me, he is delighted to hear it, especially the Vegas burger and the considerable person. He says he does agree with Joslin—the kid shouldn't be on the show. But he's pissed that David couldn't do this one little two-minute spot. Yep, he tells me, Steve Kelly is sterile and Danny Boy is not his son. I'm still none too clear about the story—or completely awake, there's a chill in the November air, and the car heater makes me drowsy. We barrel along up 405, and he tells me how "Daytime"—that's what he calls soap operas—how "Daytime" works. He says thirty million people watch the shows. "Twice the combined populations of Switzerland and Sweden, Trip," he says with a grin. Every week "This Passing Night" makes $700,000 in ad revenues for the network. Lately they've had to "skew young," he says. Less housewives facing midlife, more teenyboppers coming out of their designer jeans. But it's still about happiness. And happiness is still family. Family-shmamily. Rex is excited, hasn't been to work since his father's death. He's all wrapped up in it, talks about it like it's a woman he's in love with. I remember the San Diego Zoo, when those two old ladies recognized him and he signed autographs for them. "Jessie wanted me to move on to something else," he says, drinking his coffee. "As if Daytime were a training ground. She didn't get it. As usual. Jos never really *gets* it."

He said their rating is about 8.9, whatever that means, for people who make up to twenty thou, and a strong 9 for people above that. The sponsors are not going after the Leisure World set. Summer Snow Productions owns the show, packages it, and sells it to the network. "We use their facilities, but we buy our own talent. Summer Snow Productions bought

185

out Ziegler-Daves in '69. It was always NBC, but the first two years we were in New York."

I'm not really following him. "You've done this for a long time?"

"Thirteen years."

"Always Steve Kelly?"

"Always Steve Kelly."

"Doesn't it get kind of—boring?" Shit, I wish I hadn't said that.

"No, it's not like a long run in a play, Trip, same thing night after night. It's always new, every day. Not a story. An environment."

Oh.

"It's a *place*."

Oh.

We hum along the freeway.

"And for all these years Steve Kelly has been the family Rock of Gibraltar. But now I'm in the baddest of bad ways."

I take another slug at the thermos. "Coffee's hot."

"That's intended to be a merit."

I look at him, he grins, and he drives. He's happy.

It's still dark, everybody's headlights on. I mention that I had thought Joslin lived in Mission Viejo, I didn't know she was still in that house at the top of Bluebird Canyon.

He chuckles. "Pop and I built that house. Didn't Jos take you through?"

Uh, no.

"Jos and I just made it to our tenth anniversary. Or our fifteenth, depending on how you count. Oh, my, the very thought of Joslin and me in bed. Can you imagine it, Trip?"

"I try not to."

He chuckles again. "Good man." And then he whispers, twice, "Bluebird Canyon, Bluebird Canyon."

Five minutes go by.

"Trip, when you see Marge, you'll laugh your ass off."

"Why's that?"

"Just wait."

The sun is a faint presence, ready to rise. We pull onto West Alameda, we're in scenic downtown Burbank, where they do the Johnny Carson show. Big place, looks like a government installation. At the gate Rex jokes with the guard, some banter that I don't understand, and then the old guy in uniform says, "Have a good one, Mr. H."

Rex is carrying a briefcase. We go into the studio, down a long corridor to his dressing room. Another guard is sitting there on a folding chair with the morning newspapers, and he's got an evil look in his eyes, like an old man full of bitterness.

Rex takes a quick whiz and asks me if I want to use the facilities. I don't. We go out to the set. It's a huge sucker, like an aircraft hangar, with a million big lights slung from the rafters, and down below a half-dozen little "sets"—a palatial living room with a Christmas tree, what looks like a nightclub, another more modest living room, and a nice new Buick, a Buick sitting there like it's on the showroom floor, a tan one with classy trim. Also, a dumpy little doctor's office, and a kitchen. All these sets in a row, on both sides of the huge building, and a lot of guys already at work with the lights, guys on ladders talking low, it's 5:30 in the morning. A big coffee machine and a table with tons of doughnuts. Then I see that guy Al, the one who carried the butterfly chair at Rex's party, he's jabbering away, pencils in his hair and behind his ears and spilling out of his pockets. "Rex," he says, real warmly; it is the first day Rex has been back to work since the tragedy. I see it's a solid moment for Al and him. Rex says, "Why don't we ever have decent doughnuts?" Al recognizes me as somebody he must have met somewhere, and we clarify where. We shake hands. A voice booms out over the P.A. system, "Is this the character who's going to schiz out on us today?"

Rex looks up and flips the bird.

I don't think the doughnuts are so bad. Rather tasty.

Other people show up. A blond girl with huge boobs and a tiny blood pimple right in her cleavage. She gives Rex a big hug. She's just come back from being a judge for the Miss Texas pageant. The winner was Sue Ellen Kilpert, whose career objectives were "nun" or "veterinarian." She wears a cowboy hat and cowboy boots, and says Lubbock is the absolute pits except for the Bar-B-Q in the wee small hours when you're stoned out of your skull. Rex says, "At least you got a good dialect out of it."

I have myself another doughnut.

Everybody's having a good time, kidding around, also getting work done. Rex introduces me to each person. He says, "Sergeant Oliver Bodley, Triphammer, of the Laguna Beach Police Department. We went to high school together." Like he is proud of me. I feel like an honored guest. This whole thing is a mystery, I wonder how much that fat black custodian makes, or the woman who is trying to get a camera through the "elephant door." People drift around, drinking coffee and juice. Rex takes me upstairs to the executive offices. There's a glass case with touch-football trophies and photographs of their team. The Passing Knights. Marge Stivers is a cheerleader, and there's Rex hugging some guy in the end zone. He tells me he hired a lot of ringers, semipro, a QB from

Brigham Young. I flash on that Sunday football game—"Follow Daddy!" —and he finds me a script. Up on the wall are photographs of him as Steven Kelly getting married to a stunning brunette, then another one of him cutting a wedding cake with Marge in a bridal gown. I study the script. This is Episode #3628, Production #184457, I don't know when the air date is, Rex tells me they're always three weeks ahead. Which, I figure, explains the Christmas tree in the living room downstairs. Rex is rummaging around, happy. Then the door flies open and it's a guy, real handsome, whose voice is the voice that came from the control booth, the guy who said that about Rex schizzing out. His name is Neil Robinson. We shake hands. He says, "She's such a smart cookie. Vacuuming her studio in Malibu. She's twenty-one. I'm forty-one. She thinks I smoke too much. I say to her, 'Honey, I have been smoking since before you were born.' She says, 'Why did you take it up so late in life?' "

Rex laughs.

Neil Robinson shakes his head. Face like a magazine cover. And a nervous wreck. "She assaults hippies in pay phones. Her tits are so cold. How can she say the things she does? Imagine the things she *thinks*. She says she'd like to be a poet, and will be, once she finds a subject. Oh God, I have a terrible love life."

So handsome, and talking like a little freak. Odd combination.

Then he says, "Rex, I was so sorry to hear about your father. But you look fine. Look fine."

Rex stares at him for a second, and I turn away to the touch-football trophies and Marge the cheerleader. And, look, there's David, bright eyes, a little kid, holding the trophy up, real happy, about five years old.

Now there was a crowd in the big studio, actors, lots of technicians, people from "wardrobe," a couple of youngsters furiously writing the actors' lines on big cue cards, wide red Magic Markers just flying away. Al Marcus, it turns out he's the director, was preparing a scene for a kid, perfectly tanned with long air-blown hair, and a real petite chick in a clingy blue dress who had auburn hair down to her ass. These actors are so handsome. Another gorgeous woman comes around the corner and pales a little when she sees Rex. She goes up and kisses him, and they talk a little. She has great boobs and red hair, just what the doctor ordered. Well, the reason they get these jobs is they look like that. Why would audiences want to look at plain people? Still, it's unreal. And then I see old Jack MacKenzie, in a purple sweater, big belly sagging down, that cowboy movie star. Al Marcus arranges him in the palatial living room with that nice lady Jack danced with on the beach at Rex's party. They sit there in elegant furniture with scripts in their hands. So I grab up the script Rex gave me, it's lying beside a demolished doughnut box. I watch Jack MacKenzie and that woman, Ruth, and I watch the script at the same time.

(FADE IN: INT. BOB AND DAISY'S. MORNING. THEY ARE IN BLACK.)

BOB (Half-whispering) Well, darling, we can always treasure that candlelight supper she had for us last month.
DAISY They were so much in love. It seemed—somehow—that everything would work out at last.
BOB I was a new grandpappy again . . . Al, Christ, I can't say *grandpappy*. Can I have *grandfather*?

Al stepped in. "Whatever you're comfortable with, Jack."

DAISY Jenny was always—always Jenny. Remember when she was in the Peace Corps, in Africa, she wrote us that lovely letter?
BOB Yes, yes, weaving baskets with the women of the village.
DAISY She wondered what she was doing five thousand miles away from home, weaving baskets in a little African village.
BOB She needed Africa. Better to weave baskets in the dark continent than weave them in a—a home for—
DAISY (Cutting in) We never know until it is too late, do we?
BOB (With obvious emotion) This morning I was remembering, all those long years ago—when I had my little girl on my knee, and I read her Dickens's *A Christmas Carol*. And later, those months of her illness, I read her *A Tale of Two Cities*, and I—the last was *David Copperfield*. (Sighs) We never finished *David Copperfield*.
DAISY How she loved her "Pappy." . . . Say, Al, shouldn't we keep *grandpappy* in, if I'm going to say *Pappy* here?

Jack MacKenzie said, "Oh, Christ."
Al said, "No, leave it."
"Al, leave it which way?"
"Let Jack say *grandfather*—you can still say *Pappy*."
Beside me Neil Robinson said, "How about just *Pap*? That's what we serve up!"
Al glanced at him. "Keep going, people."

BOB I suppose—I don't know—I took such comfort in holding my little girl. But perhaps—perhaps I held on to her too tightly. Perhaps her life

189

would have had more—oh, sometimes I wonder if she was looking for a father figure. Like the father who read Dickens to her. But then how did she ever get trapped with that erratic, unstable boy?

Al says, "Stop—three beats on that one, Jack—*erratic, unstable,* one-two-three—*boy!*"
Jack: "Put some anger into it?"
Al: "Yeah. Anger."
Jack: "Check. Erratic, unstable—*boy.*"

(SOUND: FRONT DOOR OPENING AND CLOSING. STEVE ENTERS, OBVIOUSLY VERY INTOXICATED.)

STEVE   Speaking of erratic, unstable *boys*—

I looked up from my script and there was Rex walking across the carpet. He sighed, bored, and said, "Hiccup, hiccup, hiccup."
Al said, "O-*K.*" And then he checked with his "floor manager," made some notes, talked with technicians.
I looked back down at my script.

(JOSH ON THE PHONE—IN LIMBO. BEHIND HIM IS SISTER CATHERINE, ENCOURAGING JOSH, BECAUSE THIS CALL IS MEANT TO THROW BOB OFF THE TRACK COMPLETELY. INTERCUT PHONE CALL.)

JOSH   Dad—hello—it's Josh.
BOB   Hello, son.
JOSH   Just wanted to let you know I found him. He's with me. Our worries were all unfounded.
BOB   Nice try, Josh. But he's here now.
JOSH   Oh Lord, then—you know.
BOB   (Long pause)   Yes, Joshua—now we all know.

But Al Marcus didn't do that scene next. He swung over to the living room on the other side of the studio, not nearly so palatial, and there was a seedy-looking creep standing next to him.
On the set was the good-looking kid and a pretty girl with her hair in curlers and a yellow scarf around her head.
Al said, "OK, kids, step through it quick for me."

DANNY   But why did Amanda have to tell me?
DORIS   It was cruel, it was so cruel. That woman is poison.
DANNY   He was my dad—

190

DORIS He *is* your dad, Danny, he still *is.*
DANNY But—but Uncle Josh—oh my *God.*

Al says, "Johnny, don't say 'Oh my God' like '*Oy* my *gevalt.*' Just breathe it out, a sigh."

Johnny-Danny said, "Oh my Gawwwd."

"Good, good."

DORIS Now we know why—why, after all these years—you couldn't marry Sarah. Because she was—she is your—
DANNY *Oy* my *gevalt,* take two.

Al said, "Right." He turned to his guys. "That's the prologue. Easy, quick. Fade to black." He looks up. "Fairy castle forlorn insert, commercials two and three. Now get going—goddammit, why don't we ever get enough doughnuts? Who takes them all—Florence?"

The seedy guy laughs. "Listen, Al, she's making progress. She bought a comb."

Al says, "But how do we get her to use it?"

I stand there feeling stupid. All these people rush around me, wearing jogging shoes, they go squeak-squeak. Time is money.

Neil Robinson is talking to Rex. Neil says, "She's a girl-woman. A girl-woman. She tries to be educated for me. She went to an estate sale and said she bought a darling piece of 'Lamaze' china. She meant *Limoges.*"

Rex said, "Maybe she meant Lamaze."

Neil said, real quick, like Groucho Marx with an imaginary cigar, "If you can blow glass—you can pant and blow china."

Rex smiled. "Neil, I'm gonna miss you."

A frightened look came over Neil's face, then a little anger. "Just 'cause I cuckolded you nine years ago—"

"When I first heard that word, I thought a cuckold was somebody who held your cuck."

I drifted away and found Al Marcus with a beautiful brunette—Christ, these people are *all* so beautiful. Why didn't I ever get into this business? I could be a cameraman or something. I open my script with the blue cover and flip through it. But I can't find it, they're not doing the next scene. I zip pages back and forth. And then I just watch—the brunette and a statuesque blonde.

THE BRUNETTE   You lie a lot, Amanda. I've known that for years.

So I think, this is Amanda—the one who spilled the beans about Danny not being Steve's son. The actress is yawning into her script, and the two of them speak without any emotion at all. They aren't acting, they're just reading out loud. Bored.

AMANDA   When did you make this momentous discovery, Karen?
KAREN   I think it was when we were in design school together. We had lunch in the cafeteria. After lunch we were coming out, and Alex was on his way in. He said, "Anything good today?" And you said, "Yes, I had the tuna salad sandwich." And then you looked at me, you realized I had watched you eat a roast beef sandwich.
AMANDA   Oh, what a dreadful fib.

Al said, "Ladies, could we get into it just a little bit?"

AMANDA   Oh, what a *dread*-ful fib.
KAREN   But that's the point. You lie without even knowing it. You don't know what the truth is.
AMANDA   Well, I don't know what tricks your memory has played on you, my dear. But I can assure you of one thing. I don't lie about lunch . . .

I've found it now, in my script, and I follow along.

. . . and we know about *your* ability to separate truth from reality.
KAREN   That's a cruel thing to say.
AMANDA   Sometimes the truth is painful.
KAREN   What would you know about truth? Your life is all dreams—dreams of carriage rides over country roads on moonlit nights. The hoofbeats of the horses. Beautiful errands and sacred vigils. . . . Al, come on. I can't say that, I'll never be able to say beautiful errands and sacred *vigils*.

Al said, "Give it a try."
Karen said, "Couldn't I say 'You're mad as a hatter'?"
Behind me, Rex's voice: "Jesus, Linda, you're a high school English teacher. You could say 'beautiful errands' and 'high vigils.' " He walked right onto the set, kissed both women, and lingered over the Amanda one. "Mornin', puss."

192

She said, "Oh—where's David, is he here?"

"Naw, bitch wouldn't let him come."

"Oh, Rex, I'm sorry." Amanda got up, and they went to talk by the stairway, and Al Marcus threw his pencil in the air.

Karen, marooned on the set, said, "What *is* a beautiful errand? *Errands* aren't beautiful."

Neil said, "Only when you go to La Maz, China." He popped a pill.

Al Marcus said, "Get me Roy Peterson, let's do the Buick."

Neil said, "Roy doesn't get the Buick. *I* get the Buick."

Al said, "Neil, if you'd read your script—"

"We wouldn't both have Buicks."

At the other end of the studio there's a disaster, one of the huge ceiling lights falls down, it's like an explosion, glass shattering and sparks flying. Everything went dead-quiet for a second. I turned around, and Neil Robinson had fainted, flat out on the floor.

But he was up pretty quick, heading into the dressing room to lie down. Rex went with him. I went on over to the Buick. Roy Peterson, big guy, I think I've seen him in some Gallo wine commercials, he was talking with Jack MacKenzie. Roy Peterson said, "None of the pros work anymore. I did a 'Charlie's Angels' with Farrah, and all these kids run around wanting new faces. New faces, it's all they talk about. Kids—kids are taking over the industry."

Al pulls a podium thing on wheels down to the car. "All right, folks."

This really was the next scene, according to my script. I go along with one eye on the Xerox, the other on Peterson, who has this woman Jessica with him. It says JESSICA in the script. I figure that means she's Joslin. This actress is about the biggest stunner of them all. Not the best-looking, it's the way she carries herself. Bitch power. She says, "Don't make us get into the car, Al."

"All right, do it."

MIKE   What are you thinking about?

JESSICA Three guesses.

MIKE   Amanda.

(MIKE REACHES OVER AND TAKES JESSICA'S HAND.)

MIKE   Peter couldn't handle her, in the Little Theater, the Penny Players.

JESSICA I thought the problem was that he did, two-three, handle her, two-three, if you know what I mean. Al, do I really have to overstate that? Do I have to add the "know what I mean"?

Al said, "OK."

MIKE Oh, I do know what you mean. Well, Al, wait—if I—
JESSICA Shit, why don't we get some decent writers around here? I could do
better than this. Do I have to do every fucking thing myself?

It upsets me because they had brought out a little girl, six, seven years
old. I don't like foul fucking language in front of little girls.
Al: "Come on, Hillary."
"OK, OK, so I light my cigarette." She strikes a match.
"No, not there. Wait till the pleaser. Don't light a match."
She said, "But Al, I only did it in honor of our hostages in Iran."
Now I am really on her side, I hate her.

By 11:30 everything seemed to be going OK. Al Marcus was like an
orchestra conductor, all over the place, talking to three people at once.
Seemed to me he was the one person really earning his money.
It's like I have fallen into another world. Don't understand anything
at all. And hopelessly lost in the script. I watch the kids making cue cards.
Little demons, putting all the words up there, then washing off the old
cards, hosing them down in the parking lot, sponging them with big pink
sponges. I stood outside and looked at what little you could see of the
distant hills through the smog of downtown L.A. What a life. Crackpot
ego-freaks, spoiled brats. But they were pulling together now, different
from when we arrived, floods of people coming in on all sides. It must cost
a bunch. A spooky fag from wardrobe looked in on the dressing room and
asked Neil Robinson if he was a 42-long. Neil said not even when erect.
And the fag tippy-toed out, he was real stringy and obviously intelligent,
you could see it in his eyes.
I was wondering about all the strange things people do to make a living
when suddenly from behind, woops! I knew who it was immediately. Her
arms turned me around and she gave me one of those smooches, her big
boobs comfy in my chest.
"Hi there, Trip-o."
I was really glad to see her.
"You come up here to see Rex freak out?"
I shrugged. Neil Robinson came out, and Marge introduced us, and
Neil said we'd already met. Marge wanted to know what the matter is,
Neilly. And she held him in her arms, her eyes kind of lively with mine
over his shoulder.
Neil said, "Marge, I can't bear it."

194

"But, hon," she said, "you told me she had perfect pins."

"I'm not the leg man, I am the walrus."

"Oh, Neilly, why won't you ever be good to yourself?"

He turned. "You know this man. Why does everybody know this man?"

"We all love Trip, Neilly."

He scowled, rather gruesome. "Is this Trip necessary?"

"Neil—now—you come and tell me everything about it." She looked back over her shoulder. "Trip—lunch?"

Sure. Doris-Phylis and Mike-Roy and Amanda-whatever all standing around gabbing and making private jokes and smoking cigarettes in the corridor. I went back onto the huge hangar stage. Al was still at work with Jack MacKenzie and Rex. Jack had slips of Kleenex around his collar, he had makeup on, and he was saying, "I objected to this before."

Al said, "Jack—trust me."

"It's not in Bob's character. Strike his own son?"

Daisy-Ruth was saying, "But Jack, you're afraid he might harm *me*. That's the whole point."

Rex was staring at his script.

MacKenzie said, "It's simply not credible."

Rex muttered, "Listen to Ruth, Jack."

MacKenzie, this tremor in his head like palsy. He began to read again. "No *wonder* a decent woman can't live with you."

"*No,*" Rex said. "Not with '*you.*' With 'him.' You say the line to Daisy. Don't you see the truth of that, Jack? It justifies the punch."

MacKenzie sits there staring, trembling.

"You're not talking to me, you're talking to her."

MacKenzie shook his head. "Christ, the mail I'll take on this one."

"Of course, Jack."

The palsy tremor was getting worse. "How can I slug my son when he's down?"

"Please, Jack, let's try it."

They acted it out. Steve-Rex picked up Daisy-Ruth, and stood there holding her, and Jack MacKenzie came across real slow with the stagy punch, slow motion, and he pulled it, and Rex snapped back. Ruth got down out of his arms. She said, "And falling to her knees, oh, Bob, oh, Bob, don't—"

Rex said calmly, "Hell of a right cross for a seventy-year-old man."

"Seventy?" said Jack MacKenzie. "Al, am I really seventy?"

Al said, "Keep it, keep the rhythm."

"Christ, *what* rhythm?" Jack MacKenzie waited, and then he said, "I'm sorry, son—I'll carry that punch to my grave."

Rex said, "I didn't drop her."

"I'll carry that punch to my grave."

Al said, "And we fade out."

I am quite taken aback. Memories on my mind and this in my eyes. Lots of conflicting signals. I mean, Rex told me this story, didn't he? It was about J.O. Ruth is Leela.

Rex said, "You cocksucker. You complete cocksucker."

Daisy-Ruth said, "Rex Hooker, my word."

Jack MacKenzie said, "Exactly. It's like a burst of obscenity. It's not credible, it exceeds the bounds." He was pissed off and old. "These interim writers."

Rex said. "You asshole, you asshole." Very sweetly.

Daisy said, "Rex, maybe Jack is right."

Rex looked at her. "No, little mother."

Al said, "It'll be just fine."

Ruth said, "And we clear on my sobbing?"

Al nodded. He turned and raised his voice. "OK—way late—let's do the blocking for the puppet talk. Come on, Freddy, the car has to be back at three." He is a dynamo.

Jack MacKenzie sits there, his head shaking, his neck swabbed with Kleenex. He digs in his trousers and hands Rex some change. "Will you get me a *Times*?" He smiles. "Haven't even seen the morning line."

The commissary is jammed for lunch. Whole place packed with soldiers, cowboys, doctors, and nurses. The "This Passing Night" contingent has a big table for about twenty. Rex hails me over, steals me a chair. I have gotten as close to a Vegas burger as I can, a big Hawaiian thing with pineapple. Marge is just dandy, having a friendly argument with the guy Roy who plays Mike. I try to make a little casual conversation, I think I remember where I've seen him. I say, "Didn't you play a psycho on 'M*A*S*H' once?"

He says no, he has never done a "M*A*S*H." And clearly resents my asking.

Well, excuse me. From his attitude you'd think I'd asked him if he played the Indian on "Ma and Pa Kettle Go to Shit."

Marge is the great lady here, having a dagger-eye contest with that Jessica-Hillary woman. They all know each other, I guess they've lived with it for years and years.

Jack MacKenzie comes in humming. "Dancing in the Dark." He tremor-pours nondairy creamer into his coffee, which is the only thing on his tray and has been brought to him by a black waiter in a white coat.

Probably what I think is extravagant behavior is normal for them. But I am mixed up between real names and characters' names, I don't quite know who they all are. I say to Mike-Roy, "Are you a good guy or a bad guy?"

A silence—and the whole table bursts out laughing.

Jessica-Hillary burns a hole through my face with her eyes. It makes me topple my Coke. Which produces more laughter.

And then I feel kind of accepted. One of those things you sometimes fall into by complete accident. I am the country bumpkin who tells the truth about the Emperor's new clothes.

Mike-Roy looks at me a second time, his tongue exploring his lower teeth.

Neil says, "And I'm the guy you love to hate."

Hillary says, "You're the man we are obliged to pity."

That frosts it again.

"Wow, you'll excuse me"—and she leans down to Neil, growls at him —"I must go show my boobs to the crew."

She leaves, one beautiful bitch.

In the silence Neil says, "Well, nobody ever denied it."

Rex says, "And no gentleman would ever mention it."

Neil gets all horrified again. "Sex symbols *always* spoil my lunch."

Marge says, "As long as we're all here, let's form a Commission on the Arts."

Neil says, "And Rex gets to be treasurer."

Jack MacKenzie humming "Dancing in the Dark." Barely able to get the coffee cup to his lips. Tremor City. I wonder what his medical problem is.

Daisy-Ruth comes to the table with her diet-plate tray. She says, "I declare, you folks are making such a commotion—the civilized virtues are gone with the wind."

Everybody laughs again. Jack MacKenzie turns to her and says in his big bass voice, "Ah, most radiant lady, Beautiful Lady!"

She says, "Don't you go thinking that kind of talk will get you a bite of my peach."

Another ripple of laughter; I join in myself. But suddenly I get a glimpse of Joslin in my mind's eye. I try to picture her at this table, and I can't do it. Except as a kind of loneliness. It jams my roller coaster, stops it dead. They chatter on, all around me. Rex says the beef stroganoff is so full of salt he can't hardly get spit. He throws his silverware on the plate. Marge suggests a section of lime. I turn and look at her. Marge with her elbows on the table grabbing bites of this and that from other people's plates. You feel like you can count on her, you know she'd be a friend. She is worried about Rex. I raise my glass, shake the ice, check her out again. Yep. Real loud, brassy dame. But I can feel the way she is helping Rex. The love between them.

We walk back to the studio through the parking lot, Rex and Marge in front of me, all casual, arm in arm. I still think he ought to marry her. These two, if the phrase ever had meaning, were clearly meant for each other. It's as plain as the nose on your face. People go through whole lives without that kind of love.

Daisy–Ruth was teasing Bob–Jack MacKenzie. It's hard for me to keep them straight when they have trouble with it themselves, half the time real people and half the time characters.

I said to Neil Robinson, "So you're Josh, Steve's adoptive brother, you screwed Steve's wife, and Danny is your kid."

"Oh," he said, "usually we just get banjos for background, but when Jessica and I created Danny, we had a thousand violins."

Daisy-Ruth said, "We never had banjos."

This seems to me the best line I have heard all day.

Neil says, "Ukeleles. Whatever."

I look up at a huge storehouse.

Neil is right on top of me. "Those are the scene docks. That's where we warehouse the other sets."

"You've got more of them?"

He gives me a funny look. Seems to find it hard to believe that a normal person would not watch their show. He asks me what else I'd like to see. But I don't know enough about it to know what I'd like to see. Which is a pet theory of mine. Some people don't know enough to know what they don't know. Horse-hockey individuals have airtight theories because they are so ignorant. They have no idea of the world as it really is. They make zip-lock sense. Like extremist groups. Don't know enough to know what they don't know. But I tag along. I say to Neil, "This is a big operation."

He says, "Our ad revenues are seven hundred thousand dollars a week."

That will always be a rather large figure for me to get my mind around. So I guess I'll just ask him. "How much do you make?"

Neil Robinson says, "Rex picked it up when the old lady died. I saw him do it. I got left in the cold, you don't see me making five."

"Five?"

"At least five, maybe six. He's such a bitch with money."

"Oh, my. Five hundred a week."

Neil thinks that's very funny, he looks at me like I'm in kindergarten.
And then I get it. Five thousand. A week.

I see Charley Darling, I see people who work their hearts out. Five thousand a week.

"We support," Neil says, "a lot of classy prime-time stuff. We're network's bread and butter. And every day, millions of people out there depend on us."

I think of myself. I think of the Chief in Laguna. It's like I have made a mistake, flunked out once again.

Neil Robinson tells me about contracts, how they paid you for a certain number of shows in one twenty-six-week segment. If they don't use you, you can get paid anyway.

I calculate the car I could buy.

"Rex learned, very early, how to placate the bureaucrats." Neil has a snarl on his face. "He's a company man. Although nobody denies his talent." He turns. "Let me show you some tech stuff."

I follow him down a long corridor and we go upstairs. He bangs on a heavy door. Inside it's like the control tower at an airport. All this sophisticated electronic gadgetry from floor to ceiling. One little guy in there. Mickey Davis. We shake hands. He looks like a bum, poorly dressed, unshaven. Neil says, "Mickey is a genius. Ask him anything."

When Mickey Davis talks, all the bum disappears. Probably is a genius. He and Neil have a little discussion about dollying and zooming. I don't follow. Mickey Davis sees I'm confused and explains to me how dollying is better because it gives you *depth*. Objects fly by on the edge of the screen instead of just the picture getting smaller. It's dimension. He says to watch for it on shows, when they move in for a close-up, watch whether it's just the picture getting smaller or whether you feel drawn into it. Watch the edges of the picture. I say I will. He talks about airplanes, and computers, and Orson Welles. Sleepy little bum who knows everything. He doesn't much like Neil.

He's got four monitors, and he works them like an electronic painter. The primary colors are red, blue, and yellow. Photographic primaries are magenta, cyan, and yellow. He spells *cyan* to me. Then he explains the difference between transmitted light and reflected light. And something about electron beams. I feel like a dunce, and I thank him.

In the hall Neil says, "So. What else?"
I don't know.
A freaky-looking woman comes around the corner, her hair a rat's nest,

199

rings on all her fingers, her face so made up she looks like a witch. "Neil!
Al's going crazy. Where have you been?"

"Shit, I'm in trouble." Neil Robinson runs downstairs with the witch.
I follow, and when I get to the stage Al Marcus is chewing Neil out. Beside
the Buick. Neil looks like a naughty little boy. Al whirls around. "All right,
now where has Hillary gone to? Come on, people, this is *dress*. OK, now,
OK, look, camera two, look at this—" and he's talking to the black
cameraman, who nods.

Right behind me: "So, Trip, how's it going?"

I turn. There's Rex in a tuxedo. He pulls me toward the nightclub set.
I whisper, "Now I know why you're weird."

He's got a big smile on his face. "Eggs-actly."

"Neil seems to be at the end of his rope."

"Well, he dies on New Year's Eve."

"But then Danny loses his father."

"Yep. Loses two fathers in one month. As they say, holidays are the
hardest times."

"Why did Amanda tell?"

"Because that's the last connection. Ruins all the leverage between
Steve and Jessica."

"Because—uh—because they still love each other and she's jealous?"

"No, Trip, Jessica just wants the money."

"Oh."

"That's why she's having me committed."

"Huh?"

"Hi, guys." I turn around, and it's Marge Stivers, except she's a nun.
In dark blue with a pink-white collar at her throat and a hood with a
pink-white border. A crucifix. She sighs, looking at me. "Shit, it's only
temporary."

"Yeah," Rex whispers, "she's trying to kick the habit."

She kicks him instead.

I don't get this, I'm stunned.

Marge says to Rex, "Ready to flip out, hon?"

What a thing to do to her. I remember her drunk on her ass out at her
farm. Screaming at me. I remember her singing "Let It Be" at J.O.'s
funeral.

Rex crooks his finger. He tippy-toes out. Marge grabs my hand, and we
follow him into the corridor, and the big steel door swings shut. Rex is
laughing, pointing his finger at me. He says, "Oh—Trip—your face!"

I look at Marge, and she looks at me. She's smiling. I look her up and
down, from toe to, uh, hood.

"He's still doing it!" Rex really laughing.

Marge smiling, glad this is happening.

I say, "But—but I thought you were—you were married—"

"It didn't pan out."

"Come on," I say. "What happened?"

Rex wiping his eyes. "Tell him, Good Sister Kate."

Marge says, "I comfort myself by thinking about all the rabbits that didn't die."

Amanda walks by, in bra, panties, and high-heeled shoes. Mumbling to herself, coughing a real deep hack, she's not especially steady.

Rex and Marge watch her go into the can and slam the door. They exchange glances. Rex looks at me. "Marge and I have no sympathy whatever for anyone with a drinking problem."

Marge says, "Goddammit, I wanted to play golf tonight, and we're already an hour late."

Rex says, "We're not going to get the Buick back on time."

I say, "Danny's not your son?"

Rex says, "We've been getting mail for years. One guy even sent me a photograph some bugger took on Maui—of me and Marge—'member, babe?"

The nun looks at him.

" 'Beware. Your son is not your son. Your brother is his father. I see you are honeymooning with your new wife. But beware. What Jessica and Joshua may do with Danny. You will lose him forever.' I get letters all the time, Trip, marked 'Private!' See, everybody on the show and in the audience knew Danny wasn't my son. Everybody but me. And all the time the ratings go up, uppity, up. When and how is Dr. Kelly going to discover the terrible secret?"

Al Marcus comes out the door with that creep behind him. "Ready, Rex." Then he's up to the control room. He's the only person around here who never takes a break. Behind him come Hillary and Neil, yelling at each other. Neil says, "It was a mechanical problem. The light was bouncing off the goddamn car mirror."

"Horseshit," she says, "you were a thousand miles away."

"Was not, was not," just like a child.

Hillary stomps down the hall.

Neil looks at Rex. Neil says, "Actually, I wasn't a thousand light miles away. My mind was nearby in Malibu. And there *was* a light problem. I couldn't see the cards."

I thought he said he didn't need the cards.

Neil looks at me. "It's the nature of the beast." And he walks away.

201

Beats me. I wonder what these people do when they go home. Actually, I'd rather not think about it. I turn around and Dr. Kelly is necking with a nun. Down our corridor, here comes a policeman. In makeup.

It's Rex's big scene. In that nightclub. Red walls, chandeliers, half a dozen tables, a bar, and a little stage. Very elaborate, with strobe lights and mirrors, they check them out to make sure they're working, blue and green and yellow and red—what Mickey Davis showed me. They shut it down when Al Marcus yells at 'em. Rex has whipped into a smoking jacket at the piano, and he sings:

> Jessie, you are the world to me,
> And that's what's wrong,
> But you are my song.

Then he picks up a big bottle of Jack Daniels and says "Chug-a-lug-a-lugga," and then throws his head into his arms and says, "Boo-a-hoo-a-hoo-a." All the cameras are there. Al's got his wheely podium. Floor manager is taking notes.

Rex says, "Now I understand. Now I understand. Oh, physician, heal thyself." He absently plays the piano. And then he really plays it, "Danny Boy," and sings:

> It's I'll be there—
> in sunshine or in sha-a-dow—
> Oh Danny Boy, Oh Danny Boy
> I love you so.

Al says, "OK on the tease. The break. And we come back."

STEVE   You must come home for Christmas, Jessie. We owe it to Danny. We owe it to ourselves. I cannot bear Christmas alone, belovedest. (Drinks) Belovedest—we first started calling each other that when I was interning, and we had that little top-floor hideaway on Bleecker Street. We were happy. We were so happy. You were going to be a great dancer. We were alive, and young, and the whole world was just—just indescribably delicious.

Al: "Rex, uh, indescribably delicious—"
Rex: "Sorry, Al. I'll do it. Let Mike come on."
Al: "OK, Mike?"

MIKE   Well, Dr. Kelly, some people are pretty worried about you.

STEVE   I'm pretty worried about me myself.

MIKE   A little odd, isn't it? On a Sunday morning? To be in a nightclub?

STEVE   It's my nightclub, I own it.

MIKE   I understand you've been under considerable stress. Your sister died last
         week?

STEVE   (To the bottle)   And my son died last night.

MIKE   Excuse me?

STEVE   Nothing. Nothing.

MIKE   Been drinking pretty heavily, have you?

STEVE   I have been spilling more than drinking.

MIKE   How did this happen?

STEVE   Poor hand-to-mouth coordination.

MIKE   No, Dr. Kelly, I mean the drinking.

The hairs on the back of my neck are coming up. This is it, this is when
I took Rex to Hans Brandsma on Labor Day. This is when I first saw him
again, after twenty years. Oh, this is just swell.

STEVE   Just forget it. As you say, I've been under a lot of stress lately. And
         depression.

MIKE   It won't help to treat depression with a depressant.

STEVE   Thanks. Say, what do you mean by coming in here?

MIKE   Your ex-wife called me. She thought you were in danger.

STEVE   Oh, she did? Listen, I'll take care of— (Dawning on him) Who called
         you?

MIKE   Your ex-wife.

STEVE   Where—where is she?

MIKE   She didn't say. I assumed—

STEVE   No assumptions. All my one-two assumptions have been torn apart this
         week. Where is she?

MIKE   She didn't say.

SISTER CATHERINE   (Entering)   She's right here.

STEVE   Oh—oh—oh.

WE CLOSE IN ON CATHERINE'S FACE, FADE.

They discuss it, Al and Roy and Rex and Marge, and I retreat. I walk over
to the palatial living room and have a cigarette. It says NO SMOKING, but
everybody is smoking. I am upset, trying to figure this out. Did he put it in
after—or did he know it was coming? On Labor Day? David said the
"Bible" is six months in advance. So he knew. Except the actors don't

203

know. But he is the producer. And then, when Jack MacKenzie was supposed to slug him, and MacKenzie objected. I remember Rex telling me that story, on the driveway. This whole thing seems stupid and heartbreaking and a bad joke. Or insane. I stamp my cigarette to death. And go back.

A nice girl was standing there with Al. I could get into that. She clicked off her stopwatch. Al talked to Roy and Rex. Marge was sitting there in her nun's clothes, she let out one of her terrific belches. I love the way she does that, kind of to remind us we're all subject to planetary forces.

Beside me, Hillary grabbed my arm. "Who are you?"

I looked at her. Hillary-Jessica-Joslin. I said, "A friend of the family." She said, "Sure." She looked at me. "Who are you?"

"I went to high school with Rex."

She said, "Bullshit."

CATHERINE   Steve, you've cut yourself rather badly. You said you were going to kill yourself.
STEVE   No, no, just kill that—that faker in the mirror. (Turns to the mirror) Look.
CATHERINE   No, Steve, *you* look.

(STEVE LOOKS. CLOSE SHOT OF HIS REFLECTION. THEN STEVE PICKS UP BOTTLE. THROWS IT INTO MIRROR. GLASS SHATTERS.)

Only Rex doesn't do that. This is rehearsal.

Al Marcus says, "Right, right. Murray's spending enough on this one. You do it, Steve, and we cut to the Buick, do the tease, and then we continue. All right, people, keep it down. No, no, don't use the champagne until we tape. Give him a Fresca or something.

STEVE   I remember when I was taking Danny to a Boy Scout Jamboree. There was an old Burma Shave ad beside the road—you remember those little red signs every fifty feet? These signs said:
> Don't Lose Your Head
> To Save a Minute
> You Need Your Head
> Your Brains Are in It.
CATHERINE   Oh, Steve.
STEVE   Burma Shave.
CATHERINE   You must not let this terrible discovery break your spirit. Al, can I just say, "Break you"?
AL   Sure, Marge.

STEVE For all those years, as she remembers them, it was me doing the talking. But I wasn't. No, I was listening. I sat and listened. That's the real reason I wouldn't allow TV in the house. Jessica was my TV. I was hooked on her. She was my TV, my movies, my night at the opera— she was my—my invitation to the dance.

CATHERINE If I ever had any doubts, they are resolved now.

STEVE (Drinking) What the hell does that mean?

CATHERINE Look who's coming through the door.

(CAMERA, ON JESSICA, HER FACE. CROSSCUT, ALL THREE. STEVE PLAYING DANNY BOY ON THE PIANO.)

Al says, "Just fine. Just fine. Rex, that's lovely, 'my invitation to the dance.' I'd like a long three-beat on that. Very nice."

Hillary said, "I won't dance—don't ask me." She began to sing it.

Rex said, "Good—OK, *good*—say it flat." He stood up at the piano. "Can we have that, Al?"

Marge Stivers, nun, was staring at Steve-Rex. She scratched her armpit, really dug in at it. "I don't know, hon."

Rex said, "No—do a voice-over. Oh, eerie, Al. How about that? Just Jessica's face, and that voice-over, "I won't dance—don't ask me. I won't dance—don't ask me."

Rex was really excited.

Al Marcus looked at his podium, looked at them.

"Come on, Al—it works."

Al shook his head.

Rex said, "Amanda walked out of that house alone. Peter finally saw it, Peter finally understood—he saw the woman as—as *florid*. Saw the prima donna. Al, you got to go with that."

Al Marcus looked at Rex. Al still the executive, doesn't want to lose his rhythm.

"Al, listen to me—it's Jessica, it fits—mental disarray, her life as a starring vehicle—we've absolutely got to do this. 'I won't dance, don't ask me. I won't dance, don't ask me.' " Rex turns. "Hillary, don't you buy it?"

Jessica-Hillary says, "Yes." Looking at Rex. Her eyes like a cash register.

Al said, "Well." He had already decided, and was writing in his script. His gray head went up and down.

Hillary looked across the stage. "You're an asshole, Hooker, but you're not ungenerous."

"And, granola-tits, kisses to you." Rex was holding himself in, it was only rehearsal. I thought he had something on his mind, he looked at me every now and then.

They test the strobe lights again, all of them going round and round splashing color on everyone's faces.

I wonder about Steve-Rex being committed to a mental institution. I just cannot seem to put my feet on solid ground. If Sheila were here, I'd stand back and let her go for an extra game, pinball herself to death on show biz.

Al Marcus gives us five minutes. He's getting this new line in with the "v.o." and the "fade." And then Rex is jumping on him. "Al—Al, let me —when she enters—could I?, after Marge makes her exit, I'll grab Hillary, and we will dance, a dance-rape, I'll *make* her dance."

Al looks at him. "No way."

"Aw, come on—"

"No way, Rex."

"All right, I'll dance around her. You can catch it on camera three, come on—"

"Too frenetic, Rex. Now you've had one bright idea, don't—"

"Nobody never lets me have no *fun.*" Rex stands there. "You're right, it is too frenetic."

Rex comes over to me, whispers, "I'll run it right by Olivia Katz on Monday. Livy won't know. Right, Trip?"

Right.

"Have her breathless in my arms, right?"

Right.

He looks at me. "You don't have an opinion, do you?"

Right.

Al calls them. "OK, let's go straight through now, I want this done. Jessica, Steve, Catherine."

They come back.

CATHERINE   I have to be going.
STEVE (Looking at Jessica)   What is this?
CATHERINE (To him)   Be careful, Steve.
JESSICA (Moving into shot)   Hello, Catherine.
CATHERINE   Jessica.
JESSICA   And what, may I ask, brings you—

   (JESSICA SEES, FROM CATHERINE'S EYES, SHE BETTER NOT PUSH IT; SHE
   FALLS SILENT.)

STEVE (Drunkenly) Isn't it nice that we could all be together again?
CATHERINE Good-bye.

(CATHERINE STARTS OUT, WE TRAIL HER, AND THEN WE SEE WHAT SHE SEES
—THE POLICEMAN. TRAILING SHOT, THEN POLICEMAN'S FACE.)

CATHERINE Oh.

(ALARMED, SHE TURNS, STARTS TO SPEAK, THEN EXITS.)

Al Marcus: "Cut. Marge, it's flat. We've got to give you some business.
Pep up that exit."

Marge comes back from behind the set. She says, "When in doubt, go
to the faucets."

Al says, "Right. No. No, she wouldn't, not at this point."

Marge, "I could take his gun."

Al: "Come on, honey, I'm thinking."

"How about I flash him?" She starts to lift up her skirt.

Al's rattling a pencil on his wheely podium, it's like he's playing a snare
drum. "If you crossed yourself—"

"Al!" Marge wails.

"Dear, I'm thinking . . . I got it. We need another shot. Camera three.
Look—" and he takes the third camera and pulls it around. A big electrical
cord gets all fouled up. "We dolly in to the piano—come here, Harry.
. . . look, Marge, you'll come all the way out, follow me, darling, to the
ladies' room, and you'll stop—get that palm tree out of there—no, leave
it, everybody knows that fern. You'll get out to here"—he puts his foot
down, and his floor manager takes a little yellow strip of tape off his leg
and tapes it to the floor. He's been running around all day with those
yellow strips, like feathers, on his pants. "And you'll stop right here,
Marge, sigh, break down, and pray—come on, for *me*—"

Marge does it, and it looks pretty good. Although you can see she
doesn't exactly have her heart in it. First she has her fingers straight out,
flat, and then she clutches them all together. She bites her knuckle, chews
on it, her head rolling to the side.

"Perfect. That's perfect," Al says. "That's the pepper. And then *bang*
—right back into the shot with Steve and Jessica. Steve—" Al moves
through the set. "Rex, count six and then just call, 'Kate!' OK?"

"OK."

"That's it, that's it." Al is fussing with the floor manager and yelling
to the booth, "You got this, you got this change?"

They're really cooking now.

Al says, "Now then, up to close-out. Go."

STEVE   I will not allow you anywhere near your father's money. That money is for the new hospital wing—he wanted it for the clinic, the psychiatric institute.
JESSICA   Not if you're incompetent.
STEVE   Incompetent?
JESSICA   Mentally, one-two, and emotionally, one-two, incompetent.
STEVE   Nonsense. I'm drunk. But maybe so. I've got a bad case, after all this, of loving you.
JESSICA   I'm not your disease.
STEVE   We'll see. I think you are my disease.

And then, wham, he slapped her, not really, he just explodes out of his place there at the piano. She shrieks. The cop comes forward, it's the stupidest uniform, there are six different things wrong with it—

JESSICA   Officer Stanley—help—he's going *crazy*.

(REX THRASHES ABOUT, THE COP SUBDUES HIM, JESSICA RUNS OUT OF THE PICTURE.)

Al says, "OK, OK—quick cut to commercials eleven and twelve, two thirty-eight, and then back to the big one—"
Rex sits there and plays the piano.

> "Jessie, you are the world to me,
> and you know what that does,
> you should be picked up by the fuzz—"

Suddenly people all around the set laugh. Even I chuckle. Fuzz. I can see Hillary hanging by her pussy, and then I ask myself: What am I laughing at? I am the fuzz.

STEVE   I know, I know. You're here to give protection.
COP   There's an ambulance outside.
STEVE   What? No. But when a patient's judgment is seriously impaired by illness, he may be admitted and retained against his will. I know the law. But I'm impaired by booze. I'm getting drunk in my own club. I'm going—

(COP TOUCHES HIS GUN.)

208

STEVE Oh no. Oh no, I'll stay right here. No gunplay. I don't know what bill
       of goods she's sold you—
COP You're drunk, pal.
STEVE But she can't—she can't put my mind behind bars.

Christ, it gives me the willies to watch this. It scares me, it makes me
ill. I think back to Labor Day. All that ruckus. How seriously it affected
me, how spooked I was, and how sad.

STEVE Don't—please, it would be a crime. Don't let Jessica put my mind
       behind bars.
COP Seems to me she wants to save your life.
STEVE She's done everything she can to destroy it. But she can't put my mind
       behind bars. Please, Officer—please *help* me.
COP I follow orders.
STEVE You can't drag a man out of his own place. I mean, if I were driving a
       car, or a public nuisance, but I'm not—I'm—

I'm very, very upset. And then, without the slightest hint that it's
coming, right when Rex starts to play "Danny Boy," I let out this huge
sneeze.
   Everybody stops and looks at me.
   I am embarrassed as hell. I go outside with my hanky, as if I've got to
blow my nose.
   I walk around the parking lot. I feel like an impressionable little kid.
I lean against a blue Porsche.
   I see Rex come out. He walks up to me. "So."
   I glance at him; beats me.
   Rex says, "Dig that—Officer Stanley?"
   I look at him.
   "Stanley and Oliver. Stan and Ollie. Laurel and Hardy?"
   I groan. I say the word *groan.*
   "Precisely."
   Rex lights a cigarette.
   Those kids with the cue cards work like illegal aliens, sponging and
scrubbing.
   Marge the nun comes out. "They're ready," she announces.
   Rex goes inside.
   I looked at her in that nun costume.
   She said, "What is it, Trip?"

I shook my head.

She said, "He told you, didn't he?"

I looked at her.

"It's the breakthrough they've been hoping for—for so many years."

"It is?"

"Like looking for a needle in a haystack—how often we've heard that."

I stand there.

"It's no bigger than a pinpoint. A tumor right at the base of the brain. The doctors want to operate immediately."

Excuse me?

Marge took a cigarette. "Leela's been like a second mother to me. She —you never saw her in her glory days, before this hit her."

Leela?

"Wouldn't it be something? Like magic? A miracle? She was more a mother to me than my own mother."

What? I thought she had a cold, or flu, or pneumonia.

"I have even called her 'Mother,' for years." Marge stood there, Marge Stivers, Sister Catherine. "She's so precious, and if he lost her—too—"

I nod my head; inside it's going round and round.

Marge is wearing low black heels, like a nun would. She says, "I remember when we told Leela that Steve and Catherine—"

I am paying attention, real close.

"She was so joyful—she said, 'You are going to marry?'"

Ah—

"She said, 'It was always my hope.'" Marge standing there. "'It was always my hope.' And now they've found the needle in the haystack."

I'm trying to give her the look she wants.

"She—Leela is a little blue bird. A little blue bird." Marge picks at her sleeve. "He's so scared—you have to help him, Trip—he is so—scared."

It was, I thought, about the most intimate thing I'd ever heard. I looked at her. She's a big woman, physically large, I can imagine her at the Shadow Mountain Club, playing backgammon with the Gabor sisters. Or out feeding horses, kicking up her boots, carrying buckets of oats.

My kind of nun.

Rex bolts out the door. "Jack's not handling it—he's off, he's off. He can't read the lines."

I stand there.

Rex looks at Marge, at me. We look at him.

"Babe," he whispers to her.

Marge looks at him, and at me, and then she slowly goes in.

He whispers to me, "We base the whole thing on the assumption that she is never—Marge is never in the dark."

Jack MacKenzie comes out and says, "Rex? Rex?"

Rex says, "It's OK, Jack."

Jack MacKenzie, my cowboy here, says, "I clipped you good." His belly hanging there. Tremor.

Leela is old, too. She can't stand surgery—she'll die.

Jack MacKenzie has a Salem. "I'm tired of being Good Old Dad. All this patient understanding." He turns to me. "So you're a police officer? I hit my son, square on the jaw—take me away." It's not the usual tremor, it's like he's remembering when he was a lion.

He says, "We relax the curtain of rage—we draw the veil of grief." And then the tremor returns.

"Sometimes I wonder what I have lived for." And he hums, Jack MacKenzie, like Theodore, hummmmmm, an old man.

Dancing in the dark.

So now it's the "taping." This is what they put on the air, what millions of people will watch. The seminormal girl, Livy, who has the stopwatch, she told me the best place to see this is in "the booth," so I go on up there. Probably just my imagination, but I thought she looked at me a time or two. I couldn't see if she had a wedding band on. I imagine us at a little restaurant with a checkerboard tablecloth and red wine and some linguini and candles. A relationship would develop. She'd come to Laguna on weekends. I was bopping along, making up my own little Bible. She's thirty-five, maybe. Classy. Undoubtedly has done things I can only dream about. It'd never work out.

The extras looked forlorn. Like used furniture. They sat around in drab clothes, not even talking to each other. A teenaged boy, a teenaged girl, a middle-aged man, a real skinny, homely blonde. They were in a scene at "Kelly's." The kids, I suppose, could be wanting to break into the business, but I couldn't figure out the middle-aged man. How could you just sit there all afternoon?

And then a little guy with a real ugly trimmed beard and a white turtle-neck sweater came into the booth and started yelling at everybody. It's the producer Neil Robinson hates, Murray. Yelling about how Daisy broke a tureen he paid $300 for, and Livy said, "There's no ladle—if you paid three hundred for it without a ladle, you deserve to get burned." And that makes me like Livy again. Murray said they'd told him "upstairs" they needed the studio for a Big Event, at five sharp, and so why is everybody an hour and a half late? It's three o'clock now, they already have to pay an extra day on the Buick. Unpleasant little dink. He whines, "That scene's flat, Al, no punch at all. How can you let Max get away with this loafing around? I really need this trouble." Everybody in the booth hates him. And then a real kind grandfatherly guy, fat, who hasn't said a word, gets me a sort of highchair so I can see over everybody and watch the monitors. Silent as a clam he goes back and sits in his own chair, and it says MAX HERZOG on the back. I remember from my blue script that he's the head guy. He picks up a phone and talks softly, and then says to Al Marcus, "It's all right, we have the stage until five-thirty." In this real quiet kindly voice. He looks over at me and says, "Can you see all right, son?" I check him out during the taping. He's so intent on the monitors, all caught up in the story. He looks like a combination of the Godfather and an overweight little boy at a magic show. His hands are big and strong, he has hairy wrists. I think he is a man you would not cross. A gentleman, but look out.

Max Herzog said, "Al, Amanda's champagne looks like beer."

Al shouted through his microphone, "What's the matter with the champagne, why has it got a head on it?"

A voice piped into the control room, "Al, it's the lights—the lights are heating it up."

Al, back through the microphone, "Well, get it out of there, looks terrible. And get Amanda's chair back on the mark. Floyd, I give a shit about the silverware, leave it alone."

It's all different on the screen, on the monitors. The people don't look the same. They mellow out and their facial features blend in and don't look so sharp. Their eyes are bigger, I guess it's the makeup and the lights. They look even more handsome. More natural and calm. They also act better. I guess they saved the real acting for the tape, that's natural, you don't want to shoot your wad in rehearsal. Now it all flows together, the language is cleaned up, it's a story. Real live make-believe.

You'd never suspect that Neil Robinson is the wreck he is. Not for a minute. On screen Neil Robinson is a fine fellow.

JOSH   I don't know, after all these years—I can still remember that first night.
JESSICA   We mustn't dwell on the past.
JOSH   So, m'dear, we are told. But it doesn't seem like the past anymore. Not this week.
JESSICA   I can still see you coming toward me, taking the drink out of my hand—
JOSH   It was raining. Big buckets of rain.
JESSICA   Putting the glass down and—and taking me in your arms.
JOSH   Pain brings people together.

212

JESSICA And love keeps them together.
JOSH It was wrong. It was very wrong.

The dialogue looked awfully corny to me when I read it, but now it doesn't matter somehow. It's just them on the little screen, driving along in that Buick. Car lights and the sound of trucks going by—how do they do that?—just two people who have known each other a long time, and have a sordid history, but are responding to an emergency. I get a real kick out of it. The upcoming shot is on another monitor, so you can watch what's going on now, and what will happen in just a second. Al Marcus was going to town, he'd snap his fingers—*click*—the other camera would come up—and then *click*—back to the first one—and then *click*—the second. He had it all timed to perfection.

Josh-Neil's eyes, you really would believe he was driving a car. Even though I knew it was just that Buick sitting out there absolutely still, not fifty feet away. Jessica and Josh did the whole scene real well, the floor manager said "Clear," and Al ran out onto the set. He came back in and wanted to do one part of it again, but Murray said, "Shit, no, we'll loop it, Al, I can't afford these." Al said into his microphone, "OK, we'll catch it wild, thank you, folks. Move to Amanda and Karen." I slipped out for a cigarette. The red light was on over the big door to the stage, DO NOT ENTER, PROGRAM IN PROGRESS. I was just smoking beside a plant when Neil Robinson walked by.

I said. "You were real good."

"It's crap," he said. "Absolute crap."

I look at his face, think how weird it is, the difference between the face on the screen and this face. You'd know it was the same person, but it's like the difference between fingerprints and fingerprints that have been burned off. I go back in. It's four o'clock—these people have been working for ten hours. Now they're doing Rex and Marge, and Rex looks terrible—which is the way he is supposed to look—but it's the eyes. You're not comfortable with those eyes. They're unearthly, the blue eyes I saw on Labor Day. But Marge, even in that nun suit, my, she lights up for the camera.

CATHERINE Steve, you've cut yourself. You're going to kill yourself.
STEVE No, kill that—that faker in the mirror. Look.
CATHERINE No, Steve, *you* look.

Al Marcus is going *bam! bam!* with his hands and *click! click!* snapping his fingers, the cameras change on the monitor from Steve Kelly standing there and Steve Kelly in the mirror. All the strobe lights kicking away. Impressive. A real nightmare. *Click!* Steve, and *click!* Steve's reflection —except it's even more confused in the control room because I am watching both monitors, the shot that's on and the shot that's coming. Rex picks up the bottle and throws it into the mirror and the glass shatters, this huge explosion of glass, and Al Marcus goes nuts.

The voice comes over, "Clear."

Al and the whole control room are quite ecstatic. The ratty-haired wardrobe lady says, "Jesus!" in a whisper. I look at Livy, who has her arm around Al Marcus. Max Herzog with a small smile on his face. Murray said, "I can't believe it, Al. I just knew we'd have to do it twice. Hot potatas."

On a monitor Marge is kissing Rex. Rex is pleased with himself, like he just threw a no-hitter. I think I really ought to alert Hans Brandsma to this. Not to mention Joslin.

That brings me down. I wonder if Joslin watches. I think about it and a big hole opens up. And Leela? Leela, the needle in the haystack, she has a pinpoint tumor at the base of her brain?

It seems cold in here. They've got air conditioning, but you can't hear any motors or fans.

A lot of people, cast and crew, come out onto the stage and into the booth. To watch Steve Kelly crack up. For several years he has been the Rock of Gibraltar. And everybody knew that his son was not his own. Al is going *bam-bam click-click*. Rex lets out the stops and does the Burma Shave part

Don't Lose Your Head
To Save a Minute
You Need Your Head,
Your Brains Are in It—

Except it's different now. You can really feel a father and son driving along and shouting it out together. You feel the warmth. Marge is glowing for the camera. I remember the stuff she wrote in his high school yearbook. She says, "You must not—Steve, you must not let this terrible discovery break you," she says it real slow, but not draggy, just sad. "I have enough guilt to last me the rest of my life." Al speaks through the microphone to his floor manager. I watch Rex on the monitor that shows the next shot. I'm afraid there's real bourbon in that Jack Daniels bottle. I wonder if Jack Daniels gets a kickback for it, or if they pay to display the label on TV.

STEVE She is the one who is aggressive. Not me. And she doesn't understand
       that.
CATHERINE Yes she does, Steve—Jessica always knows what she is doing.
STEVE But she is trying to kill in herself the thing I love most in her.

Out there Rex says it real low, real drunkenly, and in here Al goes *click*,
and the camera moves in on Marge. Goddamn, real tears, you just feel
this Nun-Woman-Wife in Anguish. I'll bet people at home get tears in
their eyes when they see that. I almost do, and I'm in the booth.

STEVE For all those years—as Jessica remembers them—I did the talking. But
       I didn't. I did the listening. I suppose that's why I wouldn't allow
       television in the house. Jessica was my television. I was hooked on her.
       She was my TV, she was my movies, she was my night at the opera—
       oh, Kate—she was my invitation to the dance.
CATHERINE And where did that—you always speak as if I left you—but where
       did you think that left me?
STEVE I know. Oh my God, how I know. What you and I had, and have, is
       Love. What Jessie and I had, and have, is—addiction.

Al Marcus says, "What the fuck is he doing? That's not it."
Murray moving around. "It's right—it's all right."

CATHERINE Look who's coming through the door.

(CAMERA ON JESSICA'S FACE.)

STEVE What? Who's coming? Oh, oh—

Rex started to play "Danny Boy" on the piano, and we heard "Clear,"
and then Al ran onto the set. We could watch it in the control room, Rex
saying, "Al, the lines here are *wrong*. Listen to me, Al."
Murray says to us, "He's right. Rex is right."
Al comes running back in, spraying pencils. "He's right."
People laugh.
Al wants to know what's funny.
They say that that's what Murray said.
Al smiles, can't be bothered, he wants to do the v.o., "I won't dance,
don't ask me." And we do that.
The final scene with Steve and Jessica. The little bit with Sister Cathe-
rine, Marge, going to the lady's room to pray; her face is just perfect
sadness. I think about where the sadness comes from, and how much

Marge loves Rex, and Leela, and a needle in a haystack. I watch the monitors, and of course there's none of that my little pickle-warmer or an eggroll and a blow job. It's a real scene. Nothing about being picked up by the fuzz. Just Rex in his strong singing voice:

> Jesss-eee,
> You are the world to me,
> And that's what's wrong,
> But you are my song.

The strobe lights play around—the "cyan," as I have learned to call it, the yellow—this is really a nervous breakdown. Very effective, very lonesome. Big splashes of color wash over Rex's face. That stupid policeman wearing a uniform that wouldn't pass inspection in the Uruguay National Guard. Steve Kelly, psychiatrist, out of his mind, sitting at the piano, not wanting gunplay or argument. Officer Stanley—that bugs me, Stan and Ollie—standing next to him. Al going *clickity-click bam-bam*. Rex is supposed to go into this routine about how Jessica just wants the money, but now he suddenly comes out with something else. Nobody's ever heard it before. The control room tenses up, the cameras are rolling. Neil Robinson bops in and stands beside my highchair. On the idle camera I see Mike-Roy and Jack MacKenzie and Ruth at the side of the set. Quite a crowd.

STEVE You're serving her. You're helping this woman to put my mind behind bars. You want to know what she did to me, Officer Stanley?

Which was all in the script. But then—shit, then—

STEVE I came back to the house. Hoping our marriage could be saved, anticipating a quiet dinner. I opened the door—and—and what a shock—Jessica had moved out. She took the TV set. I was so hurt. You know what she left me, Officer? One fork, one spoon, one knife, one plate, one cup, one saucer, some ice cream in the freezer, one bath towel, one sheet, one blanket, one pillow, one roll of toilet paper, one broken can opener, one alarm clock. She took the shower curtain.

Al said, "What—what?"
Livy: "Oh, God—oh my God."
I may faint.

216

STEVE   Put my mind behind bars? I can't bear her cruelty any longer. One fork, one spoon, one knife, one plate, one cup, one saucer, some ice cream in the freezer, one towel, one bedsheet, one blanket, one pillow, one roll of toilet paper, one alarm clock. She took the shower curtain. I lived there for a year, I bought some odds and ends. I used to go back and sit there. And now she has taken the one—the one thing that's kept me alive.

> Oh Danny Boy,
> Oh Danny Boy—I love you so.

Rex sat there, his hands resting on the piano keys, weeping.

The floor manager said, "Clear."

Al Marcus said, "God in heaven."

Livy looked at her watch. "And the bastard brought it in five seconds early. We can make it up on the crawl."

Al on his headset: "Earth to Rex—Earth to Rex—?"

People around the set are applauding.

Rex stood up, beside the piano, tears on his cheeks. The applause kept going.

I think I have never been so shocked. Never in my life.

Al said, "Earth to Rex—beautiful, baby, just beautiful, that's a wrap, that is one goddamn wrap."

And Al Marcus ran out, through the applause, and gave Rex a big hug.

Murray said, "Un-be-*liev*-able."

Neil Robinson was crying. Jesus, everybody does go to faucets.

We were in Medjuhl when I told him. I remember how he brightened up and asked me to say it again. And being a fool, I did.

On the monitor I could see people crowding around him.

Marge the nun.

He has planned this for a long time.

What an asshole. I have been *used*.

It was sort of spectacular.

It's my privacy.

Max Herzog said softly, "And she took the shower curtain. Such a life." With that faint smile on his big old weathered face.

Hillary, of course, was pissed off. Just storming. "Jessica wouldn't *do* that. Christ, what is this ad-lib shit? Nothing—nothing we've seen—"

But since everybody hates her, she's already beat.

People actually like to see her get it in the gut.

Rex talks to her a little, seems to be explaining. I'm watching all this

217

on television, in the control room. Probably the worst moment in my adult life—in my whole life—has just been put on a soap opera.

I suppose I should have been angry, but I was so dazed.

Hillary yelling, "We have never seen anything like that—it's not *true*—" and Mike-Roy trying to calm her down.

I looked at Neil. He said, "Rex is a genius. Only Hooker could find that."

Livy was still staring at her watch. "Five seconds." She put her feet up onto the electronic panel. "Hot damn!"

On the monitor I saw Jack MacKenzie dancing with Daisy-Ruth. "Not for just a day—not for just an hour—but always."

Rex quieting down Hillary, talking to her, Hillary listening suspiciously. Me too zonkered by it to feel anything—it is just so strange.

Everybody leaving work—5:30, quittin' time. A lot of cheery good-byes, costumes spilling around in the corridor. All this big system closing down, Mickey Davis comes downstairs in his bum's clothes. Amanda half-gone with that terrible cough, in dungarees and a lavender sweat shirt with big white letters across her boobs, COMING ATTRACTION. I looked at Livy and she looked at me, and she could tell I was interested, but then nothing came of it. Marge Stivers pretended to play Chicken with us in the parking lot, yellow 'Vette against red Mercedes, and then squealed off on those big radials.

Earth to Rex—Earth to Rex.

We were on the Ventura Freeway when he said, "Do you mind?"

12

How COULD I possibly?

I say, "I hope Sheila doesn't see it."

He is weaving through traffic. "I guess I could have said, one Porsche, one condominium, one portfolio, one Keogh Plan—"

"Hey, I think that's enough."

"You found it offensive?"

"Yes. I have to say I did."

"Me too."

"I mean, it was a shock."

"Who's to know?" he says. "Really, who is to know?"

"Me."

"That's one reason I asked you to come. I don't do nothing behind nobody's back. People shouldn't lie to each other."

"Still—" I am thinking. Several million people are going to see that. It doesn't seem fair, it's too close to home. I say, "I guess I've got to watch the show."

"Well, watch with Mother. I told you, she never misses an episode."

"Marge told me, about the needle in the haystack."

He slumps at the wheel. "I hope. I hope. Christ, if this doesn't work—"

"It's a pinprick, a tiny tumor?"

"This new body-scanner picked it up. It's a two-million-dollar machine, just invented, they couldn't do it before. God, what a blessing—to have Mother herself again. For *her*, to have herself again."

I said, "They really applauded you."

"Contracts get renewed, contracts get canceled. Of course they've got to kiss my ass." We're stuck in traffic, all lanes stopped. "Trip—people are no damn good."

I say, "I have had some experiences in dealing with the shadier side of the human race."

Rex says, "Let me make a note of that."

I say, "Doesn't seem funny to me."

Rex turns. "Did I hurt your feelings?"

"I'll have to think about it."

"But your gut reaction—when I said those words?"

Well, I am not fond of it. To realize I was telling him something so personal and he was taking notes. But nobody will know. Unless Sheila sends me an arsenic Candygram from Albuquerque.

Our lane moves again.

"Trip, I really loved you when you said that."

We pass the Garden Grove exits. He says, "And Jos wanted me to do legitimate theater, films. She doesn't get it. This is all I want to do. It's family—family-shmamily. I aspire to no other medium. I lust for no other pulpit. She says I'm a fascist, that I invade territory. She actually called me a fascist once."

"That's a little extreme."

"Things hit me too hard. Max Herzog says the soaps speak Humanese. He's a nice old man, isn't he?"

"Yes."

"Hard as nails. I've seen him go up against the studio. But always remembers the basic rule—the one who can hold his cool longer than anyone else, he is the one who wins."

I look at the dumb houses clustered off the freeway. People going home, barbecue on the patio, Marriage Encounter, Shyness Workshops, people with creamed corn for brains. I wish he had not used my life that way.

He zips around a silver van with black spider decals.

Right out of the blue, except it's kind of smoggy, I say, "It's pretty clear why Joslin divorced you."

He goes into Red Alert. Not a touch of it in his driving, just in his head, I think I know him now. I think I am beginning to understand several things.

We drive along without talking. He's shaken up. Hurt. I feel a little guilty because I suspect that long day was fairly taxing.

J.O. is on my mind. Standing there, big, very big. I wonder what he thought about soap operas. About his son being in that business. *Build Therefore Your Own World.* Did it hurt J.O., or did he not understand it? I look at Rex's face. Very vulnerable. This is fine, he violates my privacy, and I feel guilty about violating his. I'm more fucked up than anybody in the world. With the exception of Neil Robinson.

We scoot down 405, it's a lovely car, real responsive, very warm piece of machinery.

The Chief is pissed. A fight with his girlfriend, over money. He tells me his side of it. I watch his face and pay attention to his words, but I am thinking of Charley Darling out in Indio. I get depressed. And I'm already depressed, I have inquest duty. I hate inquest duty. Standing around, some old guy should do it. I'm not a bailiff. Today it's fifty-four pointless minutes of people talking about some illegal alien in a language he can't even understand. It's a waste of time. Fifty-four minutes. I count each one of them. I see three or four familiar faces there, Butch Ravelling and some county guys, laughin' and smokin'. I bring Antonio Delgado in. He's cuffed, his gray hair is tousled, a little scrawny guy dressed in blue jeans. That word JAIL printed on his right pants leg, dirty brown loafers and no socks. I'm not even thinking about him, I'm thinking about Joslin in 126, talking so intimately to me about her wedding night. Who am I to her? A policeman. She didn't tell me one thing about her own life. All she talked about was Rex. Where is she in all this? I am of two minds about her. And I don't like either one.

The coroner's jury arrives, six men, one woman. Some guy from the county talks to Antonio in Spanish and then leaves him alone.

At 2:10 the jury is sworn in. They are informed that Jesus died sometime during the evening or early morning of November 20. The cause of death was four wounds on the skull. A syphon pipe with red stains on it and a strand of black hair were recovered 125 feet from the makeshift grave. A second weapon, an open pocketknife, was beside the grave. It is identified as belonging to the victim, "Hay-soos." Butch says alcohol was still present in the corpse's blood.

That clock has died, let me out of here. Rex was so afraid they'd put his mind behind bars. I'd like to check mine in a locker. Mark Leach, owner of the ranch, is called to the stand. He's a nice old incompetent fart. I pumped his septic tank for him many years ago when I used to have to do jobs like that because I was falling behind in my alimony checks to

Sheila. I'm pumping septic tanks and she is taking tennis lessons. Leach says that two of his boys came up to the house at approximately 8:15 to say Antonio had killed Jesus. They then called the Sheriff and went to look for Antonio. Found him in the Laguna bus station, waiting for a bus to Tiajuana. Leach says Antonio came along with them and was very obedient. Now they try to call Antonio to the stand, but the interpreter has left.

We clear the room so the jury can reach their verdict. In the lobby a guy offers Antonio a cigarette. The jury takes five minutes. Antonio doesn't even get to finish his cigarette before they set the preliminary hearing for Friday at one P.M. in Justice Court. I take the poor fucker away. Somebody says, "Adiós, amigo," and Antonio turns with a pale little smile, but the guy was talking to somebody else.

I don't know why that fifty-four-minute rigmarole repulses me so much. Everybody should get a fair trial, his day in court. But this is hopeless, it isn't a day in court, it's over before it begins. A charade. I didn't go into police work for this.

I know what's bothering me. The smile. When that guy said "Adiós, amigo," Antonio smiled, and the guy wasn't even talking to him. I saw his face and I'm going to dream about it.

On Tuesday I wasn't on duty until three, so I got to watch my first episode of "This Passing Night." I was excited, actually. Sat in my black Barcalounger with potato chips and a Hershey bar. On comes this other-worldly scene, looks like England with Richard the Lion-Hearted's castle, all misty and romantic. Organ music. Jack MacKenzie sounding majestic:

"The voice I hear this passing night was heard
In ancient days by emperor and clown. . . ."

I remember that cigarette lighter Marge gave Rex, "Emperor and Clown."

"The same that oft-times hath charm'd
Magic casements, opening on the foam
Of perilous seas, in faery lands forlorn.

"This is Jack MacKenzie asking you to join us on this passing night."

Then we had to get relief from the painful itch of swollen hemorrhoidal tissue. All through the show mothers compared Pampers and complained he never asks for a second cup at home and were flabbergasted that he prefers Stove Top, and ran off to corner the market on Stayfree maxi-pads.

222

The first half-hour I didn't see one single person I'd met with Rex. I knew "Jenny" had died, that was clear from the show I saw them tape. But since it's always three weeks later, now Jenny was alive, kind of glassy-eyed, and she kept saying things like "Wild horses couldn't keep me away from that baby shower." Music would come up ominously, like "Shit, she's *dying*, get it?" A friend of hers said to her, "I'm afraid the tumor is not only inoperable, it has already metastasized from your lymph nodes." Everybody says shit like that. To your face. The friend said, "You don't know how hard it is for me to say that." I said, "Oh yes I do." There weren't even any of the sets I saw—it was all other places, different living rooms, kitchens, and a scene in a park. Nobody told me they did stuff outside, I thought it was all done in that studio.

Who has time for such foolishness? I almost turned it off after Jack MacKenzie told me to stay tuned and they flashed to the fairy castle again. But while I was taking a dump I peered around the corner at the set, and part two started off with Amanda, the actress with the drinking problem. She was in her antique shop talking to Jessica-Hillary-Joslin about the terrible secret that Danny isn't really Steve's son. I finished my business and returned to the Barcalounger. It was open war between Amanda and Jessica. Real bitchy, threats about money. And just before we broke for Spray 'n Wash, old Neil Robinson came to the door and stood there staring at them. After the commercial, Josh-Neil took Jessica's side, and they walked out together—I liked that, seeing as how Hillary and Neil feel about each other.

Finally good ol' Rex himself appeared, Steve Kelly. Joshua was with him, trying to smooth things over. They were brothers, the Rock of Gibraltar and the Black Sheep, talking about the good old days when "Kelly's" opened. Rex played the honky-tonk piano, and he and Neil sang about how they'd go through everything together, through thick and through thin. You believed they were brothers; I felt a little foolish because I realized I was actually smiling, there in my trailer. And they sang pretty well.

At three minutes to one, Steve Kelly confessed to Josh that he guessed he'd always love Jessica, and he started playing and singing

> Jesseeee
> You are the world to me,
> And that's what's wrong,
> But you are my song.

The camera went in close on Neil's face, and there was one of those v.o.'s —"But Steve, what will happen if Amanda tells you? Will it destroy your whole world?" And then the camera switched to Rex, playing away, not knowing.

I liked it. So I figured what the hell, I'll call Rex. He answered the phone just like J.O., that half-word, " 'Lo." I told him I'd seen it, and he seemed pleased. Although, he said, Leela was upset, she saw the end of things. I thought she meant her life, the operation, and it flashed in front of me—tumor, brain, Leela, Jenny—but he meant the episode, Leela was worried about Steve Kelly. Sometimes in her drugged state she gets it a little mixed up with reality. As if, I think, the rest of them don't.

I signed in at three. First thing, I got a call about a sniper up in the bell tower at Saint Catherine's. On my way there I try to think about the physical layout of Saint Catherine's, I've been there a dozen times, Saint Catherine's Catholic Church on Temple Terrace, in Laguna Beach, California. But instead I'm thinking that must be where they got Marge's nun name, Saint Catherine, Sister Catherine, I'm sure that's where Rex got it, goddammit. I race up in my blue-and-white, and sure enough I spy some sucker up there with a rifle. I call for a backup and try the front door. It's locked. I think, Holy shit we got trouble, we're gonna need a SWAT team. But I check my gun, go around to a side door, and slip in. I make my way stealthily up to the bell tower, and here's an old janitor sweeping eucalyptus leaves, the rifle's a broom. Takes me the better part of an hour to calm down. My ulnar neuropathy is all better from the Bute, but that ulcer is acting up again.

When I check in at the station there is a message for me, from Joslin. So I call and she's completely fucked up. It's David. He's had a "terrible experience." But Joslin won't tell me what it is. Her voice is real guarded, and all I can get out of her is that he's not hurt physically. He has to talk, she says. And she can't find Rex. I think about how wonderfully well I've handled it in the past, when the kid had to *talk*—shit, all I do is make him cry. And today I'm blowing away janitors in bell towers anyway. But Joslin's voice is so goddamn weird and desperate, I say I'll get Butch or somebody to cover for me, I'll be there around nine o'clock.

I go back onto the street and take out my uneasiness on a dweeb in a Corvette who's showing off for his girl. And then I see an old lady coming straight at me the wrong way on Cypress. I hang a U and talk to her for a while about her family that sounds like it could go on "This Passing Night." I look at the sky and remember when Jenny picked up a baby and hugged it to her and contemplated her lymph nodes. I heard the voice of the floor manager, real soft, "Clear." You'd think they could edit that out. Or loop it. Or catch it wild. I'm still standing here on Cypress with this lady whose dog looks like a cross between a cat and a gopher, terrible little thing. She worries about her grandson, that's why she was so upset and going the wrong way. That dog should be put out of its misery, disgusting sneezy-coughs. She says he tried suicide once, which seems sensible to me, but she means her grandson, not the dog. I wonder how people get through the day.

I wonder how I do. I'm getting too old to have kids. When my daughter gets married, I'll be sixty, when I give her away, and that would be if she's born tomorrow. Life has passed me by, I have missed out on the big experiences. And don't pity myself a bit. Riding around with my eyes open, thinking. What I call thinking. I grab myself some liver and onions at Denny's. I wish I weren't so afraid of doctors, I need a complete physical—this utter weariness suddenly comes over me all the time, and a craving for sweets. Where did my reserve engines go? And the perspiration at night, I wake up sopping wet and have to change my pajamas.

At eight o'clock, Butch gives me shit with his eyes. Doesn't like being called in to cover. But he has sense enough not to say anything. We change clothes in silence, pretty much. I don't even tell him where I'm off to. Butch has been shunted off the Hooker case. He has all he can handle with his forays to the female mud wrestling in Costa Mesa. Says it's the funniest thing you ever saw. Someday I'll have him down to the trailer for beers and reruns of slides of the cast on "This Passing Night." We physically avoid each other around the lockers.

I point 1 GROUCH toward Bluebird Canyon up there. I park in the driveway and look around at the Hollywood juniper and the ice plant, it's dormant now, won't bloom until spring.

Joslin must have heard my car—she opens the door right away. Wearing a purple bathrobe, deep purple and black. Her long black hair and her ice-green eyes. We made some small talk at the door, and went in. She showed me around. There was a tremendous aquarium in the living room and on the patio a huge mobile maybe six feet around, completely made out of cutlery, with forks and spoons all swaying in the breeze. The walls were covered with paintings and there were statues, sort of, made out of wood and metal. Joslin flipped a switch and one of them went into live action, antique fans moved about by pullies.

A big old pinball machine in the cabana, and I noticed the remains of dinner on the kitchen table and in the sink and on the stove, a casserole with mussels and sausage and clams and shrimp. Joslin took me out to the pool, through an Oriental arbor covered with bottlebrush, it climbed all overhead, and little round stepping stones on the ground, you were sur-rounded by the bottle brush, all bright red and gold. A Siamese cat, Grunion, had one blue eye and one brown eye, looked at me like it had hated cops since the day it learned algebra. We came to a swing set and a merry-go-round like you find in elementary schools, and a Jungle gym, and a sandbox. Down below, the property went wild, bushes and trees. Joslin had a worried look on her face, biting her lip, barefoot in that black and purple bathrobe, tossing her hair. This is what Rex said they were supposed to share. The dream. Bluebird Canyon.

Finally she says, "I don't know what to do," she's on the verge of tears, and she looks at me hard. "Please help me." And she goes back into the house and comes out with the kid.

He's a mess. Gray eyes all glazed over. Like he's seen something grue-some and can't stand it. Can't even stand the thought of it. Joslin said —real shaky—"You guys work it out."

OK. Right. You bet.

I watch her go back into her house.

And then look at David, right here beside me. I can't read him at all.

"Walter Winn," he says. He glances at me, nervous, like you shouldn't tell last names to a policeman. I sit down on a little bench. I think at this point it might be a fight he had at school or something.

He says, "Walter's fat and doesn't have a tan at all. He's real *pale*. He looks like Moby Dick—except Walter, he looks more like Moby *Duck*."

"I see."

"Dad gave me a puzzle called that." He sniffles.

I hand him my pack of Kleenex. He wads one up after he blows. He throws it in the sandbox and says, "Toot-toot, don't pollute." We sit there and look across Bluebird Canyon. You can see the black ocean. He's holding his arms over his legs, like a teenager, except he's eleven.

He says, "In this little garden, outside their house, we were playing Stretch. You know? It's with a knife, a hunting knife. The goal is to stretch the other guy until he can't make it. Which I figured would be easy with Walter. But I didn't like the way he smiled before he flipped the knife. And I don't want any more stitches." David wiggled his foot in the weeds. "I hurt it in—the fire."

"I know."

"And I also did not like the way Walter called me weird things. Like 'my little mustache cup' and 'my little Brussels sprout.'"

David took another Kleenex. Wiped his face. Heaved a sigh. "His Mom was at a dress rehearsal. We fooled around in the kitchen. Walter is a nut

226

on cooking. He showed me how to make banana cream pie. Like it is something I have always been dying to learn."

I smiled at him. He was looking at me furtively.

"Walter said, 'Come hither, my little paprika,' and I wanted to tell him what Dad says the wise old owl of life always says. 'If you can't push it anymore—shove it.' But the pie was good. I had one pretty big piece, and Moby Duck took care of the rest. No wonder he has pimples. We talked about sex, and he told me a couple of dirty jokes. Except one of them was really mean. He had little pieces of pie crust on his white chest, and he'd pick at them and nibble them off his fingers. He says he has actually *done* it, with three different girls. He did clear up something that has bothered me for a long time."

"What's that?"

David looked at me. "Don't make fun of me, OK?"

"No problem."

"Well, my idea of a vagina was always like a big belly button—only lower down. And when I get a hard-on, in the bathtub that always happens when it hits the warm water—it always sticks straight up. So I was worried that screwing would hurt. It always hurts me when I try to bend it down into fucking position. But Walter said that women's holes go up, not across. It really 'tickled' him— that 'his little snowman' had made that 'error.' He has a lot of nerve calling me a snowman. With my noble tan and his pasty round bod. I have to admit it is a dumb mistake."

I smile in spite of myself. Kids are such hopeless cases.

"Of course, you have to be careful. For your own sake and the girl's. Walter showed me the rubber in his wallet. My dad has not used rubbers in years. Doesn't like 'em. His women always have their own protection. The pill and those Frisbees—I think they're called diaphragms, that's what my dad says, dia-fra-gums. He called Mom's her 'yarmulke.' Walter asked me if I would like to see how a rubber is used. He had this special red one. It has little dingies on it to give the girl more pleasure. Is that true? The girl gets more pleasure?"

"Well, uh-huh."

"Are you sure?"

"Yes."

"Well, how I am supposed to know? Why should dingies give her more pleasure?" David looks up at the sky. Wads the Kleenex in his hands. Tears off little gray bits. "I would certainly like to give the girl all the pleasure I can."

"That's generous of you."

227

He smiles and gives me another look. He's embarrassed.

I stretch my legs, light up a smoke, and then I sit in the swing, it's strong enough.

He stands facing me.

"So—so—we sat on his bed, and he took off his pants. He began working on his whanger. He said it would help him get it straight if I rubbed his arm. I said no thanks, and he pouted and got nasty. He said, 'My little poompkin, stroke my arm.' I said no again. But while he was working on it, he reached up and tugged my hair. And I—I let him. Just so long as it didn't go any further. I mean, I guess I don't care if he touches my hair."

I leaned forward from the swing and kind of swatted at his hair.

"And then Walter put the rubber on. He rolled it down, I always thought rubbers were white, and this red one was so—so *vivid*. He was breathing hard. He stopped beating at it, and said, 'Come on, David—finish me off.' I said, Oh no, and he said it would be very cruel for me to let him get to that point where he showed me everything and then not to let him have 'release.' He said that was a good thing to say to girls, in an emergency. If you get them far enough down the path, then you say you are 'in pain.' And they just might be dumb enough to take pity on you. But we *didn't have any girls*—"

This is swell. He's tearing up the grungy Kleenex. Below on Bluebird Canyon Drive, the little tram bus goes by. The driver is a spastic epileptic, a guy who should not be hired to drive in the canyons. He might have an attack and send his whole senior-citizen busload into the Torrey Pines. But he's a kind man. Considerate. Used to work for the postal service. I look up at the moon. It seems pretty important for the kid to have somebody to listen.

"I kind of caught a glimpse of it under his belly when he started. Like a dead baby slug. He said, *'Please,* David,' and I thought I could say I would do it if first he would run around the block three times. I figured that while he was doing that I'd make my getaway."

"Not a bad idea."

"But then I thought about the Mad Feelers. Two guys in Scouts. In the middle of the night on a jamboree they were—you know—discovered. In the same sleeping bag naked. We got 'em with our flashlights. Nobody told Mr. Sherman, but we sure teased them, except I didn't, not directly, I felt they probably suffered enough. But Walter isn't a fairy if he's done it with three different girls. And it certainly wouldn't hurt me just to grab hold and yank a few times, and he did have a point—"

We smiled at each other.

"Dad says most people can't help the way they are." David looked at me. He sighed. "But I *couldn't*— I don't know why. I got off the bed, and I don't know why, I just *couldn't*, Walter lay there, he whipped the rubber off, there wasn't anything big in it anymore. He put the rubber on his pillow. I thought it was kind of a dramatic gesture—like he gets that from his parents and it's not his fault. And then he said, 'David, my man, I'm proud of you.' "

"What?"

"After all those things he had called me—'my little this' and 'my little that'—it was really strange to hear him say 'my man' in a kind of older voice. All naked sitting there with his legs crossed, smiling at me. Like those statues of Buddha. I guess I didn't want Walter Winn to be alive. Not that I wanted him to be dead or to hurt him, I just wanted to think that he was not alive."

I rock back and forth in the swing.

"I started looking for my tote bag. I had put it somewhere in the living room, with my swimsuit and towel. Finally I found it, in their bathroom —the bathroom walls are all papered with photographs of movie stars, a kind of collage, and my tote bag was there beside the toilet. And—and Walter said, 'Come on David, it's a joke,' and I said, 'Shouldn't you be *dressed*?' I mean, Mr. Roly-Poly was all naked and following me around. And I said, 'Well, my little whinnymoomoo,' I don't know where I got that dumb word, *whinnymoomoo*, I just felt like saying it, I said, 'You can't just splatter around *nude*.' I had my tote bag so I said, 'Thanks for the pie.' Walter said, 'I'll make a deal with you. I'm not afraid of what you call me. I'll do *you*.' And he made a big hole with his mouth and made his tongue come out and he wiggle-waggled it back and forth, and his eyebrows went up and down. He said, 'You're just like your father.' So I held on to my tote bag. I said, 'What's my father got to do with anything?' And Walter said, 'Oh, always going to the booby hatch. You probably picked it up from him.' He—Walter—said, 'Your mother had to put your father in the loony bin.' And I know—I know that's the *show*. 'This Passing Night.' So I said, 'Tell me something I don't know.' Dad says that. But Walter said my real mom had said Rex Hooker—not Steve Kelly—had to go to an asylum." The kid looked at me. "Walter said the police took my dad away. Because he's *insane*."

Shit, now what do I do? I drag my heels, stop the swing.

"Walter said my dad was trying to commit suicide and my mom had him arrested. They tied him down in an ambulance and took him to the nut house. He was wearing a black coat and shorts."

Sergeant Bodley cannot meet the kid's eyes.

"And Walter seemed so sure of himself. He opened this little wooden box on the coffee table, and took out a cigarette. He said, 'Want one— or do you have *no* vices?' So I—I took the cigarette. I can't smoke. I don't even want to. And Walter can French-inhale, you let the smoke out your mouth and suck it back through your nose. He said, 'I feel sorry for you. It must be hard—having a father like that.' I tried to get just a little smoke down into my lungs. And not cough."

Shit, I don't know what to say. I stare at my shoes. The sand.

"Walter said, 'That man is not safe with man, woman, or beast within reason.' " David stopped, and sighed. "What is a beast within reason?"

I see lights in my brain.

"Did you, Trip? Or did you hear about it? Was Dad strapped down in an ambulance? Did Mom ride to the hospital with him?"

I've got to do this somehow. Stonewall it. Stonewall the sucker. I say, "It never happened."

"Walter was so sure of himself."

"Sounds to me like Walter has a few loose objects in his attic."

"What?"

I keep my eyes on my shoes. "Look, I'd know about it if something like that happened."

"But you'd lie to protect my dad."

Shit. Shit, shit, shit. "I think Walter's behavior kind of speaks for itself."

"I know. He said, 'Let's kiss and make up.' And I said, 'Kiss and make up? You are a fairy.' And he said no, he was advanced. Walter said people in America are afraid of their sexuality. Is that true?"

"I'm scared to death of mine."

He did his little heh-heh laugh.

I look everywhere other than in his eyes.

"Walter said Dad was a fairy. He had to go to the *fairy* loony bin."

"He saved your life. Don't you remember?"

Now the kid sat down in the old sandbox, moved his hands around. "Fairies don't save lives?"

I had a pang. Simon Goodheart Liberal says, "I don't know too much about fairies. I just know your dad's not one."

"Because he saved my life?"

"No. No, he's just not—not smart enough."

The kid smiled at me. "Are you intelligent?"

"No. Feeble-minded."

He liked that. He put his hands on the sand, braced himself. He sighed. "Is Walter a—a 'sickie'?"

230

I looked at him. "Maybe it's not his fault."

"It's not?"

The kid looks up at me like I have the Gospel Truth.

I say, "Do you have the address of the place?"

"Sure. I—" and then he looked at me. "I don't want to get him in trouble. You said maybe it's not his fault."

Joslin and Rex may frequently be the pits, but they did one thing right. David looked up at the night sky. He said, "You have no idea what a joy it is for me to play outside." And then he looked at me embarrassed. Like those words were a little much.

Emotionally I was all thumbs. I wouldn't be a good father. Couldn't do the day-by-day shit. Too many times my kid would see how foolish I am. Incompetent. But come to think of it, I never thought my uncle was less of a man just because sometimes he screwed up. Old J.O. himself must have had his awkward moments. The main thing is honor. And this kid knows honor in his bones. And he's so serious. Always believing the best in people. I have no hopes for him as a grownup. Good luck if he ever really understands. I don't want him to go to Stanford and repeat his father's mistakes. Shit, I don't want him to grow up at all. Just stay this way.

But tonight's job is finished. He's OK. Joslin was right—he had to talk. *Say* it, get it off his chest. Now it's time to rejoin his mother.

And Officer Bodley will soon have a little talk with Walter Winn's parents. Heh-heh.

David and I walk through the bottlebranch arbor and go inside. They have this Home Entertainment Center—like at Summer Snow, like at Medjuhl—and Joslin asked me, since I was in civvies, if I'd like a drink. I surprised myself, said OK, Scotch. David chirped, "I'll make it," and she sighed, and David said, "Soda, water, or neat?" and I said, "Ice and a little water." The kid played bartender while his mother looked at me, getting signals. We had a whole conversation with our eyes.

David brought in my drink, on a silver tray. I took a sip and, Jesus, it must have been all Scotch. I started to say, "Well, your dad must have taught you how to tend bar," but I just said, "That'll take the paint off your car."

Joslin said to him, "OK, Mr. Man, two chapters and bedtime, it's almost ten, you got school tomorrow."

She spanked at him, and he danced out of range, playing bullfighter with the silver tray. He said good night to me, he hoped I enjoyed my drink, and his mom laughed. She said, "It sounds like you're wishing him happiness in later life." He kicked her in the butt, that purple robe, and then she ran upstairs with him, yelling and playing around.

I sat there. Bluebird Canyon.

I'd like to sleep for a long time, like Rip Van Winkle, and then instead of waking up to a completely new world, just wake up to the old world put back together.

So I sat, and smoked, and thought about David. How his mother knew to call me, and how I fixed it up. By doing nothing. I've done it before, on my job, just provided a sympathetic ear. Listen, keep your wits about you, nod, be there.

I guess I'm—happy—that she called me. I try to imagine how Rex would have handled it.

I don't know.

But I do know kids can go through the most horrible experiences, and what you do is give 'em a chance to bleed it out. Pain comes when you squelch it. Bodley's Plan to Save the World—let all the kids talk. As long as they want to. In every country.

Joslin comes downstairs and stands there looking at me. She says, "David is wonderful—he just sweetly says good night, and he goes right to sleep." She comes forward. "Thank you."

I'm embarrassed. I look up at the forks and spoons in the mobile, delicate and solid and silver. I should leave now. Mission accomplished. The kid goes right to sleep. I should leave. I sure as hell don't want to do anything wrong.

A little chill hit the room, and Joslin went to fix a fire in the grate. I said I could do that, and she let me, and we had a nice fire there, in the dark. She brought out some marijuana. I'm a bit startled by that. I watch her fuss with it. She says, "I should get drunk. But I just fall asleep. I need something." She kept it in a little silver case with an orange sunrise and black palm trees. I smoke one with her, and I can't believe how it takes hold of me. I stare at the huge aquarium, life swimming in front of my eyes. Also fish. I'm hungry as hell. And scared. The black lines on her purple robe begin to get up and walk around and blend in with the furniture.

She asked me if I wanted something to eat.

I said no— and there I was starving to death. Trying to be cool. Suddenly hard of hearing. My eyes and ears have made a mutual agreement and left me out of it. Poor David.

Time goes in and out. We sit here. Joslin and me. The dope was hard enough on me at the party, why did I do it here? Joslin herself is not the greatest dope smoker in the world, she does it as amateurish as me. I tell her about Antonio without quite knowing what I am saying. I describe the scene at the inquest and how I couldn't keep my mind on it, how I was all fidgety. I do not know why I am telling Joslin this. I try never to tell women about my work, I don't want to put that burden on them. And here I am doing it. Antonio's tousled hair, and *"Adiós, amigo."* His smile when he turned around, and then how he saw that it wasn't even said to him. His life is over, it's prison now, a life behind bars. I think about Rex, afraid of his mind behind bars. Afraid that she, Joslin-Jessica, would put his mind behind bars. I don't know what's going on.

Yes I do.

Her face in the firelight. She is just quiet. I am looking at Joslin's feet, the toes. She doesn't paint her toenails. Sheila did. Come on, Trip. I accept the joint as she passes it, in this big bejeweled roach clip. Time passes. A sinking feeling. I look up over her black hair in the Japanese lanterns by the pool and the floodlights on the bottlebrush trees. I think I should excuse myself, I think I better go home.

She says, with a shy kind of smile, "When you were at Medjuhl, did Rex say that David should hold on to that 'parcel of ground'? Did he say it was 'pure gold'?"

I nod.

"It's 'Daddy's land,' " she said, " 'Daddy's land.' Oh, he eats you alive." She moaned, in her regal robe.

I look up from my Scotch-marijuana firelight fog. I see Labor Day, taking Rex to the institution in the ambulance.

Silver forks and spoons in the mobile. The fish in the aquarium. David asleep upstairs. Walter Winn. Jesus!

Joslin seems to be in such big pain. He gave her Bluebird Canyon. *Gave?*

I tell her a story. It seems like half an hour, but it only takes five minutes. About Officer Stanley—Laurel and Hardy. One cup, one spoon, one saucer, one knife, one fork, one blanket, one bedsheet. Now my sorrow for her is my own self-pity. Shit. I tell her how Rex did that, on the set, and everybody applauded, because it was so good.

She comes up with a brandy bottle and slides into the couch, the suede. I'm out of Scotch and do the very thing I should not, pour brandy into my glass. There's a comforter on the couch, I never even noticed it. I remark on the pretty rust color, with gold, and she says Leela made it. I admire the handiwork.

I think I better be going.

She tells me about her miscarriage. How it was put on "This Passing Night." She says, "Rex makes such profit on his own confusion." She sips. "And the rest of us pay rather heavily for it."

She gets up, goes to the stereo. After a minute I hear real soft classical music. She says, "The man I love is an impossible man. He actively seeks out—the—the—" Joslin standing there. She fixes the fire. She says, poking, "I never know which of the three men I'm dealing with."

"Three men?"

"First man, he's a bully. Second man, he's sensitive and intelligent. Third man is a star—and the star has no use for me."

Oh.

She turns, the fire behind her kicking up. She stands there, dark hair flowing down her shoulders. "Rex said, 'It's a thankless job.' " She shrugs. "I thought he was going to say, 'It's a dirty job, but somebody's gotta do it.' He always says that. And I was pleased he didn't, that time. But then I saw he meant *his* job, not mine. He said, 'You can walk out on them, but they stay here with me, and they all go to sleep with me.' " Joslin shook her head, black hair swaying. "I told him no, I won't sleep with them. Not until they make up their minds who they are—I'll sleep with the one who makes up his mind."

I stare at her. I have never met a woman like this in my whole life.

I suppose it must have showed in my face. Because she was looking at me strange. She came back to the couch, never taking her eyes off me. She sat down.

Then she looked away. She said, "One knife, one fork, one cup, one spoon—"

Goddammit, everybody is taking my life away from me. It's my own fault. I shouldn't blab. But I hate it when it gets to be theirs, and stops being mine. It doesn't mean what it's supposed to mean anymore. I have lost it. I was just sharing a painful moment. It's Rex's fault. He does eat you alive. I feel a flash of hatred for him. That is when Sheila walked out on me forever. When the hair on my balls started to grow inward. And now several million people are going to be entertained by it. This marijuana-Scotch-brandy has me all mixed up. I just lunge from room to room in my mind. Bedroom. Bathroom. Laundry room. I remember the trip to the San Diego Zoo. We saw that big orangoutang fucking that other orangoutang, what was his name? Sabang. And those old ladies recognized Dr. Steven Kelly, shit, Rex thinks he's so fucking important. And it's nothing but a dumb soap opera. It's not dumb. Poor David. A Washboard Weeper. Rex thinks he is so irresistible he can get away with anything.

Joslin never talks about herself, always about Rex. They have really done

234

a number on each other, it is a shame. They just should not be around each other. She ought to move away. And then I think about David upstairs. She could move to San Francisco.

"In the early years, he took such delight in my work—"

"Your work?"

She looks at me, sharp, with a bitter little laugh. "Didn't it ever occur to you I *work* for a living?"

I'm sorry. No, I mean, I just assumed—I mean, he makes five thou a week, he—

"That pisses me off." She says it real fast, like one word. "That pisses me off."

Silence. Finally I say, "What do you do?"

That seems to have made it worse. Please don't be mad, I— Joslin walks over to the bookcase, pulls out a big book. She comes back, and drops it into my lap, and I catch it and look at it. It has a purple cover, the color of her bathrobe. Its title is *Reflections III*. What the hell is that? I stare at it. I read the name of the guy who wrote it, and stare at that. She is very annoyed. She reaches down and opens the book, and points. "Translated by Joslin Breuner." It takes me a second to bend my disordered mind around that. She takes the book away from me. I say, "You translate books?"

She puts it back on the shelf. "When Rex met me, and charmed me, I was living in New York, working at the UN. The Hooker charm. When we—"

"Breuner? Your name is Breuner?"

She stands there. "It really never occurred to you that I might have some meaningful life separate from—"

"Say what?"

She sighs. "In 1966 I assumed that the husband's career comes first. If he goes to the Coast, we go to the Coast. L.A.'s a big city, I'll find something. I bought it." She looks at me, and I can't tell whether she's more pissed at me or herself. Finally she sits down. She takes a slug of brandy, and I mutter something inappropriate, and she says, "Oh, put your pennies away." If I were sober, that would probably send me right out the door. Bad enough she called me a teenager. Shit, put my pennies away. But I'm confused and weary, I think I deserve whatever I get. My foggy mind staggers back to Room 126, and then it troops over to the costume party, so I can get spit on again.

I wonder what her nipples look like. Don't *do* that. Oliver, look what you are doing. Dope and booze and here and her—don't do it. Better not, better not, Ollie, you will regret it. My pants getting big. It will happen. I am going to know.

Now Joslin's onto a new track. She says, "In the early years, in New York, I would go to the studios with him, at NBC, and it was a big party, a merry-go-round. Then he would come to receptions in my world, at the UN, with my band of *parisiennes*—he was Mom and Apple Pie, and I was Existentialism and Diplomacy. We were the Odd Couple. The Magic Couple. UNBC, he said. We were so *proud* of each other." She takes another drink, a big one. She has tears in her eyes, but she does not want to cry. She hates to be soft, I don't know how I know that, but I do. Then she stands up and crosses the room. She comes back and puts something on the table. It's pretty, it's a little model of this house. A jewelry box. She says, "He gave it to me on our first anniversary."

I stare at it. Really a nice job.

"Go ahead."

"What?"

"See?" She reaches down and opens the roof. Oh, I get it, it's a music box. It plays a melody. Tinkly melody. I don't recognize it. I ask.

" 'Bluebird Canyon,' " she says. "He wrote a song called 'Bluebird Canyon.' You know how he does?"

"No."

"He numbers the piano keys, C-1, D-2, E-3, F-4, and—" She bends over it. "For this song he used numbers of our telephone number on Seventy-sixth Street. Blue-bird Can-yon. He wrote lyrics too."

"I imagine he'd have to."

She turns and smiles at me.

Bluebird Canyon plays.

Oh, Lord.

She can't help it, she's crying.

But she stops herself. Closes the roof and takes it over to the shelf. "He said to me, 'See, Jossie, "Bluebird Canyon" will include everything—even our phone number in New York!' He thought it was terrific. Oh, the way he says that word, *terrific.*" She comes back. "It's the Hooker Story, the ongoing saga of the Hookers. I can't let David be on 'This Passing Night.' I don't want that for him. I worry every time he's over there. I never feel he's safe. Rex is a magic father—but he's not a good father."

It's all whirling around for her. And it's also whirling around for me. Why me? Don't tell me all this. I really shouldn't smoke marijuana. Don't tell me things I can't do anything about. All I can do is my job. Rex is the way he is. I'm sorry I never gave a thought to your having work of your own. Maybe I am unconsciously prejudiced. It's interesting the way those forks and spoons all balance each other like that, ingenious, took somebody a lot of time to work it all out—one fork, one spoon—oh, shit. I can't deal with all this, I can't. Leela's breakfast arrangements, one is a house on fire, Leela's cold, Leela's tumor—I can't deal with it. What I will do is change position. I cross my left foot over my right knee. I can do that.

She says in a low voice, "You have no idea how painful my miscarriage was. Not my miscarriage, though that was painful enough. I mean watching Hillary have my miscarriage. On 'This Passing Night.' She expelled the fetus in the car on the way to the hospital. Just as—just as I did."

I hate Rex, and watch the fish.

She says, "Once he said a terrible—terrible thing to me."

"What was that?"

"He said—he said, 'Relax, Jossie, nothing bad can happen to us—it's all material.'"

I hate him even more.

But I am only getting her side of the story.

She says, "And I really didn't have that much of a problem with J.O. Really I didn't. He was an impossible man, but—I suppose—I suppose I secretly admired him." She looks at me startled, like she's seeing it for the first time. Her ice-green eyes all wide. "Remember the funeral, at the graveside—singing 'Home on the Range'?"

I nod into my brandy. I also remember singing it with Rex out at Medjuhl, at the corral. Rex. I wonder where he found someone to make that music box. Well, I imagine you can get anything done in New York.

I've got to get going. Except I can't. I'm not even sure I can drive. I feel shaky, nervous. Bluebird Canyon. Bluebird. Blue. I say, "What color is a horse of a different color?"

She laughs.

Then I laugh.

Then we both do. She repeats the question.

I think to myself, My, my, Oliver Bodley, what a witty gentlefellow you are. You are positively the Wizard of Oz.

"The trouble is," she says, "that every color implies a different color. That's a good riddle. J.O. would have enjoyed that."

"He sure was full of riddles."

She nods, dreamy. "But he wasn't one."

"Excuse me?"

"J.O. *asked* riddles—Rex *is* one."

"Oh."

She laughs in my face.

I wonder what I've done wrong.

She says, "Your face, when you said, 'Oh.' "

"Oh."

And we both laugh at that.

I think of Rex laughing at my face in the studio, when I saw Marge in her nun outfit.

Well, I'll be sauntering out to 1 GROUCH. I don't feel grouchy at all. I feel terrible, but I don't feel terrible. I could talk this way for the rest of my life. All right, I haven't been in love for a long time. Actually I was in love only once. With that worthless whore who took my shower curtain. And now all of America is going to hear about it. It'll probably—how do they say it? I remember English class at Stanford—it will "pass into common usage." It'll become an expression. "Man, she really took your shower curtain." I can just hear it.

"I never could talk with Leela, I don't know why. Both of us tried. Her emanations were always clearer to me than her motivations."

I said, it just popped out of me, "Marge Stivers does real well."

"Oh—Marge." Joslin seemed sleepy. Not jealous or anything. She said, "Rex doesn't even understand that. Emperor and Clown."

Shit, nothing's sacred.

"Rex doesn't know who he is. Who he are. But he can charm people right out of their skins. The *liar*."

Not sleepy no more.

I have an idea about heroes, about how they should behave. I've probably seen too many movies. Never go anymore, though, I haven't been to a movie in a year.

"Our marriage is dead."

She's slipping away. I don't like talking. I don't want to be a failure. Talking is failure. I feel it getting big in my pants, and I dread it.

She looks at me.

Probably on "This Passing Night" Amanda would say something about "chemistry" with a sly wink. And turn around and sell somebody an antique. A music box. "Bluebird Canyon."

Suddenly there's a loud mechanical noise outside, and I half-jump out of my clothes. Then I realize it's the automatic sprinkler system. The Hooker houses all have them. You'd think I'd learn to deal with it.

Joslin chuckles.

I'm no Emperor and Clown. Just Clown. I don't like Rex, I really do not like him.

I like her.

238

She says, "He's insidious. He started as an actor—and now he practically owns the show. He loves to *own* things."

Maybe he thinks he bought the shower curtain. The whole of Southern California is full of assholes who went to Stanford.

She says, "But he's helpless. He's virtually helpless. Sometimes I'm afraid that he'll—he'll just die."

"Die?"

I think about my own death. I won't be expecting it. I'll be thinking about something else and then I'll be dead. I hope I die in the line of duty.

Why didn't Rex just love her, with all his heart?

But that's the trouble. He did.

Maybe a black widow spider will sting me on the lip in my sleep. Couldn't we stop talking? Stop thinking? When I'm making it with a woman, that's the only time my mind lets me alone. It's the only time I'm not Oliver Bodley, I'm just *there*. We are here—Joslin Breuner and Oliver Bodley. Jos and Trip. Not the Magic Couple. Us. It's probably midnight. In Bluebird Canyon.

She blurts out, "I'm so tired—I'm so tired of it—I just want somebody to take good care of me. All my life I've taken care of myself and—and my brother, and Rex, and David—it's my turn. I hate to admit it, I have a horror of—of being a lonely woman, but I am, I want someone to take care of me."

I will. I move, I go for it. I know it's right.

I kiss her.

I am ready for her to jump up and say I've made a gross mistake. But she does not do that. She opens up. I can feel her tears on my cheeks. We kiss and kiss and kiss. We are both depressed, and I stroke her robe, and she touches me. I feel so tender toward her. I'll take care of you. Good care. She unbuttons my shirt.

I take off my pants, and my underpants. But I still have on my shoes and socks. So I take those off.

She pulls that purple robe over her head, and her breasts are kind of low. Beautiful. And her belly, and there, and her legs. I am astonished. We lie there. She is crying, and I am so sorry for her, but at the same time I think this is probably what I have been hearing about. For all the sex I've had, I've never really had it. She smells so fine, and the firelight, the music is still going, violins. She grabs me by my hair and looks at me. Those green eyes. We are on strange ground. Her black hair is all around me, you can nestle down together and not be hurt. Dark freckles on her shoulders, I kiss them. It hasn't happened yet, but soon. I won't talk to myself, I'll talk to you, I can't think about this, I won't think, there is no point to it. I am completely lost, it takes hours, we are going into a whole other place. Somebody's heart is pounding, in our arms, in the upper part, and I think I understand—sex is shame, it's needing somebody way beyond what you need them for—

A light went on. Hello? I rolled over, half off her, and tried to focus my eyes. There was Rex—Rex—in his stocking feet, all dressed up, carrying big gold boots in one hand, and a big orange poster in the other. I squinted. The poster said in big black letters

Dr. Steve Kelly
(Rex Hooker)
Today

Rex walked toward us, past the aquarium, his face completely pale. He started to say something. On the phone his voice sounds like his father, J.O., but now he—he looks so much like Leela, he looks like his mother. And he is walking toward us.

Joslin jumps up, naked. She screams, *"You can't do this to me!"*

I have never put on my clothes quite that fast. My shirt, my pants. I tied my shoelaces like rigging.

What is this?

Rex put down his boots. He held on to the orange poster:

Dr. Steve Kelly
(Rex Hooker)
Today

Joslin says it again softer, "You can't do this to me."

I start for the door.

Rex says, "Trip?" He sounds forlorn.

But I couldn't manage it. I went out of the house and got into my car, started her up. There was Rex's red Mercedes, ROLLEM, its lights still on. I backed out of the driveway and drove down Bluebird Canyon. Then I drove back. Rex came out and turned off the car lights. I drove away, and then I came back again, with my own lights off, and I sat there. Hating myself. I got out and walked around. I always keep a pack of cigarettes in the glove compartment, just in case, so I had one, and looked up at the stars. What kind of fool have I been played for?

I probably stood there for half an hour. I looked at my watch at 12:05, and then all of a sudden it was 12:25. I must not have this right. *You* can't do this to *me?* And Rex not seeming at all angry. Shit, I would have killed me. I calm down, cool off, try to be intelligent. Christ, I remember that waitress at the Surf 'n' Sand. I let her use this very car for a few months. She lived in a shack out in the development. I never saw her there, she had three little kids. But one weekend her hubby went to a family reunion and took the kids. She called me at work and told me to pick her up. As I recall, I didn't get off until midnight, so she said, Come to the house and we'll use the bed. We had always done it in the car. So we had a couple drinks, watched TV, necking on the couch. It was an awful couch, she probably got it on sale at Pep Boys. Pale green and hard, with a broke spring that got you right in the thigh. And then a whole hour in bed, she's on top, getting her jollies, when halfway through, all of a sudden there's bam ka-bam-ka-bam, she says who the hell can that be? She gets off me and looks through the curtain, and there's her hubby standing on the porch. He begins to holler. So I put my shirt on, buttoning it up wrong, all askew, and my pants, and my socks. I start toward the back but he comes tearing around from the front. We wrestle a bit in the yard. I could've laid him out, a little weenie sucker. We went round and round, but my mind kept coming back to one word, *job*, my *job*, I am not going to lose my *job* over this foolishness. So I say, "Don't touch me." The sucker hears the menace in my voice and backs off. I waited outside while they had a scene in the shack. Finally he comes out and says, "How'd your superior officer like to hear about this?" He had been checking up on me, apparently, for some time. I've always wondered if maybe she told him. Well, I figured it was safest just to keep my mouth shut. It turns out the sonofabitch had been under the shack since six o'clock that night. Maybe he heard everything we said, huddled up right under the bedroom, heard everything.

We actually lived together, Judy and me, for a year or so after that. I never got along with the kids. I had a semipleasant relationship with the older girl, but the boy never liked me. I was screwing his mother. The husband did not return. But when you are caught like that, Ol' Lonesome George goes right through the floor. She didn't seem too surprised about getting caught, actually, maybe that is what she wanted to happen. It's no way to live. I was relieved when it fell through. She'd take the kids to his parents on weekends, and I always suspected she was seeing him on the side. It's terrible getting caught. Makes you feel like a child, a hand in the cookie jar.

But I promised myself it would never happen again, never. And now it has. And so much worse.

I sit in the car, shifting the shit out of my brain. This is terrible, I can't see any way to fix it.

Then the door of the house flies open, and there's Joslin, naked, absolutely naked, she runs past the red Mercedes, Joslin nude, blood streaming all over her face, running down the driveway. Rex comes right after her, with his arms up. Joslin, her low tits bouncing, and her absolutely naked body, running. I jump out of the car and catch her. She's covered with blood.

I'll kill Rex.

He says, "She fell—she fell."

Joslin sobbing in my arms, "He pushed me."

We all three stagger back into the house. David is now awake. He stands there barefoot in his Superman p.j.'s, completely horrified. His mother sobbing, covered with blood.

"You can't—you can't *do this* to me!"

She doesn't even see the kid.

Which is a blessing. Rex takes David upstairs and I guide Joslin to a bathroom. I don't know if we should call a doctor. I can't see the wound, or how severe it is, it's on the top of her head, I don't know if she needs stitches. She is sobbing out of her mind.

Rex comes down and pushes by me. He looks at her, yells, "Ice. Ice, Trip!"

I go in past the casserole still on the stove.

I get some ice, smash open a tray. There's a dishtowel, blue and yellow, only it's not a dishtowel, it's an apron. It says in white letters: TO KNOW ME IS TO LOVE ME. I wad the ice in that and bring it in. He's standing with her at the blood-spattered sink.

"Jesus, Trip, zip up your pants."

I back out. I zip up my pants. And go into the other room. The music is still playing. Rex's boots and the orange poster

DR. STEVE KELLY
(REX HOOKER)
TODAY

and the dying fire and the fish.

Rex comes in. Behind him I hear the shower go on. David must be just peaceful as hell up there in his room.

Rex picks up her snifter of cognac, drains it. He says to the wall, "I haven't been sane since she left me."

He stands there. But he's somewhere else. Then he turns to me. "I must say, Trip, I expected better of you."

I can't look him in the eye.

242

He takes a few steps toward me.

Can't look at him.

"How could you let her use you this way? I told her I'd be here at twelve. On the dot."

I can't look at him, I just can't.

Rex goes up to David. I hear Joslin in the shower. I watch the fish. And I leave—just leave.

I'm in my car, but my hands don't work right on the wheel. I have to brake at places that I would usually slide through like Paul Newman at Riverside Raceway. I am not well. I hated him, and now I hate her. Also I hate myself. I have been deceived. Yes, that is the lesson for today: I have, once again, been deceived.

And probably seriously hurt poor ol' Rex. What was I thinking of? I don't deserve the uniform. I was so totally wrapped up in her, and all the sorrow, and I believed her—damn, I have been used. He told her he'd be there at twelve? On the dot? Well, she timed it just perfect.

You can't do this to me.

I stop at the Bluebird Canyon playground and try to walk off the energy.

She played me for a fool.

David. His face. I look up at God's sky again. All those stars, life on other planets. I could pray, if I believed in anything. David's gray eyes, the expression on his face. Shocked out of sweet dreams. Shocked out of sweet dreams into panic city. Because of a cop, to whom he had delivered a triple Scotch on a silver tray. The cop who listened to him. The cop he trusted. Me.

13

I LIE LOW. What else can I do? Just make myself scarce and play the whole scene over and over in my mind. How could I allow such a thing to happen? She is really a bitch. He had everything to live for, Mr. Hot Shot, nobody could climb up and stop his clock. Except her. So she did it. Like he said, he hasn't been sane since she left him. Well, if she had to leave, then—but doing something like this—when he told her he was coming over—it's one thing to knock a guy down, but then to kick him in the balls. And I guess I myself feel just a tad let down. Here I was in a romantic fog, all ready, and then I see what a fool I have been played for.

All you can really do is lie low. Watch the reruns in your stupid mind. I wish my mind was a dog and I could train it to go sit. I shift around in the seat of my patrol car. I'm fairly sensitive about some things and do not need to be reminded of my foolishness and lack of loyalty and how my horniness and optimism always work against me. I try to make it into a farce and tell it to myself as a stupid joke, ho-ho-ho, Ollie, were *you* surprised, getting caught like that with your bare ass in the air—but it won't work. It's not funny.

The bitch, using me like that.

But wait a minute. That's not true. It was Rex. The sonofabitch. He had perfect timing, came just at the right moment. Before I did. It's like he stepped in there and said, "No you don't, this isn't yours, this one's mine, it's Bluebird Canyon." How could he do that? Like on Labor Day, when I couldn't believe he was back at the house, I couldn't figure out how he got there. And he looked up and said, "Well, Trip, how the hell are ya?" At least he didn't say that this time. What did he say? He didn't say anything. Because he was waiting for her to say something. And she did. She said, "You can't do this to me."

That's what happened.

Bluebird Canyon.

I bury myself in my job. We get a call, some sweetheart has been at work painting swastikas and Jewish stars on the Temple Judea and on two local Jewish business establishments. So I spend most of my shift using that antidefacement spray, but I can't get it all off. I'm wondering who is sick enough to do this. I'd like to get hold of him. Probably some dumb kid who wouldn't know Hitler from Napoleon. At noon I sneak down to my trailer and catch the second half of "This Passing Night." I want to see Rex. I wonder if I will ever see him in the flesh again.

But the Kelly family isn't even on this segment, it's a whole other cast of characters. A red-headed career girl blows two lines, she's no good at all. First time she's phoning a lot of people about a local election, and she sighs and says, "I hate having to call all these nameless faces." You know she means "faceless names." She just screws it up and goes right on. Later she actually gets a character's name wrong—she calls Miss Osborn "Miss Hollings." Miss Osborn draws a blank, and the redhead tries to cover by saying, "I don't know what's wrong with me today." I do, lady, you're sixty cents short. I would think they'd go back and fix that stuff, but they don't.

There's a "location" scene, only it's fake. They've got a speedboat, sort of like the Buick, we only see the top of it, the lovers are supposed to be on a lake. Their hair blows around—probably an electric fan behind the camera. Some dink floor manager no doubt piddly-paddling the "spray" from a bucket. Some of the "spray" splashes up on the sky. The sky is just painted canvas, and the water sits there, shiny, and begins to dribble down, these runny streaks. "Water on the Sky!" I mumble, "Water on the Sky!"

I turn off the set and try to write Rex a letter. There is nothing to say. I tear up the paper and think about Thanksgiving. I just hope I'm on duty so I can be making money while I'm feeling sorry for myself.

There's a pretty girl hitchhiking on South Coast Highway. I pull over and pick her up, give her a little lecture about the perils of hitchhiking while I drive her to Main Beach. Just as I go past the Jolly Roger, here comes the Chief in an unmarked vehicle. I hear over the radio, "That's cute." Just those two words. At least I have my hat on. But you are not supposed to have females in the seat next to you. "That's cute." Sure enough, when I get off, there is a memo on my locker. "In the future, when escorting lady guests around the beach, you will refrain from having them in the front seat." And his initials. Never his name. He's quite the disciplinarian.

I get home after my three-to-eleven, I'm still in uniform, dog-tired after doing hardly any work, my feet killing me, and the phone rings. It's Marge Stivers. She's in the El Dorado suite at the Laguna Hotel. Can I come immediately? There's trouble. She's crying and loaded, I can hear it. So I'm gone, out the door and down there within five minutes. I pull into the parking lot beside her canary 'Vette, and go inside, trotting.

She's sitting on the king-size bed. "Oh, Trip," she says, all breathless. She's got a big tumbler in her hand, probably a gin and tonic, and she hands me a little piece of stationery. A note in Leela's beautiful "script." You could tell she was just flying:

> Margie,
>
> I'm to Medjuhl—Rex called—says he's going to cash in his chips—sorry to break our date—
>
> > Leela

I stared at it. Rex is going to cash in his chips?

Marge went to the vanity. There was an envelope there, propped up against the big ceramic lamp. The envelope had MARGIE on it. She gave it to me. Her blond hair was kind of all wild and spraying out from her face, her eyes dull with the booze. She said, "Rex and I had a terrible fight —he was just *crazy* about something. I had to talk to Leela about it. Don't look at me that way. But when I got here, Trip, I called you just six or seven minutes after I—I didn't see the note at first—" She spilled some of her drink on the thick carpet. "Stop looking at me. Trip, we've got to do something. She hasn't driven that car, she hasn't driven any car in at least five years."

"What car is it?"

"The Caddy. You know, the—"

"She know the way?"

"But she's on medication. And the freeways are all new— please, Trip, we have to go after her. And—I'm in no shape to drive." Marge was grumbling, she slowly tottered to the big glass windows. "What if she runs out of gas? What if she has an accident?" Marge wanted to move but didn't know where. She went into the bathroom. "She didn't take her medicine with her."

Well, we have to go.

We walked through the Arcade to the hotel parking lot. We take the car. The 'Vette. On the way we check all the off ramps, peer into gas stations. At one point I saw a pink Seville, I hit the brakes, got the next off ramp, and went back. It wasn't Leela. Marge said, "That woman is just amazing." And later she said it was a good sign that Rex called; if he called, that meant he wasn't going to do it. I am thinking all kinds of crazy things. Like would he cash in his chips because of that scene with Joslin and me? Don't tell me that. Here I am, in my sweaty uniform, my hat and my gun and my stick, driving a Sting Ray. With this gorgeous drunken lady, who is really so *alone*. This lady who is in love with Rex Hooker, who just walked in on me and his wife fucking. My presence is clearly going to calm everything right down.

Which is why I told Marge. When she asked me what could have set Rex off. I told her about me and Joslin. Of course I shouldn't blabber-mouth, that's wrong. But I realize I have been aching to tell someone. Even so, I don't tell the truth. Or I leave it out—that Rex got there just in time. I tell myself I just don't want to go into the gory details. But I know that's not why. Shit, I *hate* myself. I say, "And Rex came in and found us there."

It certainly sobers her up. When I finally have the courage to glance at her, she's staring out at the night. Thinking. She says, "And David was upstairs?"

Oh, shit. I wait, and I say, "There was kind of a ruckus." I wait. "David woke up, and—"

She groans.

We talk about it some more. The only thing that makes any progress is the car. Marge is disappointed, I can't tell whether in me, or in who, or in life itself. I try to explain my behavior. But you can't explain the inexcusable, you make it worse. I swear, I do not know what is the matter with me lately, I am not myself at all. I have no business in the world telling this to Marge Stivers. And so that's exactly what I did. I watch the road fly by and think of her in her nun costume, Sister Catherine. And I think back to Hans Brandsma's office on Labor Day, when I first heard Rex was still seeing her. And the three-pizza story. And when he wouldn't go to the hospital and said he should get one call, and he wanted to call Marge. And that night in Medjuhl, what she wrote in his high school yearbook, and the lighter, Emperor and Clown. He says he doesn't know why he never married her, they're like brother and sister. Too much for me, I can't deal with it. I don't know what happened to my "Most Inspirational" trophy. Sheila probably took it.

Marge says, "That's really awful."

I know.

"How could Joslin—how could you—?"

And I yell at her. I don't want to hear about it, so I just let loose. That cuts her off.

On we go. The silence in here only weighs ten pounds per cubic inch. If you've got bad trouble, just call Sergeant Bodley. Then you'll have a disaster on your hands.

Rex wouldn't cash in his chips over that.

I let him down twenty years ago. And it was sex that time, too. I didn't want to lose my virginity with Marla Talis.

Coming down through the Pass, we killed a jack rabbit. It was frozen in the headlights, its eyes glowing, and the ol' sickening thud was just that. It felt like an omen. On the desert I just decided to hell with it. This 'Vette can really move out, if a CHP stops me, I'll tin him quick. We were doing 120, neither of us saying anything about it, roaring up the empty road. As we pulled along My Way we saw the Coral Cad with the driver's door open in front of Medjuhl. We rushed out and went right in.

Leela was sitting in the black velvet chair, holding a Bible. Handel's *Messiah* was on the stereo, I remember singing it at Indio High Christmas pageants. The music was just going. The two of us stood there, Marge Stivers and me, and Leela looked up. Clear eyes, spaced out, and she said, "He's resting. I looked in. I think he's asleep." The chorus filled the room, and I watched Marge take Leela into her arms, carefully, Leela clinging to the Bible, a big old family Bible.

> And his name
> Shall be call-ed
> Wonderful
> Counsellor—

Handel certainly did let himself go when he composed. I followed Marge out into the driveway and breathed in the dry desert air. Marge was moaning to herself, "Oh—Mother," and she closed the door of the pink Seville and leaned against it, with all her weight.

After a moment I said, "You OK?"

"Sure, Bucky," she said.

And then she threw up.

Rex said it was all a big mistake. He looked fine at breakfast. Didn't seem to mind my intruding—in fact he was pleased to see me. Shows you how valuable all my brooding is. He actually thanked me, for emergency service. He explained that Mother had misunderstood, he only meant he was depressed, he'd been doing some tape-recording work for the show and was talking about Steve Kelly cashing in his chips, not himself in real life. Uh-huh. I guess. But he said it just shows to go you, when you got a mother like Mother, and friends like Marge and Trip, you never need to cash in your chips.

Well, I'll be moseying . . .

But then he said something odd. He just tossed it off, with a big dramatic sigh, "Well, *one* of us has to go, Steve Kelly or Rex Hooker!" When he saw me looking at him, his whole face changed. Then he asked me to stay and have Thanksgiving with them.

That's Rex. Hurt him bad enough, and there's nothing he won't do for you.

I called the Chief, and made up a shot-through-with-lies story, and the Chief bought it. Told me I could stay through the holiday. He was kind of jovial. I know the Chief's head has been turned by an offer from San Diego. I much prefer him when he's just my Chief—"That's cute." Some men do not know where their real talents lie.

One of them has to go—Steve Kelly or Rex Hooker?

He and Marge went horseback riding. I spent my time with Mrs. H. Lost her husband and her health. She's got a lot of courage to get in that car and drive over unfamiliar roads in the dead of night because she thinks her son is in trouble. At noon we watched "This Passing Night" together, in the big white room with orange carpeting, under the swan boat stained-glass window. Rex was in this one, Dr. Kelly, a very big scene. When he is told that Danny is not his son. It's a thunderbolt. He sits down at the piano and starts to play "Danny Boy" and weeps. Leela gathered herself up, her own bright eyes full of tears, she saw Rex outside prancing on Whiskey, and she whispered, fierce little gasp, "You *rascal!*"

I gave her another cup of tea and a piece of toast. She had on a lacy gold sweater, white pants, and white and gold shoes. Killed me when she said that, "You *rascal!*" She told me a long story about how when she was a little girl she thought the birds were her playmates in disguise talking about her. She told it all very slowly, looking like a little bird herself. Dark circles under her eyes. She said she had wrapped David's Christmas presents already and hidden them so well that she couldn't find them herself. She asked me what I wanted for Christmas. She was worried about the upcoming "tariff" on credit cards.

I could tell she'd had a lot of medication, but she was really active, bustling around to prepare Thanksgiving. She hauled down a cookie tray, wanted to make David some Toll House cookies, and she lost her balance and hit herself right in the mouth with the tray, raised a big blood blister on her upper lip. Hurt a lot, I could almost feel it myself.

Dibby came to the door with a load of groceries. "Well-um," he said, "well-um, this hyeah burd gwyne ter feed a ahmy." Leela was very intent, afraid the meat would be tough.

Rex and Marge went swimming.

I fed the dog, Gamble, that golden Lab. She seemed to need a few words of comfort. I sat out in the garage, talking to her, wondering about how mysterious the world is if you pay attention. It's pretty mysterious even if you just catch it on the fly. I remember when my uncle couldn't walk and could hardly talk. We all knew the end was near. He said he prayed for the Lord to take him, but nothing happened. I didn't have an answer for him either.

Rex and Marge are going to the Palm Springs airport to pick up David. Now that is peculiar, with all this driving back and forth, suddenly the kid flies from John Wayne to P.S. I Love You—because, apparently, Joslin wanted it that way.

I guess I am getting too old. I want to have turkey and dressing and a little salad and peach brandy with a deaf aunt. I feel like I'm not me. I have given up something that I didn't lose. I think I want someone who is *my* people, not *theirs*. And besides, I smell something. I know you always say to yourself, "Well, I smelled it," when you smell it ten times and are wrong nine, but it's the one right time you always remember. I walked around the pool, and I could smell it real strong.

Leela was cooking up a storm. Trying to make things nice for everyone. She's living up to her husband's memory. I heard her muttering little words to J.O., his soul in heaven.

I borrowed some crud from the medicine cabinet, shaved. I cleaned my gun and strolled out on the pad, remembering I left the lights on in my trailer.

When I came in, Mrs. H. was holding the telephone, terrified. She handed it to me, and there was ghastly male laughter. The sun disappeared behind San Jack, and the phone rang again. I braced myself. But it was Rex. David's plane had been delayed, so Rex and Marge were going into Palm Springs to do some Christmas shopping. They'd be back about nine, according to the present schedule from Air West.

Leela went back for a nap. She's very ill, in a lot of trouble.

I stared up at the stained-glass windows, watched the light leaving the sky. Then I went out to the greenhouse, picked up the hose, and did a little irrelevant watering. Christmas shopping.

The smell is strong. Nine times out of ten. This is a ten.

Leela wanted to have the home movie system ready for David, "that adorable guy," she called him.

So I got out the equipment, while she sat in the black chair. I am no expert on home projection systems, but managed to get it in working order. It was twilight, so I pulled the orange drapes. She said it is always best to be prepared, she'd like to see a few reels. I rummaged through the boxes. J.O. had labeled a lot of the stuff—REX BIRTHDAYS, ONE YEAR / SIX YEARS—and Leela said just to show anything, sitting there with her tea. I did. The first one was "Me and My Shadow," with Rex, and David about five years old, both of them dressed up in tuxedos, with canes and top hats —it was nice, their singing "Strollin' Down the Avenue," except it made me a little uneasy, David at five, already his dad's shadow.

When that reel ended, I put on another, and there was Leela's father, Grandfather Darr, collecting the monthly rents in one of his big courts, it was sort of a permanent motel. The film was in black and white, from the 1930s, and her father's walking was too fast and jerky, the way it is in old movies. J.O.—I assume J.O. was the camera man—had done a little trick, as he would, so Old Man Darr would go in one door and come out and go into the next, and another, and another, and then he did it all backward, double-fast. I don't know how J.O. did that, but it was funny, like Charlie Chaplin. Except it tugged at Leela. She said to me that perhaps it would be better not to show the older ones, it made her heart beat too much. So I went through the spools and found a recent one, without a label. It was just a long study of a tree snake with a weird spacy soundtrack. Gave me the shivers, the snake slithering through a tree and eating eggs out of a bird's nest. Like those nature films they used to show in school. We watched awhile. Rex must have done this when he was stoned, and now Leela and I are alone with the space music and Mr. Snake. Suddenly the scene changed to the orange staircase, and there was Joslin in a black negligee—the color was supervivid—and the music on the sound track was strip-show music, bum-bum-bum-bum bumdy *bow bow*, with a lot of saxophones. Joslin was doing a striptease. She danced, overly sexy, on the orange carpet, and let the jacket slide off her shoulders.

She had on high heels, black, and she took off the negligee, bum-bum-bum-bum bumdy *bow bow*, bumpin' and grindin'. Then she went up a few steps, turned her back to unhook the black lace bra, and she let it fall over the banister, and then she turned and you could see her beautiful tits. She shimmied, and then kind of stopped and stood there, making a face to the camera, and you could tell she was talking to Rex, who must have encouraged her to keep it up, because she sighed as if to say, "Oh, very well, but it's dumb," and went on with the bum-bum-bum-bum bumdy *bow bow*—

I looked at Leela. At first she'd let out a little "Oh!"—a startled, almost frightened sound. I thought she would ask me to stop the projector, but she didn't. She put her hand over her mouth, and she watched, as if she didn't know I was there, it was almost as if she wasn't there, like it was happening to someone else. She bit down on her hand, her teeth into the little knuckles of her fingers, and she kind of growled, "Oh! Oh!" On the screen Joslin stepped out of the black silk panties and got them hooked on one of her high heels, she really wasn't a very expert stripper, but now she was all nude in high heels, you could see the black hair, and the hair of her head all black and falling around her white shoulders. And then she was smiling—all shy and ironically wicked—and Leela stood up and walked in a kind of dream toward the screen, completely lost in the picture. She turned and the light of the projector was on her, making her face all glowy. She was heaving these sighs, and then she started to move out of the way of the projector, I was afraid she was going to fall, and I jumped for her. She leaned against me and suddenly realized who I was, and said, "Oh my," like she had snapped out of it or had been awakened from sleepwalking. The music was still going, those saxophones, bum-bum-bum-bum bumdy *bow bow* ka *Bow Bow!* Leela huddled up in my arms, huddled like a little girl.

I helped her into the bathroom. She turned on the shower, and I went back and put the equipment away.

The phone rang. I picked it up and, Jesus, it was Joslin herself, wondering why I hadn't called. She thought I was Rex. I said it was me. She heard that, and then she said very fast, "He never—he never said he was going to be here at twelve. I never—I never—" She paused. "Where is he?"

I try to sort it out, looking at the pool. She is alone, Joslin, on a major holiday. My, she looked fine. That wasn't pornography, that was what she really looks like. I say the flight is delayed and I'll have them call the minute they come in—and then I hear another phone lift up and Leela's voice, "Yes?"

Joslin: "Mother?"

252

"Oh—oh, Jos."

"Just checking up on David's safe arrival."

"Oh, dear, we were just thinking about you."

I don't know how Leela does it, in her condition. It was the most elaborate Thanksgiving dinner I've ever had. Marge helped a lot, I guess, but Leela did all the big stuff herself, she stayed up all night working away. Says she can never sleep anyway. And we were quite a crew—Rex at the head of the table, Leela at the other end, the kid and me on one side, and Marge and this baby about a year and a half old named Roger who mashed peas all over his face. Roger was the son of one of Marge's old girlfriends, and I never did figure out why he had to be brought here on Thanksgiving Day. We sat around the table in the glow of green and brown candles. There was a big centerpiece. I looked at my three salads, and it was peaceful, except for Roger. We all had to hold hands and bow our heads while Rex said the blessing. When I heard him start, "Father—we— Father, we thank—" I suddenly realized this is his first Thanksgiving without his father, and I held on to David's hand and I held on to Leela's hand.

Then we just ate and ate and ate. Washing it down with rosé wine, Rex carving the bird, David packing it in, Roger making a mess, and Leela just hopping up and down, back and forth to the kitchen, hardly touching the little dabs of food on her plate. We laughed a lot. Especially Marge and Rex, who were stoned and found every meaningless thing hilarious. The phone rang once, and David said he'd get it, but Rex said, "Hold it, son, let me," and he took the call. I watched him standing at the kitchen sink as he listened and said in a low voice, "All right," and put the phone down. He came in and glanced at me with a little nod, but he said to everybody, "Wrong number."

Leela said, "We've gotten so many of those lately."

We had dessert. I was feeling stupid in my uniform, but I didn't have any other clothes. Rex started to say I could wear something of J.O.'s, but then he thought that might not be so good for Leela. We sat there in the twilight, burping. Rex pulling on a stogie like he was a bank president. We were all full and cozy.

Then Marge and Leela wanted to get started on the dishes, but Rex wouldn't allow it. He said he and David and I would clean up, and then he said that Marge should drive Leela and David back to Laguna, to the hotel. He really insisted on it, kind of took us all by surprise. He said he and I would come along tomorrow. Marge said, What about Roger? She'd promised to take him until tomorrow. Rex was flustered. David said he wanted to stay. They argued. Finally Rex said he'd had plenty of practice changing diapers when David was little, it'd be fine with Roger. More argument with David—Rex clearly wanted him and me alone. I couldn't figure it. Leela was doped up on those pills and obviously didn't want to drive. Rex said Marge should take the Cad, for Leela's comfort. Tomorrow "the Men" would come in the 'Vette and the Mercedes. So by 6:30 we were packing the ladies in the car, and off they went down My Way.

Took Rex and me a couple of hours to clean the place up, while David took care of Roger, playing Peek-a-boo. We put Roger to bed in David's old room, which was still like a nursery, with a big stuffed panda bear and little wooden trains and a crib. Rex changed Roger's Pampers, put a little blue p.j. shirt on him, and then stayed in there, patting Roger and singing a lullaby or two. Then the three of us watched the Turkey Day highlights on the big TV, and Rex and I had brandy. He seemed preoccupied. When we took out the garbage, he freaked over a scorpion in the driveway. Then David got his feelings hurt because he was zipping into the bathroom during a commercial and didn't know his dad was already in there. I heard Rex shout, "Stay *out,*" real short-tempered, and David came back and sat on the couch, sullen. And then I could hear the shower.

The phone rang again. When I said hello, there was a pause before a voice said, "The night is full of death." Click.

Swell. I sat beside David and tried to calm myself.

Rex came out wearing a blue robe and apologized to the kid for being snappish. He put his arm around him.

We had a pool tournament, and David wiped us out with the baby stick. Rex was bearing down pretty hard on the brandy, now that Leela and Marge were gone. And then the kid wanted a swim before bed. I said I'd skip that, and Rex and David went toward the back of the house. Then the doorbell rang. I started to call Rex, but I figured, What the hell, I'll get it, I opened the front door. Nobody was there, but in front of the door, on the patio, was a big green plastic garbage can with a huge dead dog on it. The old Lab, Gamble, lying there staring at me, on fire. The flames were bursting up from her poor back. Her mouth had been propped open with a stick so the fangs showed, the two front paws sticking out.

"*Rex!*" I yelled. The heat wasn't so bad, but it was quite a sight. "*Rex!*"

He came tearing in and stopped dead. Stood frozen for a few seconds beside me. Then he went out and kicked the garbage can over, the dog's body fell off onto the patio, and the can rolled down the driveway. I watched that green plastic can roll about twenty feet and then off onto the sand. My eyes flew back to the animal blazing away. Rex was headed for the phone when he screamed, and I saw what he was looking at.

Another fire out by the pool. You couldn't see exactly what it was, maybe another garbage can, you could only see the flames. We both started for that when I grabbed at his arm, because there was another one. Way down by the big cement wall in back of the master bedroom, you could hear that one, like an explosion.

Rex ran to the front door, slammed it and locked it, then ran back to his study. When he came out he had a gun, a .38. He stopped, then flew to the service entry, and he pulled a .22 pistol off the wall. He called, "David! Get in here." The kid had heard the explosions, he was scared. Rex gave him the .22, then looked at me. "Move it, man." I tore into the guest room and put on my gun belt. Checked my magnum and came back past the orange staircase. Now David was in Roger's room. Rex saying to him, "Just wait—you wait in here." Then he whipped out toward the garage.

What is this? I really don't think the kid should have that .22, Rex and I can handle it. I move out into the greenhouse, then back into the hall. I catch a glimpse of Roger, the little suck is sound asleep, I can't believe it, sleeping away in his sky-blue p.j. shirt and his overnight Pampers. David takes a few steps over to the crib, peeks at Roger, and I see that, without knowing it, David has the .22 pointed at him through the crib railing. I take the gun away from David. I step up on a chair and look out the little slit window. The fire is still burning down by the master bedroom.

OK, OK, cool it now. I check my weapon. Roger sighs in his sleep. I look toward the fire at the pool, but I can't see anything. Then I catch sight of Rex, he runs up and kicks over that fire. He keeps on kicking it, some of it goes into the pool. Rex stops and just stands there, and then he shouts, "Here I am!" He waits, and shouts it again: "I'm here, I'm here!" He raises the .38 and fires, fires it straight up at the night sky, and waits again. Then runs toward the garage. I open the little window and pull back the screen, but then I think, No, that's not right. I close the screen, close the window, draw the blue drapes. Shouldn't advertise this room. I'm afraid the old .22 will misfire in my belt. I try to think. How can we squeeze him? I should be outside, but Rex is so frantic, not to mention boozed, he might open fire on me. I could come around a corner and buy the big one right there. Shit, I wish he'd come in and let me handle it myself. David is pale as a sheet, trembling by the crib.

I have got to go out. I pause at the door and look hard at David. I whisper, "Do not leave this room." I say it again, each word separately, and he nods and gulps. I try to lock the door behind me, but there's no lock on it. I step back in for one more look out the window. I hear Rex's voice. Then silence. I stumble over David's old wooden train and hit that monster black and white panda. Roger stirs in the crib.

The front door of Medjuhl blasts open. Jesus, the fucker is in the house. I let myself out of the nursery. I creep through the greenhouse and look out at the swimming pool.

There he is. I know him. It's Peter Ingalls. Standing on the diving board. He's dressed up in some crazy Robin Hood costume. A cap with a long feather in it, maybe a peacock feather—flash on the burning of the bird. Peter has a torch, and he's hopping up and down. A shot rings out, but Peter isn't hit, he hops off the diving board. Robin Hood nimbly runs for a retreat into Sherwood Forest. Only he's running straight to me, to Medjuhl's greenhouse. I can see him so clean. I back up, something's behind me. I lash out with the .22 and drop it, adrenaline pumping, some kind of rubber tree leaf in my fingers. He sees me and he runs back to the pool, almost skipping. Then there's Rex coming after him, we've got him boxed in, Rex has a big butcher knife, he must have picked it up in the kitchen—and suddenly I see Peter's got a gun, Jesus, it's a Luger, a German Luger. Rex comes out and chases Ingalls along this side of the pool. I march forward, both hands around the magnum, and they are tearing around, Peter trying to get toward this end of the house. Rex shouts, *"Trip—don't!"* and he stops running. Peter Ingalls is only about twenty feet from me. Flashing that Luger. I can see his face all wild and breathless. Rex shouts again, *"Don't!"* But I have no choice, I know it, I breathe that chemical smell, Summer Snow, you complete fucking asshole, you insane sonofabitch—and it stops right there, frozen. The shot sounds like it's behind me, like it always does. My weapon kicks, and Peter Ingalls had just started to turn around so I don't see what the magnum does to his face, I only see what it does to his head.

Rex is standing with a .38 in one hand, a butcher knife in the other. He drops the knife, rushes past me into the house, calling, "Da-vid! Come on. It's all right!"

It is not all right. I knew I'd have to someday. All those days, year after year. The Riverside Academy. It is not all right. I have a cigarette. I sit in a pool chair and smoke. I don't think. Everything looks strange and pretty.

I could hear crying, Roger waking up. I went inside just as Rex came out and threw himself into that black velvet chair. He almost went over backward, he threw himself into it so hard. Then he looked up, all alert, the .38 still in his hand. He aimed right at a spot on the carpet and fired the gun. A chunk of carpet blew away.

"I've gotta—I've gotta—" Rex said. And dropped the gun.

Roger still crying.

Rex blundered into the kitchen and tried to dial the phone, but he couldn't.

He looked at me.

I called in a 10-79. Then I called the Indio sheriff's sub-station—funny, I almost dialed my old chief's home phone. I was coming down off the mountain. I looked up Charley Darling and called him.

Rex was smiling at me. Strangest smile I have ever seen, a thousand things at once. His teeth were so big and bright. Then he made this *Ssssss* noise, almost a whistle, just a long *Ssssss*.

David, all trembling and in shock. He came into the living room with Roger, who wouldn't shut up, was sopping wet, and David was a total loss at changing the Pampers. Roger squirming around so much. And David was completely wiped out, he could only get the wet Pampers off. I watched the whole scene. Like that was all in the world I had to do. David said to Roger, "You're not helping." Finally David just let Roger stand up for a while, yelling. Then Roger fell down and yelled some more. Rex went into the kitchen and rubbed his hands on a batch of paper towels, muttering to himself. I turned and Roger was on his hands and knees, bare-assed, with that little sky-blue shirt, going like a tank across the orange carpet. He had stopped crying. Rex stared at the child and reached into the refrigerator, pulled out a bottom tray, shut it, and closed the door. He knelt down by Roger. Rex said, "Want an apple?"

Roger looked at it, and—it was kind of funny, I guess—he looked at the apple and whispered, "Oh, wow!"

Then we heard the sirens.

David stayed in the living room with Roger, rolling the apple back and forth. A sheriff's deputy talked to me some, then stepped into the green-house, and talked to the men by the pool. I was still on automatic pilot. A deputy said, "Cute kid," meaning Roger.

More sirens, and Charley Darling arrived. My knowing him, being in uniform, helped. David took Roger back to the nursery. The medics brought the stretcher in through the house, but after they loaded the body on it, they didn't come back through. They went around the side. Rex was talking a lot, sitting now in the black velvet chair. Staring at the bullet hole in the carpet.

Out of courtesy and by the rules of the game I surrendered my weapon. I called my chief in Laguna, gave him quite an earful, then looked in on David, he was lying on a little couch. Roger in the crib snoring, his ass in the air. I sat down beside David for a while. Nothing to say. I patted him on the shoulder. His eyes were doing scared-to-death outer-space stuff. I went out and mentioned it to Rex, and he went on in.

I feel all hollow in my chest, and my arms don't work so great. There's this grinding in my shoulder sockets. I don't really see that I had much of a choice.

Next morning, sitting in the black velvet chair, David answered Detective Paul Overstreet's questions. Detective Overstreet was about fifty, he wore little half-spectacles for writing and reading. David did just fine, his dad standing beside him. I had had no sleep. But I did my number, and I told Overstreet about the blazing peacock, the party at Summer Snow. Overstreet was taking it all down. We were in fairly steady communication with Laguna. The Chief almost came out in a chopper, and the boys in Sacramento were hooked in. Overstreet had us all sign our voluntary statements. We used his gold ball-point, pressing hard for the court copy and two carbons.

I, _____, am _____ years of age, born on _____. My address is _____.

David was a little shook by the words "under penalty of perjury." He kept looking from Rex to me.

The D.A. showed up about 1:30, in a brown suit, crew cut, my age. Talking "justifiable homicide," playing buddy-boy with me. Rex is shaking like a leaf. I stayed calm, volunteered very little. But this was not the most subtle thing in the world. Pretty open-and-shut really. My shoulder sockets were still popping and grinding. I had the torque in my jaw.

Rex made the call to Joslin. She was completely beside herself, hysterical about the effect it would have on David. I talked to her, but there wasn't much point, no understanding on either end. And by now, My Way was crawling with minicams and reporters, vehicles parked all over the road and in the sand. The area cordoned off, microphones jammed in my face. Roger's mother just loved us when she picked him up. Pretty little brunette with a flat face. I am feeling very bad. My clothes stink, the uniform is just hanging on me. I stumble over my words for Channel 2, and then Rex comes on, very serious, he's Dr. Steven Kelly. I can still feel it. I am going to live this over and over for the rest of my life. I closed my grip, the last juice of a lemon, and the magnum barrel kicked up.

They waived what could have been a mandatory bail. I cried in the bathroom. A juicy broad from Desert Cable TV wanted to know how I got the nickname "Triphammer." I said that was what I had been called since high school, which clarified things for her. The media vultures loved it, their follow-up on the death of J.O. Hooker, the Great Architect, and Rex Hooker, the star of "This Passing Night." I don't seem to hear distinctly. I am chain-smoking.

A veritable circus.

But now it seemed a little clearer. Peter Ingalls had been telephoning Rex for weeks. Kept saying things on the phone like "We have an appointment in Samarra" and "The last chapter has yet to be written." He said he would send his "representative" if Rex would send his *consigliere*— these people have just seen too many movies. Everything happened so goddamn fast I hadn't even had time to think about that phone call I got just before Peter attacked. "The night is full of death." Peter had dyed his hair white-blond and pretty clearly was trying to make himself look like Rex. In the darkness I saw that hair but did not realize it was dyed, I was focusing on the Robin Hood cap with the peacock feather. Peter Ingalls. They found three whole sets of I.D.'s on him.

And finally we had a few hours to ourselves. Medjuhl quieted down, Rex and David and I sat by the pool, the last of the people gone. I have taken a human life. It does not please me. Except it does, I wasted a killer, it had to be done.

I look up at the clean desert sky.

Rex is real tender with David, walking and talking, talking and walking.

But something is not right here. Something is not right, I can't put my finger on it. So I smoke and smoke, one after another.

14

THE AIR conditioning in Marge's 'Vette was on the blink. David wanted to see some outer-space Disney movie at the Saturday matinee. Rex said he had a lot of things to do, including a talk with Dibby before we went back to Laguna. I was in charge of the kid and the car. The 'Vette was easy, just a dollar fuse, we got that done in a jiffy. I dropped the kid at the movie theater on the highway, just a mile from Medjuhl, and then I felt like driving around for a while in the restored 'Vette air conditioning. I wonder when I am ever going to have the money to get myself a mean machine like this. Except I really want a Porsche Turbo 928. I killed a man. I drive aimlessly. I have kept a scrapbook for ten years, all the arrests and auto wrecks and drug busts and promotion notices, nothing too small to go into Officer Bodley's memory book. Now I am splashed all over the fucking papers, and I do not want to put any of it in there. I killed a man. I have been going up and down on a roller coaster. One minute I am high with the thrill of accomplishment, the next I am completely down because I have killed a man. I replay it in my head. I get sick, and then I feel all right.

The Chief called this morning. They're going to have a special commendation—for me. The Chief says that determination and persistence always pay off. He says, according to the *L.A. Times,* that "Triphammer Bodley" has been with this investigation from the beginning. He also says in the *Times* that Oliver Bodley, police sergeant, is a graduate of Stanford University.

What?

He tells me he read them the data on my vita. The data on my vita. Well, it's true I did attend. But I sure didn't graduate. If Rex sees it, I'll tell him I was expelled for riding a motorcycle in Wilbur Hall. I can't tell him I flunked out. How could the Chief tell them that? Data on my vita, *da*-ta on my *vi*-ta, like what the shits yell on the schoolyard, a-*dop*-ted, a-*dop*-ted.

I am rapidly becoming unable to get satisfaction out of anything at all. What would have happened if I hadn't been there? Peter Ingalls would probably have gotten into the house and killed them both. And Roger, too. The Indio *Daily News* played up my past history, my service on the force there, way back to high school and Most Inspirational. I detect Charley Darling's hand in that. What was Rex doing with a butcher knife? Please leave me alone, I killed a human being. I wish my uncle was alive, sitting on the porch, coughing out his emphysema lungs, the old deerhunter.

I wonder if after the commendation, the Chief could give me a week off. I don't take much disability leave, I never seem to be able to do it, just like my uncle—I used to tell him you can't save it up, but he would always say that when you are well, you work. He had no use whatever for slackers. And I always told him it's a useless way to kill yourself. So here I am doing the exact same thing. Maybe it is inherited. Except my uncle and I are no blood kin. Not to my knowledge. He might have fancied my real mother, though. A thought I have always tried to repress. But he could have done it once and my aunt figured it out. And for all those years, every time she looked at me, she saw his face in my features. No. Never took place. Never. How do you know where you come from?

I killed a man, blew his head away.

I could use a week. Just to go somewhere. Like Vegas, where I have never been, get laid and lose all my money at the blackjack tables. Drink, look at movie stars in the lounge. I don't want to stay here, be a local celebrity for killing a man who was insane. I should have shot him in the leg. I could go backpacking in the Sierras, all by myself, up my tent and lie on my back looking at the stars. Just be off by myself in the wilderness. A little fire, eggs and bacon sizzling.

I don't feel any sense of release. I am still in it. I met an officer from the L.A.P.D. once, out at the Riverside Academy, who had killed a guy.

261

He described it to me, the "nigger" going down with his knife, and he said it was "beautiful." No, it's not. But Peter Ingalls did set the fires, at Summer Snow and Medjuhl, he had to go. I do not know what I am complaining about, I agreed to this responsibility when I put on the badge.

I give myself a little pep talk. I stop the 'Vette and stand looking out across the desert and say a few words to my uncle, my father. I bet that's just what happened, and my aunt never mentioned the indiscretion. That's what happens when you kill a man, your mind wanders. You see deep secrets in the past. You ache and ache. Try to make something that ties together. Not for one minute do I think adoptive children have the right to their records.

The desert is really beautiful in the fall.

I wish Marge would get this 'Vette tuned. I wish I hadn't told her what I told her. I hope all those women are all right. Leela and Joslin and Marge. Joslin has not held David in her arms. He's safe at the movies, eating popcorn, or Milk Duds.

I start inside Medjuhl, and then I stop and listen. The door between the house and the garage is open, so I can hear voices, a tape recording, one of Rex's thousands of tapes. It's blaring through the whole house, Rex must have the volume way up.

I go in, but Rex isn't there. He must be in the study. The tape is his voice. But it's two voices—he's talking to himself in two slightly different voices. I don't know whether he's recording back in his study or just listening to it.

"You weren't faithful. You said your marriage wasn't based on fidelity."
"I'm not sure about that."
"You aren't?"
"Oh, fuck off. You really bug me, Kelly."
"Would you like me to turn it off, Rex?"
"No, Steve, keep it going."

I sat down at the breakfast bar in the kitchen. Rex Hooker and Steve Kelly. One of them has to go. I get it. He's psychoanalyzing himself. His soap opera character is taking charge—taking charge of him. I start to stand up, to go find him, but then I hear:

"Triphammer. I found Joslin sleeping with Triphammer. And David was home—home, upstairs, asleep. How could she do that to me?"
"Sounds like Triphammer was doing it to her."

"When I caught 'em at it, she stood up and said—oh, my, I really can't bear this—somewhere long ago—and my darling son—I always knew. I always knew."

I sit there in the kitchen.
I can't listen, and I can't not listen.
Oh shit.

"I was at Cal State Fullerton. A communication arts festival. Soap opera! I was the featured speaker. I love doing colleges—I give good college. I'll never forget, those years ago, her voice, her voice, her scream. When she saw blood in the toilet. Food turns into blood. I can see it begin to coagulate."

"Back off, it's too hot for you."

"She should not have done that to me. Dammit, she knows I take it so seriously, she should not have done it to me."

"Do you hate her for it?"

"No."

"Why can't you hate her?"

"I don't know. I can't hate people. I'm too frightened of hate, it makes me weak and dizzy. I am not equipped to hate. Pop hated. He was good at it. And his rages. I remember when I was a little boy, I knew exactly when to stay out of his way. Just stay out of his way. Pop was beautiful in his hate. Because he loved people. But they, they, they so frighten me. I think my inability to hate is not good. It is a sign of something wrong in me."

"Maybe. Maybe that is even true."

"Talk to me. It's like hot water in my limbs. It does terrible things to me. Triphammer. I hate him, but I must not hate. It's like hot water in my limbs. Do you know that the woman I love most in the world called me a fascist Christ?"

"And what do you think?"

"I think she is unacquainted with the Blood of the Lamb."

"Do not let her degrade you."

"She has. Has already. Hear my *yiddishe gesundheit.* And now David is leaving."

"David is leaving?"

"It's all crashing down on me. Dr. Kelly, please, please speak words of wisdom, Mother Mary comfort me. I'm not here. Do you realize what I have done? Pop, dead. Jos, gone. Pop, dead. Ernest, Jos's brother, is in a very bad way. And now Jos wants to yank my boy out of school—midyear

—and take him to live with her in Ernest's apartment in New York and Ernest's house in Connecticut, while she takes care of Ernest, who can't take care of himself. How can Joslin take David away from me? How am I going to live without seeing my boy every week?"

"How are you going to live?"

Rex talking to himself, and me listening to it in the cold air of the kitchen. Rex talking to himself. It's awful.

"I have already begun to damage him. The other day he came bouncing into the house, and he said, 'Oh, Dad, I'm so happy today—you're not—' and then the little guy said, '—tired.' What he meant was not drunk. And a really terrible thing—a ghastly thing—is the knives."

"The knives?"

"Well, I've got Peter on my mind every second. I don't know where we went wrong, this family. Family-shmamily. We were only trying to help. Pop figures he let Peter's pop down, didn't stand by him when Peter Senior was in trouble. The horrible time. Oh God. The horrible time with Peter—it's our fault!

"It's not your fault."

"The whole world's my fault."

"Rex, people who think the whole world is their fault are people who think they run the show."

"I do run the show. 'This Passing Night.' I do run the show. And I've wrecked it, ruined it—oh, Pop—Pop—"

Silence.

"I'm afraid of Peter, so I've been hiding knives everywhere, especially when I'm drunk, I sit with my drink and I hear—I hear Peter breathing —it's like he's inside me—and I go, I go to the kitchen, and I get a butcher knife, or a steak knife, and I—I *hide* them—in some magazines, the back of a closet, the piano bench—"

"You hide knives?"

"Shut up, Kelly. Yes. I hide knives. But listen to me. It's not my hiding them—my mind's going. Jos can see that. It's not Ernest she's going to —it's me she's running away from. Clear across the continent. She wants David away from me. I'm a 'magic father, not a good father.' I'm too ill to be a good father. David can't have an invalid for a father. She has to take him away from me. And when I saw the knives, shit, I knew she was right."

"Saw the knives?"

"Early one morning. I was sitting on the carpeted staircase, huddled up there with my morning waker-upper, huddled around my sauce, and David came out of his room, you know how he is in the morning, can't wake up, and he sat on the old ottoman. In his pajamas. He reached for a magazine, and there was a carving knife, I watched him from the stairs, and he looked at it, turned it over in his hands, and then he went into the kitchen and put it back. He didn't know I saw him. But I did."

"You saw him find a knife."

"No, Kelly, you don't listen. Not that he *found* the knife—what killed me was that he *put it back*. I mean, I mean, he could have asked me about it. I'd have made up a cover story. But he never asked. And that means he was afraid to ask. Me. He's already got an invalid for a father. I'm an in-valid father."

"No, you're not."

"I am. I can't live for the boy I live for. He has to put my knives back. What does that mean about what he's carrying around in his head? Jos is right. She has to take him away from me. I can't run the show. I can't be the head of the family. I can't protect my loved ones. I'm Peter."

"You're not Peter."

"I hide knives. Jossie's got me. She's won. She knew what she had to do to win, she had to make me ashamed of myself. And I am. All I can do now is take care of Mother. And that I will do. After the operation there's going to be a lengthy convalescence. That's something I can do. Jos is right. It'll take all my time. She and David have to go. I'll just put all my energy into caring for Mother. Family. Family."

"Family-shmamily."

"I know. Why does Joslin carry on like that? You know what she said to me once? She said, 'I've finally figured it out, Rex. Why you have to keep telling the Hooker Story. Story after story. I've figured it out.' "

"And?"

"You know what that bitch said? She said, 'Because secretly, you're ashamed of your family.' "

"And?"

"*And? And?* That's only about the stupidest thing I've ever heard. Ashamed of Pop? Ashamed of Mother? They're only the inspiration of my whole fucking *life*."

"But if you're ashamed of your*self*—"

"Oh, shut up, Kelly. The one I'm ashamed of is her. Bitch. How could she do that? I thought I told her—I know I told her—midnight. She must have known. She *had* to have known. It was a setup—"

"Clever little bitch."

"Is that it? Is she clever?"

"Of course. Look at you."

"What?"

"Look at you—she's got you."

"Got me?"

"You can't eat, you're losing weight again. She's got you right where she wants you."

"Yes. I mean, no."

"You want it to be a setup."

"You know, Dr. Kelly, it would be easier for me to handle if I truly thought that—isn't that funny?"

"No. It's your opera. It makes sense. Because then she was doing it for you. Not a liaison, an aria. For Rex."

Silence. On a tape, a silence.

"Right. Dr. Kelly, you are right."

Silence again.

"Rex, tell me, why are you in such pain?"

Talking to himself, Rex talking to himself. And me listening, in the kitchen. If I had any decency, I'd get up and stop it. But I can't. I don't.

"It was eleven fifty-four. I saw it on the big digital clock on Downey Savings. I thought to myself, I'll make it, I'll just make it. Midnight. I remember thinking that in the car—by the way, to answer your question before you ask it, I did stop on the way, I bought a pint, I had been drinking on the way back from Fullerton, I already had a few drinks in me—"

"You're drinking all the time again."

"Not at crisis time. Never at crisis time. I just drink for something to do."

"Sure."

"But that's true. Once I asked Jossie if that was it. If she divorced me because of the drinking. And she said no. She said she divorced me because of a deeper addiction. To my *family*. What does that mean? You destroy family because of your addiction to it? Is that it?"

"You said that, not me."

"Destroy family because your addiction to it is killing you? So I *am* guilty? Stop that. Oh, I can't blame her—I can't hate her—"

"You buy her line."

"What?"

"Rex, you do believe you're responsible. She's got you."

"Just because I'm ill? It doesn't mean she has to commit adultery on

266

me, in front of my own eyes, in the very house Pop and I built for us. With our son asleep in his room. Not with my dear friend, not with the guy I got beat up with twenty years ago—not—not Bluebird Canyon."

"Very clever of her. Very clever."

"Stop. Just stop. And you know something funny? When I came in? I was expecting it."

"Expecting it?"

"Like it was no surprise. I knew. And I knew it was Trip. I knew before I saw his face. When he jumped up and was struggling into his pants, I knew. Those gold boots Pop bought me, the Florsheims, they were too tight, so I took them off in the car, I had them in my right hand, and in my left I had this orange poster from Fullerton—I was going to come in at midnight, and Jos and I would talk about how brilliant I was, being you, being myself, Kelly and Hooker—I tell you—*one of us has to go*—"

"You always say that lately."

"Well, it's true."

"Consider how it makes me feel, Rex. If one of us has to go, I know who—"

"No you don't. Shut up. I'm paying for this. Think if I had missed the show. Imagine that, if I had missed their dirty little show. I find them afterward, just sitting around. Trip goes home, and I want to make love, feeling all brilliant after my performance. Would she at least have taken a bath? I wonder about her bath. Trip's sperm would be in her body, and then my sperm would enter her body, and would they mingle? Trip's sperm and mine? Whose baby would that be? Superfecundation! No wonder I hide knives. She has no regard for her body. No regard for family. Family stops at the body's edge. How would she know who the father is? What kind of person is that careless? Look, Kelly, let me tell you. I remember a little incident when we were first married. Joslin's chapters in the Hooker Story are the dirty parts. She met this guy from France, an attaché at the UN. She met him at a reception, and he said the party was too noisy, he was only in the States for a few days, could they continue talking in his hotel room? Why doesn't Jos prick up her ears? Why doesn't she hear? And then, in the hotel room, he told her, in French, that her feelings were at war with her brain, and he said he was in love with his wife, too, but his dark French eyes invited a new love experiment. She stood up to leave and—these things are organized better in France— he pushed her onto the bed and pulled out his uncircumcised cock and stuck it in her face. I know, I hate knowing this was all in French, I hate the sound of it, Jos's chapter in the Hooker Story, the dirty parts, are all in French. And then she comes back to our apartment

267

on Seventy-sixth Street quite shaken and asks me to comfort her."

"And did you?"

"No. She was teasing him and she got caught. Why should I *comfort* her?"

"Nice going."

"No honor to it. Dis-honor. No man can honor the mother who does that to her child."

"Huh?"

"You must *trust* those whom you love."

"I'm not following, Rex. I thought this happened in New York. David wasn't born yet."

"Yes he was. David is *always* born. And he can't have French eyes, goddammit."

"What are you talking about?"

"She has done that to me, over and over again. And yet—and yet— I just—*die*—when I see her goodness."

"Rex, you're killing yourself."

"She lied to me. He stuck his uncircumcised cock in her face."

"Are we talking about New York, ten years ago, or Laguna last week?"

"Yes."

Silence.

"She has a career of being unconscious. She thinks she is an independent woman. She's not. She's a criminally irresponsible girl."

"In your mind."

"No, not in my mind. The world is not in my mind. *The world is not in my mind.* Excuse me all over the world. *Oy gevalt miércoles!* Must not put my mind behind bars. If I lose my mind—if I lose *me*, I'll be *you*. I don't want to be *you*. Now, you listen. Look, my hands were full of poster and gold boots—when I walked in, I could smell the dope right away, it was all dark, and I could hardly see them, they were on the couch by the fireplace, the firewood—and David could have seen that, could have wanted a glass of water and come downstairs and seen that. I thought about how I brought the wood in when I stopped by that morning, I said we'd have a fire when I got home, unless I stayed overnight in Fullerton, I'd call at nine-thirty, and if I didn't call at nine-thirty, I'd arrive at twelve midnight—I'm *sure* I said that, and she is sure I did not—"

"Well, did you or didn't you?"

"Only my head shrinker knows for sure. The horrible time with Peter. What that did to our family, family-shmamily. David—David—"

"So this is about David. What the two of you can't do in front of him. She can't fuck, and you can't drink."

"*Jesus*, Kelly, what an asshole you are."

"You hate your imagination."

"Rex Hooker Today, but Triphammer Tonight. Oh—oh—and the music. Brahms. Brahms is *me*. Why couldn't they have been listening to Blondie?"

"And you don't hate her?"

"Of course not. I love her. But how could she ever say that?"

"What?"

"That I'm ashamed of my parents."

"It really bothers you, doesn't it?"

"Yes, asshole, yes, it bothers me. I adore my parents. Why doesn't she *thank* them?"

"Thank them?"

"For giving her *me*?"

"Rex, if you don't think that's funny, we aren't making much progress here."

"Maybe they weren't even . . . I mean, when she called him to come over, maybe she wasn't planning to fuck, lots of women don't realize that men—"

"Oh yes—"

"But I hope to say, I mean, wait a minute. One thing led to another. One thing led to another. And she was so out of her mind with grief—when I go down into the deep dark holes—I mean, give her credit, give her—"

"She makes your bones water."

"She makes my bones water."

"And now?"

"She makes my bones water."

"Rex, you have to let go."

"She makes my bones water."

"That may be, but—"

"That may be, but—"

"She had that blanket, that comforter—she was dishonoring, I mean, like now, Mother grieving for Pop, there is a time for grieving—how dare she?—How *dare* she?"

"She's not family."

"She's Bitch. I thought Dishonor, I thought, oh—junk, junk, junk—shit and garbage, garbage and junk—leave me alone, Herr Doktor Kelly, turn off the tape. No—don't—Steve is my brother, just wait and see, Rex Hooker Today and Dr. Steve Kelly Tonight, except that's not the way it works. Grass in my nose, and Mother's comforter, Jossie just suddenly grabbed it to her, and she cried out, as I was moving toward her, in a dream, she cried out, *'You can't do this to me!'* Isn't that incredible? Isn't that just amazing? 'You can't do this to me.' And her eyes, those deep green eyes of hers on fire with panic and rage. *'You can't do this to me!'* Those words, those eyes. Those words, those eyes. While poor Trip was climbing into his pants."

"Did you think how he felt?"

"Well, what's so complicated about that?"

"How he must have felt when he heard her say, 'You can't do this to me.'"

"What? What? Tell me."

"He's not trapped, Rex. He's not just surprised. I wouldn't want to be that man climbing into his pants. He must have felt pretty foolish."

"Pretty *foolish*?"

I wince in the kitchen. Shit, he knows. He's got me. He knows.

"I don't mean, I mean, what would she have done—David might have awakened, you know, just awakened in the night, and he would have found his own mother—I mean, it's crazy—it is simply not in that woman's character to do that—she would not do it. Not in Bluebird Canyon, not like that—she's not evil or mean or careless—it's—she just would not do it in Bluebird Canyon."

"That's why she did it."

"What?"

"She's done a complete number on you. And you're letting her do it."

"But she's my wife, I love her—"

"She's not your wife. She's your ex-wife. A few minutes ago you called it adultery. It's not."

"It *is*. We are married—till death do us part. We said so. We—we promised."

"What would you call a woman who'd do that, Rex?"

"A desperate—"

"Yes?"

"A desperate—and a desperately unhappy woman."

I am listening to him talk to his mind. I hear him say that. I am getting a feeling, a death smell. Nobody can talk to his own mind like that. He's two-three-four steps ahead of himself. He knows *her*, for sure. The poor bastard.

"You're too easy on her."

"No. No, Steve."

"The two of you—you're sex junkies."

"What?"

"Sex junkies."

"That's beautiful. Sex junkies. I like that, Steve."

"You're very ill, Rex."

"Well, thanks a lot."

"You're welcome."

"What kind of thing is that to say to me? What are you saying? You're saying my mind is diseased? You want to put my mind behind bars?"

"You're in real trouble. You ought to be in—"

"A hospital? My mind *behind bars?*"

"Don't pour another."

"Stop with the talk, stop with the talk. If I were a part of the human body, just one part, you know what part I would be?"

"The asshole."

"No, no—the *mouth.*"

"And there we are . . . blip-blip . . . for some reason, and she took the shower curtain, help me—I am in *pain*—for some reason, after Trip cleared out, and Jos and I were alone, and I had sat for a spell with David —I immediately killed what was left of the brandy and went on with more, I called Turfbinder—"

"Turfbinder?"

"Yeah. You know, Mustang Turfbinder. I needed to tell someone, right away. Weird. I had to tell. So I called Turfbinder—"

"What's his real name again?"

"Misha Spiro."

"That's a better name than Mustang Turfbinder."

"I know. Misha Spiro is a terrific name—well, I called him and said We've Got Big Trouble Here, and I blabbed it all to him, and he said, 'Well, Rex, if I were married to you, I'd sleep with someone else,' meaning he understood the trouble she was in, the hell I'd put her through, but I remember—I can feel it now—his face earnestly close to mine, and I said, 'Well, Turfbinder, if I were married to you, I'd *certainly* sleep with somebody else,' and we laughed. Dammit, right *there* I had it demystified, I was OK right there. My mouth was ahead of me, way ahead."

"But you can't live with it."

"It was an incredibly painful night."

"I gather."

271

"Don't give me no primal trauma crap. Sure, I pushed her. Sure I did. But that's all. Pushed. And she fell, she hit her head on the fridge, really hard, there was blood on the floor, she went racing out into the street, naked, down Bluebird, and I ran after her, I was afraid she had hurt herself—"

"You were afraid she had hurt herself?"

"Of course. Her head hit the fridge. Then running naked on the street like that."

"You didn't beat her up?"

"What am I supposed to be—the Outraged Husband? That is what's so awful about it, she turned our marriage into a bad novel, a joke. One of the oldest. There's a cartoon like that every month in *Playboy*. How dare she? How dare she make me into a laugh line in a Myron Cohen routine. Husband comes home, finds his wife naked on da bed. Husband sez, 'Dohlink, vy is you nekid?' She, de poor dear, she sez, 'I got notting to wear.' He goes to de closet, and he sez, 'What do you mean, you got notting to wear? Look here—you got da blue one, da green one, da red one, Hello Sam, da yellow one, da purple one. . . .' And now *I* am the one who has to live with it, *I* am the one who has to carry that shit with me for the rest of my life, it's in there, in my head, I have to carry it for the rest of my life—"

"Now you've got it."

"What?"

"Are you going to let her win? Are you going to carry it around in your head for the rest of your life? That's all that counts."

"That's not all that counts. Man, I appreciate your giving me air time —audibilize my feelings—but I really should have other things on my mind. Big deal, I found my friend, Triphammer, my old friend, sleeping with my wife—imagine that, just *imagine* that. My ex-wife. But that is only unfortunate, I don't know why I put so much energy into it. I really should have only two things on my mind."

"Two things?"

"Mother, first. Mother first. To take care of her. And—and—"

"And?"

"Well, I've been getting these phone calls from Peter. Sorry, wrong number. Peter in my head—from that horrible time, oh dear, oh *dear*. If I can just get hold of him and stop him—"

"But Rex, he killed your father."

"No, oh no, no. My father did not stand by his father. Pop abandoned him. It wasn't Peter Senior's fault that he didn't have what it takes. And the horrible time. Pop had his brutal side. Don't sentimentalize him. I have seen him take men apart for the fun of it. *Build Therefore Your Own Robot.* What he did to me, to that poor boy. But that is wrong. I dwell, I dwell. Pop was in *Who's Who.* I'm not—because I'm asking, *Who's Who?* I know something Pop didn't know. I believe I detect a whiff of Christian charity. Or the Siamese twin of it—Christian Cruelty. Oh, if I just do not *break*—if I can just *hold on.* But I'm the one who is somewhere responsible."

"Rex, you ride a high moral horse."

"And have saddle sores. Goddammit, Doc, I'm caving in. And I can't. Not for Mother, not for Mother. And not for David. I have to—by brute force—I have to stay sane. But each day I feel it slipping away. My mind *behind bars?* What if *I, Rex,* really do become a crazy person? What happens if I lose me? What happens if Rex *disappears?*"

Then I looked up and he was outside, at the pool. It was strange, because that tape had been going, and I had been completely lost in it, and now Rex's voice went on again, but there was Rex himself, naked. He dived into the pool. I watched him butterfly, shoomshoomshoom down the pool, and he grabbed the end and hopped out. He stood there looking around, like he was puzzled, and he went and stood where Peter Ingalls's body had fallen. He planted himself there, and then he must have needed that cold water, he went in again, swimming underwater. There was something on the tape I couldn't make heads or tails of—about Peter Ingalls and the horrible time. Whenever Rex gets to that part, his voice goes weird and fast and I can't make it out.

"How could she? How could she?"

"She was trying to tell you something."

"Well, pardon me, I don't care for her rhetoric."

"You're a funny man."

"Cure me, Dr. Kelly. Make it all not happen. Make my sick mind well. I gone down where the dragons live. Their reptile cold steam is in my blood. On my tongue. I've gone down there where the dragons live. And now I am a dragon. I got—bit."

"You're in love with melodrama. Too much—cold steam—in your pipes."

"Ah, but what I hear."

"What do you hear?"

"Voices. Voices. I mean, what she thought she was doing, if David had walked in on her—Jesus, I still can't believe she did it, in *our home,* Bluebird Canyon, it doesn't make sense—"

"It doesn't make sense to do it anywhere else. She wasn't, after all, having an affair."

"She wasn't?"

"No."

"Oh, I get it. Yes, she had to do it there. But I hate it, I have that right, I just want to burn the house down, just burn all the corruption out of it, *burn* the sonofabitch—"

There in the kitchen I jumped, I heard him say that. I was scared to death. I looked out and saw him lying naked on the cement with one arm in the pool.

"Pop, my darling father, he is dead, Home on the Range—Jesus Christ, Pop isn't here anymore, I cannot believe the grief, the *grief*—how can I live without him? He was everything to me, and now—now—oh, *Pop*—"

A spell. Rex casts a spell. If I can just pretend I never heard it. Maybe I can slip out into the garage. I watched Rex tightrope walking on the edge of the pool. He lost his balance, probably half on purpose, and went flying into the water. Just fooling around. He went way down to the bottom and pushed off, hard, then came halfway out of the water, like a dolphin. I flashed on that Mexican, his crippled legs, his canes in the sand, Joslin, the setting sun. Rex went butterflying again, shoomshoomshoom, so powerful, a beautiful flip turn, and then came back with the 'fly, tearing along.

"I ought to change my name."

"Oh?"

"I want to be Prometheus Homebody."

"Nice."

"I want to live the life of ultimate discovery—to put my feet up by the fire, the sweet fire we split logs for, and now relax in the glow of—Jesus, it was my wood, she was fucking Triphammer to my wood—sit by the fire, and go over the day's business, and look in on David, and, and, and—oh it hurt me so bad, so *bad*, you must be right, Dr. Kelly, I am barely hanging on. Who's Who? Please don't move. Let me look into your eyes. The script of our marriage was corn, pure corn, cure porn, and the parts were so badly played, I should never have married a Jew, not a Jew—they don't know how to behave, they have no grace—Christ, see how cheapness has invaded me, what do I mean Jews have no grace? How can Rex Hooker with his fine mind say that? Just a bull-roar anti-Semite. Help, I am going to throw up."

"You are scary to watch."
"I am?"
"You are scary to watch."
"Why?"
"You are scary to watch."
"Stop saying that—stop saying that—"

And then Rex was there. Dripping wet, naked, moving slowly through the door from the greenhouse. I looked at the place in the carpet where the bullet hole was, where Rex fired the .38.

He was still walking, the tape booming on—

"I don't think I can go over it, again, I am getting so tired of it—I am fading away—Mother—Peter—the horrible time—"

On the tape he was crying. His voice said, "Oh my God." Then just a lot of crying and finally the swish-swish-swish sound of a played-out tape. Rex didn't see me. He was just standing there in the room, naked.

And David came out.

David—oh, Jesus—David came in from the back bedroom. How did *he* get here? The poor little suck has big wads of Kleenex in his hand. He's been listening to it, David has been listening to it. Back in his bedroom. I thought he was at the movies. You can sure see what he thinks about it, all that Kleenex in his hands.

Something wrong about all this, it's completely fucked up.

Rex walked slowly to the bathroom. He hadn't said a word. He came out with a big beach towel, patted his body with it. He was staring at David.

"Dad?" the kid said. He went over and hugged his father.

Rex let the beach towel fall on the orange carpet. He kissed the top of his son's head.

"Dad?" David whispered.

Rex raised his head. He saw me, and stumbled backward. That made David turn, and then he saw me.

The three of us, all of us in shock, I suppose anybody could have said it, but it was Rex who screamed, "What *is* this?"

We were trapped. Rex stood in the living room, in the colored sunlight coming through the merry-go-round ceiling.

"Dad?" the kid said again.

"Son," Rex whispered. "Son?"

I stood up, in the kitchen.

"I thought—I—thought you were at the movie—Trip?" He patted

275

himself with that big towel. "David—how long have you—?"

"Dad."

"Have you been listening? Have you both—been—listening?"

"Dad, I didn't mean to, I guess I made a mistake."

"Well, I guess you did." He looked at me.

I said, "I thought he was at the movie, too."

"Dad, the newspaper wasn't right, there's no Saturday matinee."

"But didn't—Trip, didn't you see the movie was closed?"

I stepped forward, a little. "I thought we were early. The fuse only took a minute."

"The fuse?"

"In the 'Vette. The broken air conditioner—it was a fuse."

Rex looked at David. "But how did you—"

"I walked. It's just up the road. I tried to hitch, a couple of cars—"

"But how long, how *long* have you both—"

"I was in my room, Dad. I was doing my report, for school. I didn't mean to listen. But I heard—I heard it was about *me.*" The kid looked from Rex to me. "The first part, I mean."

"What—what was the first part?" Rex went over to the black chair. "Oh—what a shame—what a shame." He started to walk into the greenhouse, and then he stopped. He went to the eggshell couch. "What a *shame.*"

David was staring at his bare feet. His eyes came up, and he looked at his father.

His father looked at him. Then looked at me. He said, "They fixed the 'air' in the 'Vette?"

"It just needed a little fuse."

Rex's eyes were stopping on things, looking for clues. He said, "I don't remember all of what I said on that tape, Steve and Rex. It was—I'm so—"

"Dad, it's OK."

Rex stood there for the longest time. Searching the room for a clue. But he made his eyes jump over my face. He didn't want to look at me.

Silence.

Finally David said, "Let's all pretend it didn't—you know—we can pretend. Is that OK?"

Silence.

Rex stood there naked. Then moved to the piano and sat down on the bench. He played three notes. Played them again. Waited. Again. I know. The music box, "Bluebird Canyon."

Rex said, "I thought I was alone in the house—I thought—"

Silence. Rex standing there naked.

"I don't understand why you listened"—he turns—"either of you. Don't you know some things are private? They're private."

He shivered. The air conditioner. The Medjuhl thermostat was down at the bottom.

"Well," he said, "I suppose I've got to clear up some things."

David said, "I don't care."

Rex looked at his boy. "Honey, come sit down."

I am included. Rex asks us both to sit down.

I have done all the wrong things. I should have seen that the movie was closed, I should have waited. Instead of driving around. Killing a man, again. In my head.

David went back into his room. Big wads of Kleenex on the carpet. Rex gathers them up and puts them in the wastebasket. As he goes by me, he says, "How? How could you do it?"

I said again I didn't know the kid was in the house. And then I thought, Or you mean everything? I look at Rex. He looks at me. He sighs, and then he says, "Joslin—whom you now . . . *know*—says I love melodrama." His speech is very low, very precise. He stands over the wastebasket. Looks at me again. "And I do not know why it constantly runs me down in the street. I do not know. It is some monstrous"—and his voice hits rockbottom—"illness."

David comes out, with another Kleenex box. He fumbles, drops it.

Rex says, softly, "Klutz."

We sat down.

Rex said to David, "You remember when the obstetrician put you in my arms? That's a big chapter of the Hooker Story. Remember when you were born, son? You had an incredibly ugly pointy head."

David looked at him.

"But that's the way all babies' heads are. Pointy. Ugly. From traversing the vaginal walls—you know, coming out of the womb, the melodies of the womb. Babies' heads are always pointy. Jesus, m'man, you really looked like a dunce."

David trying to smile.

"But the doc told me the head smoothes out. I said, 'Is he going to be smart?' The doc, bathing you, said, 'I haven't had time yet to give him an IQ test.'"

David did smile.

"So I believed him. But now, you know, Mother, Leela, she has to have this operation on her head. And I'm real scared about it."

"I know."

"She'll make it, all right. It's a little tumor."

"The size of a pinhead."

"That's right. But these things are very scary, and it will take her a long time to recover. And I'll have to be there, on call, every minute. I'm not doing it because I have to—I could hire a nurse for her—I'm doing it because I want to."

"Yes."

I am not exactly included in this conversation. I'm just sitting here. Watching it. I think about the time in the Hotel Laguna card room, when David asked about God. Rex was talking to him then like he's talking to him now, but that time he lost it, he went crazy. I am also thinking, How the fuck is he going to get out of this? How is he going to explain what was on that tape?

And I know that's on Rex's mind, that's what Rex is thinking about. As he looks the kid in the eye.

I'm watching Rex think.

"And so, son, your mommy and I have talked about it. Leela has to have this surgery, this tumor has just about ruined her life, and we all have to help her as best we can. I'll be by her side. And you can help by going away. Mommy is going to Connecticut and you'll join her, after New Year's."

"To where?"

"Well, sometimes family—family-shmamily—takes you away. Uncle Ernest is not well. So you'll go to school for a semester, for half a year, in the East."

"I will?"

"She hasn't told you?"

"No."

"Well, maybe she wanted me to tell you. Which I now do. It's OK. It's right."

"And leave Top of the World School?"

"Oh, you'll be back. It's just a different environment for a while. Try it—you'll like it."

"I don't want to."

"It's all right, son. We'll see it through. OK?"

"No."

"Come on, m'man, everybody's got to pitch in."

David looked at his feet.

"I've got to help Mother with the operation. I have to do that. I won't be able to spend time playing with you."

278

Just looking at his feet, the kid.

"Well, file that, OK? I want to move along here on our agenda. I want to tell you about this nincompoop, Triphammer."

The kid glances at me.

"Now, Trip has been a friend of the family for years. Years and years. He's always been good to us. To all of us." Rex sits forward. "If Trip hadn't been here, that crazy Peter could have killed us, like he—like he killed—Pop."

The kid offers the Kleenex box to his dad.

Rex takes one and blows his nose. Throws the wad onto the orange carpet. "Now we have to think clearly, son. Could I hear a vote of confidence on thinking clearly? Thanks, folks, 'preciate that. Now, look, son, don't cry—I've told you that it's OK to cry, but please not now, because I want to be rational." Rex goes into the kitchen and pours himself some whiskey. He comes back, puts his cigarettes on the glass coffee table. He picks one up. Lights it, looks at me. "It's a lie. Get it, son? It's a lie."

David's head snaps up.

"I'm awfully sorry you heard that tape—it wasn't meant to be heard by anybody except myself. As you know, for many years, I have been trying to do a good job on 'This Passing Night.' So I make things up. I make them up in my mind, and I put them on tape. I use those tapes for *memos* —to explore ideas, wild ideas. On that tape I was talking to Dr. Steve Kelly, me and Steve—it's all a mind blowout. For the show. You know how I need new situations for the show. So I make things up. They're not true. They're made up. Imaginary. Folklore. Tall tales. Not *real.*"

David wanted so much to believe him.

Rex was obviously freezing. Looking at the bullet hole in the carpet. He had the kid, he had a very heavy power trip going on the kid.

And I am sitting here. I take a cigarette and use the table lighter. David looks at me sideways.

"See, son, I talk to Dr. Kelly—because—that's a way I have of knowing who he is. I give him crazy stories. To see how he'd react. Now—now—do you follow me?"

David, gallant little boy, going for a Kleenex.

"There would be no point in my lying to you, honey. Trip saved our lives. That's a fact. A clear fact. You can't quarrel with facts."

David looks at me. He's scared.

How can Rex put his son through this? But, given the situation, how can he not? The man works hard, I have to grant that.

"Now Mommy and I do have our differences—"

279

"I know."

It's sad, touching, under other circumstances it would even be sort of funny, the way the kid whispers those two words. He's squirming, wants to go out and play. Doesn't want adults to talk about their problems, doesn't want to have to deal with them. He wants to swim, or run, ride his horse—but he's tortured, he also wants to believe.

"I was telling Dr. Steve Kelly crazy stories, to help me get a latch—a latch, a hook, a key—to the character on 'This Passing Night.' To see Who's Who—to make stuff up for the show. Triphammer—he wouldn't do anything like that, not with your mom. Trip's our bestest friend. We trust him. And when the chips are down, he's there. I was just trying to think, so I could play the part right, how would Dr. Steve Kelly react? Because, as you very well know, what Steve Kelly has to realize is that his son—you—are not his son, not mine, because I had mumps. So I use the tapes to figure that out."

"But, Dad, I saw Mommy—"

"Yes, of course you did." Rex is into it now, he's got the signals. But he can't quite get around this one, so he leans back and smokes, and he says, "What do you think you saw?"

David's at a complete loss. Doesn't know what to say.

Rex not doing so hot either. He goes into an act that I can see through. But David can't.

And Rex lies. Jesus, he lies like a flamethrower. "It was *Peter.* He made an assault on the house."

"An assault?"

I'm watching Rex think. I don't get it. What's he doing?

"Your mom didn't know about it. But Trip and I did. We were trying to trap Peter."

"But—Dad—I saw—I saw Mommy—"

"Yes?"

"Well, you know."

"What?"

"Dad—she was—"

"What?"

Kid whispers, "Naked."

Kid's got him. Kid's got him. But no, shit, it frightens me, Rex moves so fast, I could never think that fast.

Rex says, "Mommy was in the shower."

"What?"

"Trip wasn't even in the house. If they'd been—well, if they had been

280

—Trip would have been naked, too. I hate to break this to you, honey, but it takes two to—tango."

"Dad, cut it out, this is too *serious.*"

"But don't you see? Mommy was in the shower, and Trip was outside, looking for Peter."

"But—why would Mommy be taking a shower—if she knew Peter—"

And I think again, Kid's got him, kid's got him. But Rex is ready, he must have thought it through while he was talking about the obstetrician. That's why he tells stories—so he can think ahéad. Rex says, "She didn't know."

"What?"

"We didn't tell her."

The kid thinks about it. "Why didn't you tell her?"

That's where Rex wants him. Rex says, "Because of you."

"Me?"

"That's right. Macho shit. Protect the women and children. Actually, m'boy, there's something to be said for macho shit. I didn't want Mommy and you to know because you'd worry and be scared. And when she wanted to shower—well, I had to let her. If I told her not to, she'd ask why. And I couldn't tell her why. So I let her take a shower. And then she heard noises, and ran out and slipped—"

"But Dad, she said—I remember that part—she said you pushed her—"

"But that's true."

"What?"

"I did push her."

I can't believe this. I'm sitting here watching, and I can't believe it. Rex is thinking, How am I going to get out of this? and it's like he's on speed. He's doing it, he's doing it for the kid, he's doing it for Joslin. It's like he's on the soap opera, like he is on the set of that soap opera thinking a million things at once. Shit, what we've got here is Rex's mind, and it is a fucking runaway train. You can't put his mind behind bars. You can't put a runaway train behind bars.

"I *did* push her. I thought Trip had found Peter, and I was afraid of what was going to happen. I was trying to *protect* Mommy. Peter Ingalls was after us. He killed—he killed our very own Pop. And he was trying to kill the rest of us."

David's eyes so big. The world is worse than he thought. So much worse.

"But Peter's dead now. He's dead, he can't hurt us no more." Rex leans

281

in. "David, it's too terrible for you to have to contend with. You're eleven. But you should know that I do, and say, unreal things. For the show. Keep the real and the unreal separated in your mind. You can't mix them up or you'll go nuts. That tape—the tape you heard—was only for the show —look, for pity's sake"—and he looked at me—"this is our own Trip."

David wanted to believe it so much that he cracked. He actually did believe.

Rex said, "Listen, m'man, you and I are going to have to bear this thing. One fact you heard that was not a lie was that I love her, I am totally devoted to her."

David said, "Well I know *that.*"

And then we kind of laughed.

One by one by one.

Rex went back into the bedroom and put on chinos and a blue sweat shirt. David gathered up the new pile of wadded Kleenex. Rex strode around the room, combing his yellow hair with his mother's jeweled comb. "I'm sorry, son, that you had to pay for a lot of show-biz crap."

I made myself useless in the kitchen. Putting pans away. Probably in the wrong places. Then Rex came in and made sandwiches.

The storm had passed. We talked about the Lakers, how they could win it all this year. Then Rex suddenly says, "If you doubted your mother, I think you should feel overpowering guilt."

David smiling.

They exchange sarcastic looks.

Talk about cleaning up a house. We are demons. We have scrubbing contests. Rex tells us, as he polishes the linoleum, the life history of his long-lost dead wombat, Charles. Rex dries all the glasses we have used.

We go for a swim. I agree this time. I know there are congratulations awaiting me in Laguna. Goddamn Chief, he will never understand things. So I agree—after all, I will be alone in the 'Vette, and the two guys, father and son, will be in the Mercedes. Where they belong. I wasted Peter Ingalls. Because I *had* to. I'm tired of feeling guilty about it. What is a policeman supposed to do—stand idly by? I had to do it. Life is doing things correctly. If my shoulders complain, I must quiet them down. I didn't quite follow every turn. And Rex accomplished that.

We're all naked, no ladies present. What the hell, it's the YMCA. We swim, and we swim, we play Blind Tag. Even the tiniest bit of chlorine always hurts my eyes, but I ignore it. We jump all over this white and blue inflatable boat. We throw around a red and white football, plastic, with holes, Rex goes down and out, and I loft it. David intercepts, Aww-*right!* We play Minnow and Whale, which Rex calls Seal and Hippo. David finally goes in to shower down. Rex goes into his shoomshoom butterfly business. I really have too much water in my sinuses. And then Rex and I just sit in the sun, in the plastic green and white lounge chairs.

We sit for maybe half an hour. Here in the great lower desert. In the bright sunshine. Medjuhl. I think about J.O., I always liked him. "Have they captured the wolves in Pasadena?"—crazy old codger. He built all this himself. I imagine him and Leela when they were young. I dream in the sunshine. I bathe in the rays, sacked out on the chaise longue. Rex tells me a Polish joke that I have not heard before. I laugh. I could almost fall asleep from sheer body comfort, baking away. I say, "That was a good job—the way you got his feelings about his mother out of the hole."

"Little piss-ant doesn't know the truth. David must never know the truth. Trip, let's face it, I'm a shit, but one thing's for sure—I'm fast on my feet."

And then David suddenly appears right behind our lounge chairs. He throws a piece of paper onto the cement and stamps off toward the greenhouse. He turns and shouts, *"Daddy, I hate you."*

Rex sits forward, dripping. He picks up the paper, it's a folded card, with crayon printing:

A LITTLE SOMETHING FOR YOU

Rex opens it and reads it, passes it to me. It says,

MY HERO

and inside is a cut-out round yellow badge, with BADGE written on it in blue ink.

I look at it, and watch the glass door closing.

I look at Rex.

All that work for nothing.

15

So I drove the 'Vette back to Laguna. I wondered what was going on behind me, between father and son, in the Mercedes. They stayed at Medjuhl for a while, I guess. I didn't go very fast—and I stopped for a taco and Pepsi at that place where David and I had stopped before. But I didn't see them. It must have been a real honey of a drive. Now that the kid knows his dad's fast on his feet, everything Rex says will be met with suspicion.

Marge isn't at home when I return the 'Vette, I just step in the door. Then I hitch back to town to pick up my Cutlass in the Laguna Hotel parking lot. I see the red Mercedes. I hope they're in El Dorado with Leela. I have an itch to check, but all things considered, I think I will pass on this one.

I show up at work a honcho. Butch congratulates me. The Chief takes me into his office and says it's a feather in my cap. A feather in my cap? But I figure I might as well take in a little emotional gravy, it doesn't pass by your plate all that often. The Chief has all the newspapers, says some TV people wanted to talk to me. He notices I'm not too elated and asks me if anything's wrong. I say no, it's just been pretty draining, and I ask him if I might have a week, right now. Suddenly he looks at me different, maybe now I'm going to be a prima donna or want a raise. The change in his attitude is immediate, I go from Golden Boy straight to Problem Child, I see it in his eyes. He says Lord knows I deserve it, but right now he needs me more than ever. These assholes from the state are still gung-ho on joint police-fire operations, and we can't allow that. He wants me to work up a report that emphasizes all the negatives. When am I going to do this? Between killings? I say nothing. Lately I've been looking at floors a lot.

I resume work, take my turn in rotation. But I think I've broken down. Does the public notice this? Do I look funny? What is wrong? "A monstrous—illness." Rex is right, it's not all in his head. And it's certainly not in mine. But it *is* melodrama. Things are just happening strangely. You try to stand back and let everything calm down, but it just speeds up and gets worse. Every accident seems like part of a fiendish plot. Who is responsible for this?

Butch relieves me at three. He says, "See, Trip, Mickey Mouse and Minnie Mouse go to a psychiatrist. The psychiatrist examines Minnie for an hour. Then he comes out and says to Mickey, 'You're wrong, Mickey, she's not crazy.' And Mickey says, 'I never said she was crazy—I said she was fucking Goofy.' " Butch is all right. I like him. But did he look at me funny, or was that my imagination?

I popped in to see Leela, in the El Dorado suite. She was knitting a big blue turtleneck sweater for David to wear in Connecticut. Says she can't work on it too long at a stretch because her fingers ache. Besides she said, "Eleven-year-old boys don't want *clothes* for Christmas." We had tea and corn muffins. She wondered if David might like some kind of game with guns, looking at my magnum, but she was afraid of giving him something that his mother would disapprove of. So panicky about offending, and clearly petrified about her upcoming brain tumor operation. She had a big scrapbook filled with the messages, the sympathy cards, the notes from around the state and country that she'd received since J.O.'s death. She'd spent hours and hours putting it all together, in a big leather album, brown and gold. She was trying so hard to live. I left when Father Darcy dropped in. He bowed slightly to me, and turned his attention to the "First Lady." Father Darcy and me, two men in black uniforms.

On my way out I decide I should really check Rex, I'm here anyway, so I go up to the desk, and yes, Mr. Hooker still has 126. I fidget in the elevator, then saunter on down the hall. I realize I'm hearing it in my head —"Daddy, I hate you," it must've blown him away. I knock on the door of 126, my head is all spacy, I'm thinking about Joslin and Grandmother Darr, I'm thinking about everything and nothing. There's silence, and I

285

start to turn away, let him sleep it off. But then I hear him, "Who is it?" I don't know whether to identify myself or not, and while I'm playing Joe Fumble-Fuck with myself, the door opens. Actually, what he does is open the door back into himself, which only results in his knocking himself down. The poor bastard is really gone. I step in and crouch down, somehow he's gotten his underpants on, but as I gather him up I kind of take in the whole room at once: full of pot smoke, the bottle of Cutty Sark on the dresser, and Marge Stivers half-sitting up, naked, her terrific tan against the white sheets clutched around her body. On her face is this incredible expression of shock and shame, it almost knocks me over. They'd shoved the two single beds together.

In my arms Rex mumbles, "Well, Trip—" but that's it, he can't make it.

On the way out I realize I'm walking on tiptoe.

The Chief is waiting for this negative report on the Police-Fire Mutual Community Protection Programs, so I go back down to my trailer to work on it. The Chief has been making all sorts of innuendos about the opportunities facing a man of his age and station, how he'll have to "turn over the reins." So I am being put through my paces. I am Senior Man. With his recommendation I might have a shot at it. But they are very reluctant to promote from within, usually they hire somebody who did well elsewhere. Still, I did get a lot of attention for the Peter Ingalls thing. Not that it adds up, my investigation didn't really solve anything. I just happened to be there. Except if you work on it 99 percent of the time, you'll probably be there the 1 percent of the time. I never would have been there if Leela hadn't flown off in the Cadillac, and then Marge called me, and Rex asked me to stay for Thanksgiving. It had nothing to do with police procedures. But the outside world doesn't know that. They just hear fact A, fact B, facts C, D, and E, and then they think it's a coherent thing. When I was little, I thought the wind was created by trees swinging their branches around.

At noon, Friday, I had been expecting it, it was partly described in the TV guide. So I sat in my trailer and watched it. Every single scene. Jack MacKenzie and Neil Robinson and Marge. Pieces of it had faded a little, what with all the intervening events, but now it was all sharp again. Marge in her nun outfit, the Buick Electra, that Hillary bitch, Jessica. I could imagine Al Marcus snapping his fingers in the control booth, and that rummy-looking guy all alone in Mission Control, with the color monitors. My sneeze. The commissary for lunch, my Hawaiian Vegas burger. That

286

whole day came back to me as I sat in front of the tube in my trailer. Rex in the nightclub singing "Danny Boy," and Officer Stanley, for Christ's sake. And then that horrifying surprise, Rex's words—one cup, one saucer, one plate, one knife, one fork, one spoon, and she took the shower curtain.

We've been sucked up into some huge brain, and it's having this nightmare about us. Water on the Sky. I'm not Oliver Bodley anymore. I'm Oliver Hooker. I belong to them. But I never really was a Bodley, I was adopted, and I don't know how to be a Hooker. How did all this happen?

Danny is not Dr. Kelly's son. David. That tape at Medjuhl—listening to that tape.

Rex Hooker talking with Dr. Kelly. And I am still carrying around Peter Ingalls's life, his death, carrying that around inside me, no way to let it out.

I sit here and my hands shake so bad it takes me a long time to light a cigarette. I also seem to have caught cold in my neck. I experience considerable pain when I try to turn to the left. I am so afraid. I feel death coming, like a huge wind.

Why me? Why did the Chief pick me? I'm no good at this. I sit in my trailer with yellow legal pads, doing cost estimates, making columns of pros and cons. The state's screwball plan for joint police-fire units, it's fallout from Prop 13 and Prop 9. And the Chief doesn't want to give away any of our slice of the pie. I have clever little inspirations, but I don't know how to run a scam. I'm too honest. But I want to be chief, I don't want to have to please a superior anymore. Maybe I just don't have sufficient education. Assholes can run rings around me statistics-wise. But how do they factor in the knowledge you pick up by doing the job? Although I notice my chief is not doing this work. And he'll get all the credit. I am not cut out to be chief. A superior sergeant can be your most valuable man. But no chance for the big bucks. What am I thinking about? This society is too hung up on hierarchy. We pay our figureheads more than our trench workers. Which is a funny thing for a quarterback to say, but I look at a figure like $946,860 and all I can think of is what I could do with it in small bills.

So I think about Joslin. I scrunch my left shoulder to my left ear, ten times. It's painful, probably only a kink. I talk to my dead uncle. I have a Hungry Man beef dinner. I think about today's speech; a Mexican officer came in to outline the differences between Mexican law and U.S. Law. In Mexico, *difamación de honor* is an offense, the police are required to do something about it. Wife beating is not punishable if she has fifteen days to recover between attacks, In Mexico you can't enter a man's house. Even if there's an incendiary inside, you cannot enter a man's house. And Hispanics in the barrio—he was really an effective speaker—you can't cuff 'em in Mexico, it has to do with their attitude toward slavery. Which is not uncommon in underdeveloped countries.

I have seen some bees buzzing around my outside cooler. When it's dark and they're nesting, I go out and blast them, bee bodies all over the ground. Peter Ingalls. I used to love to go deer hunting, but I don't want to anymore, I guess I don't want to kill things. But that only means I have passed my sexual peak.

It's self-pity, pure and simple. I have never spent so much time feeling sorry for myself as I do now. I always just bopped along doing my job, taking things on faith, believing in authority. But now I pause all the time. I fall over my own feet. Things I used to do easily I now do with difficulty. Because I am distracted by my own awareness of things. A little learning is very dangerous, it makes me scared I can't do my job. And then, when I've got it all worked out and am a complete liberal, somebody will come along and tell me I don't know how to play hardball. I'm between two worlds. And not at home in either one. I really would like to think seriously about things. The brain was invented to think. And is also an excuse not to get to work. I could resign, hit the books. They let middle-aged people go back to college now. I think I should be an anthropology major. Become the world's leading expert on Turkish kin groups. Unless somebody's already taken it. I'd love to go to college. Spend all day thinking. But we can't all be twits in libraries. Except I would rather like to be a twit in a library. Chicks love it when you're a brooding intellectual.

I'm thinking in the chilly evening, making real progress on my police-fire report. About eight o'clock Joslin calls. She's out of her mind. "He picked David up—Trip, please—he's blind drunk, he should not be on the road."

I stare out my trailer window. Water on the Sky.

"Rex and David—they're at Summer Snow. Trip, Rex can't let me *leave*." She's all upset. "Don't let any harm—go to Summer Snow—he's *crazy*."

"But I can't—"

"Get me my David!"

"Hold on, hold on, now."

"David is the one who'll have to pay for this."

She's frantic. She obviously didn't know who else to call. But doesn't she remember, even for a moment—if, in fact, it really was a setup and I really was a pawn.

"He pushed me—and David didn't want to go—David didn't want to go—Rex said, 'Get *in*, fucker,' he—he said that."

There's no way to deal with it, nothing I can do. I say, "I'll get on it."

Her voice: "Please? And call me?"

I'm not dressed for duty, so I get ready. Buttoning down my collar, the black holes for the black buttons. I put on Brut and use my breath freshener, for no reason except it's what I always do when I put on my uniform. I'm a creature of routine. I head for the Cutlass. I'm confused, I don't know where my allegiance lies. But Rex has taken the kid, and I guess that's what it is—my allegiance is to the kid.

Rex will probably drive up on a freeway divider, wrap the car around a lamppost, end it all in a drunken traffic accident.

Daddy, I hate you.

In the driveway my headlights hit the red Mercedes, ROLLEM. I parked and got out. Lots of ladders and tools around. Front door all sanded down to its natural blond color. Summer Snow didn't look so ghostly with all that repair work going on. I poked around, the workmanship was first rate. Yep, they will certainly be back in here by Christmas.

Now where are Rex and David? They can't be inside, the house is all dark. I pick my way down the path to the rose garden, past the bed of Summer Snows. I turn and look up at the windows of the Solarium and the Music Room. The Hooker Story. They live in a dream of themselves, not in what your casual passer-by might call reality. No wonder they're crazy. I hear Rex's voice.

They're sitting by the pool. The kid all huddled up in himself, obviously not enjoying it one bit. Rex in a Levi's suit, coat and pants. Wearing those gold boots. With a bottle of Jack Daniels and a pack of Camels. Complete wasted asshole. He sees me and says, "Well, Trip, how the hell are ya?"

I'm really tired of that.

I say hi to the kid and pull up a chair.

Rex says, "What brings you here?"

I sigh.

"Goddamn her," he says. He lights a Camel. There's already one going in the big glass ashtray. He looks at me and a kind of big sadness comes over his face. He stares at me, shooting the sadness into me, like I've broken a promise to him or something. Which, in a way, I have. But I've kept some promises, too. Fairly big ones. But he's lost in hootch and trouble. So I hate him and pity him and generally just want it all to stop.

"She's not worried about me at all, just about him." He turns to the kid. "And why worry about you, shithead?"

David twists himself up. "I still don't know what I did wrong."

"You lied."

David looks at him. "About what?"

"God."

"God?"

Rex smokes. He looks at me. "See, Trip, at Thanksgiving, I was going over it with him. The meaning of God. Remember Pop's funeral, when this boy recited the Twenty-third Psalm?"

I don't know what this is about.

"So in Medjuhl, at Thanksgiving, I give him that old family Bible, and I ask him what things mean. Really mean. Like 'annointest my head with oil,' I ask him what that means, and he says, 'S.T.P.?'—shit like that."

"Come on, Dad."

"And what a staff is—thy rod and thy *cane,* he calls it—and I say, well, son, what is it about, what does that verse *mean?* He looks up at me with those beautiful eyes and says, 'God's tender and constant care.' Trip, it took my breath away. I thought, What a wonderful son I have. I let him go out to swim, and sat there thinking about how an eleven-year-old could ever express that, on his own, 'God's tender and constant care,' and—"

David says, "Oh, I get it."

Rex turns on him. "Yeah. Yeah. I picked up that big Bible and looked, and there it was in the margin. 'God's tender and constant care.' You didn't say it—you *read* it."

David scrunched in the chair. "But I wanted to go swimming."

"Not supposed to crib on the Holy Scriptures, man, not supposed to trick me about God's word—"

I think about the card room in the Laguna Hotel. I'm sick and tired of booze. I'm sick and tired of just about everything. I say to Rex, "Leave the kid alone."

David says to me, "When he gets this way, he doesn't know what he's saying."

Rex says, "Shall I remain seated—while you two discuss me?"

Here we are, again, the three of us.

Finally Rex says, "Well, Jos is correct—she is correct to worry just about you, m'man. It's what I would worry about. You have to remember that, David, your mother and I never disagreed about anything. Except America."

The kid is having a great time. He's a hostage.

"So you must remember, David, you must remember—don't hate your mother, love her, love her with everything you've got."

"Don't worry."

When the kid says that, Rex looks at him. Really startled. And says, "I've—I've lost you, haven't I?"

"Dad—"

"Please, son, I'm virtually helpless."

"Dad, can I just go home?"

"Honey, where do you think you are?"

"Dad—"

It's miserable. I hate to watch it.

Rex turns to me. "Does she want me to blow up any balloons for you? I'm fresh out of mints." He hardly knows where anything is, including himself, and flips his cigarette into the pool.

"Should I," he says to David, "give you some sexual advice, man to man?" Rex looks at him. "Lemme see—don't fire until you see the whites of their eyes, OK? Son, you know what being drunk feels like? I'll show you." He gets up and falls into the pool. Clothes and cigarettes and gold boots and everything. Like a body, a dead body. He stays down for a long time, then gradually drifts to the shallow end and comes up.

David watching him.

Rex walks back, squoosh, squoosh, and sits down. "Got to get to work," he says. Reaches into his pocket, struggling with those sopping Levi's. At last gets out his comb and combs his hair. Leans forward in the chair, spattering the cement with water. He takes off his boots, empties them, and stares at them.

I remember him carrying them in his hand.

I wish it would be over.

Rex puts his finger next to his nose and blows the pool snot out of one nostril, then the other. "Gutless wonder," he says. "That's what I am. And now just making an ass out of myself. But that's not true either. I'm ill. I'm *ill*. Believe me, son, booze is a lot worse than this. It's—it's eerie. And I don't mean Pennsylvania. It's terrible eerie. Sinister. We don't understand it. Honey, as you can see, your father is all wet."

Rex is a smart man. Why can't he see what he's doing? I have never known a man who so much needed comfort, and yet is so unable to accept a helping hand.

He's looking for his cigarettes. When he finds them, he sees that they are soaking wet. So he throws them over his head. We hear the pack land on the cement. He sighs. "When a person becomes your whole world to you, son—that's what happened. You have no idea how brutal it is—to love someone with your whole heart, and not be loved back."

"Yes I do," the kid says. "I do, Dad."

It startles Rex.

291

I'm rooting for the kid.

"I try to keep things from you, believe it or not, since you know ten times more than is good—or healthy—for a guy your age to know—but —oh, I'm gonna hate myself in the morning—drunks always say that, son —but they don't care, they say 'I'll hate myself in the morning,' as if that took care of it—and I feel, fuck her, she left me, what right does she have to you?—you're *mine,* look in the mirror, look in the mirror—oh, what's wrong with this family, we can't"—and he coughed—"we can't—let go of each other."

I sit there.

"Your mom said to me, 'I can't be your sanity for you—it's wrong to ask it of me.' She's right. As always. God, I'm so fucking tired of that woman being right."

And we sit.

Rex turns. "You see, with Pop and Leela it was always OK. When I was growing up, the first twenty years of my life, I'd watch them and the way they were with each other, damn, it was so fine, the beautiful way Leela and Pop *were* with each other, I didn't know it, what confidence it was giving me—oh—Pop—Mother—"

"Dad, don't."

"She just burned it all away, scorched it—"

"Dad, you didn't—did you? Did you have anything to do with setting the fire? You know, could by accident you—could you by accident or something—"

Rex just stares at David. Then his eyes go wildly up to the house. All the air seems to go out of him. He seems, it must be a kind of hallucination on my part, but I swear, Rex is getting smaller. His whole body crunches up. He begins to whimper, "My son thinks—my son thinks—oh, please, please just go away—go—" and he can't talk anymore. He gets down on his knees in front of David. He puts both hands out on the aluminum arms of David's deck chair. He leans on it and it gives, it is about to break. "Oh," he whispers, "oh, my son, are you out of your mind? What the hell do you—how could you think—my God, are you crazy or am I? I can't believe what I'm hearing. I—"

"But, but Dad, I didn't mean you *meant*—"

"Meant? *Meant?*"

"Please, Dad." And David is just killed, his head thrown back. The kid's in agony.

"Meant what? Oh, the world is crazy, not me. Not me. I know your mother demonizes me. Son, Mommy blames me if it *rains.* Oh, my son, after all our years together, don't you know who I am?"

David, poor David, completely shot.

Rex suddenly cries out, "Hit this old man!"

"What? What, Dad?"

Rex is frantic. He says, "How could you think your own father—I mean, how do I defend myself? I've given up trying to defend myself against my mind, but you—*you*—how could you think—"

"I don't think it, Dad. There's just been too much. I can't think straight."

"Oh, easy, easy, my son. I'm just trying, trying—I mean, what you just said—it says so much about *me*. I don't know what—what is the matter with me that I inspire so little trust—in the people I, I love most. Hit this old man!"

"Hit this little boy!"

"Don't say that, don't *say* that, David—*please!*"

Now the kid screams it, *"Hit this little boy!"* He can't breathe. *"Dad, hit this little boy!"*

Rex stands up, begins to back away. He says, "Please—please, Trip, take him back to his mother. I've lost—leave me, leave me. Oh—" Rex keeps backing up, and then he turns and staggers up through the garden. I can see him stop in the moonlight, looking at Summer Snow. And then goes in.

The kid writhes in his chair. I grab for him, but he jumps up and follows his father. Rex has closed the door. David rips it open. I see him slip in, and I run up there. I hear the kid's voice, echoing in the house, "Dad?"

I forgot my flashlight, left it in the Cutlass. Maybe I should get it. But they must have installed the wiring, the house is almost ready. I grope my way in.

"Dad?"

I see David, but as I get close to him he darts away. I am gradually getting accustomed to the dark. Without drapes or anything the moonlight allows a little visibility. The Grand Entrance Hall, this old house. How the hell am I going to get them out? Follow Daddy, follow Daddy.

"Dad, I'm sorry—please, *Dad?*"

I see the walls, and the ceilings, where they've been sanding and painting. Just the faintest hint of that fire smell. Ashy odor, mixed with the smell of new paint. I walk slowly across the living room floor. It's white, all freshly sanded down. Rex is not going to jump out this time. "Die, commie devil!" They're through with games. Except it's always games and mysteries and riddles and jokes and breakfast arrangements. The whole flam damily, family-shmamily, it's enough to burn you out. Oh, swell—burn you out.

"Dad? Please?"

I thought the voice was coming from the kitchen. I made my way in there. Follow Daddy, my ass. How can he do it to the kid? I looked out the kitchen windows to the beach. Maybe he just went through the house, isn't even in here anymore, just wants to be left alone. When I was a little boy, going from room to room on my birthday night, my aunt would say, "Warmer, Ollie—getting warmer." I'd stop, like I'm doing now, and turn, and start. My Aunt would say, "No, cold, colder over there." I'd be all excited and I'd get close to where my present was hidden, and she'd say, "Hot, Ollie—hot—burning hot!"

"Dad—please, Dad—is this—is this why Mom had to leave you? And we don't get to live in Bluebird Canyon? This is it, isn't it, Dad? Too much of this . . ."* and the kid's voice trailed off. *"Dad, tell me the words so I can find you—"*

At the edge of the kitchen, I brushed by a sawhorse in the darkness. I looked, and the goddamn stairs were out, the sawhorse was barring the empty hole. That fire smell. This house. I think of the night Sissy hanged herself in the garage, and David and I played pool, and I took him home. I can't take this darkness.

It sounded like David was in the dining room. He was trying a chorus of his old song:

> Going West, in a covered wagon,
> Get along mule, in spite of the danger,
> We're going to cross—the Cumberland . . .

*Dad? I'll say any*thing."

I go back into the Grand Entrance Hall. He can't be upstairs, the Honduras mahogany isn't there. Unless he knows some other way. I heard a skitter-skitter swish and I thought, for a second, I saw a shape at the window, a shadow.

"Dad, I hit a wall. With my head. I'm going to hurt myself, it really hurt, Dad, and it's your fault. If I really hurt myself, Dad, it'll be your fault—"

And then Rex called. A whimper. He was in his room.

I bumped into the doorway and stood there. David came in past me, real slow. He stood next to Rex, crumpled there on the floor in the moonlight.

"Don't," Rex said softly, "don't hurt yourself."

He waited a minute. Coughed. "Son, what you said, you must think your father is—a—psychotic—son—"

"I know, Dad—I know."

Rex reached up. His eyes lifeless. Pleading. In the moonlight.'
"I—I just get scared, Dad."
"When I was a little, little boy, I used to sit right here." He moved his hand over the sanded floor. "I used to sit here late, late at night, and look at the stars, just a very little boy, and now I feel like a very little boy. If you thought—"
"But I don't think it, I—come on now, Dad. Can't we—"
He shook his head.
I watched it. Rex was a little boy and David was trying to reason with him. David the father and Rex the little boy.
"Oh, just a moment, son, just a moment longer." Rex let his head go back, *thunk,* against the wall. He said, "Listening to you out there, calling me, hearing your footsteps, your voice. I just—I just love you so much, my son. And I was thinking you were right, it is so bad for me to put you in danger, but you—you knocked me completely off balance, I'm—just all cut up, man, I'm all bleeding inside and *cut up*—"
Rex raised his eyes and saw me. He shuddered. I felt his stare going into me. Rex whispers, "King's X, guys."

We sat in the aluminum chairs by the pool.
The kid said, "You *are.*"
"What? I am what?"
David whispered it: "Fast on your feet."
"Oh," Rex said, and looked away. Then he said so softly, "I know why you said 'I hate you' at Medjuhl when you heard me say I was 'fast on my feet.' It's because I was congratulating myself and my heart wasn't in the right place. Isn't that it? That's why you said it, isn't it?"
"Yes."
"I'm not dumb, honey. And I don't want to hurt you, I don't want to hurt anybody. I'm so sorry you heard that tape about Mom and Trip. Because it's worse than a lie. It's a lie to myself. Somehow it's easier for me, emotionally, to concoct a wild story like that, and put her in the wrong, than—to accept the simple huge fact of failure."
He's still at it, he won't let up. And it gets me again, like it did on Labor Day—he's drunk, but he's not.
"Pop always said—he was such a proud man—Pop always said, 'Do Your Worst, World, Here We Stand.' The trouble is, son, the world was listening. Oh, sweetheart, I know I shouldn't lie—I hate lies—and, oh, I loved Pop, I so loved him, I remember when I was building that Edifice Rex, I tried to make some little figures to go in it, little monsters, sort of half-frogs and half-wolves, ceramic figures, devils. It just worried the hell

295

out of Mother, she wondered what was wrong with me. And Pop said, 'It's simple: Our offspring is psychoceramic.' " Rex laughed. And was quiet again. He began to sing, "Too many skeletons, de heel bone connected to de foot bone, de foot bone connected to de ankle bone, de ankle bone connected to de leg bone, now hear de word of de Lord—"

"Dad—"

"Dem bones, dem bones, dem dry bones," Rex was singing it, "dem dry bones gonna stand up and walk around, stand up and walk around—"

Shit, we can't get the sucker to pass out on us.

"That's California, son. If you ain't prepared to see all your nightmares realized, don't settle in the land of dreams come true. For every Summer Snow there's a madman crouched in the prickerbushes. Oh, Christ. Enough. White Father Speak Linoleum." Rex stands up, wobbles, stares at the house. "God, honey, I loved Pop's rage. And his kindness. Oh, the way he played bridge, 'Cold Mathematics and Hot Chemistry.' And his understanding. He took pleasure in everything that happened. I remember when I was your age, and kind of all baffled by girls, confused, I asked him about it. I said the girls seemed so much older than me. I said, 'Pop, some of them are already mensturbating.' I remember the delighted look on his face."

Rex sits there, lost in memories. Unbalanced. But if someone came up right now they'd just think he was chatting with us in the evening. It's the damndest thing.

"I remember when he was supposed to have his first hernia operation. Pop said he was chicken shit, some people could have a hernia operation and not think much about it, but it was a gut issue with him."

David takes a second. Then gets it. He says, "Before you get Pop's puns, you'd just wonder what he means. And then when you *do* get them, you think—" and the kid goes thumbsdown. But then he brightens. "Except they're fun to remember."

"And his eyes," Rex says. "Pop never called for help. I've seen him, I saw him several times, with tears in his eyes, but a sparkle, too, and a kind of defiance. It—it's so fast and easy in the mind, honey—he never called for help. How I wish I could be—be like him. And I will. I'm going way, way back. I'll have time to do that, when I'm alone with Mother, when you and your mom are in the East, I'll take stock. We know your mom is OK, and I must be OK, too, because we made you together, and you're terrific—"

"I'm not terrific. I'm just—"

"I am not talking about you, I'm talking about me. And your being terrific is not an arguable point with me. Oh, let's not talk."

"That'll be a relief," the kid says. "No talk."

Rex laughs. "Jesus, I talk, don't I? It's terrible."

"But Dad, you seem to think that if you know it's terrible, then it's not terrible. But it still is."

Rex nods. "Your mom had to leave me, I know that—I'm lost. I don't have any guts."

"Does Mom have guts?"

"You bet. She just doesn't have any brains."

"Come on, Dad."

"Sorry, old man." He looks up and says, "Come on—gents, let's stroll on the beach."

So we walk onto the sand. Stand there staring at the surf. Rex puts his arm around David. "Beautiful," he says. "Laguna is so beautiful. We've got to keep this."

I look out to where you can't tell the difference between the sky and the ocean. All blackness.

"Pop—all his life he worked—he worked—that's it. Work, m'man, it's a—it's a great savior."

Rex hasn't put his gold boots back on. He lets the surf slide around his feet and ankles. He's still soaking anyway.

"I'm going to take care of Mother. That's my job now. We'll live in Summer Snow again. And then I'm going to leave 'This Passing Night.' "

"Dad, you can't do that."

"Aw, I'm getting tired of it. I used to love it. But when Steve Kelly lost his Danny—well, he's going to be in the nut house for about three months—we might as well just abandon him there. Hey, Trip, did you see it on Friday?"

"Yes, I did."

"And?"

"I got a kick out of it."

"You're not pissed? About 'one cup, one knife, one fork'—"

"Yeah, I'm pissed too."

"Oh, good."

David between us, looking from Rex to me. Trying to follow.

We turn and start back. Rex says, "Well, according to the Bible, Dr. Kelly will waste away in the cackle factory for three months, but I—I dunno, I kind of prefer to let him die there."

"Die?" David says.

"Yeah," Rex says.

"He can't die."

"Would you believe permanently insane?"

297

"Oh, Dad, we couldn't do that."

" 'We' couldn't?" Rex smiles. "You're right—I'd love the death scene. I once did a great death scene, in *Cyrano*—at Stanford. Where you're going, honey. You're going to be a Stanford Man."

"Well, I might not want to."

"You'll want to. There's nowhere else out here. And beware the East. So that's settled."

"Well, I do want to go. I just don't want you to tell me to go."

"OK, go wherever you want. Go to hell in a handbasket. Go to Duke, Vanderbilt, Columbia, Ohio Wesleyan—go anywhere—no, I think we will go to Stanford."

" 'We' will, will we?"

"Pecker-head, you're fast on your feet. Ouch. Yes, my Cyrano died so wonderful. Maybe I could die, and then Jessica would realize what she had lost. That would be nice. And Sister Kate would light a candle for me." He stopped. "It would be so weird not to carry Steve Kelly around with me every day. I mean, I've done it for twelve years. You're right, I suppose I can't just abandon him—I've got to kill him." He smiled, that crazy smile. "I wonder how I'll kill him. Now, there's a puzzlement. How do I kill Dr. Kelly?" He turns to me. "If I really kill him good, will you arrest me?"

I think this talk is getting dangerous.

"I know—he sacrifices his life so that his son can live. You guys buy that?"

"How?" David says.

"Well, we wouldn't do anything rash."

"Oh, no, Dad—no, you'd never do anything *rash*."

Rex chuckles.

I do not understand. Rex swings from awful pain to quiet satisfaction. It makes my skin crawl. We go up into the Edifice Rex. Through the winding walls.

"Forgot my boots." He toddles back down to get them.

David looks at me and rolls his eyes.

Rex is singing, down by the pool, "Dancing in the Dark."

David yawns. Not like he's bored, like he's exhausted.

Rex returns with one boot on, one boot in his hand. He sits on a little brick seat. "All I wanted, honey, was that, while I was growing up, the love between Mother and Pop—the love between them—I—I wanted for you to feel about me and your mom the way I felt about Leela and Pop. I wanted that. More than anything in the world. Because it is the—the most beautiful. Family-shmamily. The very most beautiful. But—but"—

he put the other boot on and stood up—"you have to let the people you love, you have to let them *go*. I know how to do a lot of things, but I do not know how to do that. The—the freedom of loved ones is a scandal. I don't know how to love someone without violating their air space." Rex finds a huge old spider web. It's night and the thing has come out to feed. We sit there and watch him eat the little creature he's trapped. David wants to save one of them, a little winged thing. He works at it.

Rex says, "What you thinkin' about, ol' Trip?"

I guess my face must be pale. I was so scared in that house when David sang "Going West." You do not love someone really well, the way they need to be loved, if you allow a scene like that to take place. I wonder if Rex knows what happens as he goes thundering by. He's all caught up in his own momentum, he can't see us. I don't remember my uncle for all the great things he did. Not that he did any, except be as good a man as he could be. For himself. For my aunt. For me.

I guess Rex is just hurting too much. He's not in his right mind. But J.O. hurt. My uncle hurt. You don't get anywhere by saying "I hurt."

Rex says, "Summer Snow will be what rescues you, son."

"The house?"

"Well, no, not the house, but the feeling—the size of the emotion the house incarnates."

"Dad—"

"OK, come on."

We wend our way out of the Edifice Rex.

"Poor Mother," he says. "God, you should have seen her, when I was little, you should have seen her play charades. Probably the all-time greatest charade I've ever seen was Mother doing *The African Queen.*" He sighs. " 'This Passing Night.' If the night won't pass, or if I pass, on this passing night, what becometh of a twenty-four-hour day? How do I git a good night's sleep? I better check on Neil and Buzz in the LM—lunar module. The ground seems to enjoy the TV a lot. Judging from the fan mail coming into Houston."

"Dad, what are you talking about?"

"It must be eerie for you laymen to see me floating in all directions past the endless panels of switches."

I think I better say something. It's up to me to say something. But I can't, I don't know what to say. I'm bored and sick of it. And scared. I don't know. I can't do anything about this. Now he's talking about the moon shot? I'm not quite sure David is right. That when his father gets this way, he doesn't know what he's talking about. I think he does know. And I don't know how to stop him from knowing.

"See, son, the emotion is *housed* in Summer Snow. And Summer Snow and I become, as it were, coterminous."

"Dad, are you being funny?"

"Yes, I'm being funny. You can only encompass it if you reproduce the condition of it. That was my mistake on 'This Passing Night.' Am I going too fast for you boys in the back? It's a paradox. Like the man doctor who married the woman doctor and they became a paradox. Get it? Pair o' docs. King's X means the game has to stop, the real world has intervened. I seem to have too much fluid in my secondary coolant system."

"Dad, please stop."

"But, honey, I'm talking about you. About your very first steps."

"What?"

"Your mommy and I, she was so pregnant with you, we were lying in bed, in New York, our place on Seventy-sixth Street, the summer of 1969. We were so afraid it was going to be another miscarriage and we wouldn't have you, we'd never have *you*. That sort of puts a strain on the marriage, son. Little anxiety there. We were lying in bed watching the lunar landing. And we had begun to breathe easily about it, we weren't going to lose you this time, we were going to have our baby. She'd carry you to term. I could hardly see the TV screen over your mom's belly—you, asshole, were in my way."

Kid looking at his dad.

"And Neil Armstrong stepped down on the lunar surface and said those words, 'A small step for a man and a giant step for mankind,' and your mommy whispered to me, real soft, she whispered, 'Oh, *baby*,' and it was two things in one word—it was me and it was you. She took my hand and put it on her belly, and I could feel you in there, a ripple, this wonderful ripple—a small step for a man, a giant step for mankind, and a wonderful —wonderful step for my son. Oh my."

We stood there in the big circular driveway. The three of us between the Mercedes and the Cutlass. David reads the two license plates aloud —Rex's ROLLEM and my 1 GROUCH.

Rex is still looking at the house. He can't bear to leave it or to leave it alone. He says, "Real good reconstruction, eh, Trip? I'm very pleased with it. Going to be just fine. Of course, you can't get some of that stuff anymore, no Honduras mahogany. And the cruddy plumbing they use now—but we'll have her ready for Christmas." He turns. "And, honey, that house is all paid for, there will never be a problem with taxes, or utilities. It all goes automatically and in perpetuity—perpetuity—it's all taken care of—Pop and I and our Mafioso CPA in Rancho Mirage. Never —never *rent* Summer Snow. Nobody ever lives here except family. If Jos ever changes her mind, I want it always to be here for you, and for her. Trip—both you guys—listen, let us here put our holy bond, our sacred word and honor—" Rex puts out his hand, David puts out his small hand. I don't know what to do, I have to go along. Rex says, "Pledge, gentlemen —nobody, never—never nobody lives here except—us."

It's the kid, David, who makes the three hands go up and down.

It makes me uneasy. I hate to promise anything I can't deliver on. I'm not family, I'm not family-shmamily. This is not really my business.

But it is. It's mine now.

I guess I have known that for a little longer than I am ready to admit.

Rex turns and looks at the cars. He's annoyed remembering why Joslin sent me on this errand in the first place. He says, "Look, Trip, would you mind? I promised—uh—one of the guys on the crew, I promised him he could come over and look at the Mercedes. I wonder if you might, uh, drive us—we'll drop fart-face here off at—at—home—and then I'll get back to Mother at the hotel." He looks at me. He knows he shouldn't be on the road.

I say, "I could do that."

So I do. We all three sit in the front seat. David between his dad and me. I am actually half-smiling to myself at the way Rex handled that.

We talk about the soap opera. The kid still doesn't like the idea of Dr. Steve Kelly wasting away in an insane asylum. Rex says, "Oh, I don't know —somehow all the air's gone out of it. It's worse, it's poisoned for me."

"Why, Dad?"

"I only liked it when we could all talk about it. Enjoy the good shit and make fun of the bad shit. But there's—there's nobody to talk to about it anymore. It's just so, so dangerous—and—so unserious. I don't know, honey. You can't even watch it anymore, not with school and—"

"I watch it when I'm sick. Sometimes I even pretend to be sick when I'm not. And Mommy lets me stay home from school, and I watch."

"I must alert your mother to this dastardly subterfuge."

"Dad."

"Shit, though, I wish I didn't have to take her to the airport. I always used to enjoy airport scenes with my Jos. It's on a school day, her departure —would you like to play sick so you can come watch Mommy and Daddy say bye-bye?"

Stop, I think. Stop.

"What do we do after Mom leaves?"

"Well, she has to take care of Uncle Ernest. She's going to live in his apartment in New York."

"I thought Connecticut."

"That's later, after you join her Uncle Ernest has a house in Darien. But now he's in New York Medical Center, Cornell, so she'll stay in the place on Fifty-second Street. Remember that?"

"Not really."

"We visited. In seventy-four, I think, you were five. Oh well, she'll stay there until after the first of the year. You'll have a place to play, in Connecticut. But first we got to have Christmas. Excited about Christmas?"

"Sure."

I'm going along Glenneyre. David didn't say "Sure" with all that much enthusiasm. I wonder what Rex thinks he has accomplished tonight. Scare his son to death—drive Joslin out of her mind with worry.

"I sure hate the airport. Your mom and airports. Oh, once at the Paris airport, Orly, Mom went ahead to find an apartment, and I came along a month later with you, only ten months old. The plane had to land in Scotland and was delayed and I ran out of Pampers. And then London was fogged in and the engine caught fire and we had to exit by the chutes with me holding you, sopping wet. And by the time we got to Paris, Mom was frantic and didn't even see you and me in the squash of the crowd. Everybody was speaking French and I just said, catching her shoulder, "Not to worry, lady," and Mom collapsed into my arms full of wet you."

We go up Bluebird Canyon Drive, Rex still talking, talking. The Hooker Story. The endless Hooker stories. He's an alcoholic. He's an addict. That's what Rex is doing—he's getting his fix.

"And at LAX, after our first separation, which was very brief and harmless, when I hadn't seen you for six months, nothing harmful about that—"

"Dad," the kid says, like "Lay off, Dad, I got it now."

"Your brain probably was damaged, traversing the vaginal canal—well, honey, you were kind of confused, being only three years old, when you saw me waiting at the airport, you shouted, 'Mommy!', which blew my mind extremely, what a nerd you were to call your father 'Mommy'—"

"I really said that?"

"Yep. And at the Palm Springs airport, when Mommy and I were reconciled, the desert wind gusted up and blew Mommy's skirt over her head—it was like Marilyn Monroe in *The Seven Year Itch*. Mommy was so embarrassed, trying to push down her skirts, and this middle-aged lady with bug-eye locust sunglasses said, 'Oh, isn't that cute!' She saw me laughing and Mommy catching sight of me as she was trundling along, blushing."

"God, Dad, all those times."

"Not to mention the Orange County airport. When Mommy came down the steps, and I was grabbing for her, and you were with her, honey, we all had trouble not crying—her face was all spasms, and I guess I didn't even realize how much I had been missing you both, I had been working real hard on the show, acting, writing, producing—I was just pouring my misery into my work, which is one way to solve problems, but not mine anymore—and her arms were around me so tight, we were finally home —her arms so tight around me—and we all three had to sit down for a minute. We were feeling so many things. Except it was complicated, in the heart, the body, the mind. It—honey—it was, in the way down-deep body, just like we were three deer—three deer—frightened in the forest, at least in my stupid head we were suddenly a family of deer—crowded together, hearts pounding—I—"

"Yep," he said, "I remember that one."

"You do?"

"Yep."

"Oh. Good."

Here we are at Bluebird Canyon. Here, Joslin, I picked up your kids for you.

Rex says, "Trip, how many knees does a horse have?"

Shit. "Four."

David says, "No—not four."

Rex says, "Trip, you dummy. You ever contemplate a horse's hind legs? Look a little more carefully at horses, will you, Trip?"

"Pastern," David says.

"Of course," his father says, kissing him on top of the head.

16

I HAD lots of bad dreams. Sheila didn't exist, and never had, and I adopted a child that turned out to be this kind of orangoutang, a nasty little thing, but if I didn't love it fully it would always be a source of guilt to me. My dreams make me disappointed in my own unconscious.

I can tell that once again 'tis the season to be jolly. They put up the big glass triptych at Main Beach that shows Bethlehem. All the bells and wreaths on the lampposts. Merchants making big bucks. Another Christmas at my throat. I've taken to watching "This Passing Night," its troubled souls are a comfort. One air-head woman on today's episode said, "That is potently ridiculous." I couldn't believe it. Even I know it's "*pa*tently ridiculous." She was egg-beating some batter, and the microphone must have been inside the egg-beater. Sounded like a giant dentist drill, and I yelled out loud, "Stop!" At the end of the scene, she was arguing with her father. He said, just before the music, "Isn't the point that you really don't want to see me involved with another woman?" Since I am developing this habit of talking back to the boob tube, I said, "Fuckin' A it's the point, dipshit." I don't know why they have to shove it in your face, it's insulting—as if you are not smart enough to figure it out yourself. And Dr. Kelly wasn't on. It's potently ridiculous.

But I did see Rex one evening up at Summer Snow. They are making fantastic progress, it will definitely be ready by Christmas. Rex was standing in the driveway, stoned. Not drunk. Comfy stoned. All covered with strings of electric green and red lights. Had them wrapped around him and a Modesto ash. There was a big wooden sleigh, a Santa Claus, and a crèche. Big green letters covered with fake snow and icicles. A white angel-hair Christmas tree. Boxes of ornaments. He was really a sight, I had to stop and laugh at him. "Goddammit, Trip, Pop always did this—and *he* hated it." Rex was trying to untangle the string of lights. I didn't help a bit. I just enjoyed it, poor bastard, sighing, trying to think. He knows J.O. always did this, and now he has to, for Leela and David; he's a little bit sad. But there was something all right about it. He seemed rather peaceful. He said, "Trip, if you would like to make yourself useful, goddammit, hand me the BVM." I said, "What?" He said, "Goddammit, the BVM." I said, "What?" again, just to irritate him. "The Blessed Virgin Mary. Pop always puts her on the mailbox."

I got a call and left. Solve your own problem for a change.

The next day it was all up, real nice. I chatted with a guy on the crew who was retiling the bathroom. He laughed, said Hooker worked all night, by lantern. I looked inside, and they did have a fairly nice staircase. Nothing like the Honduras mahogany, of course. But nice. Painters were in the family room, working around the angel-hair white Christmas tree standing all alone with its pink balls.

On December 21 we had our department office party. Sauterne punch in a plastic bowl. The Chief drew me aside and said I'd done an "overwhelming" job on that report. Butch Ravelling was a tad gassed, too. He sidled up to me, overly chummy, I haven't seen that side of him much, he knows I'm next in line. The secretary won't speak to me, she studiously avoids me, as I have studiously avoided her. A spacy woman in black and silver and pearls says to me, "Well, now, here's the handsomest man in Laguna Beach." Is it the Chief's girl? No. The D.A.'s estranged battered wife? No. It is the mayor's wife, she's a bit addlepated. Last year she answered the phone at the mayor's home, it was from a black guy from VISTA. And she said to him, "You leave my husband alone, you jigaboo —you dirty jigaboo." We took some flak on that one, but she's just mentally ill. She says, "Oh, Sergeant Bodley, we have so much to be thankful for, with you in our midst." Be thankful for me. The craziest lady in town thinks I'm the handsomest man in town. Draw your own conclusions.

I always get this way at Christmas.

On December 23, I sent a big poinsettia to Leela. I picked it out myself, it cost me thirty-five bucks. It was real full. I just wanted her to have it. I don't know, she touches me.

They invited me to dinner on Christmas Day. I was on duty from seven to three, but Rex said they always had Christmas dinner around five. I didn't eat all day the 24th, then the 25th I dressed up real spiffy after I got off work. Summer Snow. Lights winking in the trees, the BVM on the mailbox, Santa roaring down the roof in his sleigh. The whole house was a kind of wreckage, ribbons and boxes and wrapping paper all over everywhere. Huge fire in the main fireplace. Marge Stivers in a red wool suit that accented her tits and clung to her butt. She gave me a big Merry Christmas hug and a smack. Leela was dolled up in a green gown with roses all over it. The kid wearing that blue turtleneck sweater that Leela had knitted, lying on the floor playing some electronic football game. Rex has on a nightshirt that Leela had given him, worn over his clothes, and a stocking cap. The dining table all set up with Christmas dishes—only about ninety dishes, all with a Christmas design, I never saw Christmas *china.* They were just firing gifts at each other, they'd been doing it since David woke up at six to unpack his stocking. Whole house ringing with Christmas carols on the stereo.

Leela had to give me a gift right away. She was all flushed with excitement. I told her I felt empty-handed, but she said, "Your very presence is a gift." She had my poinsettia in the room, on a table. It did look rather nice. She gave me a home-repair book from *Reader's Digest* and a cardigan sweater with leather buttons. I had to model it, waltzing about with my eggnog. Rex said the eggnog had always been J.O.'s specialty, a secret recipe. First Christmas without Pop. Rex had given Leela a gold candy dish with a card, "Lee, Love, Jack," which J.O. himself had written long ago and Rex happened to find. It was made in Florence, very elegant.

Now Rex had to give Most Gross Gift. A family tradition. The recipient was Marge, and he gave her a coffee cup about four inches high, blond color. It was the lower half of a woman's body, a naked fat woman's body sitting cross-legged with orange high heels on her fat feet and an orange purse slung on her bulbous arm. Words were painted on the cup, in orange: PUT ME BETWEEN YOUR LIPS. Gives you a whole new outlook on bad taste.

Marge threw a present back at him. A silver crown that he put on over his stocking cap, with engraving on it: FACETIOUS ABSTEMIOUS. Rex strutted around, explaining to me, "Pop once said the only word in English with all the vowels in the right order is *facetious*"—and he stared, and

306

stared, and then he saw the two words, *A, E, I, O, U.* Rex kissed Marge, kissed the life out of her. I thought, "Emperor and Clown." The phone keeps ringing, calls from relatives and friends. Rex always takes them, sometimes puts Leela on briefly.

I take a few hits on the Maui-KaPowee that Rex offers me in the kitchen. All the food is cooking away in there like crazy. I get a gift, tied in pink ribbon. It is from Rex. Another coffee cup with printing on it:

I AM A

and then words with lines through them, crossing them out:

POLIS, PULICE, OFFIS, COP

And David gives me a red baseball cap with white lettering: PIG POWER.

Rex gives his mother an antique mahogany whatnot. It's lovely, real classy, and has to be put in a corner because it's triangular at the back. Rex also gives her a series of crystal and blue glass and pewter things to go behind its half-glass door that works with a little silver key. Leela about dies with pleasure. Everybody keeps kissing everybody. The handsomest man in town just watches. Sips his eggnog, feels the dope. Wanders into the kitchen to smell the turkey and look out at the sea.

Joslin calls from New York City. Everybody gets excited. Rex thanks her for the UNICEF calendar. David explains his most favorite gift "so far," a little motor scooter. His dad says, "Don't tell her about it, man, she'll think it's a Harley." And then Rex talks to her again. Everybody pretends not to listen to the conversation. Leela talks to her for a moment, then says good-bye, turns around with a hurt expression. "Joslin didn't like the sweater. She said it just—wasn't her."

I figure it probably wasn't. But why didn't Joslin just say thank you and give it to the Salvation Army?

Rex gets all fucked up about it.

David goes out and rides his scooter.

So much effort has gone into everything, and Joslin punctures it like a balloon. I remember her, I really remember her. Her eyes, her whole body. Probably has no idea of the trouble she's caused. It takes about an hour for everybody to get over it. But nobody inquired after her brother, asked what she was doing. I feel sorry for her. I remember her telling me her girlish dream of a knight in shining armor. And then Rex Hooker came along. She never knew what hit her.

307

Rex gives Marge a big mirror from Peru. Its frame is glass inlaid with gold, over a century old, really beautiful. Marge is overjoyed. The phone rings, some cousin in Phoenix.

Then, like at Thanksgiving, it's Scarf Time. We go into the table and we have a small problem. Leela has prepared salads. At every place setting there is what she calls a "Christmas candle." Five of 'em, each one is half a banana standing up, in a slice of pineapple, with whipped cream and a cherry on top. Well. I wonder for a second if I'm the only one who sees them like that. But I look up, and Rex sees it. Marge sees it. We can't hurt Leela's feelings, we avoid each other's eyes. We sit down, everybody joins hands. Poor Rex has to get through the blessing, but he makes it. David—shit, if the little sucker catches on, we're all going to blow it— but he doesn't, he says a little blessing. Marge gives a stifled grunt, but doesn't lose it. I take a long, long look at—mine. I sneezed on the set of the soap opera, but I am not going to do anything here. I just can't look at Rex, I'd drop my load. I glance around the table at these half-bananas standing up with the whipped cream and cherries on the tops. Leela is supersensitive, she knows what you're thinking before you do—and she knows something's not right, but she doesn't know what. She says, "Well, let's begin our Christmas candles." This is a second problem. How do you begin? Are you supposed to knock it down and cut its head off, or just lean over and suck it?

When we all manage, I feel tremendously relieved, so do Rex and Marge, I can look at them now. I feel bad for Leela, like I want to protect her. She knows something funny happened. But away we go. Six vegetables and four salads and some of these and a couple of those and a big bird. I eat as if there is no tomorrow. There are little gifts at every place setting. Leela is remembering the trip she took with J.O. to Iran. Rex says it wasn't Iran, Mother, it was Egypt. Leela says she simply cannot understand where that missing Christmas ornament is, the one that's David's profile. Rex says he looked high and low, mainly low. I love cranberry sauce sloshed all over the white meat, I make a complete pig of myself with the mashed potatoes and lush craters of gravy. Turkey dressing. Pass the peas. Rex says, "Look at us—we're the same, exactly the same, as at Thanksgiving."

"Except for Roger," David says, eating away.

Rex took me upstairs, said he had to show me something, he's being all secretive. He takes me into a study and then he gives me a knife, a beautiful knife. Must have cost a fortune, a real collector's item. Perfectly balanced, in a blue velvet sack. A knife. For me. And then he gave me an envelope. I opened it and there was all this money. Two thousand dollars. What's going on? I told him I couldn't accept it. Rex was drinking cognac and smoking a stogie, just a little too full of himself. He said it didn't matter, I deserved it, even though I had taken Peter Ingalls away from him.

I stood up. "What?"

And then, I don't know what is the matter with him, he said, "Well, after all, Trip, Peter was *mine.*"

I said, "What?" again.

He squinted his eyes and whispered, "Only one thing wrong with you, you're not too bright."

I just looked at him. I didn't know whether to slug him or throw up.

I said—I don't know what made me think of it—I said, "No wonder she couldn't live with—*him.*"

He looked at me again. And he said, "No—no—you're bright enough, all right."

I was ready to lay him out.

Then he said, "Hey, this is scary. This is fun."

I guess I composed myself. I think I said, "No it's not." But I did throw the money on the floor—with the knife—and I started down the stairs. What a fucker. He was coming along after me. "Hey—Trip, wait a minute. Hey, wait." I reached the bottom, and there was Marge, I was just steaming along, and Leela came in saying, "Oh, what's happened?" as if she'd been expecting it all along. I felt awful, I didn't want to spoil everything, but what's wrong with that puke? He grabbed me, got between me and the Cutlass. He was really babbling. I calmed down enough to speak, I said to him, "Don't you talk to me that way." He was saying, "I'm sorry, I'm sorry, I don't know what happened." I looked at him, I looked him in the eyes.

And there weren't any. His eyes were two blue holes.

So I hunched my jacket around my shoulders. I think I said again, "Don't talk to me that way." But the message had been received. We stood around outside for a while. I don't know what possessed him.

Rex plays "O Little Town of Bethlehem" on the piano. Leela goes around the room lighting candles with foot-long matches. We're all singing in a dreamy way. "And in thy deep and dreamless sleep"—Rex playing softly, Marge singing like a little girl, David swaying his head back and forth. The phone rings again. It's Dibby, out at Medjuhl. Leela talks to him, then hands the phone to Rex. Rex picks it up, talks a little, there's something he can't figure out. Leela passes a flat box to David, who seems to be in on some sort of secret. David hands the box to his father, who opens it. I see a light bulb go on in his head. He hangs up the phone and looks at his mother.

Leela nods. Smiles.

Rex displays the flat box. There's a photograph inside. Marge goes over to see. She whoops, passes it to me. I stare at it. About the most beautiful horse I ever saw. Coal-black. His name is "Dr. Kelly." A coal-black stallion.

"Well," Leela says, "Whiskey and Tequila are getting on in years, and I thought it was time—"

"Oh," Rex says, "Mother—" They embrace.

She says, "Do you like him?"

"Do I *like* him?"

Rex lets it all sink in. Then jumps up under his FACETIOUS ABSTEMIOUS crown. Says, "Well, if we're going to get into animals—"

I watch, watch and wonder. Family-shmamily.

"I did have a little gift for David." He looks at his mother and says, "Look, you guys start to clean up, I'll be back in a flash."

So we clean up. O Come All Ye Faithful. Whole house full of cards and debris. I never thought Christmas was what you point toward, it's what you get through. I scrub pots, Marge at my elbow. It is probably chauvinist of me to keep noticing her bosom. But give me a break. Besides, she's been looking at me real odd ever since that little go-round with Rex. I've been thinking, somebody's got to call the asshole on all his shit. But that face, his eyes. I don't know what it is. Marge now, she comes toward me and backs off at the same time. Like she's afraid of me. But I haven't done anything to *her*. And her eyes are weird, like she's giving me signals, but not quite. Like she's giving me *two* signals. She says nothing at all, but she's not quiet. She's hushed. That's it. I don't know why. Well, women—I would undoubtedly get it wrong anyway. Why even try? Hand me the Ajax, I'm talking grease here.

The doorbell rings. I shake cleanser off my hands, wipe them on a towel. I glance out at the sea, where it's begun to rain a little. I open the door, and there's Rex, in a London Fog. Two little puppies peeking out from his armpits.

Standing there in the mist, Rex, woebegone, and the pups all wiggly.

I look at Rex. His eyes are back. He's himself, whatever the fuck that is.

David runs to the door, and Rex lets the pups down. They scratch and mosey a bit, this way and that, sniffing. Skip on in where it's warm and dry. David picks one up, the other is all frisky. They're Labs. They snoop around all fuzzy, check out the little stinks their noses pick up.

Rex stands there like a delivery boy. Or not sure he's welcome.

I say, "Got sense enough to come in out of the rain?"

He looks at me with a helpless thank-you in his eyes. He comes on in. David gets nipped. "Ouch."

Rex says, "You got a responsibility, son."

"Oh, I'll do everything."

"Yes, you will. But first you got to name them. Think about it for a while."

David loves them. He lies down, and they jump on him, and one of them pees on his knee. I look at Rex, he's so quiet, almost plain.

"Well," David says, "they're—they keep exploring." He hiccups, pats at one. The pups are all over the house, fuzzy little golden bastards. I can't help but remember Procter and Gamble. Marge picks up one pup, kisses and snuggles it. "Oh," she says, laughing, "they're both boys." Then she sees me looking at her, and falls silent.

Rex has one more present for all of us, he meant to give it earlier, but he forgot. He leads us down into the workroom.

There's a sheet over the gift. Rex pulls it off. It is a plaster bust of Elvis Presley. About two feet high, with a kind of Greek god or Michelangelo's David look about it. I always liked Elvis. Sheila did too. I wonder what dumb fuck Sheila has given a gift to today, some urban cowboy in Albuquerque. The bust is painted, Elvis has on a lavender shirt with little silver stars in the lapels. But the great thing is that when you pass your hand near it, it sings, in Elvis's voice:

Love me tender
Love me true—

and then shuts off. Rex is absolutely delighted with it. Marge says it's the best thing she's ever seen. Leela can't understand how it does that just because you pass your hand.

Me neither.

We go back upstairs. Rex sits, looking at the photograph of Dr. Kelly.

David can't get over how those pups love to explore. He jumps up and says, "I got it—Dad?"

"What, honey?"

"I know their names."

311

"What?"

He points. "That is Lewis." He points. "And that is Clark."

I wake up in my trailer in the middle of the night. Covered with perspiration. I sit and shake for five minutes. I go over all the things that one goes over in the dead of night. Leela, Rex, David, Marge, Joslin— I go over them, like Missing Persons. I'm not getting anywhere. I'm dying on the vine.

I fall asleep for five minutes and dream I'm a woman. It scares me somehow.

I want my own life. My wife. Children. A little voice says, "You blew it, Trip." I say to the darkness, "You are potently ridiculous." But my voice lacks the ring of confidence.

I didn't see them again until Rex called and invited me up to watch the Rose Parade and some of the Bowl games. So I arrived, bright and early on the first day of the year. David was still sleeping, but Rex had been up for a long time. He'd turned the family room into a float, full of roses and silver-leaf eucalyptus and big sprays of Dutch iris. Leela modeled her new bed jacket, lace and gold, for when she goes into the hospital to have the surgery. She said she hoped the operation would finally rid her of "this pesky nuisance." Yes, "pesky nuisance"—just the word for a brain tumor that has practically destroyed your life.

The Rose Parade grossed me out. Always does. Rex said Joslin hated it too, especially the Drum and Bugle Corps, she thought she was at Nuremberg. But he could remember the good old days going up to Pasadena and getting blitzed the night before, looking for a one-night stand or the love of your life. Drinking beer, getting into fights, camping out. Then five years ago he and J.O. and David were in an Equestrian Unit.

Lewis and Clark were underfoot and knocking things over. I sat there drinking cocoa, smoking. I remember one January 2, Sheila and I drove up to look at the floats. There were all these Mexicans who reminded me of how the Catholic church deals with the poor. Floats standing around like cathedrals. Handicapped people in wheelchairs. Sheila purchased some edible panties from Frederick's. I guess they went stale, I never ate them.

Rex jumped up, pointed, "*There's* Margie!" Sure enough, with "1962" across her boobs, on a float with previous Rose Queens. Marge hadn't been the 1962 Queen, actually, but she'd been a Princess of the Court. She was filling in for the Queen, who had committed suicide. I asked Rex why Marge wasn't Queen, and he said the Queens always ball the judges.

I said I didn't know that, that's not true, and he said just don't ask Marge why she wasn't Queen. Unless you want smoke in your face, podner. I looked at her on the screen and thought of her as Sister Catherine, and remembered those odd looks she gave me on Christmas Day.

We watched the Bowl games with David, who finally made it up for the New Year. Rex told him to pay attention to the Empire State Building when he got to New York City—because Pop had been on top of it when it was just being built in 1930. He and some architect friends were hopping around up on the one-hundredth floor when it was only girders. Rex said Pop had acrophobia, but he was so goddamn interested in the structure of the building that he took his heart in his mouth and went on up there, even with all the wind. Didn't dare look down between his feet at the traffic a hundred stories below. Rex said, "When you have acrophobia, honey, you *want* to jump, you get top-heavy." David said he'd be sure to remember.

On the way out to 1 GROUCH Rex asked if I would drive to the airport with them. He whispered, "God, I hate her, taking my boy three thousand miles from where he *belongs*. I told her I never wanted to make him choose. But she's forcing it. He'll have to *choose*. Forever. No, no, no. I don't hate her. I love her. Every fool has his rainbow, and she's mine. I adore her. Cunt."

I talked to the Chief, and there was no problem with my taking the three-to-eleven on the fourth. The Chief seems more and more to want to accommodate me. He says, "Your relationship with the Hooker family has really put you in the cat bird scat." I look at him. No, I do not ever want to be a chief. Because there will always be somebody like me around to hate me. Except I would like to try. Test myself, see what I could achieve. Give me ten years, I could be a good chief.

Bright and early the morning of the fourth, I tool up to Summer Snow. Three black suitcases in the driveway. I go in, they are having breakfast. I've had mine, but I drink a cup of cocoa with them. Leela—you just can't hold her back—had done one of those arrangements. The big table set out like a miniature airport, several little toy planes and one big plane in the middle. Little wooden figures walking out to it, the one in the yellow shirt was supposed to be David, I guess. The one in the red shirt was Rex, saying good-bye. A female figure in a blue dress stood way over behind a water glass, and that was supposed to be Joslin, waiting at JFK. Little plastic suitcases and service vans and a police car thrown in for the hell of it.

They finished up. I stared at those airplanes and vehicles, the truck, and the wooden figures.

Time to go.

Leela was all dressed up, green dress with gold jewelry. Rex straight and dependable, ready to drive. As we were walking to the car, Leela said, "David, you have the best father in the world"—and she put her other arm around Rex, drawing him to her—"just as he had the best father in the world."

The phone rang, Rex went to get it, and it was Marge Stivers. So David had to run back and say good-bye to her. Then he knelt down in the driveway and said good-bye to Lewis and Clark. Leela said she and Rex would take real good care of the pups, they'd grow a lot between now and when he came back in June. She added, like it was an afterthought, "And I'll be myself again." Rex put the three black bags into the trunk of the car.

"Take care of yourself, my darling," Leela said, hugging David. "Oh, do take care of yourself, sweetheart, and take care of your mother."

Rex slammed the trunk. "Don't want to miss the plane."

"Oh, precious, *miss* it," Leela said, then caught herself, "No—no, I don't mean that, I must never mean that—get going, you guys."

Which we did.

Rex and me in the front seat, David in the back. The kid was looking out the rear window, giving the V for Victory sign with his fingers. Leela returning the V for Victory sign, she was in tears, there in the sunny morning. As we went up the driveway past the Monterey pines, Rex sounded three little beeps on the horn, David still making the V sign through the back window to Grandma. Whose brain tumor is a "pesky nuisance."

Rolling along 405, fighting the early traffic. We passed Lion Country Safari, and eventually the landing pad for the Goodyear Blimp. David folded his arms on the back of the front seat. He put his chin on his wrists. "Well, here we are, the Three Musketeers." Rex sighed at the wheel, "The Three Stooges." I don't know why I said, "The Father, the Son, and the Holy Spit." We were all feeling sad. So we played Geography. I can't believe how smart the kid is, he knows places I had never heard about at his age. Also places I haven't heard about now. I didn't believe there was really a Lake Titicaca. Sounded like something Rex would make up. But when I got home I looked in my almanac and there it is, in Peru. Titi-caca.

Rex said, "Honey, I wish you were already in college—I wish all of us were older."

David said, "And I'm already a Stanford Man?"

"I thought you were going for a football scholarship to Oberlin."

314

"Nope." The kid sighed. "I guess I'll have to be a Stanford Man."

"Check."

"You know what's best for me. You're my farter."

"Follow Daddy, son, follow Daddy."

We passed a billboard, and the kid said, "Is Nude Mud Wrestling fun to watch?"

Rex said, "Trip?"

I said that over the years it had lost its zip.

We had to stand in line for a while at the TWA terminal. Go through the detector, which for some reason kept beeping when Rex went through. It beeped even after he emptied his pockets. I thought maybe he had a knife hidden on him somewhere, and then felt bad that I had that thought. Then there was the long moving sidewalk, and the posters from Mrs. Dinklestein's Fourth Grade Class in Gardena. And on up to the waiting area where we had to stand in line again to get David a window seat in Nonsmoking.

I thought they might like some time alone with each other. I went to the drinking fountain and shined my shoes in the men's. When I came out they were starting to board. David walked right up to me and shook my hand, all business, but then his eyes went away a sec, and he pulled me down with his hand and kissed me, beside the mouth. Then he and his dad had a big hug. I was feeling the kiss while I watched Rex hand him his tote bag and say, "Off you go, man." And then David bopped along into the tunnel that hooks up to the door of the plane. A Stanford Man, Class of '91.

Rex and I waited by the window until the plane took off. Shooting up into the sky, a DC-10, on its way to JFK.

We walked out and got on the People Mover. Rex was whispering away to himself, "Don't break, goddammit, don't break."

We went past a whole clot of blue-haired ladies with leis on, just back from the magic of Waikiki. One lady spotted us, did a double-take, and then said, "Girls—girls—it's Steven Kelly—look!" and she waved her flabby arm. "Hi there, Mr. Kelly." Rex paused and turned on her, as if he were furious or something, and then he said, real loud, "Dr. Kelly."

315

17

I STOPPED by that night while I was on duty. Leela was asleep, or at least in bed. Rex and I shot a game of Cowboy down in the rec room. I was sure he would have dived into a bottle, but he hadn't, he was all right. He'd even spoken with Joslin and David in New York. Tomorrow mother and son were going to the observatory on top of the Empire State Building. Rex smiled, lined up the three-ball. "On the plane he had a seat beside a 'Feather River Roughneck.' That's what it said on her sweat shirt." He made his whinny noise. I cut out after Marge came in. I'd hoped she'd be able to lend him a helping hand, but naturally she was looped.

So for the next few days I just ran around doing my job. The Chief has given us every sign that he's pulling up stakes. Butch heard a rumor that Our Leader was offered something in Sacramento, with the state. I know of nothing in the Chief's background or training that would qualify him. But maybe he's going to school on the sly—God knows he doesn't put in the requisite time here. I always thought he was up in his hot tub balling his girlfriend. I can just see 'em, the Jacuzzis, Cerritos and Titicaca.

Leela was scheduled for surgery on the ninth, with a specialist at the big medical center at UCLA. I've never been there, but I've heard about

316

it, I guess it's top-drawer. I called a couple of times on the seventh and eighth, but got no answer, so I went up there. All the Christmas decorations had been taken down off the house. Nobody was home. Summer Snow all locked up. I suppose they had to go out there a few days before the actual operation. Nothing for me to do but wait. And then the way I found out was Rex, a telephone call about 11:45 P.M., in the middle of Johnny Carson at the desk with Ed McMahon, doing some clever little routine. I was half looking at that, and chuckling, when the voice said:

"Oh, Trip—I've been calling you—oh, man—*fuck.*" He sounded just terrible, and when he said *"fuck,"* I knew. I stared at my navy blue socks on the red linoleum, and listened.

He told me they'd had her on the table for fourteen hours. Three different surgical teams. The "pin-prick" tumor wasn't pin-prick at all. More like a walnut. I don't understand how X-rays and ultrasonic sophisticated scanners goof up like that, but apparently you never really know until you physically go in.

This was January 10. She's in the I.C.U., awaiting another operation. Except it's clearly hopeless, they told him after the first one: It's irreversible.

"They say"—I could hear Rex trying to get his mouth around it—"they say—vegetable." He was very quiet, very formal and not hysterical, I had never heard him like this. Real edgy-precise and far away. "But she—she does not look like a veget—she doesn't look like that, Trip. She looks like a—mannequin."

I stood there with the phone to my ear. After a while I said, "What can I do?"

Silence, the long-distance effect you sometimes get between L.A. and here.

"Nothing."

"You want me to come up?"

Silence, that stitching in the lines. "That's kind, Trip. Thank you. No. Marge is here. I'll keep you posted."

I wished Johnny Carson would shut up. I looked at my socks. I said something more, Rex said something more, and then I hung up, slowly, hearing his end go down. I turned off the TV, and sat there in the dark.

Rex called a few days later. He said she was being moved out of UCLA and back to the Laguna Hospital. I thought it meant an improvement in her condition. But Rex said no, UCLA needed the bed.

She didn't want to live, not this way—she had told him so before she went in. And he had promised.

About 3 P.M. on Monday, I went to the hospital, I passed Father Darcy in the hall. And Margo is there, she looks like she has seen a ghost. She has. The damage is so complete, there's no way to bring back many functions. It was the size of a walnut, and all their twenty-first century equipment couldn't see it. I make myself look at her. Her eyes are open, but not seeing anything. Tiny body, its heartbeat turned into green lines up on a screen. All those tubes in her. It seems like dishonor to look. Leela. A mannequin.

I go out. Rex's yellow hair, his head bent down, waiting. Christ, he's lost a lot of weight these past months. He's hardly there, his clothes hang on him. I know hospitals exist to help, but somehow I blamed the hospital itself. The silence like a faraway noise of heavy machinery buried deep in the earth. It's no good. Rex and I walked out into the fresh air of the parking lot.

We stood by the red Mercedes, smoking. Rex suddenly blurted, "I can't—Pop would never, I'll never—I won't—I'd fucking die first!"

And then something really weird happened. For a split second it was like one time twenty years ago, after practice on the Indio football field, half a dozen of us hanging around in the twilight kicking field goals for dollars. All of a sudden we were lying on the ground. An earthquake had just lifted all six of us off our feet and knocked us flat on our backs. I saw that same twilight sky in my head when Rex—*wham!*—it was like something hit him, threw his body against the red Mercedes, and he bounced off it and fell down on the blacktop. It was so goddamn strange. But before I could say anything, he got right back up. It's not like Rex jumped or anything. More like the pavement buckled up and threw him. Now, staring at the blue sky, his head cocked, he whispered, "I'd—truly—die first."

I began making periodic checks on Summer Snow. On the night of January 20, I tooled into the driveway. The fog was thick and Rex's figure startled me, vague in my beams. He was bent over, dumping Alamo into yellow bowls for Lewis and Clark. He hardly seemed to see me. We stood there in the fog. And then we went into the house. He had a nice fire going, and the door of the Solarium was yawning open to the sea. He poured me a cup of coffee and then settled down on the big couch. I sat with him. Except he wasn't there, really. He was in some other place. Wearing J.O.'s robe, the red silk with the black velvet lapels. He had called Joslin, he said the conversation didn't go smoothly. His whole face, his body, no flesh on his arms. He couldn't look at me.

I have been through this, when my aunt died. It was on a joy ride, just outside of Tacoma, she was up there for vacation. The car went round

318

a curve and it was head-on. I was splitting up with Sheila at the time, and I didn't go to the funeral. The family has resented it ever since. I have a cousin who refuses to talk to me to this day. I was so wasted with my own problem that I failed. I know I failed. My aunt was dead. And Sheila had said good-bye. My aunt—who brought me up like her own son—they buried her there, in the state of Washington. My aunt who was my mother. The family never understood my not coming. My aunt was killed instantly. She was always so warm and comforting, probably had a couple of beers in her, I know how she would try to be gay. Sort of a heroic lady, actually. One example, she put up with my uncle for life. They were my parents. Aunt Babe took care of the funeral arrangements. I wasn't there. It can eat away at your conscience. Makes you think your whole way of doing things is wrong.

Rex's voice startles me. "But—but, I *began* in her—I lived in her belly. She brought me into the world. Pop—Pop? I won't let you down."

Rex looked at me, Rex sitting there in J.O.'s robe. Hit this old man. Hit this old man. Rex in the firelight.

He doesn't use tapes anymore. No need for tapes now.

"The first time Jos came into this house, she said, 'I think we're not in Kansas anymore.' "

The fire blazing away. Lewis and Clark, done with their din-din, the pups come in sniffing about our chairs. I don't know whether I should leave or hang around.

Rex stood up and stoked the fire. Bending down in his father's robe. "Pop said to David, 'What am I, my boy, when I fall out of my chair? I am a Pop-over.' "

Rex walks around the room like he is picking over a disaster area, a member of a government inspection team.

His voices, his two voices. " 'Rex, do you think we have to say good-bye?' I don't know, Dr. Kelly. Joss-ee, you are the world to me and—and —I found this old pamphlet, this old pamphlet, a *Welcome to Laguna* that Mother wrote for the Pageant of the Masters in 1947. Listen up, Kelly. Mother wrote this: 'The older homes on the sea hills are Carpenter's Gothic, perched in polite groups, odd old maidens decked in lace who have gone through two decades of wind and fog and sun, and come out of it all with a certain serenity and charm.' Mother wrote that. Mother wrote that."

I'm looking at him, and listening to his voices, and thinking of breakfast arrangements, an Arab caravan, camels, each one carrying a real medjuhl date on its back. The eyes don't blink, they don't see.

The voice of Rex Hooker. The voice of Dr. Kelly. He says, "I don't know. Marge has been so faithful. These days, these memories. She—My Little Margie has always had this falling-off-the-edge-of-the-world quality. You know Margie, the tears in her eyes, the way she hauls ass, the catchy tilt of her head?" Rex stands there. "Take care a yourself, sis." He just stands there. "Joslin didn't fall out of love with Rex—Joslin just didn't believe in Rex anymore."

I sit listening to him. He begins to walk again, slowly. It's like all the voices are in his head, all the time. Skipping all over the lot.

"Joslin says, 'Our marriage didn't die—you killed it—you murdered us.' "

I feel completely helpless sitting here. I know a little of the feeling, when I heard the news from Tacoma. But this is different. This is real different.

"A couple of times Pop said thank you to Rex. With his eyes anyway. And I wonder—I wonder if David—if it would be better for David if he didn't have to grow up with an invalid for a father. 'Rex, don't—don't.' Shut up, Kelly, I'm through talking with you. I'm going away now. 'Don't break, Rex—don't break.' What do you know about *breakage*? I wonder about it. Perpetuity."

He stopped walking around.

"I don't want David to see it. He was with me. We were doing a little shopping. The day before I had to put him on the plane. We were in the Safeway at Boat Canyon, in the express line—nine items or less. I was standing there with my son, confident of my ability to deal with the world. And this gray-haired old man behind us muttered, 'You're way over nine.' And I wasn't, Doc, truly I wasn't. And I turned on him. In front of my son. I said to the old man, 'Shall we count them together?' And I did it —'One—two—three'—the OJ and the Joy and the Raid—and then I said to him, 'Do you know where you can put your asparagus—stalk by stalk?' The old man looked at David, and looked at me, and said, 'I won't argue with you.' He hadn't shaved, he had this white stubble. And I said, 'Do you buy pornography or just live it?' In front of *David.* The old man could have been Pop—'You're way over nine.' An old man, he could have been Pop, and I vented all my rage on him. My own son saw me be a bully. If I make a mistake like that—with *groceries*—and listen, listen now to this whine in my voice. 'Rex, Rex, you've got one job, not to break.' No —goddammit, I don't got *one* job. Oh, the morning Mother and I left here for UCLA, she came to me, in my room, just at dawn. And Mother said—she said, 'Oh, precious, did I waken you?' Well, she had. I sat up right away, still in my dream, it was like kittens crying, little calling moans, and it was Mother, and—in this thin gray light—she was sitting at the foot of my bed, all huddled into herself, in a white gown. She wasn't looking at me, she was staring at the new drapes. And her eyes, those eyes so deep-set, that head, so all tortured, I thought. Why does God do that to her? Why won't God let her *alone*? And she said, 'Van Gogh. *Starry Night.*' I watched her trembling there at the foot of my bed, and in this very soft slow voice, you know Mother's voice, she said, 'I couldn't sleep. I was reading Vincent's letters to his brother Theo. And in one letter he says, "God did not put us on this earth to be happy. He put us here to experience great things." ' Mother said it so—so quietly—and then—so quietly—and then—she turned and looked at me, and her face—Mother's face was so radiant, it was glowing in the gray dawn light, and she said, with her bags packed for UCLA, she said to me, 'I'm going to live to be ninety.' And—and I was too *fierce*. I pulled off the covers, and went to her, I grabbed her, and I hugged her too hard. She was all broken in my arms—oh, how can human beings do it, do everything, you have to believe in God, you have to. 'I'm going to live to be ninety.' I hugged her too *hard,* and you tell me don't break, don't *break.*"

We sat there. He said, "At Pop's funeral I wanted to whistle 'That Silver-Haired Daddy of Mine.' Have I told you this before? Not the words, the whistle. I whistle well. I should whistle more. Throw whistles at the sky. Have I talked to you about this, son? Our next entry is a father-and-son whistling team from Bluebird Canyon."

I look at him. Let him talk.

"And we don't blame Joslin. If David ever commits suicide, Rex won't blame his mother. But David won't ever commit suicide, that's dumb. Rex Hooker is thinking in big blocks of time. Dr. Kelly is a subtext of Rex Hooker. David's father, Joslin's husband, J.O.'s son, they—Leela's son—they are Rex Hooker's subtexts. Don't leave home without your subtext. But Rex Hooker has exhausted the subtexts of Rex Hooker. Mother, dearest Mother, I am your only son. I have only one subtext left. And he can help you. Rex has called him in special. A specialist. Just for you." His eyes go up, out of focus. He's whispering. "Leave her just like that? For years? Miracles do happen, doctors don't know everything." His eyes skitter. "But what if she's in pain? Terrible pain? And can't tell us? A year from now, two years—a miracle—she's all right. God will smile. But Mother is in pain now, she's trying to signal. Excruciating pain. No. No." He sighs, turns his eyes to me. "Hooker is a name. It is—what's the word for it?—you know, ethnic background. Your country of origin? There's a name for what that is. Why couldn't Hooker be Irish or Italian, or something juicy—Jossie—why does Hooker have to be—what's the word for what that is?"

I say, "Nationality."

He stares at me. "Well, Trip, how the hell are ya?"

"OK."

"What did you say? What was that long word?"

"Nationality."

"Oh. Right. Nationality. Thanks. Thanks, Trip. Will you think of things for me? OK? Think of the names of things? 'K? I keep forgetting what things are called. Can't seem to remember the names. Marge and Rex are brother and sister after all. Mother is English. Nationality. Right. I never thought Joslin would go east. Never thought she'd return east."

I didn't know whether to say anything or not. I said, "She divorced you. A couple of years ago."

"Oh yes, yes indeed. But she stayed in Bluebird Canyon. Your house is you. She stayed in Bluebird Canyon." He was really having trouble, his voice scratchy and empty. "David shouldn't be in the East. He should be in this house. This is David's house. Summer Snow. The house Pop built. It's my house. No, no, it isn't Rex's house. Rex's house is Bluebird Canyon. But he didn't get it. It fell through. David and Mommy and Daddy in Bluebird Canyon. No—no." He looked at me for a long time. And then his voice was back to normal. He said, "Trip, could you—could you promise me something?"

"Sure."

"Good." And then he didn't say anything else. Just nodded his head.

I waited, but he was really through. He walked me outside, and we stood there awhile, and then he walked back into Summer Snow and left me standing in the fog on the driveway. The house looked like a fairy castle. I had to shake myself. I got into my car and started away. And stopped. I cut the motor, pulled the brake. I walked back down and started for the door. Then I heard it. Whistling. I stepped back and looked up. He was on the balcony, the main balcony facing the ocean. I thought at first he was whistling "That Silver-Haired Daddy of Mine." Or maybe the song "Bluebird Canyon," the one on the music box. But no. I recognized the melody, I've heard it before, but I can't put my finger on it. He stands there in J.O.'s robe in the fog. Have to hand it to him. Really can whistle.

The Chief called me early next morning. Said I better get up to the hospital. Mrs. Hooker had died. I was shaky, could hardly tie my shoes. I parked in the section reserved for physicians.

There was a new girl at the nurses' station, really flustered, didn't want a blot on her record. She had been on duty when it happened. She told me Leela Hooker's last visitor was her psychiatrist.

Her psychiatrist? Leela didn't have a psychiatrist.

The nurse is maybe twenty-three, just a kid. She repeats it to me, "Oh yes, I spoke with Dr. Kelly myself." She points to the register. "He signed in at six thirty-five." She had a cold sore on her lip, she was pretty, and I read it, in Rex's handwriting, "Steven Kelly, M.D."

Rex once said to me that a terrible mistake is worse than a tragic error. But he hasn't made a mistake, and he hasn't made a tragic error. He's done the right thing. Only when he did it, he was Steven Kelly, M.D.

I can't quite see. Cause of death is "a sharp reduction in the concentration of oxygen being supplied."

Nurses and doctors walk around. They don't really care, its just another stiff sent to the fridge. The new nurse has such hopeful eyes. And that cold sore. And her hair braided up stupid over her head like in *The Sound of Music*.

Steven Kelly, M.D.

I interview the head surgeon. He's younger than I am and already a head surgeon. With a crinkly brown beard. Pink carbons, lab reports, all neatly piled up in a metal tray on his desk.

A head surgeon knows, like a policeman does, always C.Y.A. Cover Your Ass. He does not want to get himself or the hospital in trouble. He says that Mrs. Hooker's condition was absolutely hopeless. He gives me some fancy medical talk about the human brain; what he's really saying is that she would never have been able to do anything again. But he's very careful not to say anything that could be interpreted as approving what Rex did. I ask him what if Rex wanted them to stop keeping her alive? Would they have pulled the plug on his request? He looks at me and says, "We don't do that in this hospital." I ask him about Dr. Steven Kelly's relationship to the hospital. He draws a blank. I repeat the cause of death —a sudden reduction in the amount of oxygen being supplied. He was waiting for that. He is uneasy, has been uneasy. Looking at my uniform. But I will follow up on that later. Now I am trying to figure out the next move for Rex—

Who hasn't shown up anywhere.

I had to tell the Chief, he was shocked—to find out about Dr. Steven Kelly's identity. But I make it plain as day, talk with him for a good hour, I give my own opinion, that I would have done the same for my own mother, if I had the guts. I say that in no way was this a crime. She would never have recovered enough even to move her arm. Even to want to move her arm. Even to know what an arm is. I tell him it was clearly an act of mercy. The Chief listens, thinking, he nods and nods, drumming a pencil on his desk. I tell the Chief quite a bit, probably more than I should have. About Rex and me. He stops drumming the pencil a time or two. Looks me in the eye. My voice is not that easy to control, calm as I try to be. Finally the Chief says, "Well, I guess the first order of business is to find Hooker." And as I am going, he says, by the way, shouldn't the family be notified? The next of kin?

I realize I do not know who the next of kin are. Except Rex himself. Joslin and Rex are divorced, I don't know, I guess David is next of kin. Summer Snow is all locked up. Bluebird Canyon is all locked up. I call Marge and go out to her ranch. She's in a pretty bad way, but not drunk. She found out on her own, when she stopped in at the hospital today. She knows it was Dr. Steven Kelly. By now she's had a couple of hours to put it all together and get slammed with it. Her eyes are real bright, looking hard at something she's not looking at. I am convinced she does not know where Rex is. She looks pretty horrible for a beautiful woman. We make a list of people to contact. Father Darcy, Dibby. Marge doesn't know how to reach Joslin. I try to comfort her, but how can I? I just hold her for a moment or two.

She has a set of keys to Summer Snow. The next day Rex still hasn't shown up—I use them. I go in cautiously and prowl about, afraid of what I might find.

But all I see is that Lewis and Clark have done some fairly extensive dumping down in the workroom. I clean it up, feed them. There's no sign of life. I go into Rex's room. In the middle of his big desk is a stack of papers about a foot thick. I don't want to do it. But I have to. J.O.'s Last Will and Testament. Leela's. His. All sorts of financial papers. An address book. Lots of official documents. I sit down at the desk, take off my hat, and put it on a chair. I find what looks like it could be Joslin's phone number in New York. I call it, and get no answer. I call Marge, who agrees to come over and help me look through the stuff. I call the Chief, but he's not there. I leave a message alerting him to my progress. The lack thereof.

I'm just waiting for Marge to arrive, so I walk down into the trophy room. Mechanically play pool. Try to think. Try to get it all straight in my head. Bouncy-bouncy. I'm so tensed up, my hands are impossible to control. I look at my hands. I put them together in front of my face, and think of Rex's hands when he actually did the deed. My thumbs to my index fingers, I'm holding a tube, I press it, and pull it apart. I have just done it. My fingers. Help. Help, help, help. I focus through my fingers on the floor. It's all right—it's there—the grain in the wood.

18

I WORKED on it steadily for the next three days. Hardly took time off to sleep, didn't feel much like eating. I got permission to pry open a door at Bluebird Canyon, but there wasn't really anything in there. I looked at that big suede couch, thought about that orange poster, DR. STEVE KELLY TODAY. A scrap of paper on a pinup bulletin board had Joslin's brother's number in New York. It matched the number for Joslin that Rex had. But I still couldn't get any answer. And there had been no response to a telegram. I remembered Joslin and David were ultimately headed for Connecticut, but I didn't know the name of the town. Marge had put me in touch with the Hooker family lawyer in Rancho Mirage. His son was now running the office and came down to go through that massive pile of paper. Rex has now been missing for five days.

Father Darcy did what had to be done about Leela. He arranged for a simple little funeral. In fact, you could hardly even call it that, a funeral, but we didn't know what else to do. Without Rex, or Joslin. Marge got of lot of flowers, but to have a real funeral didn't seem right. How would we explain no Rex? So we settled on doing as little as possible. We just put her in the ground on the hillside next to J.O. Marge and myself and

325

Father Darcy and Dibby. Really rainy day, January 25. Somehow it seemed all wrong for the First Lady of Laguna.

I finally reached a housekeeper at Joslin's brother's place in New York and got the number in Darien, Connecticut. I tried it, but the trouble was I got David, he'd just come home from school. But he said his mom wasn't there. It freaked me out to hear his voice. I asked him how he was. He said great, he was in a soccer league that wouldn't really start until spring, but they practiced in the gym after school. Today he'd played with one group on ball control and one group on heading. He had already had his first time on skis, he said he was really getting into it, that practice on his skim board and surfing with his dad gave him an edge over the other beginners. He sighed the way he does and said it had been "a double-good day." He was also starting to get into stamp collecting. He had lots of 'em, from weird places like Sri Lanka, Dahomey, and Cameroon. I spoke with the housekeeper, nice-sounding lady. She said Mrs. Hooker would be back after dinner. I said she should call me, it was urgent. I gave her the phone number at Summer Snow. The attorney from Rancho Mirage was finishing up with the papers. He asked me if I knew the terms of the will. I said no. He said I would be interested, and he told me J.O. had left everything to Leela in trust with Rex as executor. She had left it all to Rex and David, with Rex as executor. And Rex had left most to David, with a big yearly annuity for Joslin. There was $50,000 for me. Well, for Christ's sake. Rex gave Joslin the Bluebird Canyon house, and left Medjuhl to Marge. I remembered he told me that's where he and Marge first slept together. Fifty thousand bucks. "Of course," the Rancho Mirage guy said, with shifty eyes, "he's not dead yet."

I hated the fuck. Of course he's not dead.

But where to find him? I'd done Missing Persons work before, mostly children and senile people who wander off, or runaway spouses. I'd already pushed the usual buttons. An APB, check with the bank, call likely hotels, motels. Both cars are still here, the coral Cad and the red Mercedes, ROLLEM.

I sit down and let it seep into me. My mind says to my mind, You know it. He's gone. And my mind says back to my mind, No, no, he's not. My two minds have quite a little conversation. About what he was not. What happened to turn him into what he became. Things he could do. What he did do. I sit and look out at the rain pounding on the ocean, pelting the water.

He's going to come back. When he shakes all this out of his system. When he's got himself together again. Of course he'll come back.

You believe that?

Marge came over to work on Leela's obituary for the newspapers. At about ten the call from Joslin came through. I probably did it wrong, I just said it straight out. The operation had not been a success, the tumor was much bigger than they anticipated, Leela was gone.

Joslin cried.

All by herself there in Connecticut. I guess she was all by herself, at ten o'clock, the kid in bed. Joslin cried and cried. She put the phone down for a time. I waited. The hard part, the two hard parts. When she calmed down I told her Dr. Steven Kelly had done it. I also explained that there was no question, it was the only thing to do. She said, "Of course, of course," real urgent into the phone. Then I had to tell her we couldn't locate him, we'd tried everywhere. A long silence. Joslin asked if she should come out. I said she could if she wanted to, but everything had pretty much been taken care of. She said there would have to be a funeral for Leela. I said there had already been one. And she yelled at me. I tried to calm her down, I said we'd been trying to reach her for a week. She said Rex would be at the funeral. I said, well, he wasn't there, I already told you, we can't find him. She said he had called her ten days ago, when Leela was in UCLA, he told her he'd call again in a week. She called UCLA, and they told her Mrs. Hooker had been moved back to Laguna. She thought that meant improvement. I said that had been my first reaction. She said Rex was so angry with her—he'd said, "Don't call me, I'll call you." She couldn't take his hatred anymore. I said, "He didn't hate you." We talked some more, and hung up. When I turned around, Marge was looking at me.

Marge Stivers.

Standing there looking at me.

"So? she says.

I shake my head, negative.

Light draining out of her eyes.

Just to make things easier, we had a number of big storms. The mud began to slide, and the cliffs gave way, and houses fell. Worse than October '78, when Bluebird Canyon buckled and a dozen homes were destroyed. This time everything was completely inundated. I was trying to follow up on all the Hooker stuff, but every man was needed on the front line. The storm flooded a pumping station, and it shut down, allowing raw sewage to flow along Aliso Creek into the ocean. Houses caved in all over the place, up in the canyons, down on the beach. We were working twelve-hour shifts. Disaster crews covered with mud, trying to rescue a herd of cows trapped in the hills above Laguna Canyon Road,

327

which itself was under four feet of water. Sandbagging on Pacific Coast Highway. Helping people move their belongings, plastering hillsides with protective sheeting. Power failures, you name it, we had a real state of emergency. For two weeks solid I was on the point of exhaustion. I ripped open my hand and had to have six stitches. I lost the goddamn Orthodics out of my boots trying to save a garage up on Alta Vista. Sprained my ankle. Caught cold from being soaked all the time. Throat on fire. I rescued an elderly gent on Main Beach who was watching the surf tear the boardwalk to splinters. Never worked so hard in my life. Or was so weary. Couldn't get any spit in my mouth. At least half of the problem, or two-thirds, is not Mother Nature. It's money-grubbing human beings. Overdeveloping the land, putting houses where they don't belong, spoiling natural drainage. All that short-sighted stupidity. Too bad only those ecology freaks make so much noise. Butch got pneumonia, a real helper. I had to work his shift. Taking people food, bringing stranded residents to safety. And all the while this time bomb is going tic-tickety-tic in my head about Rex. I checked out Summer Snow and Bluebird, but J.O. knew what he was doing, no danger of his structures bouncing off defective struts and careening down the hills. Even the Chief was doing things right. On the phone, coordinating crews, going out himself to work in the muck and the wet. It was touch and go for those two weeks, and when it was over we felt some satisfaction. We'd made some mistakes and errors in judgment, but we saved a lot of lives and property. It makes all the lousy dink-work somehow worthwhile. Although I could have done without the next two weeks of mop-up. That is a sucker, sheer drudgery, no excitement to it, they ought to hire those weenie-bastards who have yet to put in a hard day's work except on their Porsches. Get them out with shovels in their hands and litter bags on their backs. I would love to give them orders.

I had a terrible dream. My dreams are really beginning to spook me. I was holding Rex down—it probably goes back in real life to the time we took him to Hans Brandsma, when I had to strap him down in the ambulance. And I think it also had to do with a kind of underground resentment I always felt toward Rex. In my dream I was in uniform and I had him down, on the floor at Summer Snow. He was cursing at me, and I got so tired of it I began to hit him. Really hit him. And then Joslin was there, naked, and she screamed at me, "No—don't hit him, don't hurt him—you'll kill him, you'll kill him," and I thought to myself, real fast, like you do in a dream, not thinking at all because you know it anyway: Well, thanks a lot, lady, you're the one who called me up here to subdue him. I went on clubbing him, and suddenly he turned around underneath me and looked up. Only he didn't look at me, his eyes were looking to the side of me, horrified. I turned around, and David was standing in the Entrance Hall with a .22 pistol—I remember it was a .22—holding it in both hands. Rex shouted, "No, son—wrong!" But it was too late, and David blew my head off.

Because I was hurting his dad, and I'd fucked his mom. I didn't, actually. I sat in my Barcalounger in my trailer in my soggy uniform with my eyes closed and saw all these red bottlebrush trees going zing-zingity-zing in the dark.

It's amazing how the mind puts things together. When I think about it, I can explain most of the details. And then I had a similar dream the next night. It was in a different place. It was happening again—I was clubbing Rex, Joslin screaming, and David holding the gun in both hands. I woke up after being shot to death. I sat in my bed this time, telling myself I know that dream, it can't scare me. But my T-shirt was soaked through. My head throbbing from my cold and my throat scratchy. I'd slept on my hand and opened a stitch or two, there was blood on the pillowcase. I stare at the blood and I think he's alive, and in crazy pain somewhere, he's not dead, and I am going to find him, he is alive.

I'm not going to find anybody. Because I'm a sick man. I was at Summer Snow, going through some things, when Marge came in to help clean out some stuff, she'd just come from work, from "This Passing Night," she was all made up. She found me sitting in a big chair, and when I tried to get out of it, I couldn't. Nothing worked. I couldn't even reach my note pad. Marge has been giving me those strange looks lately, but this time she really looked at me. Said I'd obviously worked myself into the ground. Said I should be in the hospital. When she called the hospital, I yelled at her for requesting a private room, I don't need a private room. She drove me there in her 'Vette. It was almost midnight, hardly anybody around. They made me sit in a fucking wheelchair and they put a plastic I.D. on my wrist. They wheeled me up to a dark ward. I had to take off my clothes and put on one of those gowns that shows your fanny to the world. I was sort of sorry I'd refused the private room, my roommate was an elderly noise factory, wheezes and tumbler farts. I asked the nurse what ailed him, and she said, "Oh, he just got old."

I lay there all angry and irritated. Marge, she was wearing a mink coat, said she'd get some of my stuff if I gave her the keys to my house. I thought, no way that woman's going into my trailer, but I was so completely wasted I let her. She said, "I'll bet it's like a boy's bedroom." Probably thought it would be full of ball gloves and model planes. Bitch.

But then I let the sedative work, they put an I.V. in me, and I just fell into dreamland.

Next day Marge looked shaken, must've had a hard time contending with my trailer. But she brought bags full of stuff, shaving kit and magazines and goddamn flowers and fresh fruit. They wouldn't let me eat the fruit. Wouldn't let me eat anything. Kept me three days. Every morning I'd get pissed off, demand an immediate release. But this big bald doctor was one determined sucker, he said I was really sick. I failed a test, an intestinal scanner. My guts are foggy, cloudy like Venus. They're going to starve me to death. I do not enjoy entering the competition for stool specimens. My roommate, Mr. Welch, tells me he got the way he is by never allowing whiskey, tobacco, or playing cards in the house. On the second day he lost a razor head. I helped him look for it, and found his uppers under the bed. A fat little doctor came in with two medical students and examined me for them. When he pulled the curtain around my bed, he said to them, "Well, if he were a horse, I'd shoot him." Jesus! I was miserable, hungry, head all woozy. Had to piss in a Dixie cup every time. The Chief came by, probably thought I was faking. Father Darcy paid a visit. We had a very sad talk about Leela. And a rough one about Rex. During one of my naps I dreamed I was in Casita Hospital with Rex after our fracas with Duke Talis. I dreamed a lot. I remembered my uncle, and his dream about walking by the river with the people in gowns. Marge came in every evening after taping "This Passing Night." We had to laugh when the nurse said, "He's making real progress, Mrs. Bodley." Marge told me she'd had enough husbands. And then she got sad, remembering a time about five years ago, when Leela came into the room where Marge was and said, "Well, where's your husband?" Meaning Rex. And then Leela got all embarrassed. Marge told it so sad, I thought she was thinking about herself and Rex, but when she went on, it was Leela, she wanted to protect Leela. I know the feeling.

Well, finally they've had their fun with me. I am getting out. Said my farewells to Mr. Welch. Really going to miss those farts in the night, they're like tremors, actually. It'll be a relief to chain-smoke again. And then the tall bald doc, he looks very somber, takes me into a small conference room. He has folders in his hands, my tests, and he tells me I am a dangerously ill man. What the fuck is this? I said I get tired a lot, but there's no pain. He said, "Dead tissue doesn't cry." Thanks! But it was like he'd lived with me for a week, he knew me from tip to toe. He knew about my feet, although he hadn't tested them at all. And he knew about my eyes, although he hadn't tested them either, he knew I have to hold the page two feet away to read. My retinas are bent. He knew about everything, and he wondered why I didn't. I said I steered clear of doctors. He said I had a congenital condition. I said it was probably just infantile. But he was fucking serious. He said I was an acute and chronic diabetic.

I heard it and didn't hear it. I think I had diabetes and epilepsy a little confused in my mind. I said, well, you can treat it. He said they could arrest it. Arrest? *I* arrest. I said, well, I'm not going to die or anything. He passed. What? Then he said I was lucky. Five more years and they couldn't have done anything. I am in a nightmare. He talks about my pancreas, which is dead but doesn't cry. He says I have rocks in my guts, calcium flakes, deposits. They've been testing my urine, I spill sugar, I don't even go to plus-four dark green, I turn the damn thing black. He wants my family history. But I can't tell him that. He says we'll have to go the insulin route. I go into his office and he shows me how to stick a needle into a tennis ball. Water on the Sky. He says I have periodically gone into insulin shock.

Shit, I'm in shock all right. It shakes me to my timbers. Apparently I've been living on pure protein, sugar can't get into my cells, it just sits there. Or something. I'm too confused, I must look a little spaced out because the doc says, "You've got to take this seriously, Sergeant," and I snap to and think to myself, What the fuck do you think I'm doing? He gives me some needles and a prescription, and I get my things and slink out of the hospital like I'm a sex deviate.

I get all the way to the parking lot before I realize I've done it again. No car.

It has been six weeks now. I wondered if Rex might have drifted to New York or Connecticut, so I talked to cooperating departments. At least in Connecticut I got some help, but New York City, that's on the moon. I got hold of Neil Robinson, who had been fired from "This Passing Night." He was no help whatsoever. Drunk and sobbing about his girl in Malibu running away with an elderly professor. I checked places Rex might be working also, bars, airlines, buses, Amtrak, the Salvation Army. I wrote the IRS, asked the State Department if a passport had been issued. Kept checking hospitals, morgues, ads in the papers. I figure this guy who has been watched by millions of people on the tube every day for twelve years, somebody is going to recognize him. I get some crank calls, some well-meaning calls.

I neglect other work. But I take pleasure in some nice mail the Chief receives and shows me about my work during the rains, citizens who want to single me out for special service. The feeling settles down into my body. Which I treat like a fragile blue-glass slipper. Diabetes. Injection

331

ceremonies every morning. I'm squeamish, hate to watch the needle go in. Never give a hypochondriac a real disease.

Where is he? He has to be crazy, or he wouldn't have left David. Unless he meant what he said, that the kid shouldn't grow up with an invalid for a father. But what does that mean—he's an alcoholic? Who didn't know that? There are well-staffed places to help people like that. So I call rehab centers, pathologists, drunk tanks. I remember his cough, and start looking for people with advanced emphysema, enlarged heart. I think about how I'll feel when I find his body in some room, smelling terrible. I don't know. No man who loved his son so much would just fade out. Maybe he's being held captive somewhere. I dreamed about that, only it was happening at the bottom of the sea. Which I interpret to mean he has drowned. So I check out drownings.

The Chief is upset with me. Another month passes, and as we move into April, he thinks I'm spending too much time on it. I've got "Hooker on the brain."

I point out to him that my diligence in the arsonist case paid off, that was a pretty big feather in both our caps. The Chief looks at me funny.

Another two weeks, and I think, it's been three months, if I haven't got it, I'm not going to. But I won't believe Rex is dead. I start to spend a lot of time at Summer Snow. First I go over tapes, all those hundreds of tape recordings, listening, looking for the clue. Then his songs, lots of them I haven't heard before. And the ones I have. I go there to watch "This Passing Night" when I can. I'm no Sherlock Holmes, but I have an intuition that I know something that I don't know. That my subconscious mind has something stored up and when I remember it, I'll go right to him.

I call Joslin in Connecticut. If Rex still exists, maybe he's made some contact, maybe she hasn't wanted to tell me, but she would, of course. I'd have to use all my well-known powers of persuasion. It's 6:30 here, 9:30 there.

David answers. "How you doin'?"

"Not very well." His voice spits it out.

"Well, could I speak with your mother?"

"She's not here. *I never know where she is."*

Jesus, he's secure.

"Where's my dad?"

Wow, boy oh boy, the kid is ripped. Furious.

"I don't care about Uncle Ernest anymore."

I try to talk. "It's not the easiest time for your mom, either."

He breathes hard, trying to catch his breath.

"You've got to support each other, y'know?"

"Yes."

He's learned it's better to be mad than pathetic. He says, "I had a fight with Buck. And it's not me at all. He's mad at his father. His father beats him with a belt. So why does he take it out on *me*?"

"Because that's the way people work."

"Well, where's my *dad*?"

"He's had some trouble, but he'll swing out of it."

David cries, and tries not to. I can see him in my mind, holding the phone away and squinting his eyes up at the Connecticut ceiling. He's trying to be a man, trying to be OK.

I calm him down as best I can. But when I announce that baseball season is beginning and I hope they avert the players' strike, he gives me his opinion that baseball is a really boring sport. Still, he seems a little better.

I ask him to have his mother call me, he should write it down.

Joslin does call, and we talk awhile. She tells me about her brother Ernest. I mention Rex, he has been missing for so many weeks. And she says, "If he's not dead, he's obscene." I cannot let that go by. I say right back to her, "I think he is dead. But if he's not dead, he isn't obscene —he's insane."

That stops her. She lets the long-distance stitching go on. I think it's OK that I said it.

She says, finally, "You're right."

More stitching. I am talking to her from Summer Snow.

She says, "I'm fond of you, Trip, I think you're a good guy, but I know what you think of me—"

I'm listening.

She went on, all the way from Connecticut, "I know very well what you think, you *shit*—"

Just wait a minute.

"Oh, I know very well—but Rex never said—he never said he didn't want to find me in the sack with somebody, and I deeply regret that night, I *deeply* regret that, but you weren't a pawn, I was not using you—just forget it—*forget it*—" And she hung up.

Five minutes later a girlfriend of hers called me back and said, "Joslin is sobbing here beside me. She says she's sorry. She'll call you tomorrow."

I am dazed by all that anger and pain.

I walk on the beach with the dogs, I've got to take them to the vet for shots.

I think about David wanting to know about his dad. That means her cover story must leak. Or she hasn't told him. I am playing on their turf now. I wonder what has happened to me. I go inside and call Marge. She says, "Want me to come over, Bucky?" and I say no, no, but I would like to talk to you. We do talk, for a pretty good time, about Rex, and Joslin. Nothing really new comes up, but Marge is no slouch. I think, shit yes, I want you to come over, I'd like to hold you in my arms. No, Marge is no slouch. I sit back and consider what she has done all along. At the hospital after the fire, telling Leela. Driving out to Medjuhl in the 'Vette. Taking me to the hospital. I call her back, then hang up before it rings.

On the memo line of my alimony checks to Sheila I would write, "Blood Money" and "Tramp." The family court judge said, "Mr. Bodley, you will hereafter refrain . . ." and I had to send her cashier's checks for a year.

The manager of the Safeway at Boat Canyon called the station. He had received a letter saying cyanide had been put into two bottles of the salad dressing on his shelves. This would continue until a specified amount of money was delivered to a specified place. I go up there and check it out. One jar of Big Boy Roquefort has clearly been tampered with. We close off the section. When the lab reports come back, it actually is cyanide. Then the manager of Albertson's gets a similar note. So I work on it.

At the end of April we have a string of hot perfect days, it's ninety degrees—in goddamn April. I guess to make up for all that rain. Except this means everybody blitzes the beaches, we must have had fifty thousand in the Laguna area alone. Canyon Road backed up halfway to 405. Drunks, potheads, Marines getting into altercations with gays, lost children. About 4 P.M. on Sunday there's a big crowd on Main Beach, in the center of it a couple dozen guys in one huge fistfight. Beautiful brawl. It takes us a good half-hour to quell it. And I reinjure my hand. I soak it back at Summer Snow. And shoot up. Insulin.

There is a lot of maintenance to do at Summer Snow. I've let all the workmen go, don't know how to arrange to pay them. So I clip the rosebushes, clean out the pool. Walk along the beach at night with Lewis and Clark. I've begun to spend some nights there, in a guest room. After a while I take up a couple of suitcases, some of my stuff. I need to keep an eye on things.

And Marge is still looking at me that new way. I don't want to deal with it. She comes by to see me. One night after a graveyard I found her

334

asleep on the couch. I looked at her. Shit, she works hard. As hard as I do. "This Passing Night," and sometimes a commercial. She's a career girl, a business woman. I put a blanket over her. She's cut her hair, real short, it makes me sad, she had such beautiful long golden hair. Why'd she cut it? It's like all the steam's been let out of her. I walk onto the balcony and look at the beach. That football game we had last September, Marge in her cheerleading outfit, prancing up to Rex and yelling *"Rah!"* The letter she wrote him in his high school yearbook. Him pulling her out of the fire, how he came back in here. I wander up and down stairs, in and out of rooms. I look into J.O.'s and Leela's rooms. I think about a family's *rooms.* Marge has gone through Leela's clothes and given them to the Episcopal church. Marge is completely heartbroken. She tells me that at "This Passing Night," in Burbank, the mail about Rex has been amazing. People do not want Dr. Steven Kelly abandoned in the nut house. One night she came in with *Soap Opera Digest,* and there was Rex's face on the cover. Inside scoop about his life, a lot of the details were mixed up, and a ghastly last line: "Come back, Dr. Kelly—come back to life again!" What can those people be thinking of?

What was Rex thinking of? Nothing bad can happen to us, it's all material. Right. Marge doesn't know it, but I think I am in love with her. When Rex was in charge, producing the show, acting on it, Jerk-of-all-trades, as he said, what was he doing, acting out his own death? The idea weighs me down and makes me feel old. I stare at his face on the cover of the magazine. A photograph taken at a happier time. His sparkling blue eyes. Now he could be in a ward somewhere, at a state hospital or a county facility, sitting in a green gown in a corner. Chattering to himself. Dr. Kelly. I reel back. And I am in love with Marge.

I bring in the mail. Send most of it on to the lawyer in Rancho Mirage. Apparently there are all sorts of hidden bank accounts. Stock in Transamerica, money market things, property payments in Redlands. He seems to own a trailer park in Chatanooga.

I go up to Bluebird Canyon to have a look around. I've hired a clever Chicano guy to tend the grounds. Everything looks fine. I go inside. I figure. I should keep her posted, so I call her in Connecticut, and again David answers.

Right away he starts talking baseball. Which tickles me, he had said it was a boring sport, but he knew I liked it. He's full of news about the Yankees and their nine-and-a-half-game lead in the AL East. If you live in Connecticut, I suppose the Yankees are your home team. I tell him that in high school I watched Larsen pitch his perfect game in the series. On TV. We jabber on a bit. I ask if I can talk to his mother. He says she's not home, she's taking care of Uncle Ernest, and I say, "As usual." It's snotty, but he takes it humorously. He says he has been taking real good care of her like I told him to. I say that's good. He says school is a drag, his teacher, Mrs. Ravioli, nobody pays attention to her, her name is really Mrs. Angioli, but "we" call her Mrs. Ravioli. He says he's "Dungeon Master" for the D&D club. "My mom says it helps me develop leadership qualities."

"She says that, does she?"

We talk and talk. I mention off-season NFL contract negotiations. He says he'll never understand the Rams' front office. He says, "Trip, why should the quarterback of the eighties pull down a salary from the sixties?" I am flabbergasted. Where does an eleven-year-old get that talk? Not from his mother. But where? Newspapers, magazines, TV?

We say good-bye. I sit by the phone for five minutes, thinking. Go back to Summer Snow. The phone is ringing as I come in the door. It's Marge. She wonders if I have dinner plans, says she'll pick up some steaks and we can barbecue. I say sure. She says she'll be a little late, she has to call her parents in Switzerland. Fine, I say, fine.

I must sound funny, because she says, "Fine? Trip?"

"I mean—"

"Something the matter, babe?"

"No, no."

She bides her time. Why'd she cut her hair?

"What is it, hon?"

I don't want her calling me *babe* and *hon*. Certainly not yet. "Oh," I say, "it's nothing."

"Is it the diabetes?"

"No, it's not the *diabetes.*"

"Well, take my head off. You want to skip dinner?"

"I'd like to have dinner. I'd like to have dinner with you."

"Trip, you haven't been into the booze?"

Jesus, what kind of conversation is this?

She says, "I couldn't stand that—I really couldn't."

She's not too pleased when she lets the phone down, and I'm all out of sorts. I go take my pills. Shit, I miss David.

I make myself a Scotch and soda. It's sheer perversity. Don't stick beans up your nose. The phone rings again. What am I, a switchboard operator? And it is Joslin. David gave her the message. The feel of alcohol in my gut. Booze and women. I'm warmed.

She says her brother Ernest is not at all well. He will have to be

336

hospitalized. She says she is worried about David. "He was twelve this week."

"He's eleven."

"Trip, I know how old my *son* is."

"OK. I'm sorry. You should have told me, I'd have sent a card."

Silence.

"Look, I'm sorry." Joslin is trying to be a good soldier, I can hear it. "Ernest—he shielded me from all my parents' violence. I owe him a debt. When we were little, he took care of *me.*"

"Yes. Yes."

"I want to help him. But if I help Ernest, I neglect David. I can't let David suffer."

"Then get out of there."

"I've been thinking in Laguna I have friends, and David has so many friends. I will, I don't—I think we'll come—home."

"Home?"

"To Bluebird Canyon. In the fall."

"Anything I can do?"

"No—no, I don't think so. I have to finish things up here. I just wish David could—could get away."

Silence.

I have a wild idea. Maybe it's the Scotch. I say, "Look, I'm real fond of him. Send him out for the summer. I'll take care of him. And then you come when you're ready."

Silence and long, long distance.

She says, "I'll think about that."

"You don't want David around on your mind—"

"Oh, I want him *around on my mind.* You can't believe how sweet he is."

"Yes I can."

"He's just—just an angel."

I say, "He's not an angel—he's a gallant little boy."

She gets it, lets out a surprised little laugh. With a lot of feeling in it.

I have second thoughts about my wild idea. Not too practical. I mean, I've got to be on duty. But Marge, she loves—woop, I know how Marge and Joslin feel about each other. But Trip, I say to myself, skip that. I could get him in a Little League, now that he appreciates baseball. And there's Lewis and Clark, and the ocean, and the pool. I suppose it might be better if he didn't play Stretch with Walter Winn. I'm surrounding the problem in my mind. I say, "You sure you really want to come back here?"

"Yes."

"Why?"

"Because—because that's Bluebird Canyon—because that's *where.*"

I heard it. I said, "Nothing new about Rex."

She said, "Rex is alive."

"What?"

"He's been calling me."

"*What?*"

"He never speaks. But the phone rings, I pick it up, and it's silence."

"It's some crank."

"No, no, it's not, Trip—God, why do you have to call yourself Triphammer? It's so melodramatic, a gun, see my big triphammer—"

"A triphammer has nothing to do with a gun."

"It doesn't?"

"No. There's no triphammer on a gun."

"Really?"

"No. It's a tool."

"I didn't know that."

But I am extremely upset. "What makes you think it's him?"

"I know his speech—and I know his silence."

Woman's intuition is a magical thing. I do not pretend to understand it. Even Sheila had it. A buddy of mine, older guy, Willie Dingler, went to Mexico with his wife and wrote me a letter. Sheila read it and said, "He's got a girlfriend." I said, "No, come on, what are you talking about?" I read it several times, every word. There was not the slightest indication he was getting something on the side. But Sheila said, "He's got a mistress." And when Willie came back, a month later, he and his wife were getting a divorce because he had met this woman in Mexico. I swear, no one could have seen that from the letter. I just let it pass by, it cannot be explained or understood. Women know things.

I am being bounced around, questions are hitting me.

We have not spoken a word for a full minute.

Out of the blue—out of the dark, actually, in Connecticut—she says, "You know, Trip, for being a shit, you're not such a bad person."

I said, "Likewise, I'm sure."

She sounded peaceful.

I said, "And Rex wasn't so bad—after all," I said it fairly carefully, "he picked you out."

I knew she liked it.

She said, "And he—he picked you out."

Silence.

338

She said, "If I sent David out, could you—?"

"Nothing would please me more. I don't know how David—"

"Oh, he says only good things about *you.*" She said, "David was Ben Franklin in the school play. He was so upset. He said, 'Mom, they put rouge and lipstick on me.'"

I smiled.

"The whole auditorium broke up. King George the Third said, 'Why don't the colonists act now, if their cause is just?' And David—David in his rouge and lipstick—stuck up his finger and said, 'Haste makes waste, y'know.'"

Something about the way she said it made me feel happy. I could see David putting up his finger.

"He's so—so hopeful. I look at him, and—and, oh, Leela's photo albums, pictures of Rex when he was twelve. When I look at David—I *see* him—"

Anguish in her voice.

I feel close to her. I am with her again. I have never given Joslin a fair shake. Was never interested in her life, always took Rex's side. I say it, carefully, I don't want her to hear one sip of the Scotch. I tell her I'm sorry I took Rex's side all the time, don't know why I did.

"Oh," she says, "probably the old male-bonding crap."

"What?"

"Nothing, Trip."

Did she insult me, or was she being ironical, or what?

She says, after a space, "Do you honestly think I *planned* it? To sleep with you? I didn't want to sleep with you. But then, after you told me about Antonio—"

"What?"

"At the inquest. Someone said, '*Adiós, amigo,*' and you saw him smile. You noticed. And the man wasn't even talking to him."

I remember. Did I really tell her about that?

"And you were so good with David."

Her black stormy hair.

We say good night. She sounds calm, almost happy. I have really misjudged her. Antonio. My, my.

"Haste makes waste, y'know." All the parents were gathered for the school play, an old schoolhouse with an oil furnace. David running around in rouge.

She's kidding herself. She's really kidding herself if she thinks he's calling her. He's not. But it tells me something about her. Just because you hate melodrama, and hate all the scenes, and can't live with the

Hooker Story, once it's got hold of you and you put so much of your life into it—well, she must not quite know what to do with herself. Without him. "I know his speech and I know his silence." Good luck.

Dr. Kelly—come back—come back to life again.

Rex isn't calling her.

I went onto the big patio deck and doused some charcoal with fluid. Nine twenty-five. Twelve twenty-five in Connecticut. I got the coals going. I could have one more Black Velvet. No, I couldn't. Clickity-clickity-click, it all goes through my mind. Send David here? I have no idea how to take care of an eleven-year-old—twelve-year-old kid.

So Joslin is coming back to Bluebird Canyon. Because that's—where. And David will spend the summer with me. Here in Summer Snow.

I went inside and looked at Rex's face on the cover of *Soap Opera Digest*. I stared and stared. If he were alive, he'd be here. If he were alive and *well*. But he's not.

I go down and wander in the rose garden.

The phone again. I run up. It's Marge. She says, "I can't make it, honey, it always kills me to talk to my father—I can't come. Don't be angry with me, hon."

"You're—"

"Oh, babe, how can I deal with my father? He just doesn't *care*." She's wasted.

She says, "Babe, can I come tomorrow?"

"Sure."

"Thank you, Bodey."

That's what she says. Without the *l*. Bodey. Body. Goddamn baby talk. Goddamn booze.

I fix myself a baked potato. Toss fragments of the skin to Lewis and Clark.

19

THE *TIMES* had a story today about the new chief of police in San Diego. My chief says, "Who could ever want that job?"

Probably he botched the interview.

And I don't get my shot at being chief, at least not this time.

He calls me into his office. He gives me an enameled ashtray that he made. He says it's a token of appreciation. And friendship. He reddens. I say, "Who would suspect that underneath that flinty exterior lurks the heart of a poet?"

A week later, at the department picnic, he was quite grand. Giving a speech on the picnic table. Dropping two flyballs in left field and blaming it on a borrowed mitt. I took Marge as my date. She wore a white halter top and blue shorts. Both cheeks peeking out. She looked spectacular. People were really quite astounded. Except I still don't like the cropped hair. She plays fine second base. Goes "Woop" when she singles to right. Butch Ravelling gives me a wink.

We have the usual relays and three-legged races. The delicious smell of barbecue. Families, kids crying and fighting.

Everyone assumed, naturally, that we are together.

And then, after we take Butch home, we are.

We go back up to Summer Snow, Marge and me. I know, I have been waiting. Marge knows, and has been waiting. I empty the picnic basket, and she goes down to the ocean for a swim. She swims nude, her wonderful tits and her ass and her legs. I am going crazy on the deck watching her. Then I go down. We lie on the sand, then wash ourselves off in the pool. I look at her. We talk about everybody at the picnic.

We put on robes. I have a tan one and she finds a blue terry cloth. I make a fire. We sit together. I lecture her on her haircut. We're still a little sandy. We smoke dope. I ask her if she'll stay the night, and she does.

In the morning we have breakfast, and then I don't see her for a week. I'm frantic, she's all I can think about.

Joslin calls me. At Summer Snow. I guess I've pretty much moved in, it doesn't seem strange that people call me here. She's got David's airline ticket, he'll be coming in July. I hang up and feed the dogs with a flourish. I have a giddy nauseous feeling. It feels like the noise a water heater makes when you turn it off and all the water flushes down into the pipes, you can hear it being sucked out, a mechanical rush. There is a bond between Joslin and me. If she needs a friend, she's got one. Whatever, she can count on me.

Marge and I have a candlelight supper on the patio. Little cherry tomatoes you squirt through your teeth, big platter of chicken with mushrooms and broccoli in cheese sauce. We sit on patio chairs. Two glasses of Chablis, just little sips. She's a wonderful cook. I don't usually eat like this. When did she do it? When I stand in the kitchen talking to her, I don't even notice she's cooking. I don't even notice I'm standing there.

I do notice I'm stabbing a little spring potato, putting it in my mouth. I notice I'm taking a sip of wine.

Marge says, "Leela used to say that when she was alone in this house she was afraid she'd disappear." She says it real soft, dreamy.

I say *Oh?* with my eyes. I'm thinking, Why didn't Rex marry you? I'm thinking it real strong. Why didn't he marry you? If I'm not careful, I'm going to say it. So I say, "Why did Rex marry Joslin?"

Marge shakes her head. "Why? Why did he marry her? Because she was everything in the world that Summer Snow isn't. Because she's Jewish. Because she's not—Family—family-shmamily. And let me tell you, Bodey, *there's* a woman who sexually has been down in the dirt."

I get up. I walk away.

"Trip?"

I don't answer. I'm so mad I can't see straight. I walk downstairs and sit in the old workroom. Where the peacock was stored, where I found Peter playing with the fuse box. Why the hell didn't I notice that in time?

342

I hate Marge Stivers. I don't want her in this house. I want to live here, with David, for July and August, that's all.

I hear her at the top of the stairs. "Trip?"

I don't answer.

She comes down. She stands there. In white pants and a bright green sweater.

"Trip, I'm sorry. I know you slept with her, and—"

I blow up completely, I make Mount St. Helens look like a puff of smoke. I shout, "I didn't sleep with her, it's a lie, he got there in time."

She backs off.

I say, "You're just jealous that he married her instead of you."

"Yes," she whispers.

"You're jealous that she's the mother of his child."

"Bodey—"

"And don't call me Bodey. Hate baby talk."

"I'm sorry."

This isn't getting us anywhere.

She whispers, "I am jealous of Joslin. And more, deeper. She's ruined Rex's life."

"Rex ruined his own life."

"Bodey—I'm sorry—Trip, can we go upstairs?"

We do. We are both on edge. I think maybe we should go to bed. To *sleep*. But she takes out a joint, says it calms her down. I want nothing to do with it. Oh, all right, I smoke it with her.

"I'm sorry what I said about Joslin."

"I don't care what you say."

"Yes you do, you care a lot about what I say. That's why you hate me when I talk shit."

I hold the smoke in. I say, in a stupid squeaky voice, "This also is true." Rex said that once. This also is true.

"Rex—you don't know, Trip—what Rex was like when he was young."

"Yes I do."

"But you don't know how in love with him I was."

"Yes I do."

She sighs and sits there. "And when he went away to Stanford. I lived for the times he came home. Or when he'd fly me up for parties. The way he and his fraternity brothers talked. Bitchin' R.F. The places we'd go, the Top of the Mark, the Saint Francis. Once we went on a bat hunt in the San Francisco Reservoir. We drank crème de menthe."

"Boola-boola."

"Stop it. I want to tell you."

I look at her. She's right, she needs to talk about it. Shit, I am in love with her. Just don't talk against Joslin.

"When he was eighteen, nineteen—oh, Trip—he was beautiful. In that fraternity of his. His room up on the third deck. It had a little balcony. He had the—peacock—in there. One night he sat on the edge of the bed and read *Walden* to me, two pages, he was so excited. He was getting a college education. I remember him, sitting naked on the edge of the bed, reading *Walden*. I said, 'Sounds like Thoreau wants to get back to basics.' And he said, 'No, no—up to basics, Margie. *Up* to basics.' And we played golf on the Stanford Golf Course. And canoe rides."

"On the golf course?"

"Shut up. I'd watch him study, sitting out on the little balcony. I could see him thinking how his life was in front of him, how he was preparing himself for it. Everything made him happy. And he made everybody happy—he'd walk into a room and just light it up. You don't know, Trip. And the good time—it lasted until, oh—do you know I thought he was going to marry me all the way up until—"

I look at her. "Until?"

"Until David was born."

Oh.

She smokes another joint. I have one hit. She says, "Before it started going sour with Joslin, Rex had such a wonderful—privacy. He was playful and outgoing, but there was a joke that he shared only with himself. He didn't need to *talk* all the time. His eyes didn't have that hunted look. Once in a while, even this past couple of years, I'd see it again. He was on a talk show about the perils of drugs, and the emcee asked him if it's true that cocaine makes sex better. Rex said no, but it makes talking *during* sex better." Marge sighed. "The old gleam in his eyes. Not the hunted look. Or, a year ago, we were driving along and he saw a bumper sticker. It said, HE WHO DIES WITH THE MOST TOYS WINS. He was so—so *delighted,* he had to pull over."

"So what ruined it all?"

She waited. "I know I blame Joslin too much. I know it. But a hundred times I drove out of this house with him, and he always honked the horn three times—I-Love-You—to Pop and Leela. But after Joslin it wasn't working. She made him think, she questioned everything. He loved her, adored her—and he loved them, adored them. But they didn't adore each other. He couldn't put it together, it mixed him all up. And the harder he tried to fix it, the worse it got."

She talks, and I listen. I look at her, thinking I should be jealous, but I'm not.

"He was working so hard at something that used to be natural. Summer Snow is a miracle. But it's not Summer Snow anymore. There's Snow. There's Summer. But it isn't right. When he didn't have to work at it, he was beautiful, but when he had to work his ass off, he wasn't beautiful at all. All his friends—he'd always taken care of us, and now we were taking care of him. He knew it, but he didn't know why, and he didn't know how to fix it. He did everything wrong."

I bring the wine in.

She says, "I'm sorry. I shouldn't talk about it."

"It's all right." I pour. Just a glass.

"You're right to call me on Joslin. It wasn't her fault. She just—*thought* differently from Rex. And she had trouble with J.O., a lot of trouble with Leela. He'd do anything to please her, so he tried to think the way she did. But that meant—" Marge stopped. "I do hate her. She made him ashamed of his parents, and he couldn't stand it. It made him ashamed of himself. He'd always drunk too much, but now he was *drowning.*"

With the perceptiveness that has made me a household word, I said, "This isn't a happy story."

We stopped talking for a while. We walk onto the balcony and watch the gulls spotlighted over the ocean. I put my arm around her. I'm in love with this woman who is all wrapped up in another man. Who is dead. No, not dead. The gulls look like UFOs in the white light. I say, "Want a pizza?"

She leans on my shoulder. "Sure, Bodey, I'll have a slice."

"I'll go get one, they're not closed yet."

"Call Domino's, they deliver."

"No, I'll take the car."

"Call Domino's, Bodey."

I pull away and yell at her. "No, I'll get Salerno's. You had Domino's with him."

She stares at me, her eyes full of grief, surprised smile on her face. "How did you know that?"

"He told me."

She laughs. "Pizza? He told you about our pizza?"

"One time when you had three in a row."

"Oh."

"The sad part," I say, "was how Joslin and David found out. He wished that could have been avoided."

She looks at me funny. She shakes her head, that short hair. She looks at me. "Oh, Bodey, we aren't going to work out at all."

I say, "We aren't?" It's the dope, I say it real fast and high up, like a child who's just heard there's no Santa Claus. I know I've said it like that because she laughs and hugs me, "Oh, *Bodey.*"

And while I hold her, I'm thinking it's not right. For us to be in Summer Snow talking about him. It's not decent. But I don't know, somehow this is where we are—this is where.

We don't want pizza. We want sweaters. We sit on the balcony in the candlelight, whispering. She has to tell me all this.

She says, "He was so sad. These last months he was—defeated. He said to me, 'Margie, I know my epitaph. It's "Here He Thought He Could Get Away with It." That's what they carve on my headstone.'" Her eyes in the candlelight. "*Here* he thought—and he was already in the grave. He was moving around, at top speed, and he was already down there. One night in one twenty-six, he said to me, 'Margie, you know what I did? I made my family television. I turned Summer Snow into Daytime.' And he cried—he cried in my arms like a baby."

We sit here.

"He was dead—the man who lived every moment."

Silence.

"You really loved him."

"Yes."

"You'll never stop loving him."

She looked at me. "No, Bodey. Twenty years, of his life and mine, you don't stop that. But three or four years ago even, if I'd met him for the first time, at a party, I would have been very interested. You bet. But not —there was too much pain. He was—he was in too much pain—to fall in love with. And in bed—oh dear—oh dear—"

She says it twice, like that. And then one more time. She looks at me. "I don't want to tell you this, but I'm going to. At the end, there was something very—dead about it. And there was something very erotic about that. And, as he always said, we were brother and sister. And there's something very—erotic—about that. I can't—I can't talk about it."

We are talking about it. You're talking about it, and I'm listening.

She had complimentary tickets for the opening night of the Pageant of the Masters. So we went. Looking at *The Last Supper* I discover that Saint Luke is my barber. I wish he'd told me. I see the big bald doctor who informed me I have diabetes, and I hide out so I don't run into him. I see a lot of prominent people. I'm actually glad I have some new clothes. Marge said my wardrobe was a horror, which I couldn't argue with. But I did feel a bit strange when she took me to South Coast Plaza and picked out all these coordinated outfits. She bitched at me, "Bodey, you're so handsome when you take your clothes off. Don't walk around in that polyester shit." I am 1 GROUCH about it. In the Irvine Bowl she keeps getting stopped, talking to people. One woman seems to think she really is a nun and looks at me like I'm sacrilegious.

Marge and I go back to Summer Snow, fade into it. Marge has completely moved in. Her dresses fill up Leela's long closet. Am I supposed to allow that? It makes me queasy. We fuck in it. This is obscene, but it's not. She says, "Oh, Bodey, my poor Bodey—"

I will love her and lose her, it's in the cards. Knowing me, I probably want to lose her. Always get comfort out of defeat.

We are in a dark light. She whispers, "You are so dear to me." She says, "Oh, look, I'm crying." She nestles up, with her legs. Marge Stivers. How do I touch, how do I hold you? Your hair all cut away. I close my eyes and see a soft blur. I open them and look her square in the eye, and then all I can see are her eyes, me in them. I feel my feet, the tops of my feet, braced against her insteps. She shudders, and there are these aftershocks, you feel them coming up inside. I don't know. I look down under me and her body is simply all there, alive in the moonlight, she's so tanned, it never gets better than this. Aftershocks. I could spend the rest of my life here. You don't do it, you are it. She says, "I know you," and is crying. I'm beside myself, my arms and legs have died. She goes into a blur, whispering into sleep while I lie here like a seal. She moves, and her elbow curves into my chest.

Hours later, apparently, she whispers—her big body, big, beautiful body and wonderful face, her cropped gold hair, Marge, my fucking darling, my woman, she whispers, "Are you in love with Joslin too?"

I sit in the patrol car. Any minute I'll see some clown and run after him. That's life. I have a dismal view, morbid. People should spend their whole lives exercising, exercise until they drop. Get up and do it again. Have a life expectancy of about ten adult years, then blotto. I don't want too many of us standing up at the end.

Did Marge mean "Joslin too" like do I also love Joslin, or like Rex loved Joslin too? Or are we all just one big happy family? One big happy family-shmamily? One big happy Magic Couple? I don't like the way my mind works. I'm losing confidence in myself. And what's really bothering me—face it—is that I, who have always claimed to hate deceit, I have not told Joslin about Marge and me. I am essentially living with Marge, and Joslin is sending David out to live with me—to live with me and Marge? How would Joslin feel about that? And I, who am essentially living with

347

Marge, have not told Marge that David is coming out to live with—us. I, the man who hates deceit, am a liar to both his women.

I think about what my mind has just told itself. Both—his—women.

There he is, the asshole, big black El Dorado using up the whole street. I pop it in, peg to the floor, and I stop him. Oh, how I love to write tickets. I notice his wheels could use balancing, the tread's gone on the left front, I write that up too.

Bucky. Bodey. No, *babe*, no, *hon*, I'm not in love with Joslin *too*.

I don't know who I am anymore. I'll tell you one thing, I think Rex and Joslin ruined each other—they blew each other apart.

I don't know how to take care of a kid. What if he gets sick? Why did I even suggest it? Why is Joslin coming back to live in Bluebird Canyon? Does she know what she's doing? I think this is just when I should be strong, but I blew it somewhere. I have no strength left.

On my way home I catch Theodore sitting on a bench at the kiddy playground next to the Laguna Hotel. Old Theodore, sitting there with a brown cigarette falling off his lip. Wonder where he has been. What memories he has. Theodore. It goes with the smell of the summer sea, big blotches of kelp. I'm shooting up religiously.

On Thursday I get Gerald Moses. I had been alerted to his presence eight or nine months ago, when he attacked two Irvine coeds up at Turtlerock. And plea-bargained his way out of it. The whole criminal justice system needs revamping. This time he had been watching a teenage girl undressing in her third-story room on Oak Street. After she went to sleep, he walked eight blocks, stole a twenty-eight-foot extension ladder, returned to the house, climbed through the girl's window, and raped her at knifepoint. But I got him, found him in Luigi's restroom on a tip from the cook. Yes, I suppose you might say I overstepped the Miranda rule, but we got him on two counts rape, one sodomy. Gerald Moses is fifteen years old.

I think I ought to get out of this line of work. Don't want to put on the uniform anymore. I sit in Summer Snow, in a big gold chair. I munch on some cold fried chicken Marge made. I pull out my scrapbook, the one I have had since I worked at the Indio P.D. I used to paste everything in, whenever I got my name in the paper, nothing too small. Every stupid car wreck, certificates for being a Boy Scout safety instructor, grades from College of the Desert, all sorts of snippets and bulletins and photographs. There's a page on my buddy Fred, who used to sit with me under the apple trees. His suicide and funeral. My snotty letter of resignation from Indio. The article when I was promoted to sergeant—my photograph, Jesus, shit-eating grin on my pretty face. Badges from the National Rifle Association. And letters from townspeople.

> Dear Sgt. Bodley,
>
> I want you to know how very much I appreciate all you did for me on the night of Feb. 26 when my husband Charles was so suddenly stricken. I shall always be deeply grateful to you for being at our side so fast to administer oxygen and give Charles the assurance that he was being helped. You really did calm him down, with your very presence, and did all any human being could. As you remember, I fully expected to stay at the hospital overnight, and I was fully aware that you offered to return for me, and I knew I could call on you at any hour, and that was a real comfort to me.
>
> In sincere appreciation,
> Joyce Marks

I've got quite a few of those. I sit here reading them. I'll never quit this job.

Marge and I sit in front of the fire. It gets real chilly even in June. Lewis has an eye infection, Clark lies in my lap, drowsy.

We have been looking through the Hooker family album. A lock of Rex's baby hair. The four-leaf clover Leela found, sitting on the lawn, the morning before she gave birth. All of Rex's childhood birthday party invitations. Marge says, "When I first saw this, I thought to myself, where's *my* book? Why didn't *my* mother keep a book for me? Sissy had one. Mother said, 'Now, Margaret, the second child always gets neglected.' Thanks, Mom."

I ask about her father.

She says, "When I was eleven, I took diving lessons. I was good, mastered my swan, my jackknife, I had a hell of a half-twist. And my little cutaway, neat as a pin, never disturbed the water. But gainers—I couldn't hack gainers. Every time I went up, I'd see my teeth hitting the board. When I confessed my fear to Daddy, he said, 'I knew you'd quit when it got tough.' "

I wait for her to go on, but she's finished. I say, "So?"

"So I stopped taking diving lessons."

"You should've got mad at him."

"You don't know my father, Bodey."

"Could we go back to Bucky? I have a lot of trouble with Bodey."

She looks at me.

I want to say, "Are you in love with Rex *too*?" I manage not to. I say, "Did Rex ever ask you to marry him?"

"Sure."

"Really?"

"Yeah. But he always sobered up."

"Come on."

"I wouldn't be a good mother."

"How do you know?"

"Because I quit when it gets tough."

I let that one go by. I say, "He did drink too much."

"Shit, Bucky, you better get that down on paper."

"Fuck you."

She says, "I dried him out a dozen times, took him to the hospital. He always said, 'I can't stop drinking, I'll lose my soul.' Then once after I dried him out and he was being discharged, I said, 'See, you didn't lose your soul.' And he said, 'But I've lost interest in it.' "

Silence. I say, "That time—I've told you, you know, that time when I was, well, with her, and he came in on us?"

"Yes."

"Maybe you know." I look at her. "Joslin said it was an accident. Rex said it was a setup."

"Probably neither one knew."

"No," I say. "Really?"

"Bucky, you didn't hear me. I said, 'Probably neither one *knew*.' "

I think. Oh. Oh. Little words are sledgehammers. Triphammers—which are parts of guns?

And our evenings go on like that. Covering old ground, digging up mines. Together we do that. For weeks.

Marge and I sit in the family room. Quiet evening at home. She's doing needlepoint and I am reading the sports page. The Bodleys. I actually think that, and right away think of all the reasons I shouldn't. The Bodleys. Stop it. Don't rush things.

My mind, such as it is, wanders. Back to something I've been thinking about, something I don't want to think about, but can no longer avoid. Peter Ingalls. There's still something I don't understand. I remember that tape recording, Rex and Dr. Kelly. I listened to it in the Medjuhl kitchen. Rex talking about Peter and the horrible time. I remember Christmas. Rex telling me I took Peter away from him, saying Peter was *his*. I remember that costume party. Peter telling me he was a Vietnam veteran.

350

I look up. Everything in this room, everything in this house, is new. Even the staircase. Because Peter set that fire. And set the fires at Medjuhl. I had to kill him. But still there is something I do not understand.

Marge goes up to bed. I watch her as she climbs the stairs. I want to ask her about it. She knows Rex, the family, all the details, all the skeletons. She must know this. I remember how I smelled something, before I shot Peter. And after, I thought there was a piece missing. Marge knows. I trudge on my aching feet up to the bedroom. Marge, I don't know, I'm afraid you won't know, and I am afraid you will. I have to try.

I stand in the doorway. She's reading in bed. I say, "What about Peter Ingalls? Rex said something once—what about Peter and the horrible time?"

She looks at me, real quick, looks down. Says, "Oh, Trip, I don't know. Let's go to bed."

Her eyes tell me she knows something. And won't tell me. Right away I get angry. I hate secrets in general, but this particular one I just cannot bear. Any longer. The woman I love is keeping it from me. I raise my voice. I say I have to know. Now. Whatever you know about Peter Ingalls.

She turns away, doesn't want to talk, says it's nothing, forget it.

I say *now*. Tell me now. Everything you know.

She won't look at me.

And then I—I didn't know I was so furious—I reach out and I slap her. Hard. On the side of the head. Her hair all cut off. I've hurt her and she's screaming, she can't understand why I have to know, and I tell her, "Because I killed him."

She goes limp. She's looking at me. And then she whispers, "Of course."

I move away. She's lying there on the bed. First time she whispered it, now she says it out loud: "Of course you have to know."

She sits up on the bed, hugging a pillow to her chest. She rocks herself. The bedspread, yellow lines and green circles. I glance at her face. How could I hit her? She looks miserable. "Oh, Bodey, I don't know where to begin."

"Well," I say, "I know J.O. and Peter's father were partners. And Peter Senior built apartment houses that burned down."

"Yes, but—"

She stops.

I sit here. I wait.

She hugs the pillow, looks at me, then finally makes up her mind. "Peter's mother died when he was little. He had nowhere to go, no living relatives. J.O. and his father were partners, and his father was killed in the Hooker cabin at Big Bear. So they took him in, the Hookers took him in."

My heart goes through the floor. "They adopted him?"

"No, Bodey. They didn't adopt him, they took him in. As their ward, not their son." She sighs. "It all happened before I knew them." She starts to cry. I get her a big box of Kleenex. She gets hold of herself. And as calm as she can, she tells me the history. Peter wanted, really wanted to be adopted. To become a member of the Hooker family. But Peter wasn't Rex. Not as smart, not as tough, not as clever. One Christmas, the Hooker family was playing Can You Top This?, firing presents at each other, and all Peter can think of is to wrap up, individually, seventy rocks he found on the beach. Not pretty sea shells, not unique rocks, just plain brown rocks. And Leela has to say, sixty-nine times, "Oh, look, it's another lovely *rock!*" And at one of Peter's birthdays, a slumber party, J.O. told the kids a ghost story, "Who's Got My Golden Arm?" He got to the punch line —"You got it!"—and he grabbed the Birthday Boy, who pissed in his pajama pants right in front of all his friends.

Marge says, "They couldn't deal with him. Peter threw them all off stride. J.O. and Leela started fighting with each other. Like that ghost story, Leela blamed J.O. for telling it. The Old Man said, Well, how was I to know the little good-for-nothing would pee in his pants?

"J.O. tried discipline. Leela had long talks with Peter, trying to 'understand' him. Leela—oh—I loved her. She was *my* mother. But nothing worked. Peter became a problem child.

"He started setting little fires. Burned a hole in the workroom. Burned up one of Leela's little, you know, the things she sets up for the morning on the table—"

"Breakfast arrangements."

Marge nods. "Right." She takes a deep breath. "Peter worshiped Rex, wanted to *be* Rex. I don't know. J.O. and Leela—well, they thought Peter had spoiled it, their perfect family. He was a constant rebuke. So they sent him away. Private schools, college, Europe. They gave him money."

"To stay away."

"Yes. But he came back, a few years ago. He was crazy, impossible. Made up that Vietnam story to tell Rex, who knew it wasn't true. Peter began following Rex around. It was right after Joslin left, and Rex—he —he couldn't handle it. Peter proved something to him. Peter proved that Joslin was right. Family-shmamily. Peter hadn't ruined Summer Snow, Joslin hadn't ruined it. Summer Snow was a *disease*. David—David would be addicted, like Rex. Oh, it didn't make any sense, but Rex was creating it in his head. Sometimes it was the family, or Peter, or Joslin. It got all

352

mixed up, he couldn't keep it straight. And the morning after the anniversary party, Peter was still there, Rex was pissed about his peacock getting burned. But it was more than that, Rex went after Peter's *eyes* with a cigarette—jumping all over the room, 'You *hurt the family,* you hurt the family'—trying to put Peter's *eyes* out."

I'm looking at the colors on the bedspread, that's what *my* eyes are doing. Half the time I am thinking about when my weapon kicked up, when I killed Peter, in Medjuhl. But I'm in Summer Snow, I'm in a swamp. There are all sorts of things to do here—it's humanly impossible to do them all. It's so huge—the family, the family-shmamily—if Rex walked through the bedroom door right now, what would he say about all this? What would Rex say, if he were still alive? Still alive?

"Bodey, where *are* you?"

I look at her. I say, "You never told me the past. And now it's too late. I killed him."

Her voice, so lost. "Bodey, how could I tell you? I didn't know. When Rex was drunk, it would get worse. Sober lies and drunk lies. Lies on top of lies. Forget time. Acting. Become Steven Kelly every day, become Peter Ingalls some nights. 'Whose son am I? Whose son is David? Who did Joslin—Jessica—sleep with? It's summertime, why is it snowing? My parents are—my parents are—they couldn't take care of Peter. Who am I? They made me an invalid, an alcoholic. I'm as bad as Peter, I *am* Peter.' It was in Rex's head, Bodey. Peter isn't the problem here."

He was the problem I killed in Medjuhl. Don't tell me I'm a *murderer.*

"It's Rex. He told me, after the fire, he said—*his words were acting up on him.* He kept saying that, his *words* did it. The Peter in his head jumped out. So Rex did it—he—"

Something screams out in my head, I can't believe I'm saying this, I shout, *"Rex set the fire."*

Her face goes white. Her head snaps down.

"The fucker set the fire."

And her head comes back up and her eyes look at me, completely terrified, and her whole goddamn wonderful body is hunched over there. She whispers, "No, Rex did not set the fire. I was there that night. I was awake before he was. He was drunk, in a stupor, I had to work like hell in that fucking smoke. Just to get him on his feet. And—and, Bodey— I saw Peter—when I broke the window. I saw Peter with a red can. He was wearing a costume. No, Bodey—you killed the right man. But we've also killed the wrong man. We've *also—*"

I look down and both my hands are knotted, they are fists. I have to know this, tell me—

353

She's sobbing. "Rex convinced himself that he did set the fire, and none of us helped him get rid of it. He was banging off the walls of his own head. His words *had* acted up on him. He always thought he could get away with it, say anything, think anything, I'm a Hooker, I can think any fucking thing in the *world*, and then all of a sudden . . ." She looks up, but not at me. "Peter and Joslin all scrambled, popping up in each other's stories. Peter was David's father, Rex absolutely convinced himself Peter was David's biological father. And I couldn't listen to it anymore, I couldn't listen—I couldn't *hear*—"

She's lost it. She's gone over. It's all crying and yelling.

"And that was *before*, it was before. We hit him when he was down. Don't you get it? Rex was that way *before* the fire, he was that way for a *long time*. His wife tied him down and dumped him. And that's what *you* did, Bodey. Rex was trying to get his feet under him—under-*stand* —to stand *up*—get *well*—and nobody was helping him. He was hurt so bad. Right fucking now, he's not *dead*, he's *fatally wounded*—why couldn't you see that, when you took him to the hospital on Labor Day? On the way back, I was driving him back—"

"What?"

"Don't you remember, Bodey? He was wearing little white shorts—"

I know, I know, I know. Margie. It was Marge who got him back. But when did he call her?

"All anyone could do was hurt him until he couldn't stand it anymore, and then dump him—and he'd call for me and, goddammit, I'd go get him. He was crying in the 'Vette, beside me. Mumbling about how 'that was a little close' and he had to be ready for Mom and Pop coming back from Scripps, he was all cut up, all *cut up* on his face and what was left of his body—"

Body—Rex Hooker's body—I'm not going to find it. We've got an hysterical actress and a hysterical police officer here, and they're screaming, the actress is doing it out loud.

"He's not dead—my Rex is *alive*, right now, this very minute, and Jesus, my baby is fucking *nuts*—"

Rex has walked through the door. He's in this bedroom, and he's got her. He's killing her, spasms running through her body, he can't do this to her, goddammit, you cannot have her this time—

I go to her and grab her. Marge is babbling and babbling, it's all I can do to get my arms under her. I lift her up.

She gets her breath back. We're sitting here. But she looks at me like I'm way far away. I kiss her on the forehead.

She stands up, goes to the bathroom. I sit by myself on the bed. A long time. Finally I hear her in there. She pees and cusses.

She comes back in, sits beside me on the bed.

We will never get to the bottom of this. Is no bottom. Jesus, we got years of work ahead of us.

And that stops me. I'm already stopped dead, but that stops me deader. I look at her beside me. Exhausted and broken-hearted in our bed. Her eyes all empty of it now. She looks like a little girl.

I start to say something, and she says, real quiet, "Sweetheart—"

We got years of work ahead of us. You and me. You. Marge Stivers. And me. Oliver Bodley. Sweethearts.

20

SHE SMILES at me, her loving smile. She says, "When we make love—did any woman ever tell you?"

"What?"

"Well, you—"

"What?"

"Bucky, I hate to break this to you—"

"*What?*"

"Well, you say 'Oh shit' a lot."

I heave a sigh of relief. I say, "If you're going to talk about that stuff, I'm leaving."

"Well, you do. And you're so handsome—you're twenty years old."

"Look, I find this sort of conversation sickening."

"I've never before felt that a penis was—*also*—so good for me."

"That does it. Happy Trails." My mind full of the cliché known as 'filled with joy.' I'm not twenty, I'm ten. I feel like I've just been introduced to Babe Ruth. I'm *childish*. Do I really say 'Oh shit'? In the huddle they told me I said 'holy shit.' See? I'm grown up.

She says, "Tell me something about yourself, Bucky. Tell me something important."

"Don't like to talk about myself."

"I know. That's why I'm asking."

"OK—I'm the strong silent type."

She says, real slow, in a low voice, "Really—I want you to tell me."

I try to figure this one out. I'm not cut out to live with anyone—I could tell her that. Shit, I don't talk out loud because I talk to myself all the time. And I bore me. Boop-boop-boop-boop. I really like your cooking. I like everything about you. I love you. No way—I talked to Sheila like that and look what it got me. A shower curtain. Look, Marge, I'm helping you through a rough time. That's all. I'm your friend. I say, "My life is sort of a long walk."

She laughs out loud. She looks at me with that smile she gets on her face when we're in bed. She says, "Your life is a long walk—and you're afraid it's not worth the—*Trip.*"

Oh shit.

She says, "Come on."

I think if I tell the truth to a woman, if I really spill my guts, pour my heart out, she'll think, Well, I can do better than him. The Bodley Story is a bore. At least the Hooker Story had some zip to it. Well, OK, I'll give her a chance.

"Something important?"

"Whatever, Bodey."

"Well—shit—"

"Something trivial. And at the same time important."

I say, "Well, I told you I flunked out of Stanford. Because I wrote 'Yes' as an answer."

"I agree with you, I think you should have gotten full credit. Oedipus was guilty."

"Well, it was a lie."

"What?"

"It wasn't a smart answer. I was just afraid to write anything else. I didn't flunk Western Civ. I flunked English, too. The first English theme, the subject was 'Where Am I in Time and Space?' "

She says, "I knew there was a reason I didn't get into Stanford."

"I wrote this flowery shit. And the professor, he was a T.A. actually, went over my paper with me. He said, 'Your mind is full of clichés.' And instead of listening to him, I thought, 'Fat little asshole, I could take you out in a minute.' "

"Good for you, Bucky."

"Can I stop there?"

"Would you be more comfortable if I knitted?"

357

"OK, OK. This guy who sat next to me, his name was Howie Browne, he got an A. I told him I got a D minus, told him the T.A. said my mind was full of clichés." I pause, I know I'm going to regret this. "I was hanging out a lot at the Oasis—that's a—"

"I know the Big O, Bucky."

"You do?"

"Sure."

This fucks up my story. I never saw her in there. I did see Rex once, with his "brothers." I cleared out fast. OK. OK, now. "Drank beer all the time. Neglected my studies. The place was always crowded. Great burgers. I was in there one night, drunk, when Howie Browne comes in with a pretty girl. I stagger over to their booth and slobber around. Uninvited, no class at all. I actually put a few moves on the girl. Howie gets pissed. I say to her, 'Ol' Howie here is a real brain. We had a guy like Howie in my high school and we nailed his briefcase to the floor.' And Howie says to me, 'At least my brain's not full of clichés.' "

"I'm with Howie, Bucky."

"Of course. But I was steamed. I say let's settle this outside, and out we go. Howie can't fight worth shit and I'm drunk on my ass, already ashamed of myself. So I don't hit him, I walk away. And the next English class, I try to apologize, follow him around, fall all over him. But he won't shake hands. So we make a contest out of it. We never miss English class, and never speak. I don't even hear what the teacher's saying, all I do is sit and look at the back of Howie's head. I know. He's in the right, and I'm in the wrong. But he won't let me apologize. I think my mind isn't full of clichés, my mind is full of shit."

"That's right, Bucky."

I look at her. "You really think so?"

She says, "I like the way your mind works, Bucky."

"No you don't. You're trying one of—one of *me*—for a while."

"Check that. I don't like the way your mind works at all."

"But that's the point—I don't like the way my mind works. I'm ashamed of it."

She says, "Can I tell you the moral of your story?"

"Why not?"

She says, "The moral of your story, Trip, is that you're in love with me. And you're scared. You're scared that I'm going to leave you."

I look at her. I knew it. I knew there was a reason I don't talk to women.

She says, "It scares the shit out of you."

What if she's right? I know I'm getting red. I tell myself, Ollie, you're not supposed to mess up a good *thang*. I say, "Well, you—"

She says, "What?"

I say, "You. I may say 'shit' a lot when we fuck. But—and, by the way, even with that tan you've got there—you get these—well, big splotches all over your chest, above the boobs—"

"Me, darling?"

"Yeah, you. I may say 'oh shit,' but you—well, the noises you make don't sound like they come from someone who could master the art of reading."

"Hey!"

I jump. "I'm sorry. I swear I've never said anything like that to a woman in my life. Ever."

She's laughing at me.

I blush. I know I'm blushing.

She laughs along. "I wonder what it's like to be in your head."

"Oh, it's all right."

She says, "Do you wonder what it's like to be in my head?"

"Sure."

"I give good head, Bucky."

"I know."

That twinkle in her eye. "Want to do it again?"

"I can't."

"Why not?"

"Because I'm a diabetic."

A month goes by. We're still in Summer Snow. I think we should move out, somehow it's indecent to be here. But we stay.

Margie takes her shower and comes into the room. She looks nervous, worried. What is it? She's going to tell me she's moving out. I knew I never should have talked to her.

She stands there. How I wish she hadn't cut her hair. She says, "I've got to tell you something."

I nod my head mechanically.

She's crying. Shit, what is it, what's wrong?

"Oh, Bodey, I don't know *how*—" She stands there, tears coming down that tanned face. I want to go to her. "I'm not careless—I'm not careless—"

"Take it easy," I say.

"Bucky, I didn't want to do this to you."

"What?"

"And I haven't been drinking. I haven't. You know how hard it is for me to stop drinking, but you said you'd had trouble with liquor, too, so I stopped. For us. I don't get drunk anymore."

"Yes, I know."

"Well, you never said anything about it."

"Don't like to talk too much." What is it, dammit?

She sighs. "Do you know, Bodey? Oh, of course you don't." She says it real, real slow. "I'm afraid—I know—Bodey, we're—oh, I'm so sorry —I'm pregnant."

My uncle used to tell a story about a guy who said to him, "My wife just had a baby—you have no idea what I've been through!" My uncle laughing and shaking his head about it.

It's her abortion—and look at me. I've had four days to get ready, now it's Tuesday, and I'm running around like a lunatic. OK. Checklist. Two-hundred-dollar cashier's check. I *know* you can pay for it, Marge, but I want to. You have to go through it. OK. OK. 'Vette gassed up. I know, Marge, I prefer 1 GROUCH, but if you prefer the 'Vette . . . yes, I'll drive home—you'll still be woozy from the Brevitol or whatever they call it.

Every once in a while I think we could keep the baby as our own, but no, we don't know about *us* yet. Of course you could have the baby and then give it up to be a-*dop*-ted, a-*dop*-ted. That wouldn't phase me at all.

"Ready, Bucky?"

"Ready. Just a minute while I finish these dishes."

I'm sorry I ever thought you were a tramp. You're an orphan.

Rex at that party, tears in his eyes, "Do you know how alone Marge is? You know how *alone* she is?"

You're not alone. I'm here. I'm having a little trouble locking the door, though, it's because I'm putting the key in the wrong lock.

OK, here we go for a Tuesday spin in our 'Vette.

"No, Bodey—*MacArthur!*"

"I know, I know, I've got a biker on my fender."

Drive much, Officer?

It's a nice little place, like a complex of dentists. I just wish they'd get rid of that drab woman standing on the sidewalk with the big rubber doll crucified on those sticks. Marge, in her black toreador pants, I know they're not toreador pants, and a short-sleeved maroon sweater. Marge just walked right by her. Me too, but I took a pamphlet, I reminded her not to wear jewelry. No food or liquids after six last night. She's dying for a cigarette. I read the pamphlet:

> On Jan. 22, 1973, the U.S. Supreme Court judged that the unborn child
> is not a person during the nine months prior to birth and may be legally
> killed.
>
> Over $150 million of tax money has helped to destroy more than 1
> million babies a year.

I wonder if anybody can tell I'm a cop. If I show my badge to the woman
with the fetal Jesus, maybe she'll move on.

The name Marge gives at the desk is Bodley.

This place must do a land office business. At least a dozen couples in
here, and six or seven single women. You're supposed to leave your
children at home. Why would they have to tell anybody that?

She sits beside me. "You don't have to wait, Bucky."

"I'll wait. You said ten minutes."

She laughs quietly, digs for something in her purse. "No. Two hours,
Bucky. Ten minutes asleep. You can be awake or asleep, but I prefer
sleep."

"Why?"

" 'Cause it hurts."

Right. I look at the macramé wall hanging. "What's that supposed to
be?"

She turns. "A map of Micronesia."

"Really?"

"Bucky, I think you ought to go buy some jogging shoes."

"Shut up." Why are we whispering? Do they get matching funds from
the state?

Oh, swell. It's noon, and those three couples are watching "This Passing Night."

Marge and I look at each other. What if she's recognized? Nuns usually
have their abortions in the convent.

> Most pregnancies are not detected until the sixth week. By then, the
> baby's heart has been beating for three weeks, brain waves can be read,
> the nervous system has been complete for two weeks, and he or she is
> sensitive to pain. At nine to ten weeks, the developing child can swallow,
> get hiccups, and make a tiny fist.

"Bucky, maybe I can find you a *U.S. News & World Report.*"

I crumple up the pamphlet. We sit in the air conditioning and listen
to Jack MacKenzie's voice on the tube. The Hooker Story *is* a soap opera.

Marge is too hard on Joslin, all she asked Rex to do was grow up. But he didn't know how. I should talk. Look at all those people. I'll bet Marge and I are at least five years older than any of them. Marge and I are slow learners.

'Cause it *hurts*. At nine to ten weeks he or she can swallow and get hiccups?

"Really, Bucky, just be back by two o'clock. I don't want to come out of there and not see you sitting here."

Nurse appears and says, "Nelson?"

The girl who troops in cannot be a day over sixteen. Do you have to have a note from your parents?

"Want to play Geography?"

"No, I'll just memorize my mother-pleaser with Hillary."

"You didn't bring a script."

"Bucky, I *explained* that to you."

"Right."

I look out the window at the 'Vette. I remember when I fixed the dollar fuse.

"Bodley?"

We kiss. I watch her go in, carrying a canvas sack, her shoulders slumped.

Her feet in stirrups, she's unconscious, an Electrolux sucking out a little jelly polyp that can make a *fist?*

I sit there a couple of minutes. Can't stand it, get up, go into the men's and read the poster on the Pill, Rubbers, Diaphragms with and without Foam, Rhythm, and Nothing at All. A Moral Majority militant has defaced it. I look in the mirror. I go out, "This Passing Night" is still on, I think I need some fresh air.

Gorgeous day. Perhaps I could strike up a conversation with the doll on the cross. The woman looks at me, her husband's probably having a beer down at the Klavern.

I sit in the 'Vette, then back out, get on 405, and a few minutes later I pull into South Coast Plaza. I want to get her a present. A card, flowers, anything. No, something special. It's hard to pick the right thing. Presents. You can't please Joslin. The sweater Leela picked out wasn't *her*. I'm sorry, Joslin. When Marge talked dirty about you, I stood up for you. Always will.

I take the escalator down to ground. I inspect a yellow 1916 Buick. Real craftsmanship, in the old days everything was done by hand. Magneto.

When I was on the Indio P.D. I figured I might someday have to assist in the birth of a baby. So I made a little study, learned not to cut the cord immediately. It doesn't have to be cut, shouldn't be cut, actually, for oxygen supply. Just get mucus out of the mouth, and put him on Mom's stomach to keep warm.

I want to get her something really nice. What? I wander around in gifts. A diamond brooch perhaps.

I have to remind myself, she's in perfectly good hands. Nothing can go wrong. It's not a back alley and a coat hanger, it's a nice office. If it weren't, they'd close it down.

Marge. I'm a schoolboy head-over-heels in love. When I see her on the tube I die, that commercial, when she says, "I can tell you how to turn your home into money." And her hair swishes.

No, not jewelry.

"Excuse me, I was lost in thought."

The matron smiles at me. She thinks I'm a clumsy oaf. I am, I run into goal posts.

This situation has been having a negative effect on my work, I can't concentrate anymore. J.O. was a Pop-over. He had a musty smell, an old man with a twinkle in his eye. I'd like to have met him here some Christmas Eve, his arms full of presents for Leela. He'd come up to me from behind and say, "Sergeant, commando units will put a stop to this collective bargaining." Or something, I don't know. I want to get her something *precious*. So when she lies in bed, recuperating, she can wake up and look at it.

Like those pretty candles. No, not candles. It's 1:10.

"May I help you?"

"No, I'm just looking around."

"I like your shirt."

"Thanks." I stagger into silver. You do? I wasn't sure about it, I don't wear a lot of pink. I did in '56, we all wore a lot of pink and black. My uncle always said to save your ties, save your ties, Ollie, ties go in cycles.

And Triphammers go in circles. How could Joslin think a triphammer was a gun?

That.

That vase. It's her favorite color. Mulberry, plum, whatever. But I don't want her to think I bought it for the house, for Summer Snow. It's for *you*, Marge.

I know it's right. I want this vase.

Sixty-seven dollars? For a vase? Jesus, I'm a cheap bastard. OK, I'll get it. "Could you wrap this for me?"

"Not at this counter, you can have that done upstairs. Oh, it's lovely."

That's why I'm buying it. Yes, they do accept personal checks.

"And could we have a phone number?"

Sure. If I can persuade my hand to form Arabic numerals.

"I was hoping this would find a good home."

Lady, you should see it. "Upstairs?"

"Yes, behind housewares."

I hold the package gingerly as I ride the escalator. I'm afraid I'll be late, she'll come out and I won't be there.

The girl in Gift Wrap looks for a big-enough box.

Red roses for a blue lady. Do *you* like my shirt? A 1916 Buick. We've got to get the Buick back on time.

"What color paper?"

I look at the rolls. "Yellow."

"And ribbon?"

Do yellow and pink go together? "And I want one of those big bows."

She fusses with it. Probably a summer job to help defray tuition. Shit, I forgot to shoot up this morning. I still can't turn the tape yellow when I stick it in the paper cup; my record is lime.

"No, a really *big* bow."

"Keep your pants on."

If I'd kept my pants on, we wouldn't be in this fix. I remember at Indio I'd sit at my desk and see these little holes in my black pants, my old uniform, and I would take a pen and black out the flesh, cover the little circle of leg that showed through the hole in my trousers. Then I'd go home, all ready to make love, and Sheila would shout, "Ollie, you done it *again*." I'd look down and see little black measles on my thighs.

"That's perfect."

"This is the biggest bag we have. Careful."

"I've got it. Thanks again."

What if when they went in they found something wrong, like Leela. We tried everything, Mr. Bodley, if it had been a hospital it might have been different, we operate on a shoestring here.

I'll put it in the trunk. So she won't see it until we get home. Home.

I pull in and park. The lady with the doll on the cross is now lunching in Fashion Island. On a hill far away stands an old rugged cross.

Where'd everybody go? Was there a raid? Only four people—two singles and a couple. I sit and think. It's painful to be in love. I have to have it pulled out of me. I'm a heap of twisted metal, a junk heap on the freeway that's been hit head-on. And me trapped inside. Jaws of Life.

She's drunk. When she's drunk she looks just like that. Exactly like that.

"Shall we go, Bucky?"

"Are you all right?"

"Fine and dandy."

She goes back for a minute to talk to a plump black lady. They laugh about something, touching a lot.

We walk out to the 'Vette. She has one Band-Aid on the crook of her elbow and another on the top of her other hand.

I almost hit that Riviera. The black driver yelled, "Fuckah, why don' ya look when y'all back out?" and I can't believe I said, "In your *face,* bro."

Marge says, on MacArthur, "This girl in recovery, she said she hadn't even used birth control." Marge is woozy. "She wanted to know why she couldn't have a gown with flowers on it, like mine. I said, you're so young and pretty you don't need one." She sighs.

There's the ocean out there.

She screams.

I jump, almost pull into the oncoming traffic. "You gonna be sick?"

"That man in the Porsche, he was picking his nose and eating it."

OK, Situation Normal, All Systems Go. Acknowledge, Coral Sea, Please Acknowledge.

"We can't fuck, Bodey, for two weeks."

I may never fuck again.

"I can't run or do anything."

"It'd probably hurt to fuck."

"Healing process. Risk of infection. Shit, I forgot I can smoke, where are my cigarettes?"

Emerald Bay.

"She said seven weeks. She knows what she's doing. You saw her, didn't you, Bucky?"

"That black nurse?"

"She's not a nurse, she's a doctor. She rammed her finger up there and said seven weeks. And she was right. It was late in my cycle."

I think. Late in the cycle. I say, "That means it was a boy." Then, real fast, "I didn't say that."

Boat Canyon.

I want to hold her in my arms. I am afraid for her. I fear that her whole life will be unhappy.

Do they have to shave them down there? Guess I'll find out. Can't fuck for two weeks. Can't even run or anything.

I don't want to use human speech. I don't want to hear people talk.

That place on her left breast where her bathing suit stops, pure white, and that little angel kiss. Which is what my aunt called a mole.

"You won't leave me for a couple of hours, will you, Bucky?"

"No. I won't leave. The Chief said eleven, but I'll call in sick."

"No. Go ahead and take the graveyard, I'll be asleep anyway. Shit, I feel like I've been to a funeral."

You have, actually. No you haven't. It was an error, we corrected an error.

"Could we stop? I'd like a magazine."

"Sure. Sure." I pop the 'Vette into the Laguna Hotel green zone and tell Herman we'll be five minutes, I give him a look. We walk down two shops to the little magazine store. She browses and I slouch along to the girlie magazines, they've got all the creepy ones for freaks, but I've told the owner not to put them at floor level where kids can get at them. I pick up *Blue Boy*, thumb through it, and this is just about the most disgusting thing I've ever seen. Is it supposed to be jewelry, or what? It's a silver chain. You make incisions in both nipples, the areola, I guess, and pinch the chain through there, and then, holy shit, you make an incision in the foreskin and pinch it through there. I can hardly believe it—and neither can Marge, looking over my shoulder, she screams and runs out of the store. I throw down the magazine and take off after her. She's halfway down the block when she stops, leans against the street light. I get there, and she falls into my arms, and everybody looks at us. I hold her. I whisper, "They told you not to run."

Sitting on the bed, she unwraps it real slow. Just like a kid at Christmas. A special well-brought-up kid who wants to savor every moment. She has no idea what it is, she's got the box open and still doesn't know. Tissue paper. She holds it up. "Oh honey, it's my *color.*"

I know.

"Bucky, it's beautiful—you have wonderful taste."

Damn right.

"When did you get it?"

"Couple days ago."

"Oh, it's perfect." She jumps up.

"Hey, you need to rest."

"Oh, but I want to get flowers for it." She rushes into the bathroom. No flowers in the bathroom. Not last I checked.

I sit on the bed. Tears in my eyes. Fool. Mind full of clichés.

Big trouble. A little girl, ten years old, is missing from her home on Ramona Road. It appeared she has been kidnapped. She was last seen this morning by her parents and brothers as they left for work. When her

366

mother, Mrs. Zepeda, came home, the girl was gone. The mother does not know what she was wearing, maybe a small white nightgown, all her clothes seem to be in the house. Apparently someone came in looking for money. A hundred dollars in cash is missing. We speculate that he didn't know anyone was home, and when the little girl confronted him, he took her along, wrapped in a bedspread.

We investigate. This is top priority. We patrol the area, house by house. Her mother says the girl was timid, probably would not have wandered off by herself. We study pictures, she is a cute child. Sparkling eyes and shoulder-length brown hair. Weighs just under eighty pounds. She was barefoot, all her shoes are still in the closet.

An old neighbor woman calls the office. Says she knows what happened. It must be the man who makes "lewd phone calls," she has received a few from a man who asks her, "Are you coming out?" She told me she asked the man if he wanted to speak to her husband. But the caller just kept asking, "Are you coming out?" I ask if her husband is at home. She says, "No—he's been dead for thirty years." Then she tried to sell me her car. Eccentric. Desires companionship.

The Zepedas used to have a boarder, they evicted him. A masonry contractor, the victim's uncle by marriage. A bulletin is out for him. In Wyoming. The family keeps a lonely vigil, doesn't get any sleep. We've administered six polygraphs, but nothing. The radio chatters to Wyoming. Now it's all routine work. Drudgery.

In a canyon a mile away, a pair of hikers stumble onto the remains of a young boy. The body is buried in a shallow grave, dead for about five months. But there's nothing to link the two cases.

And then, at the Zepeda house, I notice the oldest brother. Shifty eyes, he's just not cool. I think something is wrong here. I have a Pepsi with him. We watch the sun go down in the sea. Salsa music on the radio. We talk about hunting, shooting deer. He wears wide-bottom Levi's and white shoes. I see his eyes flitter and return to the same spot. Cisco Kid, mustache, nylon shirt open to his waist. We talk about horse racing. He is a workout boy at Santa Anita. I ask him what a cold-walker involves, his eyes still darting to that same place. I go inside, use the john. I come back out, I don't like his eyes, I have been watching them for several hours. I take a walk with him and talk about horses some more. When we come back, I see it again. And I see a swarm of flies on the sandy path. I tell the deputies to dig. I stand there with the boy and keep talking. His eyes are going crazy. I look down, one of the shovels hits something, and my men get down, and I see her arm.

367

Call off Wyoming, it's her brother. Man, I've got you, you horrible asshole, you did that to your sister. I've got your crazy eyes in my hands I've got you, I cry I'm so happy.

Next morning the coroner says Juanita's death was due to inhalation of foreign particles. She was still alive when he buried her.

I was fixing a Summer Snow awning when I got the call. And then I went down into the workroom and had a little nervous breakdown.

I cry like a baby. King's X—King's X—thirty feet from your own family's front door, lacerations behind her left ear. Because she saw you steal a hundred dollars. King's X, Water on the Sky. I'm crying uncontrollably. I never want to be seen again, this is the truth. I'm just crying, sobbing, and it's not just for little Juanita, I'm crying about everything. I really loved you, Rex, the traffic light where Marge was standing after she saw that horrible photograph. You know something? That was the very same place I stood with you after you slugged Virgil Ault. I can't get my breath, I don't belong in this house, all the people in this house have died, they're *dead,* everybody keeps *dying,* she was only ten years old, just a little girl, I want to scream like a fucking banshee, I'm sick, I'm a diabetic, all my life I've tried to be good, to be a good man, but I'm not, I'm a weak man, my mind is full of clichés, it's my job not to cry like this, and I'm not doing my job, don't take my *job* away from me, it's who I am, it's who I am, I'm a-*dop*-ted, a-*dop*-ted, all these people are dead, I stood at the graves of two of them, and I know you're dead, Rex, so what am I doing in their *rooms,* and it really could have been a baby, a child, a boy, like David, *our boy*—I'm sorry, I'm sorry, I'm not a crybaby, it'll be over in a minute, just one minute, it's private, every day when I put that uniform on, I just want to keep this house safe for dead people and the boy who is alive, it's wrong for me and Marge to play house, that's what we're doing, Rex, playing house, but that's not it, what we're trying to do is bury you, and it takes time, it takes time, you're too big, you take all the air out of a room, you brood over our lives, but I miss you, I do, I hated you a lot of the time, but I also loved you, and I've spent days and weeks and months looking for you, not because it's my job, because it's you, you fucked up your life really bad, man, but you tried, you tried, and I probably would have gone out of my mind too, that terrible pressure, and you're gone, you have gone out of our lives, we just piddle along having our abortions and things, and I remember at Medjuhl when you were talking to David, you were trying so hard to fix things, I saw how fast on your feet you were, and I saw what it got you, but I honor you, asshole, you're an inspiration to me, really, most inspirational, and it's hard for a man whose mind is full of clichés to think fast and strong like Rex

Hooker, but I'll try, I'll try hard, to think like you, I am thinking like you, I *am* thinking like you, goddammit—I'll think for J.O. and for you and for David, I am the custodian of the Hooker Story, I *am*—and I thought it was my job to find you, but it's my job not to find you, you don't want to be found, because you're dead, or you're not dead, you only think you're dead, no, you are dead, just because my uncle's dead doesn't mean I stop talking to him, it's OK to talk to the dead, they've got rights—and I do love Marge, I wouldn't be doing all this if I weren't in love with her, your sister Marge, I know somehow you'd want me to love her, not let her be *alone* anymore, and Joslin was right after all, Joslin was right from square one, you were going insane, and she loved you and didn't know what to do, and I'll take good care of her, and of your boy, like I promised, if you're not dead let me know, or if you are dead let me know, but this not knowing is terrible, you can't do this to me, oh shit. Oh shit, she was just a little girl who never harmed a soul, I can't bring my job home with me, I can't stop crying I can't stop crying.

21

I CAN stop crying. I can stand here on the beach at 11 P.M. and know that the light up in that room is Marge Stivers reading. I've got it all. A beautiful woman who's not mine and a wonderful kid who's not mine and an unbelievable house that's not mine. I got it made.

You can tell these footprints were made by little kids, playing in the sand. Not only because they're small, it's the way their toes curl in. They grab the sand with their toes. The surf is like cream in the spotlight. Hot night, moon up there not quite full, like an old softball. Down here on this section of the planet earth seventeen sandpipers all run diddle-diddle-diddle on their toothpick legs. The outside lights on the house are green and amber and blue. A magical environment. There's one of Marge's green-and-yellow thongs, she can never keep track of things, I slap its bottom on my thigh.

I am taking a midnight stroll at 11 P.M. A perfect night. I remember I came down to this sand on Labor Day, to collect my thoughts.

I think about that last night, Rex asking me if I'd do him a favor. I said sure, and he said good and didn't say anything else. Then he was standing up there, whistling, in the fog. I didn't know what he was whistling. But I know. He was whistling

David's fishing for a dream,
Fishing near and far,
His line a silver moonbeam,
His bait a silver star.

That's what he was whistling.

Sail, David, sail,
Over the bounding sea.
Only don't forget to sail
Home again to me.

That's what he was whistling. I have decided that. Which is doing him a favor, and that is what he asked me to do. Doing somebody a favor may mean doing them some other favor, because they don't know the favor they need. Which is why they ask one. I flunked out of Stanford thinking this way. I see me in my rat-trap apartment putting a book down and starting to think. Trying to think what thinking is. Mentally goofing off. I can't do that anymore.

I miss you, Rex. I haven't told the kid about you, what I know about you, why you've disappeared. I'll have to be the one to tell him, I'll have to tell the kid how shitty the world is. And when I do, you'll be alive again for a minute. And I'll have to see you die in his head. I'll have to see you alive in his eyes and watch you die in his head. I'll hear you scream, Rex, and I'll have to handle the kid. Because it's my job. David's going to lose you however I do my job. The Laguna Hotel card room. I won't push, or smother, or jump the gun. I'll do it right. Because you were whistling to him.

I'll make sure he knows the good side of you. Because you live in him. And he's got to love you. Follow Daddy. At least he knew football was good for you. But he's gone now. So I have to know what's good for you. Not crowd you—just let you be who you are. Because your dad asked me to do that.

My father? Oh, he was my uncle, really. He adopted me. Like I've kind of adopted you. He tried to bring me up right. Think he succeeded? You'll want to succeed with your boy, or girl, as the case may be. Pardon my thinking in clichés, it's a habit I've developed to protect myself.

Your bed is ready. I hope your pillow smells at least a little bit like sleep. I'm glad you like Marge. Because I'm in love with her. Marge isn't your mother, you've got a fine mother of your own. But Marge really loves you. I know she's a whirlwind, she has no choice. But don't worry about that, she's all right, she'll be good to you.

I turn off the outside lights.

Joslin, we will have to have a long talk in September. It won't be easy on either of us. But Rex is dead, and the kid has to know that, from Trip and Mommy *both*, one clear message. Joslin, you're a good woman. Excuse me, a fine person. No, I mean that. I do.

I climb the stairs. What we have to do tonight, Marge, is not do what got us into this trouble. Damn straight I'm afraid you'll leave me. If you do, we won't be able to fuck. And now for two weeks, all we have is the memory of aftershocks. Oh, well, we'll find something to do. But from now on, there will be some changes made. Can't go into all that beautiful doom shit anymore. Sorry. You're trying to pull your act together, and so am I, and this is part of it. My penis is—also—good for you. And you are good for me.

She's sitting there reading. No, I don't think in clichés, I say, "You oughta be in pictures."

I wake up early, Marge is still asleep.

I walk down to the sand. The water goes slush, it comes up, and it goes slush. I clear my throat. I say, "How was your flight?" Sounds terrible. I clear my throat and say, "How was the flight?" Doesn't sound much better. However it sounds, it'll have to do.

We've made big preparations for David, Marge and me. I've greased up his bicycle and the motor scooter he got for Christmas. Enrolled him for six horseback riding lessons and for Beginner's Youth Tennis. I know he can ride, but I don't think he's swung many racquets. Anyway, it can always be adjusted when he gets here. I can't stand the thought of failing him, those gray eyes. I've emptied the swimming pool, cleaned it out, chlorinated.

It's the Big Day, I'm getting dressed, and Marge hates my old checked pants. She says wear something she bought me. So I change, and then she fusses, and pulls a white sweater around me with the sleeves like that on my chest. I look in the mirror and think I'm in a magazine. I change again. When I come out she does a double-take. And then nods. I say, "I'll tell him I had a meeting." I just feel more comfortable in the uniform, he knows the uniform. I check my gun, spin the cylinders.

Get into 1 GROUCH and go. Out on the freeway, listening to my radio. It's such beautiful country. I wonder what the Indians thought, five hundred years ago. I make it to Century Boulevard in fifty minutes. I park, go into the terminal to wait. L.A. Airport. Hi there, *Dr.* Kelly. David's flight has been delayed.

372

I go into the men's and shine my shoes at the machine, I always do that. I inspect my aging face in the mirror. I can't believe I walked right out of that end zone, banged my shoulder on the goal post. When I was real little, about five, my aunt took me with her shopping. I had twenty-five cents, and spent it on the wrong thing, and then I saw this little wooden donkey with a red saddle, and I just tucked it under my shirt. I was playing with it on my bed at home, and my aunt said, "Where'd you get that?" When I told her, she marched me back to the store. I had to climb a long flight of stairs all by myself, seemed like those stairs would never end, the boards all shabby and worn. I'd just never get up there, and I hoped I wouldn't, but I did. The manager had suspenders and he said, Let this be a lesson to you, Oliver, you must never take what does not belong to you. I handed over the donkey. He looked at me through his spectacles, I was blubbering. And then he said, We'll just forget this, you may keep the donkey, Oliver, and he handed it back.

I did keep it. For years.

But I will probably never understand things. Oh well. "This world and one more." That's what my father, my uncle, always said. I'm not quite sure what he was talking about, but I think I know how he felt. That sigh. "This world and one more."

At last the kid's big bird comes in, wheels up to the gate, that enormous fantail. I suspect pilots have a good life, making that kind of money. I watch the tanned guys on the ground crew, sitting around, bored, chatting. I wonder if they could be police officers. It's all in the eyes. If you don't have the eyes, you can't do it.

The passengers begin to disembark, flushed and dazed from their transcontinental adventure, their in-flight movies and headphones and microwave entrées. I'm looking them over, looking for my boy. I say a quick prayer to anybody who may be listening, and suddenly here he is. Here is the little suck in reality. Huge blue sneaks, green tote bag over his shoulder. He's grown. He's twelve years old now, has to pay full fare. The stew doesn't take care of him anymore, he can handle this, no problem.

I pretend not to see him, turn around as though I am scanning the arrivals monitor. I parked 1 GROUCH right across from the Mexicana baggage claim. I turn back, he is sauntering toward me. David. A real heartbreaker. He is going to do terrible things when he gets into girls. He looks up at me, gray eyes, and says, "Well, Trip, how the hell are ya?"